BRAVE N...

"Goodbye," the doctor said, and the lid clicked shut. There was suddenly complete silence and complete darkness.

Blake's mind drifted. He was floating on a sea of light with darkness over him, pain pricks of stars forming and dissolving. There was more pain, then still more. His whole body was filled with needles, tearing at his flesh. *It wasn't supposed to hurt!*

Suddenly the sky ripped open, flooding flame into his eyes, driving pain into his brain. And then harsh loud words crashed into his tomb of silence.

He opened his eyes.

Looking down at him was the woman he had given up a world of sensual delights for . . . the woman he wanted to love forever.

And looking down at him was the revenge-hungry man he had betrayed a hundred years before!

CRITICS RAVED ABOUT
PATRON OF THE ARTS
William Rotsler's First Novel

Available from Ballantine Books

To the Land of the Electric Angel
William Rotsler

BALLANTINE BOOKS • NEW YORK

Library of Congress Catalog Card Number: 75-34417

SBN 345-24517-2-150

First Printing: February, 1976

Cover art by Darrell Sweet

Printed in the United States of America

BALLANTINE BOOKS
A Division of Random House, Inc.
201 East 50th Street, New York, N.Y. 10022
Simultaneously published by
Ballantine Books of Canada, Ltd., Toronto, Canada

For
Sharman DiVono
with love

□

The walls shimmered and changed colors in a flowing, liquid way, reacting to Blake Mason's body heat as he strode through the entrance hall of his office. The dark-haired young receptionist smiled when she saw him, held out a sheaf of messages, and murmured a good morning.

Blake slowed and flipped through the messages. "Call Mrs. Templeton and tell her the Coe sensatron is ready for installation. Tell Caleb I want the terraces on the Castlekeep job ready for the tile setters by Thursday. Ask Count Radovsky if we could have lunch on Tuesday instead."

"Yes, sir. Aaron would like to see you, if you have time."

Blake nodded absently, then stopped to look around the entrance hall. "Tell Libby to start some prelims on a new shocker hall. This one has been around four or five months. If I'm getting tired of it, the clients must be, too. Tell her . . . um . . . maybe something in the Martian Splendor style . . . or Mirrormaze—even authentic Early 20th, if Dutch can find the pieces." Blake looked at the Bodycomfort furniture, custom-built items that had been used for two successive decors. "Ask Dutch to sell these with reasonable return, will you?"

"Yes, Mr. Mason."

Blake went through the big dilator door, less a functional port than a bit of showmanship intended to impress the clients of his decorating and design company. He turned right, and went down a hall to the work area.

"Environmental Concepts" was a small company working with big clients and big concepts. Blake did not just decorate a house, he investigated the life-style of his clients, conducted exhaustive interviews, made tests,

1

and then designed the house or condominium, the grounds, the furniture, and sometimes even whole wardrobes. Some of his projects were not for individuals but for corporations, for public use, or for specialized use by select individuals. The hallmark of Blake's success had always been the solid background and firm foundation upon which he used the genius of his talent and intuition.

His company required space and the workroom was big. The one he entered, one of three on this floor, was filled with drawing tables, sturdy worktables, finished and unfinished scale models, sketches, photographs, holograms, books of sample material, reference volumes, and several people.

"Hi, boss," Carole said, looking up from her table. Blake stopped and looked over her shoulder. "It's the Alice-in-Wonderland thing for Alexander," she said.

Blake nodded, and pointed a finger at the Cheshire cat on a big mushroom. "Hologram?" Carole nodded. "That will work, fading away to just a grin. The rest is pretty much animatronics, isn't it?"

"Yes, the cards are going to have to be about four millimeters thicker than Caleb first thought. So much wiring has to go in, that they will be somewhat thick playing cards."

"That's all right, the effect will be good." He touched Carole on the shoulder and she looked up at him. "Everything all right between you and Mark?"

She smiled and patted his hand. "Yes, we talked it all out. I suppose he's just more monogamous than I am. It's all right, really."

"Okay," Blake said with a smile. "But if I can help . . ."

"Not unless you can bring Mark up to the twenty-first century."

"My time machine is in the repair shop. The sand was running out of the bottom."

"Too bad." They smiled at each other, and Blake walked down the aisle between the rows of worktables, nodding and saying good morning to those who looked up.

He passed through the door into the center work

area, a big high-ceilinged room where the large portables were constructed. Blake walked through the clutter and casual disarray that has characterized artists' studios since the dawn of time, but he wasn't seeing it. His attention was caught by Aaron and the big column of whitish plastic on a shiny black base.

The slim young man straightened up from a drawing board, and a worried smile replaced a worried frown. "*God*, I'm glad you're here! Look at *this*! Dawson gave me those specs for the Mohawk job, but they simply don't match the prelims. *They* want the color fountain *here*, and and Dawson has it *here*. Now, this is where you wanted the Hayworth construction, wasn't it?"

Blake looked away from the tall white cylinder and peered at the workprints. "I think he's reversed the coding. See?" he said. "Phone him and have Dawson check. Mohawk wants this whole job done by the end of July, for the opening of the Emperor Nero Arena. They are starting a PR blitz about how the Greeks and Romans tinted their statuary with lifelike colors, so all this will work in very well."

Aaron brushed back a lock of unruly hair. "Oh, I know, but after several thousand years of looking at those bleached statues, going back to fully painted ones seems positively *gauche*, really, like something that bitch Georgina Sand would do."

Blake smiled. "Ah, love unrequited." Aaron shifted some papers and made a loud sniff. "Did the molecule skimmer arrive?" Blake asked.

"Yes. Mario tested it down at the studio and it worked *fine*. It has fine and wide band adjustments and you can sculpt even high-tensile plastiment with it. It will be *marvelous* for shaping the rocks around the Shah's summer home. Looks so *natural*, just like weathering, except for the patina, of course. No chisel marks, no laser burns, just *marvelous*!"

Blake pointed at the column of white plastic. "Is Nimma finished with this fleshmolder yet?"

"Yes, I think so. Here, let me. Carl showed me the setting for the *loveliest* configuration. Watch."

Aaron punched out a code on the small ten-digit control panel on the far side. Slowly the cylinder began to writhe with a rather sinuous movement as the memory plastic reshaped itself, shifting its colors, until it was a replica of Michelangelo's *David*, slightly blurred and indefinite, as if seen through water. But the color and texture were human flesh.

"See?" Aaron said delightedly. "*Look* how he reformed the genitalia!"

Blake looked stonily at the plastic statue and asked, "Has he worked anything else out?"

"You don't like it?" Aaron asked anxiously.

"I've seen the original. I didn't think it needed any improvements."

"*Well*, Blake, really, he was just using this as a *test case*, something to judge against. Don't fret at him, *please*. *Libby* made the suggestion that he copy a few of the *classic* pieces to get a feel of the thing."

Blake nodded. "Okay, what else?"

Aaron hopped over to Carl's table, rummaged around, and came up with a code card. He bent over and punched out another code. The *David* blurred and melted as the plastic reformed into another human shape, this one the *Venus de Milo*. Carl had added the broken and lost arms, mimicking the placid postures of the period. The sculpture held for ten seconds, then once again writhed, and darkened from ivory to deep red as it shaped itself into the so-called *Colossus of Mars*—the strange, weatherworn, shrouded figure of indefinite species. It might even have been a humanoid with folded wings, but it was too worn to tell.

"Stop it," Blake said, and Aaron punched a hold. "This is where his waterworn look works. Have him try some abstracts. That effect should be exploited, because it is very good."

"Yes, of *course*, Blake, I'll tell him when he gets in. He's over at General Electronics, trying to get the new M-9 cilli nets for the casino sensatrons. They're getting terribly difficult to get these days. *Everyone* is doing sensatrons now."

Blake nodded in agreement. Those complex engineering miracles—sensatrons—used ten- and twenty-thousand-line screens, a variation on the hologram, and a computer's ability to "paint" three dimensional subjects in what seemed to be three dimensions to Alpha-wave generators and subsonic projectors played almost directly upon your emotions. Most sensatron artists made continuous loop operations, designing the action to end up at the starting point and editing the tapes and control wafers to obscure any joining, making the "performance" continuous as long as there was power. The original cubes by the artists were often quite large—as much as two meters square or cubed—and some were over two meters high. They were always rectangular, due to the necessity for the optical flatness of the screen surfaces to give the optimum apparent depth. Already, artists complained about the artificial restrictions of the cube shape, but so far neither artist nor engineer had figured out another way to achieve the same result.

"All right," Blake said to Aaron. "Check with Mohawk."

Aaron nodded and Blake went through the workrooms, and on into his own small area just past the massive freight elevator. His studio had high ceilings and strong, clear Easyeye light panels. Here he kept his own personal tools—virtually every one listed in the catalogs, plus a few he had designed or adapted himself—all carefully cased, stored, or hung. Next to a large drawing board was a shelf of thick portfolios that bulged with prelims and finished drawings for a hundred environments.

Next door, in his business office, things were arranged with less clutter. Models and photographs were displayed to impress his clients with both the achievements and the taste of "Blake Mason, Environmental Concepts." There were photographs of the Martian Civilization exhibit for the Madrid World's Fair, Shawna Hilton's house, the FSA Monument, the *Valhalla* dome, an elaborate fantasy for the opening of Caligula's Circus, and the interior of the astrobubble on Station One. Displayed with pride were tridees of Casa Corazón, forever lost in the Peruvian earthquake three years before. Most impressive, however, were the photographs and scale model of Blake's biggest commission: the Hanging Gardens of Babylon, which he designed for the Shah of Iran.

But here, in the studio, was his own private world. Few clients were permitted in, and few employees, either. Blake's business was providing environments of an unusual nature, whether reconstructions, fantasies, artistic tours de force, or merely trendy "in" designs that were kept for a season or two. Few of his customers wanted to know how he did his work. Either they didn't care, or else they actively avoided destroying their illusions by not going backstage, so to speak. Their usual questions were only "How much?" and "When will it be finished?" Blake always knew he had a really rich client when, in the best J. P. Morgan tradition, he was not asked, "How much?"

Blake had dozens of the varied tools he needed close at hand. These ranged from a simple, old-fashioned graphite pencil to sophisticated Alpha-wave projectors, from memory-plastic templates to his own coded sample books that listed everything from fabrics and metals to robotronic plug-ins, animatronic modules for constructing human, animal, and fantasy creatures, and Martian synthetics. He had a tieline to a Da Vinci Visual Computer, as well as a terminal that was used mostly for computer checks on material strengths, prices, availability, and delivery dates. But Blake's most used, and perhaps most important, tools were the pen and paper with which he roughed out ideas. With these he put his thoughts down to find direction and to hold on to parts of a concept while he thought about its other parts.

Blake stopped and looked at the big project that sprawled across a large, flat worktable. It was a multilevel, a complex harem he was designing for a famous publisher. When completed, the structure would have big orgy rooms, carpeted, cushioned, and filled with rich textures set off by soft lighting. There would also be intimate cul-de-sacs, decorated with rich fabrics, and sensuous furniture that writhed in a seemingly endless manner through the four acres of the arcolog penthouse. To the untrained eye the model was a confusing mess, with penciled notes on scale walls, bits of fabric or color taped to walls and floor, temporary partitions stapled into position. One level was raised with a paperbound copy of *The Famine Years*, and another with a heavy book entitled *The History of the Modern Roman Games*. One could see where arches and terminals had been drawn, then eliminated with a slash of ink. Conversation pits and ceiling-television panels were sketched in, cases for old-fashioned books noted, an enlargement of the kitchen area indicated with scrawled arrows, a photo of a sensatron pinned into a corner. The mock-up was now only a tool, a sketch that when finished would be given to a talented subcontractor for translation into a breathtaking scale model that would be photographically realistic, complete with tiny art objects and a few human figurines for visual scale.

Why do they come to me for these blatantly sexual environments? Blake asked himself. *Commission after commission is for something boldly sensual. Perhaps no more than 15 or 20 percent of my work is for a design without a sensual overtone. The Africaine job. The Alice-in-Wonderland project. The eighteenth-century house for Karsh.*

Can what Jacques Charlot said be true?, Blake asked himself . . . Standing there before the hologram stage —much as Oscar Wilde might have stood before an Adam mantel—Charlot, a mauve-tinted mari in his hand, dropped his acid pronouncements with his famous studied casualness. "Mason is popular, Lady Faring, because he finds sex dirty. He makes his environments so deliciously sensual for all the *wrong* reasons."

There had been a mild titter, and a few quick smirking looks were thrown his way.

"The *wrong* reasons?" Lady Faring asked, right on cue.

"Precisely, my dear woman." He patted his face with a wisp of lace pulled from his sleeve. "He's so afraid of sex, of letting himself go, that it preoccupies his entire mind." Charlot turned toward Blake, tucked his handkerchief back into his sleeve with a flamboyant gesture. "Isn't that correct, dear boy?"

Blake felt that his face must be flaming. "That's the kind of commission I seem to attract, all right."

Charlot's pale face brightened theatrically. "Exactly!

And why do you attract them? Because you do them so *well!* And why do you do them so well?" He turned to the group to answer his own question. "Because he thinks of *nothing else!* An artist with *true* dedication!"

There was laughter, and Danièle Giraux spoke over the last of it. "Not *always*, darling. He does not *always* think of sex."

Again, the group tittered, for Blake's affair with the coal-conversion heiress had been well publicized the previous season.

Charlot bowed, saying with a wry smile, "I bow to your superior knowledge, *chérie.*"

There was considerable laughter at Blake's expense when they noticed his obvious discomfort. Then Eve Bernstein spoke from deep within a Life-style chair-bed. "This is very interesting, Jacques. You mean that Blake's livelihood depends upon his sexual dissatisfaction?"

Charlot turned elegantly. He gestured delicately with his mari. *"Certainement, mon amie.* Sexual satisfaction clears the mind for other things."

"There *are* no other things!" Eve laughed.

"But, Jacques," Ellie Ripper protested. "Blake has had so *many* women!"

Charlot turned to her, the demonic smile one of triumph. *"Exactement, chérie. Le coeur a ses raisons que la raison ne connaît point.* He is unsatisfied with many women because he has not the *one* woman."

Charlot turned again toward Blake, smiling, and all eyes followed.

"I dislike being referred to in the third person," Blake said, unable to remain quiet, but without a good rejoinder. "Besides, you are wrong." You equate professionalism with obsession. Do you think an actor who plays a murderer is one? I have an *interest* in sex, Jacques, not an obsession. Or are you now above such things?"

Charlot looked stung, but before he could answer Lilly Holliman spoke. "That's right, Blake, dear, you tell 'em. Jacques, you old phony, that wasn't what you said in French. You said a heart has its reasons, of which reason knows nothing."

The focus shifted to Lilly, who enjoyed being the center of attention as always. She thrust out her ample bosom and puffed up her education—only one of which was real. Blake sat motionless and silent as Lilly, in her blundering way, took the floor away from Charlot. She began to talk about her own affairs of the heart, particularly about her adventures with younger men.

Blake stood up and slipped out of the group, glad not to be on the grill. He felt Charlot's eyes on him as he went through the doors to the terrace. Blake kept his face calm—not blank, but calm.

The terrace was wide, and the greenery grew in lush profusion from large planters faced with genuine Roman carvings. Lady Faring's condominium home was high on the western flank of the great pyramid of *Sunset* arcolog. The bubbles, domes, and windows of surrounding condos glinted in the night, glowing balls and dots across the great face of the arcology structure, home of over a half-million people. Up here at the top and on the exterior flanks were the twenty-first-century condos of the rich. Inside and below were the boxes of the less-rich, and deep inside were the burrows of the poor.

Below, the flowing rivers of light that marked the freeways between the man-made living mountains continued their never-ending movement. The *Venice* arcolog to the west and the distant humps of *Bel Air* and *Camelot* glittered and shone, rising above the hills and the petite arks to the north and south. On the other side of *Sunset,* out of sight from the Faring terrace, were the others: *Mañana, Great Western, California Tower, Casa Laguna, Heaven, Astro, Ciudad de Oro, Sun City, Maaravier,* and *Urbo Nova.* Housing a half- or three-quarters of a million each, these self-contained city buildings were designed and built with factories within and beneath. Monorails and aircars linked tower to tower. Thousands of cable-television lines linked millions of terminals in a vast information and entertainment system.

Over the Santa Monica mountains the tips of *Koma, Prudential Towers,* and the more distant *Star* could be seen. Beyond, to the north and west along the curve of shore, were *Oaktree, Santa Rosa, Camarillo City, Oxnard Center, Ventura, Skycity*, and others under construction along the coast to Santa Barbara. To the south, toward the desert, where the towers were faced with huge solar panels and the desert was roofed with them, were still more arcological towers.

Arcologs dotted the landscapes of the world in ever-increasing numbers. They were much more efficient to service, and took up less space, giving up much land that was vitally needed to grow crops. Even many of the planned park interspaces between the big arks had been filled with the overflow of people, buildings, and factories. The arcolog concept had begun with Paolo Soleri in the late twentieth-century and his practical example, *Arcosanti*, the first arcolog, built near Phoenix, Arizona. "Architecture is in process of becoming the physical definition of a multilevel, human ecology," he had written. "It will be arc-ology." The nearest early example was the ocean liner, then the first true deep-space ships.

The pressure of a growing world population and the need to use more efficiently the Earth's resources had brought about the realization of the arcology concept. In urban areas, where the pressure was greatest and land the most precious, the huge structures rose to populations of seven and eight hundred thousand each. There were also many smaller ones, some with as few as ten or twenty thousand, built in outlying districts. Some "micro-arks," housing only a couple of thousand, were built on the same principles. *Castillo del Aire*, or "Air-castle," near Madrid, had, on the other hand, a million inhabitants. Chicago's *Babeldiga* had 1,200,000. *Novanoah*, a huge floating island under construction in the Indian Ocean, was designed for nearly 2,500,000 inhabitants, who would derive 80 percent of their food from the sea itself.

Arcologs were masterpieces of design, and an individual could live and die without ever actually having to leave any one of the huge buildings. Food, entertainment, and myriad services could be brought to the door by tube, multiplex cable, jets, and electric delivery vans. Many people conducted business by television, using computer and information terminals and rarely leaving their home offices.

Blake Mason hated the arks. He realized they were needed; and at times he admired them, much as one may admire an efficient riot tank or a piece of well designed machinery. But Blake could not love an arcolog. It was too cold, too impersonal for him, despite the agile machinations of the arks' social designers.

Blake watched the tiny darting lights of aircabs and the contrails of high-flying jets, a firmament in motion that blotted out the sight of the galaxy. He walked to the edge of the terrace and looked down. The city stretched away—square mile after square mile of building blocks, all at the legal height limit and broken only by the looming bulk of the Christmas-tree-like arks.

Too many, Blake thought. *Millions. Too many, but maybe not too many if out there, somewhere, was that one . . .*

The memory of that evening at Lady Faring's was still sharp.

Was Charlot right?

Blake stroked a plastiwax figurine of the thirty-foot Sensualus sculpture he was going to install in front of the elevator doors on Landau's floor.

Was Charlot right that night? Did he touch a vital point? Am I obsessed with sex, or rather with the thought of sex? Is this obsession the reflection of my business and my art, or is my art and business the reflection of that obsession? Or is there really an obsession?

Blake twisted the plastiwax figure he held in his hands, feeling the slightly oily surface, enjoying the sensuality of the dips and curves, letting his imagination flow freely. Thighs and breasts, with nipples hardening. Cool buttocks flexing under gripping hands.

God, Charlot was right! Blake put the figure down quickly. Why couldn't he just admit it, go with it, flow with it, use it, enjoy it. *I can't be a Victorian in the twenty-first century!* "I'm not that bad," Blake said aloud. *I'm not a prude. If I disapprove of the casualness of sex today, it's on the grounds of taste, not prudery.*

Or is it? a tiny thought spoke as it scampered through his mind.

Blake picked up the figurine and slammed it down, distorting one soft side. He abruptly turned away and stared for a long moment at the framed sketches for the pleasure dome the Hughes Corporation was building on Silver Mountain. The dome had been a well-received job, with much attendant publicity. The critics, the vidtab faces, and the chic trend setters had all remarked on the effect of the colorquick walls flowing with heat-sensitive crystals in liquid suspension that reacted to body heat and air currents, shifting their colors in rippling waves. There were no straight lines, only organically curved walls. The rooms were warm and soft, with scented air in constant flux, and hidden music helped along by concealed Alpha-wave projectors working directly on the emotions. A bath for the mind, a massage for the soul, a carnival for the body.

Experienced girls would cater to every wish, every need, real and fancied. They had been picked from the welfare levels of the arks, from orphanages and broken homes. Three months of hypnotraining, of probing psychs, of field training in disciplines known for five thousand years—or in others unknown fifty years before—and *voilà!* a pleasure dome girl! There was nothing anyone could teach her about sex.

But what about love? Blake Mason mused. He ripped his eyes away from the sketches of one of his greatest achievements. In his office he had more offers, more pleasure dome contracts. Bigger domes, the finest yet: *Atlantis*, beneath the Mediterranean, and soon the new *Xanadu*, a jet hop away in North Africa. Hirahawa was doing Tokyo's *Tanoshimi*, and Bentcliffe was doing *Seraglio*, in Constantinople, but Blake himself was wanted for the two big ones.

Temples to sex, raised to a high art . . .

Sex, yes, Blake thought grimly, *but what about love? Does sex come before love? Should love come before sex? Do they have anything to do with each other? Millions of people think not. There is food, sleep, sex, work, and entertainment. Millions of people never think about entertaining themselves. That is for the professionals. Sex, too.*

Where is that noble breed of man who is going to fly to the stars, conquer disease, stop death, end famine and poverty? Billions crowd the Earth in gasping swarms, kept alive by the miracle of fusion power and the benefits derived therefrom. But they are just barely alive. The quality of their lives is deplorable. Blake knew he worked and lived among the top few percent of the population: the Shahs, kings, and energy czars. He knew he sucked at the front teat and existed precariously at the crest. "I pretty things up," he said aloud. He moved with those who had never seen the interior of a ghetto or who had never been hungry, except for the inevitable young beauties, male and female, who always surrounded wealth and power. These willing souls had been desperate to escape the dismal fate of growing old and weak and starving to death, unnoticed in the masses.

Blake knew the world did not consist solely of millionaires and haunted-eyed wretches starving in the arks' passages: there was a strong and healthy middle class. But the world only had so many resources, and even the recycling that the fusion torches and mass accelerators provided did not conserve those resources efficiently enough for the growing population. A little bit was lost on each recycling, one way or another; and only through technology had man kept his head above water for this long.

But what is the technology of love?

Blake shook his head angrily. *I'm perverted,* he thought. *I live only in the future, where there is love and peace. And that future might never come! I don't want a harem. Just one women—the right woman.*

Blake smiled ruefully at himself. *Self-pity is such a degrading emotion,* he thought. He slammed his fist down on the worktable, and a tiny round bed in the publisher's penthouse model flipped over. Blake lurched away and went into his office.

His was an office to inspire confidence. The models and photos were near the entry door, where they would be seen first. Closer to his desk, on the walls and floor surrounding it, were more specific examples of his taste and signs of his prestige. The warm-toned walls were paneled in expensive real wood and were considerably more permanent than the walls of his outer lobby, which could be cosmetically changed for effect. On shelves were relics of the ancient world, as well as the modern and near-past. He prized a pair of Mesopotamian sculptures and a Babylonian tablet the Shah had given him. A Greek head and a magnificent Sioux headdress under glass. A Picasso plate, a Coe assemblage, an intricate breastplate for a ficticious Amazon mercenary by Caruthers. A brick from the Grand Hall ruin near Ares Center on Mars. A lunar opal floating in a cube of crystal . . . The past, the present, and the future.

A painting by Otis Flu, an original photoprint by Coogan, a small Cilento sensatron repro cube, and an authentic Van Gogh paintbrush used in a collage by Powers all hung on the walls. Each had been carefully selected to impress and awe, either directly or subconsciously.

A polished cube of Tycho marble on his desk held a lighter, and a chip of stone stolen from the tomb of Cheops was fashioned into a tiny pyramid near it.

Confidence, awe, and admiration were the tools of the modern environmentalist's trade. "Trust me, I know best": the patois of the expert everywhere and everywhen.

Blake Mason snorted, thumbed a stud on his desk, and turned toward the wall as a rosewood panel slid silently upward. An enormous screen lit up, on which a dusky brunette with skin the color of burnished copper was slithering through the ruins of Angkor Wat, hissing the message of her sponsor: "Buy the aphrodisiac of the ancient east, the jewel of great price in the handy purse size or in a generous boudoir flacon . . .

Blake quickly punched another button.

A serious-faced newsreader was saying, "—esident DeVore was visibly delighted with the visit today at the Southern White House of the delegation from the International Association of Nudists." The scene changed to the pool area of the White House grounds, where a hundred nude men and women clustered respectfully around the small, smiling figure of the President. The newsreader's voice continued over the various cuts to the scene. "Although President DeVore did not disrobe, he did enjoy watching the delegation swim in the presidential pool." A pair of young girls came forward, moving awkwardly and obviously embarrassed by all the attention, to put a flower lei around the President's neck and to kiss him on each cheek. The President smiled and laughed, but Blake noticed that he did not ever touch the girls. "The Nudist Queen of the Americas and the Queen of European Nudism joined together to present President DeVore with a token of appreciation for signing the Free Beaches Act earlier today ... In Great Britain the bisexual scandal is still rocking London and today the Minister of Finance said—"

Blake snapped the set off and the panel slid back to cover the gray screen.

Can't people think of anything else? Can't they do something else?

We voted sex into legitimacy, and rightfully so; but somewhere we lost love, Blake thought. Or is it just me? Are all those couples and triples and foursomes in love? Are they even in like?

Blake dialed the window to transparent and looked out. The City of the Queen of the Angels. The tops of fifty-story office buildings were only the floor for the tall arcologs that dominated the skyline. But below, and between, the buildings were the bars and porno houses, the pawnshops and stim fronts. Live sex shows and obscene sensatrons, with highly realistic women mating with patent impossibilities: urban pagans and beasts from the jungle, their matted hair showing through the rips in the their thin layer of civilization.

I could go there and find a woman, Blake thought. Or a boy. Or a man. Or something that would go either way, be anything my money desired, whatever the situation demanded. Momentarily, temptation tugged at his loins, a mindless search for something unknown, something different, but it quickly went away.

I've never done that. I've never bought a woman.

Sure you have, a voice in his head told him. Not in

cash, not with a credit card perhaps, but with a present, a service, a favor. That Degas sketch to Danièle had started off their relationship. The visit to the hanging gardens and the introduction to the Shah and his court had so impressed the countess. *You've bought it before,* his mind-voice reminded.

But buying sex is not my problem, Blake argued with himself. *Getting laid is not the problem, it's who I'm laying.*

Is it?

Yes, it has always been the who not the what. Not whether she was rich or famous or black or yellow or talented or anything. It's the who, the woman inside, the person.

Blake Mason pressed his forehead against the cool glass and stared out at the Southern California city-scape.

"I want to fall in love," he said in a whisper. *With someone who is not an animal, with someone who is a person first and a sex machine second.* With his finger-tip, he drew a heart in the condensation on the window and slumped back into his chair.

If wishes were pennies, I'd be rich!

"Anything else, Elaine?" Blake asked his secretary, handing over a folio of signed mail and a Null-Edit tape to his accountant.

"Just your afternoon appointments, Mr. Mason. You want them now?" The trim, middle-aged woman flipped open her stenochart and looked at Mason, who nodded wearily.

"Two o'clock, Mrs. Barrows from the Landau wants to show you some holos of a gallery in Naples that used sensatronics."

"Call her back and tell her I've seen Santino's and that it is marvelous but will date very, very quickly. The impact of the sensatron is too strong for the use to which they have put it. If she still wants to come in, shift her to Aaron."

"Three o'clock, someone from Hughes wants to come check the progress on your first-draft sketches for Xanadu."

"Head him off. We're not ready yet. Never show a customer anything that isn't at least 75 percent finished."

"Three-thirty—and I'm saving the best for last—none other than Jean-Michel Voss."

"*The* Jean-Michel Voss?"

"Mr. Money himself. In person, no less. Shawna Hilton called, herself, to make the appointment."

Blake was a little amazed. "He's coming *here*?"

"Three-thirty. I guess he wants to see you in your natural habitat. Want me to deliver a dossier? He's Voss Oil, Voss Electronics, Voss Investments, Carbocon, Lunaport III, Martian Land Development—and God only knows what else."

"All right, thanks. And, Elaine, cancel all my other appointments."

17

"Yes, sir," Elaine said as she turned and left the room.

Blake settled back in his chair. *Jean-Michel Voss. What could he want with me? I did that Lunarport job for him years ago, but we never met.* Blake looked at the rosewood panels of his office, his eyes following a pattern in the grain. *Voss Investments are rumored to be behind the Poseidon project in the Bahamas, the biggest undersea dome cluster yet considered. Could he want me for that? What sort of environment would those submariners like? What would be right?*

Blake's mind went wandering along the path of visual and sensory associations that typified his approach to preliminary environmental concepts.

Poseidon. Sea god. Water. Domes. Fish. Fish tank, air tank. What would people like to see undersea? Too much water. Maybe land, hot tropical land instead of cold sea? He made a mental note to have Libby check on mean temperature in Bahama waters. *Desert environment. Contrast. Maybe cubist theme; flat, hot, textured surfaces opposing cool, fluid water.*

Voss was Interport Transfers, too, wasn't he? And didn't he own a piece of Station Three? Or was that Brian Thorne?

A space-station environment? Vast, black space. Stars. Airless. Cold. Faraway. High. Something lush and thick, rich and soft. Contrast again. A touch of luxury. All six walls padded, but with decorator fabrics. Maybe Astro Membranes could develop something more attractive than their standard gray, blue, and oyster.

Damn!

Blake leaned forward and thumbed the stud to Elaine's commline. "What is it?" he snapped.

"It's Mrs. Shure on One. Sorry, boss."

"Yeah, I know how she is. Okay, I'll take it," Blake said wearily.

He swung to face the visionphone lens and tried to get a smile on his face. He failed. He tried again for a neutral expression tending toward somber, then picked up a sketchpad to be a busy-busy prop and a subtle indicator of his business. Then he punched her in.

"Ah, Mrs. Shure . . ."

"Mr. Mason, how nice to see you. Are you feeling well? The last time I saw you you had a bit of a cold. The Andes, didn't you get it in the Andes?"

"No, in Canada, and that was a year ago, Mrs. Shure." He looked at the woman as she giggled in her prissy way, and wondered if she had ever received an obscene phone call. Ever since visionphones had become standard, the number of obscene phone calls had skyrocketed. "How may I help you?" Blake asked pleasantly.

"Ah . . . well . . . you know that lovely, lovely decor you did for my daughter Andrea's wedding reception? The psychedelic Aztec temple?"

It took Blake a moment to remember that he had never seen it. *Aaron handled that one, the crazy cackler. A psychedelic Aztec temple? Did something like that really come out of my office? I will really have to watch that sort of thing in the future.* After the famous financier and patron of the arts, Brian Thorne, had been married at the Temple of Magicians in Yucatán, a brief fad in Aztec and Mayan decor had followed. "I'm glad you enjoyed it," he said. *What the hell is her first name?*

Even as he tried to remember, the tickler-file screen lit next to the visionphone, and Elaine was punching in the information: Carolyn Shure . . . 48 . . . 4th marriage . . . Daughter, Andrea, by #1, Darrell Clive, then president of Empire State Police Services . . . #2 husband, MacNeil Busby, novelist . . . #3, Chan Xuan Thu, holder of important patent on mass accelerator . . . Daughter, Arden, by #4, George Shure, financier . . . estimated annual income from combined sources before taxes 7.4 million . . . address, 10 Hightop Circle, Camelot.

"Why have you called?" Blake asked, hoping to get her back to the point. "Carolyn," he added.

"Well, now, my daughter Arden is about to become engaged to the most *charming* young man, the eldest son of the Von Arrows, and I was *hoping* you'd be free to do the party. It's the first week in August, which doesn't give you much time, I know, but would

$25,000 be adequate? We spent fifty thousand on Andrea's wedding, I know; but after all, this is only an engagement."

Blake's eyes flicked to movement on the tickler screen. Elaine was holding up a hastily scrawled sign: SEBASTIAN FREE—DAUGHTER ELOPING—TRY FOR $40– $50.

Blake smiled and settled into his sales-talk patter to flatter her ego and to flatten her pocketbook. How could she, a pacesetter, the social leader in her ark, afford to commission anyone less than the best? The best, it was obvious and unstated, was Blake Mason. But, alas, his time was in such short supply that only a sufficiently high retainer could possibly get him to adjust his schedule. There was the Shah, of course, and the pleasure dome, and . . .

"Ah, thank you, Mrs. Shure, I'm certain that you will be pleased."

"Then you *will* come out this week?" He could see her trembling anxiety to score a triumph in having "Blake Mason," who dined with dynastic emperors and bedded vidstars, share her table.

"Yes, but I'm not certain just when. I'll have to give you a call." *Don't give her time to have more than a minimum of rich, but boring, friends waiting for me with their questions about the Shah and the others.* The tickler file flicked on again, and Blake gave it a quick scan. Money from soybeans, arcolog condominiums, a marina, a baseball team, an insurance company, garbage recyling. *God, the conversations I'll have to endure!*

The screen changed to show Elaine holding up a sign: SAT THRU TUES FREE. "Perhaps this weekend, perhaps as late as Tuesday. I'm sorry to make this so indefinite, uh, Carolyn, but the Shah wants some minor changes and trusts only me to do them." *Let her know how valuable my time is.*

"Oh, do tell that dear, dear monarch I said hello!"

You never met him in your life, lady, Blake said to himself. "Yes, of course. *Au revoir, madame!*"

"Good-bye, you dear man. I'm so happy we arranged this today. I can't wait to tell the girls!" She waggled her fingers as Mason cut the connection, then his forced smile.

Blake opened the intercom. "Elaine, my precious pearl, you have zero defects. Does that woman's husband really make that much?"

"Yup. Disgusting, isn't it? But she has part of that, too. As the man said, you can see the way the good Lord feels about money by the damn fools he gives it to."

"Steady there," Blake laughed. "I am not exactly a pauper, pet."

"I was hoping you'd say that, boss. How about a raise?"

"No raise, but a bonus if this job goes through. Knowing that her daughter was planning to elope cinched it and I could push hard enough to get the larger fee. She's just the kind of woman who likes an excuse to make a big splash and show off. But how do you know all these odd little things?"

"Society pages, boss. What do you think I fill up my time with out here?"

Blake grinned. Elaine had often come up with the strangest information at just the right moment. "Okay, mark yourself down for a dollar and a half bonus as soon as we get the retainer."

"You are *too* kind. Monday would be a good day to go out. No weekend guests, and a business day gives you a good excuse to make it a quick trip."

"Make that two bucks even and tell Sebastian."

"He'll love all the froufrou and the fawning."

Blake grunted and clicked off. Ravel was playing, but he wasn't listening to it now. His mind had gone back to the possibility of a Voss undersea project. In the *Atlantis* dome he had used a mermaid decor in one area; a seashell motif in another; a pagan throne room with gas torches; mosaics set with rocks, then laser-cut and polished and permafinished to look wet.

But he would have to come up with something different for Voss. Blake wanted to have at least one idea to throw out spontaneously when Voss brought the subject up. That always gave the client a feeling he was talking to a creative person. But the best idea, the final idea, should never be revealed quickly or casually. Although he might come up with the concept in a second, Blake liked to polish it in private, mainly to give the client the feeling that this was the best possible answer to his problem, and one not quickly or lightly reached. Blake remembered a senior environmentalist, one of the old breed who still called themselves decorators, who used the phrase "I was thinking last night," and then proceeded to improvise his thoughts of the moment. "Doing so gives greater weight to your words," he had told Blake in his student days, "And it gives you the reputation of being a thinker."

The intercom lit up. "Mr. Mason." Not "boss"— someone was there.

Blake hit the stud. "Yes, Elaine?"

"Mr. Voss is here."

"Please show him in." *Ritual and façade. Oh, what the hell!*

Voss was tall, tanned, and ugly, with that beautiful sort of arrogant ugliness that seemed to devastate women satiated with pretty men. He was quick and sure as he came through the door. Everything about him radiated money and power. *He doesn't walk as if he owns the place*, Blake thought, *he enters as if he doesn't care who owns it.* Used to the rich and powerful and their often egocentric ways, Blake was nevertheless impressed.

Voss's handshake was firm and quick, his smile wide and friendly, his eyes steady and automatically appraising. Behind him two burly men eyed Blake and the room, but then left instantly at a flick of Voss's hand.

Voss sat down in a Life-style chair and fingered his Martian firestone cuff links as his gaze took in the room. "You have many lovely things," he said. "I believe I have a Coe assemblage of that period. Somewhere."

"Thank you." *A pitiful handful*, Blake thought. *You probably have more warehouses full than I have pieces.* "Would you like a drink?" As he spoke, he thumbed the bar stud and a panel slid upward.

Voss peered at the wine behind the cooler panels, then his dark eyes scanned the array of bottles, flasks, and vintage tubes. "Ah, a favorite," he smiled. "Benedictine and brandy, please." Blake selected two small Gral goblets and poured. He left Ravel playing, but turned down the volume.

"Shawna suggested you to me," Voss said without preamble. "Her home is very pleasant. Fits her beautifully. Nothing that *I* would want, of course, but very pleasing."

Blake was silent, smiling briefly and acknowledging the compliment with a salute of his glass.

"What I have in mind is . . . unusual for our time, but very ancient, really. I want a tomb."

Blake was surprised. Voss seemed so young to be thinking of such things. "Yours?" Blake asked, just to be certain.

Voss smiled broadly. "But of course." He held up his hand warningly. "But, please, not some tacky little pillared tomb, all solemn and marble, a piece of ego sculpture. Nothing, um, tricky. You did a lovely miniature Taj Majal in something transparent for Topaz."

"Magnaplastics."

"Yes, and that Moon-orbiting casket for Ron Bellingham is really quite beautiful. It's becoming something of a tourist attraction." Voss smiled again. "But I want something that is definitely *not* a tourist attraction. More like an Egyptian tomb, quite hidden. I have the site already picked out. We'll laser the whole thing right into the living rock."

Blake nodded as if tomb design was something he did every day. *Everyone has an ego*, he thought. *They leave foundations behind, nameplates on buildings, scholarships, trust funds to operate homes for wayward cats, stadiums, museums. Some commission art. Some want political power. Some are just egotists.*

"I want the best art. Murals by Don Kains, a portrait by Paula Powers, a Coe assemblage from the trivia of my life. Sculpture by Rosenthal, Green, perhaps Mallinoux or Cordova. But nothing that needs power—no sensatrons, no electronics, nothing that can be detected. Everything must be built to last."

Blake smiled. "Are you planning to take it with you into the afterlife?"

Voss looked at him a moment before he smiled. "Perhaps, Mr. Mason, perhaps." He laughed softly. "If the pharaohs could do it, why can't I?" He nodded to himself, then looked at Blake. "This project will make you rich and famous."

Sensing a bargaining point not to be lost, Blake matched his smile and said, "I am already rich and famous."

"No, man, *rich* and *famous*—not just rich and famous." He laughed lightly, with a kind of disturbing secret amusement, then sipped at his Benedictine.

"It sounds like a major project."

"It is. I'd like you to drop everything else," Voss said.

"I have contracts I must fulfill," Blake said. The impact of the project was only now beginning to get to him. *A tomb as big as a pharaoh's, and to last how long?*

"Then don't take on any new ones. When this is finished .. hell, long before ... you'll be able to command much higher fees."

Blake hesitated, then plunged ahead. "Just how much money are you prepared to spend, Mr. Voss?" He gestured as if to say it was crass to talk of such matters, but one must start somewhere.

"One hundred million. In Swiss francs, of course." Blake's chest was suddenly tight. "To start," Voss added casually. Now Blake's chest was much too tight for his heart. "I know these things take time and always cost more in the long run. I expect we'll change our minds about details as we go along. But I want it done *right*. The hundred million is only to get you thinking in the right area. I will go as high as 150,000,000 as long as the tomb is completed to my satisfaction."

"Mr. Voss . . ."

" 'Jean-Michel,' please. We will get to know one another, yes?" He laughed again, an odd, wry laugh, as if secretly amused. "We plan for my death, no?" At Blake's expression of shock he waved a genteel hand. "No, I'm not being morbid—only ego, my friend. A mark to make in the world, perhaps. I can afford it. You might say that after I am dead who will care ... ?"

"I . . ." For once Blake Mason was at a loss for words.

The Gardens of Babylon had been estimated at 300,-000,000 European standard francs, but much of the labor had been done by the Shah's army, and the cost was borne by the treasury of a petroleum-rich nation. The pleasure dome projects were commercial ventures, with a return expected. But here was a private project, privately financed, an artistically oriented commission that was certain to bring him fame, if not glory.

"Uh . . . Why did you choose me? There are other, bigger companies. Enzenbacher and Son. Quigley and Rausa. The Corwin Company. Environments, Unlimited—"

"No. You are the best. The best for what I want. This will be more than just a tomb, it will be a home. It must be built around a central chamber, and the specifications for that will be sent to you." Voss smiled. "You look puzzled. Yes, a home. In a mountain."

"A mountain?" Blake felt stupid.

"A mountain to hollow out. It's in the Rockies, and it is geologically stable; I've had it carefully tested. The only thing that might affect it is continental drift, but nothing can be done about that. We will hollow the rock out, make it into a home where, if I chose, I could live comfortably for many years. That is why I selected you. Should I . . . um . . . decide to live in it for an extended period, it would still be a pleasant place."

Blake nodded, though still not certain what was expected of him.

"You will begin to understand as our talks progress. This mountain, I own the sixty thousand acres surrounding it. Or rather, certain companies I control do, or foundations. We'll fly up there soon and look it over. When can you go? I'd like you to get an idea of the location soon."

Blake blinked but didn't answer.

Voss peered at him. "We do have a deal, do we not? The lawyers and the contracts can get here in good time. This is the important part: the agreement, the meeting of minds."

"Uh? Yes, of course."

Voss grinned. He stuck out his hand and Blake took

it automatically. "When can you fly up?" he asked again.

"Uh, anytime next week. No, this weekend. This weekend all right?"

"Fine. Saturday morning. Which is more convenient for you, Palmdale International or the Catalina float?"

"Catalina."

"Fine. Be at the Voss hangars at, um, nine?"

Blake felt just a bit dizzy and more than slightly confused. A hundred-million-franc tomb for a living man? Hollowing out a mountain. Top artists? Pharaohs, indeed!

"Mr. Voss, er, Jean-Michel, there must be other reasons why you picked me?"

Voss stopped as he strode toward the door. "You have the right sort of engineering degrees, the reputation of being discreet, and, of course, because you were the most sensual."

"Sensual? You want a *sensual* tomb?"

"Yes, of course. No one has ever had a sensual tomb before, certainly not on this scale. Oh, a few nudes in sterile white marble—very virginal. A bed for the pharaoh's afterlife. That's all." His wry smile widened. "People don't think of death as being sensual, do they?"

"No. Neither do I, to be perfectly frank."

Voss threw back his head, and his laugh was a sharp bark. "But you see, after it is built, I will live in it, at least for a little while; and later on, too, perhaps. I may have companions. Then . . . perhaps, if I have an afterlife, the tomb will certainly be my home." He paused, came back, and clasped Blake's upper arm. "Who knows what the world of the future may be like?"

Blake left the studio that night in a state of total bemusement. The crowds that thronged the malls and corridors of the arcolog did not bother him. Usually their jostling and noise gave him a feeling of claustrophobia and loneliness. He had often contemplated moving closer to his studio, or even expanding and building a home as an extension of the studio, but the space he would need had never become available. Now he enclosed himself in the ark dweller's capsule of indifference and pushed his way mechanically through the crowds.

He stopped at a restaurant and ate a bowl of soysoup without really tasting it. His thoughts were on the project ahead.

Epic. That's what Voss wants, Blake told himself. *Something fabulous, as well as eternal. Something with a unifying sense, something that has to be taken as a whole, not just as a collection of items. The Egyptians had it because their art was of one style, with only one way of doing things, one way of looking at art. From the top down,* Blake thought as he paid for the soup.

He took an escalator up two decks and walked along the commercial level until he came to the Swain Gallery. The pedestrian traffic was very light here, for the shops were closed. A new sensatron artist had an exhibit, and an example of his art was in each window of the dark gallery. The plastic window panels were especially fenestrated with microholes to allow the Alpha and Beta waves as well as the sonic waves to come through directly.

The first cube was a pastoral, a square of primitive forest in some long-gutted section of the world. Blake could see through the thick underbrush toward a clearing in the trees, almost as if he were in hiding, watching

27

for prey. The cycle on the cube was not long. Insects crawled on the leaves nearby, a huge butterfly flopped through drunkenly, the wind sighed in the clean, green trees. Then Blake saw movement through the tree trunks, and the Alpha-wave projectors made the adrenaline surge in his bloodstream. He was suddenly tense. A deer walked slowly into the clearing, a doe with delicate markings. She stopped, looked around, dipped her head to chomp some grass, looked around again. Blake was startled when the brush before his face parted, as if his own hand had moved it. The deer's head went up, and a second later the animal was bounding away, to disappear in a few seconds. The brush stopped moving, the forest returned to its noisy silence, and the same butterfly flopped through again.

Not bad, thought Blake. *I wonder where he found such a parkland to use for his basic photographic imagery. Places like that are hard to find.* He moved on to the next window and the second sensatron.

Here was a dawn world, with strange prehistoric ferns that seemed outsized. There was a murky pool of water in the foreground, dark and topped with scum. Suddenly the placid scene erupted. The head of a great gray-green brontosaurus rose, dripping and munching on slimy greens. The reptilian head loomed close, then turned ponderously and looked over his shoulder. With a crunching sound, a *Tyrannosaurus rex* stalked out from behind some rocks, and the subsonic music quickened in Blake's ears. Another monster from the past roared challenge offscreen, and the herbivore in the foreground ducked away. There was the smell of sweat and decaying vegetation.

Suddenly Blake felt pressure against his kidney, and hands grabbed his arms. *Fool!* Blake was annoyed with himself. *After-hours on a darkened commercial level, what else can I expect but a mugging?*

His assailants twisted him around roughly. One was thin, with the erratic twitch of an Eroticene addict gone past the help of any antidote. The other, young and elegant in a cheap, trendy way, wore a sleek and shiny white suit with a fashionably padded crotch. Both were smiling, but the addict's grin had a mean twist to it.

"Your money or your life," the one in white said.

"Stand and deliver," the addict said in a gravely voice that dissolved into a high-pitched giggle.

They've been watching too many historical tapes, Blake thought. "I only have credit tabs," he said. *No one uses cash anymore, at least no one legitimate—or not often. But surely they know that, too.*

The slim one in white laughed abnormally loud, and right in Blake's ear. He waved a knife around and Blake stared at it. It shone in the light from the cubes. The *Tyrannosaurus rex* was rolling around on the bottom of the cube with a spiny-backed reptile Blake had not seen enough of to identify.

"I guess you'll have to pay a forfeit," the one in white said. He brought the knife close, and brushed the point against Blake's throat.

It had been a long time since Blake's two years in the service and his two years of militia, when he had been called out to quell food riots and fight in little brushfire wars between ethnic arks. It had been even longer since the bravos in his ark section had challenged him on the way to school. Violence was just not part of Blake's world anymore. He had almost forgotten that special surge of fear and the thrill that such situations brought. There were accidents in his world, such as a fail-safe system failing on someone's aircar, or someone at a party falling a few levels and bloodying a neighbor's dome or being squished on his terrace. But that violence was not personal, it was just part of modern living, like elevator failure or a fouled computer readout.

His adrenaline surged and Blake started thinking fast. He knew these scrubs didn't want money. Indeed, they would have been very surprised to find any. If he were a woman, they might rape—not out of passion but out of boredom, or out of hatred. Since he was a man, they would want to play games: Run and we'll chase you . . . Walk on the edge of this slidewalk, it's only a fifty-meter drop . . . Challenge one of us to a duel. Or else . . .

The zongo gangs roamed every arcolog. If the police

came they ran, knowing every chute and elevator—in this condo and out that delivery hatch; down that tube, up that access passage. They had lithe young bodies and good motivation for hiding. The police seldom gave chase for very long: they were older, and hadn't the motivation to run blindly down service halls with knocked-out light panels and deadfall traps.

Blake looked down the curve of the mall, but few citizens were in sight. The Monte Carlo section was popular at this time of night, as the gaudy, rowdy Sinstrip would be later on. Few people in *this* area now—mainly service technicians, and they were faraway, either unseeing or deliberately unseeing. They had to work nights in this section, and the gangs might return anytime.

White Suit laughed. "No loyal members of the constabulary in view, citizen slave."

His knife grazed Blake's cheek. The designer tried to stay calm, to stall until a patrol craft floated by.

"Forget it," White Suit said. "There's a Zeropop riot over in the university or somewhere."

"It's a Living Standards protest, Lennie," the addict said.

"Shut up, Weed." Lennie turned back to Blake, who had not moved. "In any case, no blackshirts, citizen slave, none at all."

He pulled Blake toward the darkness of a support column covered with violent-colored posters, shoving him against a torn placard of George Clay's Law and Order Coalition. Lennie's chuckling laugh degenerated into a giggle, as if he could not help but laugh at the future.

Suddenly Blake was afraid. Up until then he had been startled, and apprehensive, but had had no real fear. *They're kidding. They'll go away.* But they weren't going away and they weren't kidding. Now Blake was afraid. Even as Lennie patted his body, looking for weapons, Blake was composing a headline: NOTED ENVIRONMENTALIST KILLED, VICTIM OF VIOLENCE. "The sad death of Blake Mason spurs Ark Director Bloch to sweeping reforms . . ."

Death.

Nothingness.

Then, just as suddenly, the fear was gone, and anger replaced it. *How dare they!*

"Duel or chase?"

"Huh?"

"Duel or chase, citizen slave?"

The addict giggled, holding the knifepoint against Blake's throat.

They don't rob for gain, only for thrills, Blake thought. *Urban banditos!* The anger spoke. "I don't feel like running."

A wicked grin spread across Lennie's face. He stepped back, hands spread, the knife loose in his right.

The addict backed off into the mall, looking in both directions and grinning crookedly. "Uh, looks okay, Lennie."

"Come on, citizen slave," Lennie said, gesturing Blake out.

"Where's mine?" Blake said, indicating the knife.

Lennie shook his head, his eyes glittering. "Table stakes, citizen. You should carry."

Blake didn't speak, but he edged forward. He saw Weed move toward him and realized the table stakes were high. Three to one, counting the knife.

It's time to reduce the odds.

He faked a lunge to the right, then broke left toward the mall space, then just as quickly threw himself to the right, toward the wall, hitting and bouncing, letting himself twist and roll along the ferroconcrete until he was almost behind Lennie.

Lennie turned and Blake brought up his leg, kicking straight out from the knee, aiming for the crotch. Lennie twisted, avoiding it. But he stumbled, and Blake shoved at him, breaking past and striking at Weed. The addict lurched, blood on his cheek, but did not fall. Blake kicked at his feet and the twitching Weed crashed to the mall deck.

With a strangled cry Lennie threw himself at Blake. His knife cut through Blake's jacket, caught on the tough creaseless fabric, and as Blake leaned backward the knife twisted from Lennie's grasp. He stumbled and fell to one knee. Blake grabbed at the knife, but it fell to the hard deck with a clatter.

Lennie lurched up and started running, not looking back. Blake took a few steps after him and stopped. Then he turned toward Weed, who was unconscious. He looked at him, then stooped to pick up the knife. Putting the point of the blade into a crack between the support column and the sidewall of a balancing salon, he snapped the knife in two and threw the pieces down the dark mall.

Goddamn stupid fight! Blake told himself with great annoyance. *How stupid to get in that position. I know better. I grew up in these arks, I ran with gangs out of self-protection.* He knew that criminals and addicts roamed every ark in the world: mindless mini-rioters, vandals in permaplast, the true sons of Attila—each of them bored and frustrated.

The brontosaurus was still munching placidly. The tyrannosaurus lurched into the background once again, continuing the cycle that would go on as along as the sensatron had power or until something in its electronic guts burned out.

Blake headed for the nearest elevator cluster and went home.

The world had barely escaped strangling in its own waste, the planet was gutted, and only the fusion torches and mass accelerators had saved it. They mined the waste heaps, recycled the garbage in a way never before possible, shredding the very molecules with the tiny suns of the fusion torches, stripping the waste down to the atoms themselves, before separating them with the mass accelerators. This technique gave man back most of his precious elements in a form more purified than ever before. Recycling with fusion torches and mass accelerators had given man a second chance, and just in time. Given hope, the birthing masses of the world tried harder, so that although everything was still not perfect at least there was now no fear of using up the Earth's resources completely. Fusion torches didn't plant or harvest food, and mass accelerators didn't distribute it, but at least now there was material, chemicals, power—and hope.

Man had colonized Mars and had turned the Moon into something not much more than an exotic, if somewhat distant, port. Satellites now sailed in silent swarms around the planet, gathering solar power, monitoring the weather, feeding down information about the sun and stars. Man was spreading outward at last, but in a painfully slow manner. Probes had gone to the other planets and there had been a few manned missions; and now there was even talk of mining operations starting on the moons of Jupiter as soon as an efficient shielding against the big planet's deadly radiation could be developed.

Nevertheless, still the population grew. Babies came relentlessly, even though the Pope had at last reversed himself and amended the Church's historical stand on contraception. But he was too late. The more practical-minded of his flock had long since deserted him for theologies that had more relevance. Belatedly, congresses and parliaments made laws, dictators and regents issued edicts, foundations said I-told-you-so, and economists held their heads. There were too many people for the available food and available space. Ecological structures only utilized existing space more efficiently, they did not solve the problem.

Angered and frustrated, youth had little to do. Most young people took the highroad: drugs and sex, "challenges" and quick thrills. The old cliché of "Live fast, die young, and leave a good-looking corpse" was still operational for a large percentage of the young.

Blake shook his head sadly and punched out his secret code on the door lock, thumbed the sonic identifier, stood on the hidden sensor mat.

Home, sweet home, he thought.

It was a black-and-gray mountain, made of uncounted megatons of granite and immense continental-plate pressures. It had a thin mantle of decomposed granite and a skirt of pine trees in the lower regions, but raw rock above. A three-dimensional image of the entire mountain was constructed from seismic recordings, holograms, test holes, sonics, corings, and precise engineering measurements.

Voss kept everyone under constant pressure, from Blake and the engineers to the security men charged with keeping the site private. Voss even used his charm, and sometimes the pressure of his power, to obtain or hurry artists whom Blake had found difficult to handle. Blake found he admired the drive and decisiveness of the man, though he couldn't stop wondering why anyone as young as Voss was thinking about a tomb. But he shrugged it off. It was an exciting venture, so why should he care?

At one of their frequent meetings in the designer's office, Blake mentioned Voss's ability to get people to respond and to act.

The industrialist laughed. "That is one of the reasons I like you, my dear Mason. We are much alike. You, too, get people to do things your way ... and at a profit."

Blake started to protest, but Voss was already off on another subject. "Come down to Puerto Vallarta this Sunday. Rio should be there by then. I'd like her to look over the plans so far."

"Who's Rio?"

"A lady of many beauties. You'll like her."

"What's this?" Blake laughed. "A blind date?"

Voss's laugh was short. "No. Rio is mine. But there

will be other entertainment. One of my planes will be waiting for you at the Voss hangar Sunday morning."

After Voss had left, Blake sank into his chair, disturbed by Voss's comment that they were much alike. But now that he thought about it, he had to admit there was some legitimacy to the man's words. For years he had smoothed over union disputes, wheedled manufacturers into doing research on materials and processes that he could not afford to conduct himself, and persuaded cities and arcologs and cranky individualists to accept his views. He challenged artists to exceed their usual degree of excellence; he created environments that stimulated creativity; and he used the weapons of status, ego, jealousy, money, or whatever he needed to pull together the current dream he was creating.

But he also realized there was at least one major difference between him and Voss. The financier used people. Though Blake also used people, he believed that his use of them left them enriched in spirit or in money—or both. Voss did not care for people at all. They were pawns and phantoms to him, as a hundred casual comments had proved. Voss just used people—including Blake Mason.

□

The helmsman of the launch, a stolid bronzed Mexican who seemed to ignore the crazy naked Norteamericanos, swung the boat into the dock with expert skill, killing the motor and letting the craft touch gently against the stones. Two girls who had been sunning themselves on the cabin roof jumped off athletically, leaving the crew to take off their luggage. They ran across the dock and up the ramp to the first level.

Blake stepped off onto the warm stone dock and peered up through the thick trees at the red and white glimpses of Casa Emperador on top of the promontory. He could see someone waving but could not tell who it was.

He thanked the helmsman, who only nodded, and followed a crew member loaded with luggage up the slanting seawall that formed the ramp to the wide terrace closest to the water.

Two more girls came running down the ramp from the terrace above, laughing and bouncing. Only one wore any clothing, and that was a wide sunhat. They ignored the Mexican crew, who seemed to ignore them, except for the helmsman, who spoke softly to Blake.

"A convenience for the guests, *señor*."

"Hello, hello, hello," the brunette said, grabbing Blake's arm. She looked up at him brightly. "I'm Caren. With a *C*."

The blonde shoved back her hat as she clung to Blake's other arm. "I'm Debra!" She snuggled against his arm like a long-lost lover. "Welcome to Mismaloya!"

"How was the flight down?" Caren asked. "Isn't Puerta Vallarta quaint? Jean-Michel practically rebuilt it, you know; and it's becoming popular all over again."

As they walked up the ramp, Caren regaled Blake with the history of the old port's social downfall decades

36

before, starting with the murder of a beach boy by a jealous heiress. A series of small but messy situations had been capped by the discovery of a homosexual satanic coven. The jet set said, "No, not this season," and the town started to die. The resort had gone on some years, feasting off the middle-class tourists who didn't know it was déclassé; but in time they, too, caught on.

Blake knew how the Beautiful People moved from watering hole to watering hole, and how others followed, hoping that the glamour would rub off on them. The southern Peruvian villages were easily reached by aircars from big city jetports. And the tourists found their way to Lake Sahara; the pampas ranchos; the Gold Coast of Africa, with its legal slavery; the undersea pleasure palaces like *Triton*; and the plankton skimmers with their lush accommodations. So Puerto Vallarta had grown weedy and the beach boys developed paunches.

"Then Jean-Michel bought up practically everything here, tore down those dated old hotels, and redesigned the whole city from the ground up. Spanish Colonial is the motif, not bastard Grand Motel," Caren said proudly. "But this is the capitol," she laughed, gesturing overhead at the big house above. "This is where things happen!"

Debra pressed against his arm. "You're Blake Mason, aren't you? You and Jean-Michel are up to something big, right?"

Blake smiled noncommittally and looked down at her bare flesh. She smiled back and the two girls led him across the terrace to the cool shade under the big thatched roof of the seaside bar. He was brought a cold drink, introduced to a count, to the director of a large corporation, and to two vice-presidents of Voss Investments. There were three other beautiful women in the terrace lounge: Wendy, Pei Ling, and Doreen, a redhead. The girls wore jewelry and sandals but little else, and they were uniformly—almost monotonously—beautiful. The men, all middle-aged, wore brief swim suits, and some had on robes that covered their aging bodies. Blake noticed how casually the male hands caressed the unresisting women. The helmsman's comment came back to him: *A convenience for the guests* . . .

Debra tugged at his arm. "Come on, Blake, Jean-Michel wants to see you!"

Blake shrugged and got up. They went out into the sun again and up a wide, stone-stepped path under the green trees. A few Olmec stone heads were lying in the undergrowth. The retaining walls seemed to be a thousand years old, but the greenery was as fresh as morning. He could hear music, something rather exotic but unknown to him.

The climb was tiring, for the hill sloped steeply. But they at last cleared the level of the final terrace, and Blake saw the high white walls of the big house rising over him. *At least fifty rooms* . . . he thought; and knew that this was only one of Voss's homes. *And I thought Shawna Hilton was rich!*

Blake took in the terrace quickly, for he saw Voss emerge from a large and ancient double door and come toward him smiling. On Blake's right, a tanned beauty lay supine on a lounge. She raised the brim of her crushed straw hat when she heard Voss say Blake's name, and looked at him without expression. On Blake's left was the terrace wall, stone blocks capped by deep rust-red tile squares. Potted plants and an excellent Mendoza bronze lined the wall. The sea was seen beyond, through the trees. Several birds hopped about on the tiles, pecking at crumbs.

"Blake, they just told me you had arrived! Welcome. *Mi casa es su casa.* Did you bring sketches?" He noticed Blake staring at the woman on the lounge. "That's Theta, my sister." When he saw the expression on Blake's face, he laughed. "Yes, sometimes it's hard to tell her from the others. Except she doesn't make a fuss over me."

"Oh!" Blake said. He couldn't think of anything else to say.

A beautiful blonde, deeply tanned and wearing nothing but an ornate silver necklace, came out of the house bearing a tray with one drink. She saw Voss, paused to smile briefly and make a small bow, then knelt on a cushion next to Voss's sister and proffered the drink.

Blake thought she had one of the finest and most beautifully proportioned bodies he had ever seen.

Voss nodded his head toward the blonde, who was now oiling Theta's nude body, and took Blake's elbow. "Theta's taste is getting better. She's a nice one. I wonder what she paid for her."

"Paid?" Blake spoke before he thought, and Voss smiled.

"A labor contract, all very legal. Expensive, but legal. Lump sum upon signing, a weekly or monthly amount deposited in a Swiss account—and lo! a slave girl to do with as you wish. A year, three years, seven years, with options. I'd take very few for seven. They age too much. But that one, that one might be worth it. You'd have to pay through the nasal passages for her now that she's seen how it's done."

Voss gestured Blake through the big oak door, heavily carved in an intricate design with big bosses of cast silver set with jade.

"You look shocked, Blake. Don't you really know about the world of the rich? The *rich* rich? We have everything, anything. All we have to do is want something enough to spend the money." He gestured back toward the terrace as they went through the entry hall. "Everything but time. Oh, you get a *little* more time with the doctors, and the shots, and the little extras. Knapp is putting millions into immortality research. So am I, for that matter." He smiled. "The Methuselah Institute is funded by me. Warfield and Kemp have foundations researching democratic processes." Voss now came close to Blake and whispered to him with mock seriousness. "Want a slave girl, Blake? One that is your property? Want to whip her or have her do something . . . dark? All you need is money, my friend. All *they* need is money, or so they think; then they are willing to do whatever they must. Beautiful boys, luscious women, any type you want. Just hunt around." Then he laughed and stepped away. "Or if you are a Voss, they send you pictures and details. Ah, Amelia!"

Voss greeted a buxom Mexican woman in a plain dress. "Amelia, this is Mr. Mason. He is the man who is going to make me famous. Blake is going to design my tomb."

"Oh, *Señor* Voss! Why do you think of such things! Ahh!"

Voss laughed easily and turned to Mason. "Amelia is my housekeeper and my friend. She keeps the girls from stealing the silver when they don't hook a millionaire by dinnertime."

"Oh, *señor*! You are *loco*!"

Blake looked around the big main room. Life-style chairs in warm colors. A Locke table, a bad Shembo and a good Kirk Austin mosaic. A tapestry that was probably a Shannon. An oriental girl asleep on a pile of velvet cushions, her skin creamy and flawless, her breasts small and perfect.

"Which is his room, Amelia?"

"The one with the blue door, *señor*, at the head of the stairs in the south wing."

Blake turned to his host. "Why do you want to leave this and go live in a hole in a mountain? I don't mean to talk myself out of the biggest commission of my life, but I have to ask."

"But I don't have to answer," Voss smiled. Blake noticed that only his mouth smiled; his eyes were flinty. "I don't blame you for asking, though; but don't get nervous. We shook, didn't we?" Blake nodded. "This is not a whim, Blake, remember that. It is important to me."

Amelia showed Blake to his room, and Blake sat down on the bed.

The room was big and comfortable, the baronial hall of a lord, fully equipped with a wall screen in an antique frame, a colorchanger, a computerized tape library, and an information terminal hooked into the Masterlibe in Omaha.

He lay back on the fur spread and closed his eyes. He had come a long way from the old neighborhood. There hadn't been as many of the big arcologs then, and more of the untidy urban sprawl. The San Fernando Valley had been one big bedroom, twenty or thirty floors deep. His parents were middle-class—his father a hydroponics engineer, his mother a biochemist with Algae International . . .

"Art?" his father exploded? "You want to study *art?* Goddammit, Son, make yourself useful in the world. Go to Cal Trade, or some good electronics school. There will always be a need for someone to fix things. I can get you into the Hydroponic Institute, you might like that."

"That's great for you," Blake said in his teen-age voice, "but that's not for me. I want to be an artist."

"What kind of artist?" his mother asked. "Some of those fancy arks they're building are using a lot of craftsmen. Or maybe you could get a job in television like your cousin Mae."

"I don't want to be a craftsman. "And I don't want to whip up sets for *quiver* music groups. I want to go to art school."

"And be what?" his father growled.

"I don't know yet. All I know is that is what I want to do. I want to look the whole thing over. I can decide later."

"Jesus H. Mohammed," Blake's father grumbled.

"Now, Charles, some of those artist people do make a lot of money."

"It's not the money, Mom," Blake said. "It's . . . the *doing* of it. Dad, remember when you rigged that bypass and stopped that overload? You were pretty proud of that, weren't you?"

"If I hadn't acted, it would have blown the side right out of the ark."

"And no one else did it, or knew how, or even thought of it. *That's* how I want to feel about my work. That no one else has done it, that only *I* could do it, and that I'm the best at it."

Charles Mason stared at his son, his head barely nodding. "All right. I still don't like it. But everyone has to make his own mistakes."

"Be careful, Son," his mother cautioned. "I've heard some pretty odd things about those artists."

Blake shifted in the luxurious bed. Art school. Working long hours—longer than the classes had required—for the sheer joy of it. Working in the cafeteria, working for a spray-plastics craftsman, selling tickets to Arena games, doing whatever odd job came to hand in order to get by. Living in poverty and not really caring. Drawing and drawing and drawing. Sketching people, sketching dreams, painting the landscape of his mind.

Wrangling a one-year scholarship from the Ventura County Art Commission, and getting it stretched to two. Linette, Johnny, the Chinese kid whom everyone said was on a scholarship to watch for earthquakes, bisexual Georgi, big Brownie, beautiful Dora, witty Marge. The thrill of selling his first drawing, seeing his first painting hanging in the group show. One thing had led to another, to a series of murals for a group of condominiums in the *Scheherazade* ark on Lake Sahara. That had been the turning point—a slow, but steady improvement in his status. Then the Ali Baba cave commission, the Blackfoot Nation Fair, the soaring monument for the Federal Space Agency, Shawna Hilton's incredible home, and all the others that had consolidated his reputation.

And all the time his parents had never understood a thing he was doing. They had been proud of him when he started making money, and prouder still when his name was mentioned in the vidstats. But they'd never understood why.

An environmentalist was, in Blake's opinion, part artist, part accountant, part psychologist, part manager, and part psychic. He had to determine what a client really wanted, not what he said he wanted, and not what his status told him he should have. Some people wanted to be told what they were, others wanted their lives structured for them. Talking a client into what that client really wanted was often the hardest part of Blake's job, but also the most rewarding. Some clients hired him just as a convenience—hiring his taste, his expertise on what was available on the market, hiring him as they hired security services or carpenters.

Blake knew that taste was simply knowing what was appropriate, nothing more. He had to know what was *going* to be fashionable as well as what *was* fashionable. Occasionally his own efforts started a trend.

As Blake had grown more popular he ceased taking on the commercial jobs, the ones for which he was merely "hired." He would concentrate more on the challenges, the commissions where he worked on his own, or those in real partnership with someone of taste. He was now in a sense an orchestrator, the one who brought together the artists, engineers, materials, and craftsmen, and yet maintained the original vision.

A bawdy laugh brought Blake back to the Casa Emperador. He heard more laughter, below, on the terrace, and the sound of the surf far below. He rolled onto his back and let out a long sigh. The sound of a soft gong came from a wall speaker, and a voice quietly and politely announced that dinner would be served in one hour.

Blake rolled off the bed and undressed. He took a sonic shower, luxuriating in the fresh, clean feeling as oils and dirt and dead cells were swept away. He stepped out dry, and dressed.

Blake looked at himself in the mirror. A crisp snow-silk shirt, with a ruffled front, accented his skin. Snug formal black trousers, soft black boots, and a black vest with silver conchos in the Spanish style gave him a bold, graphic look. Blake stared into his own dark eyes.

Why do I feel expectant? Blake wondered. He closed his left hand slowly into a fist, then looked at his image in the mirror. Then he smiled, and snorted at his own fancies. He left the room, but an odd feeling of expectation was still within him.

From the top of the stairs he could see several of the male guests standing around the living room, dressed much as he was. Each had at least one girl at his side drinking in his every word, looking attentive.

Although the girls were still nude, their hairstyles were now much more elaborate, wound with velvet ribbons and set with pearls and delicate pins. They all wore shoes or fancy sandals of some sort, and many of them had suddenly sprouted long fingernails, some in color and some in bright designs. Much jewelry was in evidence, from diamond nipple ornaments to expensive earrings to toe rings and jeweled necklaces. All the lilies were gilded, but they were still not letting anyone forget their basic commodity: prime young flesh.

Blake descended the steps slowly, watching the

guests, hearing the laughter. He spotted Voss standing between the count and a rather corpulent though obviously powerful man—the three of them surrounded by women. He took a rapid head count and realized there were several more women present than he had seen in the afternoon. Voss had seven male guests, and there were thirteen women visible, although neither Theta nor her servant were in sight.

Caren saw him and left the side of one of the vice-presidents to come to the bottom of the stairs. Wendy also crossed the room, stroking executive backs as she passed, to wait for Blake.

"Hello," Caren said warmly, taking one arm.

"All rested?" Wendy said softly, taking the other.

Blake nodded.

Voss gestured to the designer and introduced him to Vincent Kresadlova, a name Blake recognized at once as a prominent Czech pharmaceutical manufacturer, the owner of some basic patents for Eroticene.

"Ah, yes, the young man who designed the palace for the Shah!"

"The Gardens, Mr. Kresadlova. The palace was built centuries ago."

"Yes, a nice job, very nice. Perhaps you would do a summer home for me at Freya?"

The conversation turned to the Antarctic mines, then to Voss's adventures in traversing the Jää Juosta racecourse in an icesailer two years before.

Blake stepped away from the group for a moment to stop a white-dressed Mexican waiter with a tray of drinks. A movement at the top of the stairs caught Blake's eye, and he looked up. For a moment he was stunned; then there was no reaction at all: he just stared. She had to be the most beautiful woman he had ever seen.

Her golden-tan skin was part nature, part sun. Her long, thick black hair was gleaming, and it moved with the motion of her body. Her dark eyes swept the crowd below as she stood with one hand on the railing.

She spotted Voss and she smiled, her mouth curving softly. Just as she started down the stairs she saw Blake. She faltered, looking at him with something like surprise. There was an awkward moment before she continued down the grand staircase. Blake stepped forward and stopped, uncertain and thoroughly surprised. In that brief moment when their eyes met it was as if an electric current had run between them.

The golden woman kept her eyes lowered, intent on each step, her exquisite body hidden by the simplest of black dresses. Long panels of thick, rich cloth hung down from a deep neckline. The panels were fastened at the sides, with openings that gave a hint of tanned flesh. She wore no jewelry, except for a large ornate ring. Her simplicity, contrasting with the jeweled displays of naked flesh in the room around her, was startling. Blake took a step closer, but could not detect any makeup. Her nails were of moderate length, and plain, but polished.

At the bottom of the stairs she raised her eyes and looked at him again. For a long moment no one was present but the two of them. The impact startled Blake, and he suddenly realized that the painful feeling in his chest was from a lack of breathing.

I feel like a fool, Blake thought. He found he was nervous, and fought a curious desire to run outside into the cool night air. Instead, he impulsively started toward her.

"Rio!"

Voss walked on past Blake and swept the brunette beauty into his arms, hugging her tightly. She laughed, a deep throaty laugh of pure pleasure. Blake's heart turned to lead in his chest. He started to turn away. Voss called to him.

"Blake!"

He turned back to see Voss kiss her.

"Blake, come here!"

He walked closer, the drink forgotten in his hand, a symphony of emotions playing loudly in his mind. "Rio, this is Blake Mason. Blake, this is Rio Volas, our *Rio Grande!*"

The girl smiled warmly at Blake as they shook hands, saying, "Mr. Mason, I very much liked what you did with the Martian exhibit at the Fair. Have you been to Mars?"

"No, I'm afraid not."

Her hand was smooth, her fingers strong. The ring was a crimson diamond from Mars, held in what looked like a Simpson setting. He looked into her eyes and saw tiny curving reflections of his white shirt.

"It had such a *flavor*, a sense of being there."

"Thank you," he said, watching her. Her eyes were so big, so dark—intelligent eyes that seemed to be saying something to him.

Voss spoke, an arm around her waist. "It was Rio who really sent me after you. After I saw Shawna's house, I decided you were the one."

"Thank you," Blake said to Rio.

She smiled, her teeth white and strong against her golden flesh.

"Blake, honey, here's your drink," Caren said, slithering in close. "Oh, you have one," she said without surprise.

Blake turned toward her with a slight loathing. She stood close, staking out her territory.

"Uh, thank you," he said. He looked back into Rio's eyes and saw the understanding, a swift stab of empathy that surprised him.

"Rio, darlin', you look simply *luscious* in that dress, but isn't it warm?" Caren asked.

Rio smiled with some amusement and said, "No, I'm quite comfortable."

Caren wiggled closer to Blake, certain that everyone was watching her. He took a sip of his drink, glanced surreptitiously about, feeling awkward and uncomfortable. Caren captured his arm and pressed her pelvis against his hip, making a small sound of pleasure.

A quick glance at Rio told Blake that she was politely ignoring Caren's obvious ploy.

The company president joined Voss, asking about Shawna Hilton's new triplet affair. Rio was silent, but she glanced at Blake from time to time. The conversation going on around him gave Blake a chance to recover his poise—the sight of Rio had disturbed him more than he cared to admit.

We all have types, he thought. *We respond more to one type than to another. We look for what we don't*

have, or for someone to fulfill our dreams of youth.
Blake then thought about his male friends. Caleb liked
his women small and slim, almost boyish. Kerrigan
liked them almost pre-adolescent. Tom Oldman liked
them at least warm. Dawson liked them older, in their
early thirties, when they theoretically knew what they
were doing.

And he, what did *he* like? Blake Mason knew. He
had always known, had always responded, first to the
physical part, for that was the first thing he noticed;
then to the mental part—the spirit and wit and character
of the woman.

But why had his reaction to Rio been so sudden, so
total? He knew many beautiful women, for he moved in
that kind of society. Beauty brought both men and
women to the company of the rich, and it was only the
rich who could afford his services. But his reaction to
Rio had been more than a reaction to her beauty. And
she had seemed to sense it as well, although she covered
it well. But those first looks she gave him had betrayed
her calm.

What made Rio so special?

Determined to find out, Blake waited until Rio was
momentarily alone and then approached her. "Show me
the villa by moonlight," he suggested.

She smiled, even as she took his arm. "There's no
moon tonight," she said.

"What?" Blake exclaimed as they walked out onto
the terrace and over to the wall overlooking the bay.
"Surely that is some bureaucractic foul-up. *All* evenings
at Casa Emperador require a moon. Heads will roll."

Rio laughed softly, almost politely, then turned to put
her hands on the tile-topped wall and look out to sea.
They could hear the surf and see the starlight glinting
on the water.

"Do you think Jean-Michel's idea is mad?" she
asked.

"No. Everyone wants to leave something behind, be
remembered. He can afford it, that's all."

She looked at him, her face shadowed. "Do you want
to live forever?" she asked seriously.

Blake thought a moment. "I suppose everyone has

that fantasy. Living for hundreds of years, thousands perhaps, having enough time to do everything, see everything. Why do you ask?"

Rio shrugged and turned to lean against the wall, her face illuminated by the light from the arches. "Do you like what you do, Mr. Mason?"

"Blake, please. Yes, I do. It's very interesting, I get to go a lot of places, try out a number of ideas that are my own. Once I'd achieved a certain, um, prominence, people put themselves into my hands and let me do as I wished."

"Do you enjoy that power?"

"I don't really think of it as power, but as opportunity. It's a challenge to create something that hasn't been done to death, that is even better than the client thought it might be—and to find out what a client really wants." Blake paused a moment, then asked: "What do you really want?"

She smiled. "To find out about you. You are quite famous, really, but . . ." She let the sentence die, then started to speak, but Blake spoke first.

"But the famous are not always good, or interesting, or . . . exciting?"

Rio's smile was renewed. "What is your philosophy of life, Mr. . . . uh . . . Blake?"

"I don't know. My subscription ran out. I used to belong to the Philosophy-of-the-Month Club. I used to have one, though, when I was a kid. The wheels fell off it and it died, and since then . . ." He made a gesture with both hands.

"Seriously."

"Seriously." Blake turned toward the sea again, his shoulder very close to Rio. "You mean how I separate the good from the bad, the right from wrong?" Rio nodded. "That's very difficult. What is right one time doesn't seem right another, sometimes. I suppose . . ." He took a deep breath, feeling her eyes on him. "I suppose it is in not hurting anyone, in giving pleasure, in being worthy of the friendship of people you like and admire. But to have friends like that you have to be that way yourself." He looked at Rio, but her face was shadowed by her hair. "What is your philosophy, *Señorita* Volas?"

"Rio." She smiled. "Once I was too poor to have a philosophy of life. If I had been asked, I wouldn't have known what they were talking about. My philosophy was survival." She paused, then asked, "Do you think having a philosophy of life is . . . unfashionable?"

Blake shook his head. "No, not at all. You arrive at one willy-nilly, at any rate; it's just better when you think it out. But I have a confession to make."

Her "Oh?" was carefully said.

"I think you are the most beautiful woman I've ever seen."

Rio's face sobered and she turned again toward the sea, looking down so that the twin falls of her long hair hid her face. After a moment, in which Blake held his breath, Rio said, "Thank you." She raised her face and looked up at the stars. "But it's much too serious a confession to make and then continue a moonlight walk."

She turned, as if to go.

Blake stopped her. "But there's no moon. Besides, I have many confessions to make—"

"Please, Blake, you're spoiling it." She waved her hand around, smiling. "You're ruining the moonbath. Come, let's go back in." She tugged at his arm. "Tell me, do you think Cilento is the greatest of the sensatron artists?"

Blake let her pull him back into the big living room and into a conversation on contemporary artists. But even as he talked, joined by one or two others, he kept studying Rio's face. Her eyes were large, but shadowed by lashes; her mouth was a bit wide, but smiles came easily to it. Her hair was sleek, healthy, very long and very black. Her features were flexible, reflecting her inner thoughts easily and reacting to the words and thoughts of others. Blake watched how deftly she gathered others about her, engaged him in conversation with them, and withdrew, free to act as hostess and catalyst.

Blake looked to see if Voss had noticed their short absence on the terrace, but the financier appeared as urbane and imperturbable as before.

Blake managed to extract himself from a group that was debating the merits of Boynton's laser-cutting of icebergs as an art form. Getting a drink, he drifted to one side of the room, apparently to study a Coe oil but actually to think over his response to Rio. It had been total, positive. He had no explanation for his reaction, only an uncontrollable desire to possess her, to make her part of his life. *How little we know of ourselves,* he thought, *of the reasons we do and don't do things, of our likings and aversions, often for no discernible reason.*

In Rio, Blake knew he had found the ultimate in his type of woman. Rio was beautiful, with his kind of beauty. He had never cared much what other people thought was beautiful. If *he* thought someone or something was beautiful, that was all that was necessary. But she belonged to someone else, someone important to him. Moreover, she seemed committed to Voss, and that was more deadly than being owned by him.

All he needed was Rio. And she was the one woman he couldn't have.

□

Voss raised his glass and saluted Blake. "To the future!"

Blake smiled, and toyed with his own glass as the others at the long table toasted him. He was sitting at Voss's left, with Kresadlova on his right, and Rio a light-year away at the other end of the table. He looked at her and found her smiling at him. She gave him a small, direct salute, and Blake felt himself unexpectedly blushing.

Blake tore his gaze away from her and looked at the others down the long baronial table. The count was smiling with icy politeness, annoyed at being replaced as the focus of attention. He saluted Blake stiffly and said, "There hasn't been a really fine tomb maker since Michelangelo." Blake wasn't certain whether that was a compliment or not, but he smiled back. Lizette, the girl seated by the count, gave a wiggle, causing the strings of linked metal plates that flowed over her plush body to part and allow her breasts to poke through briefly. She raised her glass and said brightly, "To Blake Mason!"

The company director, Kimsey, dressed in a deep-maroon astrosuit of tropical cut, leaned forward and addressed Voss. "This tomb of yours, Jean-Michel, where is it to be built?"

Voss waved a finger at him. "That is my secret. The pharaohs made a big mistake advertising their whereabouts. No one will really know where it is, not even the workmen."

"Are you going to kill them as the Egyptian kings did?" Kimsey asked.

Voss smiled slightly. "No, just confuse them. Sealed aircars with computer pilots, misdirection, false reports, that sort of thing."

"It sounds like a midnight holodrama," said one of the one-name girls down the table.

"It is, Fionna, it is." Voss laughed, and glanced at Blake with amusement. "Don't be afraid, my friend. Holograms of the interior will be spread all over the world, to Luna, even perhaps to Mars. Everyone will know of the glory of my tomb and your part in it. They just won't know where it is."

"In what manner are you planning this wonder of the ages, Mr. Mason?" the count asked.

Several people looked at Blake expectantly.

"In no *manner*, Count Marco, just in a unity."

The count took his rebuff with bad humor and held up his glass imperiously for a servant to refill it.

From far down the table a man spoke and Blake leaned forward to see. It was Rex Crawley, a well-known landscape painter of Earth's few colonies on Luna and Mars and a favorite of the jet set. "Are you going to use Caruthers? His "Man" series of sensatrons is really superb."

"No," Voss said, answering quickly for Blake. "Nothing electronic. Everything ageless—so it can be seen exactly as it is now a thousand years in the future, perhaps two thousand."

Blake leaned forward and addressed Crawley. "It doesn't matter what medium an artist uses. The art is what counts. It doesn't matter how long it took him, or how difficult the situation. Only the art counts. It doesn't even matter how long it lasts, except that more people can experience it. The art of Booth, Bernhardt, and much of Caruso is lost. But it once existed, and that is what counts. Mr. Voss wants the art of his tomb to be ageless, and so it shall be."

Voss smiled at Blake Mason. "Make certain they use the best materials. No cost cutting. Everything to last as long as possible. Have Permaplastics send samples of their inert protectives."

Blake nodded and said, "I've already thought of investigating a new spray sealant that *Plastics Age* reported on favorably."

At the end of the table, Rio rose. "Enough technical talk, please, Jean-Michel. The art is what is important, not the method."

As they rose Blake said, "The end justifies the means," and grinned.

Rio laughed silently and said, *"Touché, Monsieur Mason."*

There was the rustle of snowsilk and the whisper of colorquick panels as everyone pushed back his chair and moved away. Caren took her hand off Blake's thigh and stood up, ready for the evening's fun.

Lizette's metal-link dress tinkled as she spun on the count's arm, laughing gaily at something he said. Kresadlova drained his glass and let two of the girls lead him away. Rio and Blake exchanged looks down the length of the table and he read a hundred meanings into the glance.

"Where was your lovely sister tonight?" Kimsey asked Voss as they returned to the main hall.

"In her rooms. I'm afraid she finds some of my dinners too heavily burdened with business talk." Voss smiled perfunctorily, and Blake wondered about the brother-sister relationship.

In the main hall the tape of a current *quiver* group had been hooked into quadrapod color organs, filling the room with shifting masses of brilliant color shot through with the threads of muted shades and pockets of darkness. Everything shifted and changed with the rapid, humming, *quivering* quality of the music.

Two of the girls had already shed some of their panels and were standing atop a low table, quivering in the maelstrom of light and shapes. Two others were coaxing a vice-president to undress, overcoming his middle-aged modesty with laughs and caresses.

Voss came up to Blake, his arm around the darkly clad Rio, to tell him in confidence, "Everyone but the girls is leaving tomorrow, and none too soon. We'll have time to work then." Voss smiled easily. "I really want to start this project going. I'm eager to have it completed."

Blake stifled the words that would ask whether Voss thought he was going to die soon. Instead, he said, "Will your enthusiasm wear off as swiftly?"

Rio laughed softly, and Voss gave him a quick grin.

"I see your point. No, it won't," he said seriously. "This is very important to me."

"I do have some appointments."

"Put them off a few days. I want to get the basic plan laid out, and then you can start to fill in the details."

"Please stay," Rio said, and put her hand on his arm.

Caren joined them at that moment. "Yes, stay," she urged.

Blake didn't look at Caren and he didn't look at Rio. He nodded and shrugged. "A couple of days," he muttered.

Voss slapped him on the back as they parted.

Who am I? Blake Mason thought. *What the hell am I looking for in this world? Is it the expensive house with the wall screens, the Life-style furniture, the fat bank account, the servants? Do I want to live like Voss? Is it the fame, the power that fame can give? After variety, fame is the greatest aphrodisiac there is, but is that what I want? Why am I not content just to plunge into this freely offered fleshpot and wallow about?*

He closed his eyes, and the *quiver* music drove his mind into a room and shut the door.

Rio.

Rio.

The name, the face, the tiny postage-stamp glimpses of her mind were racing across his brain. *Rio. Where does she come from? Where is she going? Where does she want to go? What is she doing here?*

Blake laughed at himself, and Caren stirred and cupped his crotch again, looking up at his face expectantly. "Honey, she said, "Honey . . . ?

Blake shook his head, the colorquick patterns shifting jewel-like images across the inside of his lids.

Voss's girl.

The boss's woman. Boss Voss. The carrier-to-fame. Rio. A river. Flowing water. Freudian symbol. Life-giver.

Blake felt a body come down onto the couch next to him and hair brush across his face. He opened his eyes, but it was only Doreen.

She put a leg across his and grinned impudently.

"Hi!" she said.

"Good-bye," Caren said firmly.

Doreen ignored her as she bent to give Blake an expert kiss. Her tongue lanced into him like a snake striking.

Caren grunted something, sitting up to press herself against Blake's other side. Her tongue went wetly into his ear and her hands began to open his shirt.

Blake opened his eyes and saw all the nude or near-nude girls covering every male guest. *They are earning their living*, Blake thought. *Expert technicians in the Palace of Love. That kind of love.*

A sudden revulsion seized Blake, and he heaved himself up. But the two women dragged him back, kissing and caressing more enthusiastically. He tried again, and tore away from Caren almost cruelly. She made mewling sounds at him, but he struggled to his feet, wrenching at Doreen's hands. Both girls looked at him in shock.

"What's the matter?" Caren said. "You wanna do something else?"

"Want to go somewhere else?" Doreen said with a wicked grin, coming to her feet, weaving her glistening body seductively.

Blake put out his hands in protest. "No. No, you don't understand."

"Did we do something wrong, honey?" Caren asked anxiously, licking at the corner of her mouth. "You want us to—"

"No, no, thank you, I—"

Blake couldn't finish, and abruptly he turned away, threading his way through writhing triplets toward an exit.

Caren and Doreen exchanged glances, then separated to join different groups.

Blake found himself in a corridor, and he fled from the sounds of revelry. He passed through a couple of rooms, then walked down some steps into a room lit by bluish-green light. One wall was a huge window that looked underwater into a large swimming pool. There was no one in the room and Blake sank into a big chair close to the glass and just stared into the blue-green water, trying to organize his thoughts.

He heard a faint splash, and saw a lancing explosion of bubbles as someone dove into the water. As the figure coasted free of the mass of air it had brought into the pool, Blake saw it was Rio.

Her long black hair trailed smoothly behind her, a sleek dark tail that pulsed forward as she slackened her stroke. She was wearing a modest black bathing suit that seemed almost prudish in light of the almost total female nudity at Casa Emperador. The proper underwater lights and the filter screen in the glass wall kept her skin a perfect color instead of giving it a greenish tinge. Blake was lost in admiration of her gracefulness and the rich, ripe perfection of her body.

Buoyed by the water, her full breasts bobbed and shook in the confines of the black bra with each stroke. She somersaulted slowly in the water, then bent her back and aimed for the surface—her stomach flat and muscular as she reached up, her legs scissoring, her glistening suit a bold graphic against her golden skin.

Blake rose and stepped close to the glass, looking up to see the rippled, crumpled undersurface of the water. Then he saw the heave and twist of her body as she flipped herself down—her lungs once again full, her buttocks flexing, her legs giving two powerful kicks, her arms out, her hair streaming behind her in a wind of water.

Rio curved up, braking herself and stopped, her arms moving to hold herself steady, a trickle of bubbles coming from her mouth. She was looking right at Blake, the glass magnifying her to heroic proportions. Her hair continued to move, a feathery Medusa spreading out into a great dark crest, a black fairy crown behind her head. She stared at him, her eyes slightly startled. More bubbles escaped from her nose as they stared at each other for a long moment. Then Rio turned, kicked, and was swimming away.

Blake wheeled and sprinted for the door, running down the corridor to the stairs, and up onto the patio above.

A half-dozen torches flickered in the greenery surrounding the patio and pool. At the far end, a man-made waterfall splashed in realistic mimicry.

Rio was starting to pull herself out of the water as Blake came swiftly across the patio, his feet slapping the tiles loudly. He stopped and they stared at each other. She slipped back into the pool, but did not move away.

Blake walked toward her slowly, breathing hard but trying to slow it. He stood over her, barefoot on the wet tile rim. They looked at each other as if trying to read the mystery in each other's face.

"Would you like a swim?" Rio said at last.

Blake nodded, and Rio gestured toward the bath-house.

"There are suits there if you want one." He turned and walked to the bathhouse entrance, stopping to look back, but she had not moved. He undressed quickly and found a suitable pair of trunks among many on a shelf.

Blake walked quickly out, not really looking at her, and jumped feetfirst into the pool near her. He turned to her, seeing her wipe away the splash of his entry. Then he reached for her, pulling her to him.

She resisted for only a moment, then clung to him, her mouth opening to his, her hands clutching at his hair. They pressed their bodies together, and Blake put one hand on the pool rim to steady them. Their arms and legs were a tangle impossible in full gravity, their mouths shouting volumes into one another's mind as they kissed.

Rio broke away first, breathless, her face glistening, a shy on-again, off-again smile flickering on her face. She made a small sound of pleasure and surprise as she clung to the pool edge. Blake pulled her hips back to him, pressing her against him so that they reunited their legs, staying close and staring into each other's eyes.

He wanted to speak but didn't know where to start.

Rio's mouth twitched and suddenly she was laughing. Blake felt momentarily offended; then he found her laughter infectious and smiled himself. Her laugh was gutsy and startlingly loud in the empty night patio.

"We're crazy, you know that?" she said.

Does Voss own you? The question burned a trench through his mind like a laser gone wild. *Are you Voss's property?* He stopped smiling.

"You look so angry!" Rio said, and put her hand on his shoulder and drifted closer. She looked soberly at him. "You're afraid," she said.

Yes! Afraid of losing you! Losing something I don't have!

"If he finds out, he'll be petulant and petty," she said. "But he'll get over it."

Blake looked at her a long time before he spoke. "I want you," he said, "but not that way. Not only as long as Jean-Michel doesn't find out. Not as a loan-out from the Boss. And when it's over, you go back to being his property."

Rio's face darkened. Blake's heart sank. He had spoken with such foolish possessiveness.

"He doesn't own me!" she snapped. "I am not like Theta's wench. I'm not one of the silly little pagans running around spending their youth, trying for the big time."

Blake raised his eyebrows in a silent question. He didn't want to ask, but he had to know. *Something small and petty and weak inside me wants to know.*

Rio untangled her legs and moved back along the rim, both hands on the smooth stone edging, not looking at Blake. "I'm . . . I value myself too much for . . . for what they do. Sundance sold herself to Theta's agent because her whole family was starving up in Zavitaya, near the Manchurian border. Theta renamed her and trained her to be the pliable creature you see." She shot Blake a quick glance. "No one has trained me, not that way."

"Rio, I—"

"I know what you think. They always think that. I've had some beauties come after me. They think Jean-Michel talks in his sleep or something, and they want me to slip them little financial scraps on the side. They've sent me some gorgeous young men and beautiful young women. I've been . . . I've been offered some freaky scenes, scenarios that I would control completely, from whips to electrostims. *Anything*, just as long as I tipped them off on Jean-Michel."

Blake was silent, and the water lapped against the tiles. "But no one wanted you for *you*," he said.

"No! That's not true. I . . . I can't believe it's true." She moved further along the curving pool edge and Blake followed her. She spoke in a soft voice, almost to herself. "No . . . There have been several . . . They . . . wanted . . . just me. I know that. . . . I . . . think that . . ."

"But they were not the ones you wanted," Blake said, suddenly certain. He moved closer and touched her shoulder.

Rio looked at him with a quick, fearful expression and shoved against the pool edge. The water pillowed behind her head as she backed up. She twisted over and swam to the opposite end with a great deal of energy. She ended up under the waterfall and Blake followed.

The water crashed around them, louder now, pelting off their shoulders as they stood in the shallows and looked at each other.

"Rio . . ."

"Don't, Blake. I don't want just another damned quickie. I can't do that again. I'd rather . . ."

"I want you, Rio. More than anything else in the world." They looked at each other, their eyes slitted against the cascade of the thin sheet of water. "I hardly know you, but I want you."

Rio moved back, out of the waterfall. Her golden body gleamed with water drops in the warm night. Blake stepped free of the water and they looked at each other until Rio looked away.

Blake smiled. "I've gotten in trouble before, being so . . . so impulsive. I'm a romantic. It's the way I've been programmed, I suppose."

Rio smiled at him, a sad, weary smile. "Don't," she said.

"Yes," Blake said and moved a step closer in the water. "To hell with 'Blake Mason, Environmental Concepts,' to hell with money, to hell with Voss Investments and Voss Oil and Voss This and Voss That. To hell with a tomb for the ages."

"It isn't just a tomb." Rio stopped short, and her lips parted. "Don't, Blake, please. He can get angry. You haven't seen that side of him. He can be ruthless. He has power. He can ruin people when he gets angry enough. Ruin . . . and worse! He owns Costa Verde, he owns Bodigard and all those toughs, he owns senators and ministers and police chiefs."

"I don't care," Blake said, and, amazingly, he really felt that he didn't. "I've been looking for you . . . all my life . . . and I'm not going to lose you!"

Rio pulled further back, staring into his eyes, her face sad and frightened. "No, Blake, you . . . you don't understand . . ." She turned swiftly and dove into the pool, swimming strongly to the opposite side. Blake swam after her, but she was already up the pool steps and running across the tiles before he reached the edge. She disappeared into the house.

Dripping, wet, he trotted after her, looking each way as he came into the hall. He did not see her, and had run a few feet toward the main hall, when he saw his shed water splashing on the carpet. He looked back, turned and ran, tracing her by the dark spots on the Verneuil carpet. But the droplets ceased before he came to an intersecting passage, and he had lost her.

Arbitrarily, he took the right-hand corridor and proceeded along it until he saw an open door. Beyond it, a Mexican family sat at dinner. The women glanced at Blake and quickly looked back at their dishes. The men looked at him impassively, their faces telling him this was their territory. These were the workers who trimmed the trees, tended the garden, cleared storm damage, did the maintenance, serviced the boats, and cooked the meals. They were not the pretty creatures who served their employer in a different way; they were honest, hard workers, too polite to show their shock at a near-naked man invading their home. Blake started to speak but turned away instead.

Walking back toward the main hall, he glanced into the rooms that were open, seeing the pairings that had broken off from the mass still seething in the main room. In one room he saw Sundance curled up in Theta's arms, but neither noticed Blake. The music in the main hall did not completely mask the short, earnest gasps coming from the pile of glistening flesh. Blake looked for Voss, but did not see him in the melee.

Blake found another corridor he had not searched, and followed it. The walls and ceiling were molten metal, gleaming and flowing stripes of gold, bands of silver, streamers of bright copper, all flowing down in eye-hurting streaks of fiery rivers and cool, slow-moving swaths. Blake ignored the Guinevere sensatron panels that lined the walls like wallpaper, hurried through to the next grouping of rooms. He pushed open a partially closed door to find one of the maids, brown as a penny, polishing an intricate Steuben imitation of the Martian goblets from Northaxe.

"Where's Rio?" he demanded. "Where's your master?"

She was used to the antics of her employer's guests. She just stared at him with her large, dark eyes and pointed down the corridor. Blake whirled and plunged on.

He found Voss in a library, elegantly robed in a deep-red Webwove. The multimillionaire looked up from a computer console and flicked off the machine, as if he did not want Blake to see what he was doing.

"Hello," he said ambiably. "Why aren't you simmering in the fleshpot?"

"Why aren't *you*?"

Blake found it surprising he didn't hate the man. A quick, fragmented image of Voss and Rio in bed fell through his mind like a rock through a skylight. He forced himself to be calm, and listened to Voss's answer.

"Too much of a good thing can kill a man," Voss said.

Especially when there's Rio at night. Blake turned the knife in his own heart, and knew he was deliberately doing it.

"You wandering around looking for something in particular, or just cruising?" Voss asked with a grin, his tanned face pleasant.

"No, I . . ."

Voss laughed and said, "Don't worry about it.

You've seen the way my sister Theta lives. She rarely wears clothes anymore, except to dress for dinner on those few occasions she consents to attend. But why shouldn't she go nude, especially around here? She finds it stimulating, she says. Last year she wore nothing but jewelry by Ransom to the Daughters of Bilitis Ball."

What did Sundance wear? Blake wondered. *A collar and chain, artfully engraved "Property Of"?* Rio popped into his mind, collar and silver chain leading to Voss's claw.

"Fifty years ago," Voss sighed, "my sister would have been locked up. But then," he chuckled, "fifty years ago most of us would have been in jail, for one thing or another. Do you realize how long mari was on the illegal list, for God's sake?"

Blake nodded, tyring to form the words he wanted to say.

Voss gestured toward his video equipment. "They call me a male chauvinist, you know." He smiled crookedly and gave a short laugh. "All of us who are, shall we say, rich have women after us. Shawna has beautiful young men on her trail, and not a few women, either. Are we chauvinists because of that? I think not. These women . . ."—he gestured around, as if to include the houseguests—"they are selling a service, that's all. Nothing new about it. Men do the same thing and perhaps not in so honest a way." He stopped and sighed, fiddling with a Null-Edit tape on his desk. "Sometimes I think maybe I should not have so much money. People try to blackmail me and assassinate me, do a whistle on me." He smiled up at Blake in an innocent way. "I *give* my money away, I *spend* it, I *use* it, but I do so hate to have it conned out of me by some cheap whistler."

Blake felt a moment's fear as he digested the words. *Did Voss think he was a con man, intent on some high-stakes whistle?* But his need drove him on and he spoke.

"Jean-Michel . . ."

He stopped, and Voss politely prompted him. "Yes?"

"Listen, I want to talk to you about something. Rio and I—"

"Oh, Blake," Rio interrupted from the door, "you said you wouldn't tell him!"

She moved past Blake, regal in a yellow dress that complimented her tanned skin, to sit on the arm of Voss's chair and kiss him on top of his head. He put a hand up to pat her bare arm and smiled up at her.

"What?" he asked.

"Blake and I had the greatest idea," she said with a smile, ignoring the designer, who felt foolish with only a bathing suit on while the others were dressed. He seemed to be in an embarrassing dream. "Suppose you had a duplicate mountain? Something to confuse the tomb hunters with. Something in the same area, about the same size, with some signs of human habitation, or touch."

Voss smiled. "Yes, not bad. The trouble with those tombs of some of the Egyptian kings is that they were so damned obvious! They announced, no, *declared* where they were! The grave robbers arrived there before the body was even cold!" He looked at Blake. "Suppose we kept the exterior construction scars to an absolute minimum? We'll polarize the windows of the helicars, of course, and have a checkpoint somewhere after pickup where we can debug the ship and transfer the workers to another aircar. No traces."

"They'll know the rough area, but in those mountains it could take them years to find the spot," Rio said. "They are still looking for the Lost Dutchman mine in the Superstition Mountains, you know. And Blake had the most marvelous idea . . ." She paused to smile at them both. "When you're . . . you know . . . inside . . . we dynamite the whole mountainside and hide the entrance completely, very naturally. Maybe you could . . ." She gave Blake a look, then continued: "Maybe you could plant a thousand-year capsule with the coordinates."

Blake had to admit she had some good ideas, even if some of them were supposed to be his. They might solve the problem of how to hide the tomb from grave robbers. *But that's not what I want to say to Voss.* "Jean-Michel, I—"

"And you will bury us all with you forever," Rio interrupted with a cry, sliding into Voss's lap, throwing her arms wide and going theatrically limp.

A dark expression crossed Voss's face, and for a second Blake believed that Rio's flippant suggestion was exactly what the man had in mind. Burying servants and retainers to serve in the afterlife, in addition to taking along all the treasure that would give him a secure environment in that forever future, was a familiar concept.

Blake shrugged away the thought. *It isn't sane, and Jean-Michel has shown the business world, at any rate, that he is decidedly sane, if a bit ruthless.*

Rio came abruptly to life with a whoop, and kissed Voss fast and hard. Then she jumped to her feet with an enthusiasm Blake had not seen before. She pulled the financier to his feet and urged him to come with her.

"Come on!" she cried with mock seriousness, and Voss laughed. "That swim gave me an appetite. Let's eat!"

Back in the main room most of the guests and their girls were lying about, breathing hard, idly watching three bodies actively engaged in a complex maneuver.

"Attention, attention, attention!" Rio cried. "We're going to the Golden Iguana!"

The announcement brought life to several and they struggled up. The women hurried off to put on something more appropriate to Puerto Vallarta's biggest *quiver* club.

Rio turned to Voss, smiling like a mad leprechaun. "Okay, Boss Voss?"

I feel like a dummy stuffed with straw, Blake thought. *I just stand around and they push or pull. Push—I go! Pull—I stop!*

In the morning Blake hated himself. He hated his sulky performance at the Iguana, and he hated Rio just a little when he found she was gone. A general goodbye note was pinned to a tapestry by the archway to the terrace where everyone was breakfasting on fruit and eggs. She was off to Greece and Corsica on business for Voss.

Blake took a pill instead of breakfast and spent most

of the day lying in his room, sliding through darkness and dawns, around stars and chasing comets. He was supposed to be starting his sketches, but all he drew were a few idle scratches that looked like malevolent pyramids.

At dinner, he wore a black Darkmoon suit and a crimson stock. *Looks like my throat is cut*, he thought.

Doreen had watched him dress, then disappeared. She returned wearing a silver collar and roses in her hair that were the exact shade of his shirt.

He was silent through most of dinner, letting his melancholy pass for deep thought and responding only perfunctorily to Kresadlova's questions regarding the Shah, and the semi-secret Inner Palace of the Ali Baba cave complex in Syria. Voss seemed to note Blake's reluctant involvement and steered the industrialist away adroitly.

After dinner, Blake engaged Voss in a technical talk on the tomb, burying himself in laser penetrations, stability ratios, air-conditioning, excavation volume, and manpower hours.

Voss sat through his questions and self-answers amiably, but then insisted upon talking about basic designs.

Blake tried to talk about artists he had considered, and how others might be schooled in some combination crafts that he had in mind, as well as about some Japanese laser stone-cutting techniques that could be used advantageously in precise sculpting of large areas from miniature models. But Voss kept returning the conversation to the basic design.

Rather than admit he had not developed a full plan, Blake seized upon the one fragile idea he had. "A pyramid. A negative space in pyramidal shape. It's good structually and is evocative of tradition." Blake was beginning to employ the patois of the pseudo-artist—not his usual manner at all—but his mind was really elsewhere. "We still don't know everything about the preserving qualities alleged to be adherent in the pyramid shape. But if we are to pattern your, um, tomb on the general Egyptian style, it might be noted that the Great Pyramid of Cheops is different from the ordinary burial pyramid. We still have no true idea of how old it really is, you know. Even in the earliest writings it was considered ancient. But also, strangely enough, there is hardly a mention of the tomb in any of the writings throughout the history of Egypt!"

Blake paused for breath. He was on automatic, filling up time.

Voss spoke into the pause. Suavely and without damaging Blake's ego, he led him away from the historical aspects of Cheops to his own tomb. Then he said, "I will shortly be supplying you with the specifications for the inner chamber. This should be at the heart of the complex. All the rest—the living quarters, the art, everything—will be outside it." When Blake looked surprised, Voss smiled. "Then there will be air locks." Voss paused, as if considering his next words. "The inner chamber will have more than one sarcophagus, if you wish to call it that. I'm not certain just yet how many. Seven, I think."

Your queen? Your slaves? Blake only nodded.

The departure of the remainder of Voss's guests broke up their conversation and Blake took the opportunity to slip away. Doreen knocked on his door and called to him, but he did not answer.

He was back in Los Angeles on Wednesday. Elaine had taken care of all his appointments, eliminating and reshuffling expertly.

"I've started the publicity campaign on the Voss job, boss," she said. "Just *your* part in it. I'll leave the 'Big Picture' to Kramer and Reiss. They're handling all the personal Voss publicity. I just didn't want you to get lost in the shuffle. Say, are you listening to me?"

Blake pulled his eyes away from the moody abstraction that the color synthesizer had created on the big screen, and smiled wanly at his secretary. "Sorry, mind a million miles away. You were talking about the publicity. Well, don't worry, Voss's people are handling it."

Elaine sighed. "Doesn't it seem strange that he would want to publicize a tomb?"

"Jean-Michel spoke to me about that. He figured he couldn't keep the project a secret, and if he tried to make it a Big Secret it would only attract more attention than it deserves. This way people will just write it off as a rich man's folly."

"Isn't he awfully young to be thinking of ... you know."

"It's *his* business. And ours! Is that mail to sign?"

Elaine handed over the portfolio of letters and tapes. She stood at his shoulder, pointing out things, then asked, "Hey, boss, are the parties at that place as wild as I've heard?"

"I've seen better."

"Oh, don't disillusion me, Mr. Mason. I want to think the rich and famous have bigger and better orgies than anyone else. I want to know that *someone* has bigger and better orgies, *someplace*."

Blake looked up at her in surprise. "I just can't imagine you at an orgy, Elaine. I'm sorry." He smiled, but he meant it.

The silver-haired woman drew herself up. "I'll have you know, sir, that I was once the talk of *Allegheny* ark, the queen of the Sunflower Nudist Park, and *one time* I had three hot affairs going at once. An upper-level ark senator, a soyafiber merchant, and a vice-president of Barbara Brown Security Services—the outfit that has half the police franchises in the North-east. And not one of the three knew about the others! I, sir, am no stranger to free sexual expression!"

Oh, god, you, too? Blake thought.

Elaine bent closer, grinned with delighted wicked-ness, and said, "Did you bed down with some of Voss's private stock of sluts?"

"Don't talk vulgarly," Blake admonished. "Yes, I bedded and linked and was bedded and linked, and all of Voss's private stock is the same in the dark— terrific!" The knife twisted again: *all but the ultra-private stock . . .*

"Marvelous!" Elaine said, hearing what she wanted to hear.

"Now I suppose you'll tell your girlfriend at Fourzon Fabrics and she'll put it on the TIS and I'll have the *Inquirer* calling me up for a vidtab feature."

"Boss! Me?"

"You. That's what you did when I went to the open-ing of *Freudian Frolics* with that actress, what'sher-name, Shelley Graham."

"Publicity, boss, that's all."

"Huh. You just like having a boss who's in the news, so you can lord it over the other secretaries. You couldn't stand it when your friend Carmen's employer got that fighting robot manufacturer as a client."

"But she got to go backstage at the Circus all the time. Aw, come on, boss, you gotta have your fun in these jobs."

"Uh-huh. Here," he said, handing her the portfolio.

"When do you start the prelims on the Voss job," she asked.

"Right away, today, yesterday. I've never seen a man more eager to upholster his grave."

Elaine laughed and went out.

Blake swung around in his chair to look out at the city, but almost at once Elaine buzzed. "Mrs. Shure on Two."

"Tell her I'm not here."

"She read about it in *Celebcon*."

Blake groaned and turned back to the desk. He took a moment, inhaled, put on as sincere a smile as he could muster, and punched Line Two.

"Mrs. Shure, how nice to hear from you! I'm sorry about not getting out to your home, but I had to leave town."

"Oh, dear man, I know all about it! A Voss commission! It sounds just marvelous. You *must* come to dinner and tell us all about it."

Blake winced at the "us," but kept his face calm and smiling. "I'm afraid my assistant must take the preliminary work, Mrs. Shure. I'm certain you won't mind. Just basic details. He'll report to me, and then we can work up something for presentation. He's a charming man. His name is Sebastian. He designed quite a few of the homes in the dead Antilles volcanoes—Miller's, Frank Fuller-Wright's, the Count of something or other's, Frank Sterling's—all built into those volcano bubbles. I'm sure you've heard of them."

"Oh, yes, indeed, Blake darling, but he's not *you!*"

Blake laughed, but deprecatingly. "Sebastian did a house for Brian Thorne on Madagascar, so you know he is first-rate. Thorne picked only the most talented people."

The woman's eyes narrowed as she said, "Then why is he working *for* you?"

"Some people hate paper work. Sebastian likes challenges, but I'm afraid he needs the clercial backup, which I supply. I'm certain you will like him; he is most charming and has some fascinating tales of the Antilles people, of Thorne and Shawna Hilton, whom he knows very well, and . . . well, you can see he is completely qualified. He and I will work together on this, and I'm sure you would like what we come up with."

"Well, all right. But remember, we want *you*, just as soon as you're free." She hesitated only a fraction of a second before adding, "And bring Jean-Michel with you, of course."

Blake ended the conversation pleasantly, clicked off, punched the privacy button savagely, and turned again to look out the window.

Los Angeles hadn't looked so fresh and clean in ages. The sun glinted off a million windows and ten thousand domes. Scores of flat-sided buildings reflected the setting sun, throwing the whole landscape into sharp relief. The shadows of the mountainous arks spread across the city, merging into valleys of darkness, where lights were already glowing. The soft green of the Metro dome was in contrast to the red tower of the Connecticut Life tower in the shade of the *Sunset* arcolog. Aircars followed invisible lanes overhead. The air was clear, but there were no birds. Lights were coming on all over the eastern face of the arcology structures, and the Disneylife level of *Great Western* was glowly brightly.

Where are you? Blake Mason asked silently. *And why are you there instead of here?* Blake's chest hurt. He felt like a hand was clamping tightly around his throat. *I haven't cried since I was a child,* he thought, and felt a wetness on his cheek. One tear was a flood for a man who had not cried since he was a child.

□

Voss looked at the preliminary model critically. He squatted and peered through the various entrances into the scale model. Blake rotated the table and tilted it, removing the pyramidal top so they could see inside.

"It's only a rough," Blake said. "Just a way of visualizing the three-dimensionality of it for you." Then he grinned. "For me, too. It's very difficult to think in three dimensions, you know."

"It's fine," Voss said absently. "Will it really look this good?"

"Better. Stabilized ferroconcrete with a life span longer than they have any way of testing. If it moves, the whole thing will move. It will be stronger than the rock around it. There will be a Stibbard mosaic on the floor here—"

"The Inner Chamber," Voss interrupted. "Is this the model here?"

Blake pulled off the plastic cover. "It's in a larger scale so you can see detail better. But just as your specs said. Stabilized lead sheathing, stabilized ferroconcrete stressed walls, and the whole thing floating independently within the outer chamber on a sealed moat of oil. A sphere within a sphere, like a ball bearing rolling in oil. I only have the specs on the top hemisphere, however." He looked significantly at Voss, who ignored him.

"You can leave that to the construction crews. Special installation," Voss muttered as he bent over the model.

There were seven sarcophagi indicated, a number which had at first bothered the designer, but he had assumed that Voss was making room for members of his family already dead or who might die before he did. He had shrugged it off as plans for a common family burial plot.

71

"Excellent," Voss breathed.

"I had the impression you did not wish any decoration in the inner chamber."

"Yes, purely functional. Inert materials. The outer chamber is just . . . for amusement."

Blake nodded, not understanding at all. "It will be fully functional right up until you . . . until you die." He had to force the words from his mouth: he found it uncomfortable talking to a man about his death, even if he was designing his tomb. But Voss had seemed to encourage that kind of conversation from the beginning of the discussions, months before. "There will be a portable fusion power plant on the outside, down the hill, to provide power for the construction—and for later, in case you want to live there."

Voss stared at the Inner Chamber model. Then he spoke. "Do you think about death, Blake?"

"No more than I must. It will get here in time. All too soon, I imagine, even with the geriatric drugs."

Voss nodded. "Even with the drugs we only live so long." He looked up at Blake and straightened with a sigh. "What would you do with yourself if you could live five hundred years? . . . a thousand?"

Blake shrugged. "Learn. Experience. There are so many things I haven't done. I've had no time to pursue my studies in church architecture, and with so many of the churches impoverished, there are no commissions coming from that area. I'd travel, try different lifestyles."

"This business of the church architecture. Are you religious?"

Blake grinned. "No, I don't think so. Not in any formal way. Unless you count me as a devout hedonist."

Even as he said it, Blake felt a twinge of guilt. It was so common to project an image of a hedonist that it was automatic. Everyone did it.

"About a long life . . ." Voss asked, "what do you think about that?"

"It's more important, I think, to do something *with* your life, than to live a long time," Blake answered honestly. He smiled. "Better an hour as a lion than a lifetime as a lamb."

Voss's thin lips flickered in a smile. "Better yet a lifetime as a lion."

Blake started to reply, but Elaine's call stopped him. "A friend of Mr. Voss's is here, Mr. Mason."

"Ah, that's Sonya," Voss said. "Send her in."

What came in was a magnificent blonde, all tanned smooth skin and carefully designed sexy walk. She was encased in a sheer Starmist dress, carrying drinking glasses, and smiling. Elaine followed behind, a huge jeroboam of Château Astré from Voss's private vineyard in her arms.

"Sonya, this is Blake Mason. Sonya Vahlberg."

She smiled in a warm and extraordinarily friendly fashion, and Blake let the personality-plus wash over him without much of it sinking in. *A new one for Voss . . . Well, what else would I expect a girl with all that beauty to do: sell soyaburgers or work in a balancing salon? Why shouldn't she go for a life of comfort and ease at the top of the heap?*

Blake felt a certain sadness within himself. *Am I getting just too damn cynical?*

"How do you do?" Blake said pleasantly as Jean-Michel thumbed open the chilled bottle.

Sonya jumped when the cork exploded, and they all laughed. The wine was tasty and at just the right temperature. Elaine took one glassful at Voss's insistence, then tactfully disappeared. Sonya poured herself another as the men talked.

"The base camp has been set up," Voss said. "The men will arrive on Sunday. They are all well-trained employees from various of my companies. With the procedures we've set up—the blind jets, the deliberate confusion and so on—they won't know where they are within forty kilometers, if at all. They'll go in and come out at night."

Blake nodded as he poured them both more wine. Then he casually asked, "What's Rio doing these days? It's been several months since I've seen her." The question had been festering in his mind for weeks.

"Running around Yugoslavia, I think."

"Bulgaria," Sonya said, moving closer to Voss in an

instinctive gesture that said, *Competition is competition even if it isn't in sight.*

"Oh?" Blake said, and dropped the subject as if it didn't matter.

They talked for a moment about Sonya's last film, *Lord Frankenstein,* which Voss had financed; then about how she had lost out to an Italian import on the remake of *Captain Blood,* a part she had badly wanted.

Blake brought up Rio again. "She's well, is she? Rio, I mean."

"Oh, Rio is never sick," Voss answered.

"Uh .. give her my love when you see her," Blake said, keeping his tone light, almost polite.

"Certainly. Come, my pigeon," Voss said. He clasped Blake's hand and smiled into his eyes. "Keep it up. Don't worry about the other jobs. Your staff can handle them, I'm sure. You stay on this one." Blake nodded. "We'll have dinner on Castelli's yacht Friday and then we'll go to Casa Emperador, yes?"

Blake agreed, and they parted. He went back into the silent workroom and looked at the inner chamber model.

It was well designed and he thought it would be well made, well shielded against all sorts of radiation—almost a perfect tomb. The exterior of the site would be disguised and all traces of construction obliterated: the Mystery Tomb that everyone knows about but no one can find. Oh, someone would eventually find it, hacking their way into the tomb with a brute laser. Nothing was sacred, especially not the rich tomb of a multimillionaire.

But there was something about it that still bothered Blake. The tomb was almost *too* well made. The intricate shielding that had been included in the Inner Chamber specifications still troubled him. *Why does a corpse worry about cosmic rays or stray radioactivity?* Blake shrugged. *People are often oddly concerned about their bodies after death, as if preserving them extended their power, their memory, or their existence in some afterworld.*

But the heavy shielding still disturbed him. And the

mystery. Moreover, certain things seemed not to have been told to him. For example, he had found out about the installation of a fusion plant in the lower hemisphere of the Inner Chamber completely by accident. *Why a fusion plant?* Voss had stipulated no powered art or devices in the outer chamber, and construction power was being supplied by an exterior plant. There was just enough of an aura of mystery about the fusion plant that Blake hesitated to bring it up to Voss. He was afraid Voss would tell him it was none of his business and then a wall would be erected between them, a wall that Blake felt he could not afford. He needed good social relations with Jean-Michel Voss as a path to Rio.

Just for a second he imagined Voss, green-lit and clad in crumbling linen wrappings, carrying Rio in his arms, unconscious and with the night wind moving her sheer gown. For a moment, in his imagination, the light rippled over her flesh the way it had in the pool. Blake whipped his head to one side. *"No!"* he exclaimed aloud, then immediately felt foolish.

He heard someone enter behind him, and asked, "Elaine?"

"Was there anything you wanted before I go?"

"No, have a good night. See you in the morning. Oh, take whatever is left of the wine."

"Thanks, boss. That bottle is big enough to build a floating ark in. Good night."

Blake nodded, staring at the model of the Inner Chamber.

Why the hell would anyone go to so much trouble? When you are gone, you're gone. Even someone with Voss's ego should know that! No matter what all those religions say. They have proved nothing. Death is extinction. Give a body a decent burial to keep it from polluting the area. Or section it up for the organ banks and recycle the remains. But a tomb of this size? Elaine had reported that there was already some adverse publicity, people wondering why so much money was being spent on one man's tomb when there were people starving in India, in Central America, in Africa. People grumbled that the money could have been better spent fighting crime that was rampant in the arcos of Texas and Louisiana.

When the announcement of the tomb-building project had been made, the Voss empire took a nine-point drop in stocks and continued down for days. Voss had been prepared, and bought stock heavily before the market stabilized and the price went back up. He had made a profit of over 30,000,000, a substantial part of the tomb cost. Blake had wondered if the whole effort had been arranged for just that effect. Jean-Michel had smiled blandly at the suggestion, said others would probably try the same trick, and had then continued his intense discussion on the zero-defect aspects of the Inner Chamber's construction.

Blake had shrugged then and he shrugged again, now. He left the workroom and slumped into his chair behind the desk. The day was nearly gone, and the sunset brought Blake the melancholy that had so afflicted him of late. Not even the high adventure of this special commission had broken it.

He gazed out at the city, thinking of the high price he paid for his office to be on one of the exterior facets of the arcolog. He had considered it a necessary expense and had refused an inner office.

Money. It is always money. Money to live well, money to live at all. But that will change soon, Blake told himself. With the money from this one commission he would be able to retire, if he wished, roam the world, buy a condo at the top of an arcolog overlooking the Aegean, have a summer home with a modest helipad to receive guests, have a good wine cellar, clothes, art.

And, of course, a woman.

Rio.

Blake ripped his mind away, dialed opaque his expensive view, and sought distraction in his wallscreen. He poured himself a drink and let his eyes munch on the television.

A plainclothes detective was chasing a sweating man across the slippery top of an arcolog. Cornered, the sweating man turned and fired a laser, narrowly missing the detective, who returned his fire. The criminal screamed and the screen changed viewpoints to see a dummy fall from the crest of the ark.

Blake punched the control studs.

A crowd roared over the clang of steel. The screen cut from a wide view of Nero's Colosseum to tight close-ups of the desperate trio that faced the big French *soldat* robot, a curved sword in either waldo. One of the human fighters was a woman, bare to the waist, and bleeding from a bad shoulder cut.

Shaking his head, Blake changed channels. The Circus was getting too bloody for his tastes.

"— will bring you the latest news. Sheppard Maier, in Houston, on John Grennell's return from the Jupiter Mission and the tapes of Terry Ballard's tragic death on Callisto. Hans Sidén on the phenomenon of a rise in church attendance. Jay Kinney with the latest in sports and arena highlights. And more, after these words from Steele Security Service, the ultimate in modern protection."

Stab.

Reverend Sam's *Star of Bethlehem* satellite was seen in a long shot against the curve of Earth and the blackness of space. A slow dissolve brought into view his famous "Firmament of God" clear-plastic dome space cathedral. A man in a white spacesuit floated with arms extended in the center.

"Sinners! The pendulum of excess is swinging against you! The —"

Click.

A newstape was in progress. A middle-aged man in a conservative suit sat in a room lined with tape shelves, speaking to an off-camera newsman.

"No, no, we here at the Methuselah Institute are certainly working on lengthening the life span of man, but we are hardly creating immortals." He chuckled indulgently.

"But Doctor Carrington," the off-camera voice said, "what of the statements of those who oppose such research, such as Gil Lawrence of Zero Population Control, and Reverend Neville of the Sacred Angels of God the Glorious Church, to name but two? They say you tamper with natural laws and increase the pressure of population."

The doctor shook his head and Blake listened closely.

"No, Mr. Weinstock, there is nothing man was not meant to know. It is how he *uses* his knowledge that is important. If we were so successful as to be able to grant extended lifelines—and I must point out that this is speculation—if we were able to do that and a benefactor were to use that extended lifetime to oppress a people, then I would say it was wrong. But if a man or a woman were to use a longer than normal lifespan to learn, to gather wisdom, to help mankind, then I would say that it was good."

"Doctor, what of the rumors that you have perfected such techniques and are ready to start using them?"

Get out of that one! Blake "said" to the scientist.

"Rumors are not science, sir, they are rumors. It is true, we have been able to substantially increase the life span of fruit flies, worms, and some lower forms of vertebrates. But as to granting immortality . . ." He laughed heartily, but with restraint. "Don't be misled by our title, Mr. Weinstock, as so many have been. We are not creating nine-hundred-year-old Methuselahs here." He seemed genuinely amused.

That's all we need, Blake thought, *more people who will live even longer.*

The camera cut to Weinstock. "We have been talking to Dr. Emil Carrington, director of the Methuselah Institute in New Haven, Connecticut, where scientists seek to find the cause for aging and perhaps give us all eternal life."

Blake's fingers hit the black button and the screen went dark.

Sonya was waiting for Blake at the top of the seawall. She was wearing only sandals and an expensive necklace of lunar opals and Byzantium silver beads. She stood in a studied pose, smiling.

Blake shook his head with a smile. *Voss has done it again,* he thought. *Voss, the plucker of the best and ripest fruit!*

"Darling Blake," Sonya said with an intense whisper, and hugged him carefully. "Jean-Michel has been waiting for you. Come, darling."

Blake noticed that she didn't seem to sweat in the Mexican heat. Even in the bright sunlight, sudden death for most blondes, she was pampered perfection. But her great physical beauty aroused no lust in him, only distant admiration.

"Jean-Michel likes his guests to arrive by sea, have you noticed that?" Sonya said. "Maybe the trip was too rough?"

"No, it was quite nice."

"Then you have no excuse not to compliment me," she said, tossing back her long hair.

She laughed to take the bite from her words, but Blake saw that she was waiting. He mumbled a polite phrase, saw her expression, and expanded his words deftly into a flowery compliment that had no real feeling. It made him feel bad.

He saw Caren's familiar figure on an upper terrace. She was waving through a break in the trees. Next to her was a portly man with gray hair.

Blake and Sonya walked out on the wide tiled terrace with Casa Emperador looming above them. Theta was at her usual sun-worshipping altar, looking no darker, and attended dutifully by Sundance. Nearby were two more young women, one a slender black girl, the other a

79

small-breasted pixie. They only paid attention to Blake when Theta raised her head to view his arrival. Or possibly to watch Sonya walk.

"Jean-Michel is on the vid to New York or *Waipahu* or someplace," Sonya said. "Go on in, he's waiting for you."

Caren was standing just inside the big doors; when Blake entered, she smiled at him, very graceful and elegantly aloof in her floor-length metacloth robe. She was on the arm of the gray-haired man, who was wearing a brown playtux.

"Dear Blake," she said, "how are you? Malcolm, this is Blake Mason, the man designing Jean-Michel's tomb. Blake, this is Sir Malcolm Morrison, head of Jean-Michel's entire African operation.

They shook hands and exchanged pleasantries. Blake marked him at once as a man out of place in this infamous private temple of international hedonism.

Two girls now entered, and Caren introduced them as Nikki and Mariette. Their hair was still damp and plastered down, and they tried to get the two men interested in swimming in the warm but muddied waters of the bay. Only Sir Malcolm could be persuaded, as he tried to keep his eyes off their lithe, unclad bodies.

Caren let Sir Malcolm walk on ahead for a little distance, then she touched Blake's arm. "Be happy for me, baby. I'm going to be a knight's lady." Blake raised his eyebrows, and she quickly added, "Oh, just a registered mistress, but it's better than being a punch bowl everyone dips into!"

"That explains the dress then," Blake said. *The famous British reserve says* his *lady, even a mistress, should be decent.*

Caren laughed and made a kissing gesture in his direction as she hurried off. "Excuse, excuse, but I must watch my investment!"

Blake went on into the library and found Jean-Michel at the visionphone. "No, tell them 150 or forget it. I want Franklin to see Steghof tomorrow. No excuses. It's Condition Yellow on the Berlin tri-ark, but tell Perry he must be back from Ares Center by late October."

Voss listened again, then spoke a rapid-fire series of orders. "Have Shinoyama get those specs on the cargo subs to Schellerup as soon as possible. What? Yes, tell Steffan to proceed to Phase Two on the Neptune project." Voss hesitated, then continued in a slightly different tone. "The Ripvan Trust must be completed by the end of the month. This is *numero uno,* and don't forget it." He paused, and the machine murmured at him. "Yes, Dena is to be in charge. And send me the hardcopy on the new sailship-vane design as soon as possible. Run it through the Total Information Service computers to fill in any of the blanks."

Blake could not catch the voice on the screen, but Voss seemed satisfied and signed off. He turned to Blake at once. "You have the final designs?"

Blake nodded, and took out a packet of holograms. He started to put them into a projector, but Voss stopped him.

"Wait. Rio will want to see these, too."

Blake stopped short as Voss leaped energetically to his feet and left the room. Then he caught himself and hurried after the millionaire.

Rio! Here! Or coming here! Rio!

The hope that he had stuffed into a box in his heart exploded, spraying itself all over the inside of his body.

Rio!

Sonya joined them as they went down the hall. She was all brilliant smiles, swaying flesh—and confidence.

Voss pointed at a holographic projector, and Blake went over to it and dropped the squares into the hopper. Voss darkened the room and everyone settled down.

Where is Rio? Blake felt his body tense and his heart pound; he was like a kid on his first date.

"Hello, Blake," someone said close to him, and Blake turned, knowing it was Rio.

Her clinging white dress almost glowed in the dimness, and the fanciful ruby-and-silver clip that held her hair back on one side sparkled in a chance light.

Blake felt his heart leap. He forced down what he

wanted to say and do, and said casually, "Hello, Rio. It's very good to see you."

She moved closer to him, as graceful as ever, and took his hand, looking into his eyes. A shadow crossed her face and then it was gone. She turned to Voss and said, "Let's see the great tomb!"

Blake thumbed the controls, and the three-dimensional holographic projection appeared in the middle of the room. Voss walked slowly up one side and down the other, ignoring the *ohs* and *ahs* of the ripe-bodied Sonya. Rio paced behind Voss, equally silent.

Blake sat down in a russet chair set before one of the large authentic Martian sandstone panels, brought so many millions of kilometers to Earth at enormous technological effort. Beside the rocketry, shuttles, and special stasis cylinders, massive infusions of inert plastics under pressure had been needed to transport the museum-quality carvings from Mars to Earth without breakage. As stable as man had made them, these fragile-looking panels would probably outlast man himself.

No one knew what the panels meant. There was as yet no Martian Rosetta stone, no bilingual tablet, not even an atomic table that would give some basis for comparison. Every tablet found, every *in situ* wall sculpture or bas-relief was blurred and worn by the winds of the millennia until it was barely discernible as anything touched by the hand—or tentacle, or claw—of *Xeno ares*. The magnificent ruin of the Grand Hall, the gloomy Tomb of Kings, the fantastic beauty of the organic crystal growth called the Star Palace—all were unreadable, every stone an X-factor despite decades of study.

Blake's thoughts were brought back as Voss straightened from his close examination of the last hologram.

"Fantastic," the financier said. "Better than I had thought it could be."

Blake looked at Rio when he realized that Voss was also awaiting her approval.

She looked at him with a warm smile. "It will be fantastic, Jean-Michel." She turned her head to look at Blake. "Are you going to use the ceiling that Lennard suggested?" Blake raised his eyebrows and she smiled. "I dropped in on him in Paris over the weekend, and saw the sketches. I thought the design was excellent. Visually, it would tie together the side panels very well."

Blake glanced at Voss. "Jean-Michel vetoed it. He didn't like the idea of anything that might come loose and drop on him."

Rio laughed. "Very well."

Jean-Michel's face flushed at Rio's quick agreement, which was almost a dismissal, and there was a look of sudden, hot hatred.

Blake felt fear—not for himself, but for Rio. *There is a savage beneath all the man's suave European charm,* he thought.

"It had been decided," Voss confirmed.

"Of course," Rio said.

Sonya looked suddenly arch. "That's the way Jean-Michel wants it, dear," she said to Rio.

Rio shrugged, and made a gesture to indicate the matter was unimportant.

Blake was puzzled, for he did not think it was unimportant. Then his heart leapt and he felt a quick, dirty exultation. *They've split! They've fought! Something's wrong between them!*

Rio turned to Blake and told him his designs were superb and that, in her opinion, the final construction phase should go ahead. Voss agreed, and Rio excused herself.

Sonya spoke to Voss in a carefully modulated, intimate whisper. "She shouldn't act like that, darling. You've given her everything."

Voss crossed to the bar, his face still dark, but controlled. His reaction had been more violent and intense than the simple clash of tastes implied.

Sonya followed gracefully. She was a magnificent female construction, glossy and perfect, a spotless image of utter depravity. She put her arms around Voss and whispered something in his ear.

Voss gulped down a swallow of wine, glared once

more at the door, and came back to Blake. "All right," he said, "let's get on with it. Waste no time. Did the Henry Moore arrive all right?"

"Yes, no problem. Finishing touches on the floors this week, then we start moving things in from storage. The Inner Chamber is all but finished, too, they tell me. I haven't had a chance to go up there for two weeks."

Voss's mood changed mercurially. He smiled and pulled Sonya to him. "Sonya, my love, my passion flower, my Mothering Russian beauty, you are in the presence of the greatest pair of tomb builders since King Tut."

"Try Cheops," Blake smiled. "Tutankhamen was fifteen hundred years later and a small-timer."

"Correction noted and logged," Voss said.

He tugged at Sonya and they left, going up the stairs. Sonya had a happy, triumphal look. She made her famous bosom bounce, the muscles under the skin moving smoothly.

Blake put the holograms back into their packet, then hesitated. *Should I hunt for her? I must, I can't let this opportunity slip by.*

He found Rio on a small terrace, looking down into the foaming sea, a warm wind blowing her long hair and plastering her dress against her body. The palms were making irregular rustling noises in the wind from the Pacific and they could hear the surf far below.

She looked up at Blake as he approached, then for a long moment they both stared at several small pink-and-tan figures playing in the surf. Blake was trying to think what to say, when Rio spoke.

"He knows about us," she said.

Blake looked at her with a frown. "What is there to know?"

"He knows that I . . . I responded. That's enough. One of the teleguards in the basement showed him the tape."

"Teleguards?"

"The whole peninsula here is guarded. Dogs, men, eletronics, television, irregular patrols. There's a strong room buried down below, and a control room. There's a camera on us even now."

Blake looked around involuntarily.

Rio smiled wanly and said, "Jean-Michel is very rich. People are always after treasure. He guards himself. In this spot only, there is no overlap from the mikes. I discovered it by accident. The wind covers up our voices unless we shout."

Blake became angry. "I feel like a conspirator! I don't like it! Listen, Rio—I want you. I want you enough to blow the whole tomb job, if I must!"

The dark-haired girl looked at him in pity. "You don't understand. Voss gives away women. He takes them, he uses them, he kicks them out—gently or roughly. But they don't leave unless he wants them to leave. Not me, not Caren, not Sonya, none of them. Probably not even Theta."

"But you go around the world—"

"He has a long leash on me."

"What in hell can it be? Money? Fear? What?"

Rio smiled sadly. "No. I am his greatest ally. My own greed, my own fear chain me to him. He knows it and relishes the thought."

"It's his *money*, then?" Blake asked harshly. "Rio, I'm not rich, certainly not like Voss. But I won't starve. Come with me, you don't need him. I know, in a way, we hardly know each other. But I felt ... I *know* you did respond to me. And in an important way."

"Yes. I did, Blake. But you don't understand." She turned and sat on the terrace wall, backed by the tops of green palms growing on the slope below. "I was born poor. Grimy, filthy, dirt poor. *Hopelessly* poor! Part of the *doomed* poor! I was born in Mexico City. They didn't even have arcologs there; everyone was so poor. Endless miles of trash heaps called homes. The rich had long since moved; only the factories were left. Eleven million people ... and most of them starving." Rio closed her eyes and raised her face into the sun. "My family had been poor since the beginning of time. My ancestors built the Mayan pyramids and the lost cities, working like slaves for the priests, and dying. My sister died from malnutrion. My father died without a sound, falling into a hydroponics tank, his body worked out. My little brother Hernando was eaten by rats. I was *poor,* Blake, with no hope. No hope at all."

Blake put out his hand to touch her, but she twisted away and stood sightlessly looking out to sea, her eyes wet. "I also worked in the 'ponics. I helped my mother give birth to Hernando under a tank, with fertilizer dripping on us. I saw nothing but poverty, disease, death—and hard work. I didn't even know about a world like this," she said, waving her hand around her. "We saw the rich ones come: the bosses, the owners, the tourists. They were like gods. So clean! So rich! So beautiful! They smelled so good that I wanted with all my heart just once to be clean and sleek and smell like that."

She paused and took a deep breath.

"One day Voss came. I was begging on the steps of the Pyramid of the Sun at Teotihuacán. Begging. A ragged, dirty ten-year-old girl. I lived on the twenty-seventh level of a slum without working elevators with my dying mother and my sick brother, Alvaro—and the bugs and rats. Gangs ruled the slums where no police would enter, and they took what they wanted. Someday, I knew, I would grow old enough, and perhaps attractive enough, to be taken and used by them. But Voss came, and he saw me and asked me to tell him about the place."

She smiled. "He looked so rich. His clothes were so clean and he smelled so good. His women were fantastic beauties. He smiled at me and took my hand. The pyramid's steps are very steep, but he helped me; and we stood on the top and looked at the Aztec city below. I told him what I knew of the Aztecs, but he knew more—my own people, yet he knew more. I was shamed, and when he offered me money I did not want to take it. I took it because my mother was dying, but it shamed me. But Jean-Michel knew. And he did something grand, something greater than building all the tombs of the world."

Rio looked exalted, remembering. "He took money from his wallet and gave it to me, then started to give me more—an impossible amount of money. The numbers were so high they meant nothing to me; I had not the learning. But that, too, he sensed. He called down to *Señor* Cardona, his man in Mexico City, and he told him to take care of me. I thought he meant to give me coins instead of bills."

Rio sighed and smiled. "But when Voss left, *Señor* Cardona came to me. I was still begging by the steps. He took me himself to our shameful room in the great building. He took my mother and my brother and put them in the hospital. Then, later, he moved us all to Vera Cruz, where it was clean, and I went to school."

Rio laughed a hard, bitter laugh. "They laughed at me. Even in my new dresses I was a primitive savage from the city jungles. *Señor* Cardona visited me once a month and talked to the sisters. He got me a tutor and soon—ah, soon!—I was the smartest! I knew what they knew, and I knew more! I watched and I did not forget. When Alvaro was old enough, *Señor* Cardona put him in school with the sisters. And when *Mamacita* died, he bought her a coffin and a piece of ground in the church lot. He said *Señor* Voss would want it so ... Voss ... Voss ... I found his pictures in old magazines and I cut them out. Voss was my saint. I studied hard for Voss and for Alvaro and Mama and for myself. When I was fifteen, *Señor* Cardona sent a picture of me to Jean-Michel and was told to send me to school in Europe."

Rio stopped talking, but Blake did not speak. The palms rustled and the surf hissed. "Alvaro works for him now, in Tampico. He is to be married. To a girl from a family that would spit on us if they knew. I handle some things for Jean-Michel—delicate things, certain negotiations. I am not his whore *or* his secretary, but ... perhaps both. I do not care. He saved me."

Blake was puzzled. "But you are so ... independent."

Rio smiled slightly. "Of course. I am of no use to him if I am but another of his yes-people, another of the more-than-willing women who spread themselves for him. He made me. He found a dirty, ragged peasant and made me into a creature that men desire, that men respect, that men fight for. I am his."

Blake felt the anger in him, a tight and frustrated anger. *"No!* You are a human being! You are free!"

Rio looked at him with a sad smile. "Oh, my poor Blake. You cannot understand. If I were Wendy or Caren or Doreen, I would go with you in an instant. If I were still that ragged child, all grown up, I would go with you with wondering eyes. But I cannot do that to Jean-Michel. He knows I am flesh, that I have lusts that do not include him. It doesn't bother him as long as it does not inconvenience him. But if I were to leave . . ." Rio left the sentence unfinished, pregnant with vague meaning.

"But, Rio, I—I love you!"

Blake blurted it out, shamed by the awkward crudity of it, but relieved of the pressure.

She smiled at him, softly and warmly. "Thank you, Blake, it . . . it is lovely . . . But . . ."

"You don't love me?" Blake tried to call back the words, but they were gone into the air before he thought.

Rio touched his arm. "It's not that," she said. "I—I do love you . . . I do, Blake! But I also love Jean-Michel. He needs me."

"Needs you? What the hell does he need another girl for? He may *want,* but he can't *need!"*

"He needs me," Rio said firmly. "He trusts few people. I am one of them."

Blake twisted away from the terrace railing. He felt cheated and frustrated and awkward. He turned again to her, his face in anguish. "I have no right . . . I—we hardly know each other, but—but I love you."

Rio closed her eyes and her body swayed slightly. Then she looked at him levelly and Blake took a step closer.

"What can we do?" asked Blake. "I'm selfish. I don't want to share you with Voss—or with anyone!"

"I can't . . . do it that way," she said. "We must be careful. Already Jean-Michel thinks you are different. Partly because you are building his tomb, partly because he respects you. Nothing must seriously detract you from this commission. It is very important. Sec-

ondly, because . . . because he senses you are different
for me."

"But, crumbs . . ."

". . . are better than nothing," Rio smiled. She paused
and her face grew sober. "Perhaps I should tell you . . .
No . . . Yes . . ." She looked perplexed, then she
shrugged. "You should know," she said.

She drew Blake close to her, though not too close,
and spoke confidentially to him. "I know you have
wondered at the reason for the tomb. A man so young
and all. But Jean-Michel *is* a man. To the world he is
powerful and sure, but inside . . . he is afraid to die."
She raised her hand to stop Blake's words. "We are all
afraid. Some of us are more so, and others . . . Well, in
the slums life is cheap. To die is not to lose very much."
She shrugged. "It is the way it is. But Jean-Michel has
always had money. He was born rich and got richer. He
is not a Rothschild or a Rockefeller, but he was born
rich enough. He has seen poverty and filth, and he has a
fear of it—and of dying, of losing so much . . ."

Rio shook her head. "So much fear, that he has put
millions into the Methuselah Institute, into the Du Pont
Foundation, into the Massachusetts Institute for Longevity Research, into UCLA and Plantagenet University, into anything that might come up with an alternative. He gave *millions,* much more than people know."

She paused, took a deep breath, and continued: "And
some of it has paid off. Sabra Wood and George Engelson seem to have something." She shook her head
quickly. "No, nothing easy. But that's the reason for the
Inner Chamber. It's partly cryogenic rest, but mainly
it's cell cleansing and transformation. It is supposed to
take about thirteen and a half months per kilogram to
convert the cells. Jean-Michel weighs eighty-six kilos
right now. So that's about eighty-eight years in the
crypt."

"Eighty-eight years!"

"But afterwards, the experts estimate he will live
three, perhaps four hundred years. They just aren't certain. The laboratory mice have quadrupled their life
span. The chimpanzees are still being tested."

"But today most people live about a hundred years

anyway, not even counting organ transplants or any special treatments," Blake said.

"Most *healthy* people, but many of those spend a quarter of their lives in a state of near-senility. In those parts of the world where there are still famines and the people are undernourished, the life expectancy is much shorter. The bell curve on the Wood-Engelson method seems to give a proportionally longer maturity, with approximately the average senility curve of today on the end."

"But Voss is relatively young and—"

"And afraid. If he takes the treatment now he may remain at this age, in the prime of health and life, for three to five hundred years!"

"This treatment will change the world!" Blake said.

"Only if the world can afford it. The cost of the treatment equipment alone is over 20,000,000 francs."

Blake quickly added up the cost of the tomb and added it to the cost of the longevity treatments. *At least 100,000,000 francs!* "Is he really *that* rich?"

Rio nodded. "Easily. And this is something he is willing to pay for: four hundred more years of healthy life. He's willing to face the fact that the world will be different even ninety years from now, that he will be a displaced person. But his money will isolate him. There are foundations, trusts, bond issues that will mature by then. He has planned carefully."

Blake felt a sudden surge of hope. "Then you will be free as soon as he . . . as he goes."

Rio shook her head and touched the side of Blake's face. "No. I'm going with him in his cryogenic time machine."

It was as if Blake had been struck in the stomach. "You're . . . !"

Rio nodded. "I must. I owe it to him. He will be alone in a world of strangers. There is no way to know how the world might have changed. Could you imagine the world of today from ninety years ago? We were not yet on Mars, and the Moon was still not self-sufficient. They were only beginning to build the arcologs, and then only for the rich. There was so little hope then. They hadn't perfected the fusion torch or the mass accelerators. Organ banks were still so inefficient. Cosmetic surgery was little more than Band-Aids of flesh. Food production was so poor. Hydroponics was an infant industry. As bad as things are now, today we have a chance, a slim chance."

"But why the whole fancy tomb idea?" Blake asked. "Why not a cryogenic vault, Rio? There are others. Just deep-sleep ones, true, and not for rejuvenation."

Rio smiled. "Boss Voss has style. If he wakes up a hundred years from now and finds the world an atomic ruin, he can live out his days in relative comfort."

"But why go at all? He has *everything* here. Money, power, security ... He is a man of these times. He has everything to lose by taking such a risk. And are these methods proven?"

"He's going *because* he has everything to lose. He thinks the methods have proven out. There is research you don't know about. They have had volunteers. Only the first one showed any ill effects—a mild paranoia—and there was a suspicion of it before he took the sleep treatments." Rio leaned closer to Blake. "Jean-Michel is driven. He feels he *must* do this. He is quite certain he can survive financially as well. He has created trusts, made investments. He has something like 10,000,000 Swiss francs in the Union Bank of Switzerland; he has several million in Lebanese pounds in the Chemical Bank in Beirut; and I think he has money in Bankhaus Deak in Vienna and Bank of America in San Francisco. Millions, just waiting for him, drawing interest. Yes, Blake, he's that rich. And he'll be taking money with us in the tomb. Gold bars, gold coins, silver ingots. Guns, medicines, survival equipment, anything he thinks he might need in a possibly hostile environment."

Rio touched Blake's arm. "Blake, he's not a fool. He has calculated his chances and minimized the risks."

"But this whole process is untried!"

"Not really. As I said, there have been human volunteers, three of them. Two, six, and nine months in the cryogenic treatments. They were very well paid and will live a little longer to enjoy it. They have been pronounced in perfect health."

"But eighty-eight years!"

"He's willing to risk it." Rio put her hand up again to stop Blake's outburst. "So am I. It is settled."

Blake was silent a moment, then spoke. "Who else is going? There are seven sarcophagi."

"Jean-Michel, myself, two of his best toughs from Bodigard, two women he has yet to select, and Granville Franklin."

"He's a generalist for Astronetics, isn't he?"

"Yes. He knows a lot about more than a few things and a little about a lot, and can put things together. He's already fascinated by the idea. The two women are . . . in case the whole thing fizzles at the other end. The two from Bodigard are rather like me. They were found in similar circumstances, and given a chance. They would never betray him."

"A loyal and self-sacrificing band of followers," Blake said, unable to keep the frustration out of his voice.

"Yes," Rio said sincerely. She grabbed Blake's arms tightly. "It *is* a great adventure. We're going into the future! Oh, not like Mr. Wells and his spinning machine, no trick tape effects, no silvery spiderwork, no pulsating lights. We will just go to sleep, and wake up in the future!"

Blake pulled away and took a few steps along the terrace wall. There were tears in his eyes. "And you are going with him," he said flatly, his voice tight. She did not answer. "And I stay here. All my life knowing you are in that mountain . . ."

He stopped and looked sharply at Rio, suddenly wary. "Unless . . . unless Pharaoh Voss has us all killed—all who know of the location."

Rio said quickly, "Oh, no, he wouldn't do that!" But her eyes were suddenly worried.

Blake stepped to her quickly and grabbed her hands. "Take me with you!" She stared at him. "Have him take me, too! I'll go. I'll be with you and . . ."

Rio looked at him and her face hardened. "You are afraid Jean-Michel will have you silenced?" She shook her head. "He does not work that way."

"No? What about the Marc Duveau affair in Lesotho, in Africa? The Exxon witnesses? The mercenaries in Gambia? The Marseilles job? The *Chugoku* in Kawasaki? The *Huygens* in Amsterdam? There was blood there."

"But that was never traced to—"

"Never traced? Never *found out,* you mean! Are you certain he will not have me killed, and the rest? If this secrecy means that much to him, will he not cover his back? If he is willing to step into an icebox in the prime of his life, what might he not do to protect that venture?"

Rio was silent. Then she said, "But why would he take you? You are . . . an environmentalist, not a tough, not a warrior, not a generalist. What good would you be to him? He respects you, just as he respects anyone he cannot control, but if you get too much out of control he'll . . ." Rio hesitated, her voice trailing off.

I'll go whether he wants me to or not, Blake vowed. "I don't want to lose you," he said to Rio.

"You don't understand." Rio shook her head in frustration. "I have to do this. I *have to.*"

So do I, Blake thought.

□

"Rio tells me you know about our little adventure in time-traveling," Voss said to Blake.

Blake nodded. "And you are still taking Rio with you, even though your theory is totally unproven."

Voss smiled thinly. "Yes. I need her. She is a volunteer." He looked shrewdly at Blake. "You object?"

Blake hesitated, looking for the right words. "Yes. How many Rios are you taking with you?"

"You mean the other cryogenic volunteers? Only two women, besides Rio."

"Insurance against the dulls? Just in case things don't work out?"

Voss's smile evaporated. "Perhaps. Do you, too, think I am a chauvinist? Everyone will be a volunteer: I will kidnap no one into the future, Mr. Mason."

The use of his last name alerted Blake to the tension in Voss. "But you *use* them," he said accusingly.

"Everyone uses everyone," Voss said, as imperturbable as ever. "You are using me; I am using you. Everyone acts to his own self-interest, at least in the long run." He smiled thinly at Blake. "And this will be a very long run."

"Eighty-eight years," Blake said. "You will be a stranger in your own world."

"I was always a stranger. Only a few know how I feel—presidents, kings, emperors, men of great wealth. Everyone comes to you to ask for something. Few give. They take, they steal, they bargain, but they seldom give. Rio gives. To me. Not just her body, but her life, her loyalty, her soul." His eyes bore into Blake's. "No one will take her from me. No one."

"Death might," Blake said, and Voss shrugged. *Love might,* he thought.

94

□

"Theta isn't going," Rio said.

The signal was bounced from a satellite and was just a bit grainy. Blake touched the screen with his fingertips and traced around Rio's face.

"Why not?" he asked. "Doesn't she want five hundred years of slave girls?"

Rio didn't smile. "She knows what she has here. She isn't curious and she isn't driven. She has no need to go."

"And you do?"

Rio ignored him. "Theta's in Bombay right now. I think she's . . . hiring some housemaids."

"I find her repellently fascinating," Blake said. "She doesn't say anything, she just lies there looking through you, being waited on hand and mouth. What does she contribute to society?"

Rio raised her eyebrows. "What do any of us? Maybe it will be good we will be going away."

"At what cost to Earth's resources? A hundred million francs. You could save a lot of children from dying of starvation with that."

"People do what they must. Oh, Blake, I don't want to defend Jean-Michel by attacking you! I don't care if Theta Voss has a hundred slave girls! That's just a hundred who won't starve. She is feeding the world as best she can. But I am loyal to Jean-Michel first and to the world second."

Blake didn't know what to say. *I love you,* he thought. "They are installing the Inner Chamber equipment now. It won't be long . . . before you . . ."

Rio smiled softly. "You must forget about me— about this whole thing, Blake."

"Where are you now?"

"In London, at the Anne Boleyn, in *Tudor Towers,* but . . . you aren't thinking of coming over!"

"Yes. It's been almost a year since we met, and we've hardly had time together at all. No private time and—"

"No, Blake. Don't start. It will only make things more difficult."

"Rio—"

"No, Blake!" Rio said firmly.

He looked at her for a long time, their eyes locking together on the screen. "Why are you doing this to me?"

"Because I must. If we . . . were together now, it would only make it worse when we parted. And Jean-Michel might . . ."

"I don't care about Voss, I want *you!"*

"No, Blake, and that's final. I am going into the vault with him. You must forget me. Go back to your work, find another woman, but forget me."

Blake stared at her, his stomach knotted. He saw her hand reach for the cutoff and he started to speak, but the screen was dead.

He stared at his faint reflection on the plastic for a long time, and then finally he cut the connection. He sank back in his chair, feeling hollow and mean. He gritted his teeth and his eyes felt sandy.

He stayed there for a long time, rousing himself only when Elaine spoke over the commline.

"Boss, Mrs. Shure on Three."

Blake groaned. He dragged himself upright, passed his hand over his face, and took a deep breath. "I guess I'll have to talk to her." He thumbed the stud, and Mrs. Shure's face swam into focus on the screen. "Ah, my dear Mrs. Shure."

"Blake, dear, your Mr. Sebastian was a lovely, lovely man. And Arden's engagement party was a great success. I'm going to have him do over our old condo in Madrid. The Goya, you know. Charming place, but I think the decor needs a new face-lift, don't you agree?"

"I'm certain you will again be pleased with his work."

"Oh, but we want *you* for my daughter's wedding reception a month from now. I've told all my friends you are doing it and they are all looking forward to meeting you."

Blake took a deep breath. *So, she didn't elope after-all.*

"Arden is *so* thrilled at the idea of Blake Mason doing the reception that she is just swooning! Imagine that, swooning! Mr. Sebastian was so very charming for the engagement, but only *you,* dear, dear man, can do the wedding justice."

How much longer can this go on? Blake wondered. "How many daughters have you, uh, Carolyn?"

"Oh, just two, dear boy, just two, the legal limit. Of course, they were on two licenses—two different fathers, you know." She tried to look roguish and failed by thirty years.

"I thought you might have adopted some," Blake said.

The woman looked hurt. "Adopt? Oh, dear man, never, never! You never know where they've been! Blood lines, character, oh, dear me. No, never!" She rearranged her face and smiled brightly at him. Blake thought, *Her makeup must take hours.*

"Well, I will be working closely with Sebastian, Carolyn, so don't you worry a second." *She has probably taped the call to show her friends,* he thought.

"Incidentally, the marriage will probably take place in Germany. Mr. Shure has some frozen Deutschmarks there, you know."

That isn't the only thing he has that's cold, Blake thought cruelly. "I'll be sending you some prelims very soon, Carolyn," he said, and they made their good-byes.

Blake phoned Sebastian. "How did you like the Shure engagement job last year?"

The lean, dark man rolled his eyes. "Thanks a lot for that one, Blake."

Blake grinned and said, "I told you you needed seasoning. Bite the bullet, underling."

"Rank hath privileges, huh? Just wait until I take over this company."

"Take it, take it. Take the taxes, the overhead, the payroll, the rent, *all* the Mrs. Shures, all the widows and counts and lawsuits. Take it, take it."

Sebastian glowered theatrically. "You really know how to hurt a guy, boss. You know I hate all that spit." He sighed. "Well, I suppose I have to take the Mrs. Shures to get the Shawna Hiltons, the Thornes, and the Rothschilds."

Blake nodded. "The bitter with the sour. Now this wedding reception . . ."

"The *royal* marriage, you mean, between the heiress to four sweeper subpatents and a prime algae conversion process, *and* the heir to the Alproteina fortune."

"God."

"No, he's grandfather Richard Von Arrow. Mrs. God is the famous Patricia Stiles Von Arrow, of Stiles Seawheat Corporation and the Zeropop protests of the Eighties."

"Are mortals permitted to attend?"

"You are. Mrs. Shure will want you particularly." Sebastian laughed, an odd high-pitched laugh unlike his suave, dark image. "I'll do the work, but it is *your* head she is collecting, bossman . . . What do you think they'll want, just the inside of Westminster, or will the National Cathedral do? Or are we doing it on some algae skimmer in the Pacific with gay, mad streamers?"

"No, it's a quiet, little party at a cost of twenty-five big ones—just for the family and a few close friends. Nine hundred and four at last count, and rising."

"Okay, give me what you have."

Blake plunged into some possible plans for the party, the sort of bread-and-butter job that kept "Blake Mason, Environmental Concepts" in cake and caviar. In a few minutes they had roughed out a few main proposals and Blake left Sebastian alone to work up the preliminaries.

"File the others," Blake said. "You never can tell when we won't have time for a custom job and will have to do it with off-the-shelf components."

Sebastian saluted with one finger and Blake darkened the screen. He looked at his reflection in the shiny glass.

"Commercial artist," he said to himself, then laughed aloud. Michelangelo had been a commercial artist most of his life, turning out tomb sculptures, ceiling designs, even stairways; his letters were filled with business problems, unpaid debts, contracts reneged upon. Leonardo da Vinci had put his genius to commission after commission—all commercial art. Even Rembrandt had done most of his portraits for money. Then, because the subjects didn't like the way he painted them in "The Night Watch," his career was ruined and he died working in an "art service" for his ex-mistress. *And these three are considered the greatest artists of history,* Blake thought cynically.

What is commercial art and what is fine art? Most of the works of great literature were written for money. Is the distinction whether the work was inner-motivated or whether the inspiration came from without? A writer may use all his inner feelings and thoughts and beliefs in a script for a drama tape, yet sell it for money. A copywriter for a new soyafiber is paid to write, told what to write, and the final work is criticized, edited, and rewritten by others. Is the criteria how much of one person is involved? No film (or very few films) is ever produced by just one person.

Leonardo's "Last Supper" was a commission, he knew, yet it also appeared as a post card, a funeral factory mosaic, and was parodied—devoutly or humorously—in films and elsewhere. Alexandre Gustave Eiffel built a tower for the 1889 exposition to be just a temporary structure. It was much hated by the Parisians of the day, but it became known as a work of art and even became the international symbol for that ancient city.

One theory had it that commercial art was functional, but there were so many gray areas that Blake shoved the subject away from his thinking, with a shrug. *Inner-motivated is fine and outer-motivated is commercial. With exceptions. With qualifications. Who cares? Only the artist. Only he knows. Only he really cares.*

□

Nineteen long hard months after Voss and Blake had made their deal, the tomb was finished. A dual fusion plant—heavily shielded against detection—was located in the base of the Inner Chamber and was primarily there to provide power to the cell-conversion and cryogenic equipment. Its second purpose, for almost ninety years in the future, was to power the entire complex after the proper time had elapsed.

Voss looked over his tomb with a curious expression, breathing shallowly. Behind him were Warford and Vogel, the two husky young toughs, wary-eyed and quiet.

Blake Mason watched Rio's face, but she seemed resigned and almost serene. *No hope there,* he told himself, *she won't stay behind.*

With a little start of surprise, he realized that the plan he had been working on, the one he had been thinking of as "the alternate plan," was now the only solution for him. He hadn't planned to use it, and the time he had given to it had been sketchy, stolen from other work. It was a daring and dangerous plan that he had hoped he would never have to use. *Surely she will see that our love cannot end like this?* he had told himself time and again.

But Rio was stepping into the vault. He had only minutes.

He walked out briskly and took a thick document lettercase from the aircar, opened it, signed two papers and thumb-printed them, sealed the packet, and applied the stamps. It was addressed to Elaine. He tossed it onto the seat and walked back into the tomb.

Now that the decision was made, Blake felt a kind of heady exhilaration. He also had butterflies in his stomach.

100

Granville Franklin was roaming about with a bemused expression on his face, looking over the rich appointments, the stack of gold bars, the weapons cabinets, the stasis cylinders with the medical kits, and the various boxes and tubs and jars. He was a sturdy-looking man in his late forties, with brown hair, a ruddy complexion, and penetrating dark-brown eyes.

Sitting nearby—casually eyeing the furnishings of the tomb and being unobtrusive in their appraisals of the others—were Doreen, one of the full-figured girls from Casa Emperador; and one who was new to Blake, a stunning blond beauty named Flower. Blake had spoken earlier to Doreen as they walked in from the helicar, asking the vivacious young redhead why she was taking the dangerous cryogenic voyage into time.

"What chance? I'm being taken care of, my sister and her two rugrats are taken care of, so why not? Oh, you think it might not work?" She shrugged. "I believe Jean-Michel. He's going, too, isn't he? And it is kind of exciting, isn't it? I'll be able to visit my sister's grandchildren next week. I mean, it will seem like, you know, a sort of overnight sleep. Jean-Michel has set up a little trust to keep a message center going for all of us, for our friends and family to check in, so that we can find them, you know, later."

Blake had shrugged the conversation off. It was *her* life, *her* future. Moreover, it was only Rio he was really concerned about.

Voss spoke now. "I think we're ready," he said. He walked back outside to speak to Ken Bangsund, who was to take care of the final sealing of the tomb, under Blake's direction. When the financier came back in, he just said, "Come on," and everyone began to follow him through the Richter space lock into the Inner Chamber.

Sabra Wood and George Engelson were inside, giving the equipment a final check and adjustment. They were professionally calm.

Voss, casually cheerful, chided them. "It must frustrate you, doctor, not to know whether all this will work or not."

"It *will* work," Dr. Wood said firmly, "or I wouldn't be letting you go ahead."

Voss smiled and raised his hand, gesturing each one to his own sarcophagus.

They were all wearing plain, simple tunics made of a special inert material that would not affect their skin—the same material used in the pads and enclosures of the sarcophagi. Voss climbed in first, but did not immediately lie down. He watched each one get into his or her so-called coffin, and then he lay back.

Wood and Engelson began attaching the sensors to his heart and head. He was prepared before the others, but stopped them from closing the lid. "Wait!" he said.

He wants to be certain they are going with him, Blake thought.

The girls were next—first Doreen, then Rio, then Flower.

With a bleak heart, Blake watched Rio get into her sarcophagus. She looked over at him, smiled rather wanly, and lay down, out of sight.

I can't let them know, he thought, and kept his face in that bleak, somber expression he had worn all day.

Blake walked over to Voss and looked down into the vault. The lean, saturnine face was already softening with the drugs that were putting him to sleep.

Dr. Wood gestured him away, and Blake turned to look at Warford. The burly bodyguard was stoically awaiting his turn. He looked at Blake with flat, expressionless eyes as Blake approached. "You have the time," Blake said. He gestured back toward Voss. "He's just gone under, but he wanted you to be certain that they don't dynamite until after the doctors leave."

"The men know that."

Blake shrugged. "Well, Jean-Michel wanted you to double-check. You have time."

Warford's face never changed. He just grunted and turned to walk out of the crypt. Blake quickly looked toward the doctors, but they had not noticed. He went outside after Warford.

He saw the bodyguard speak to the construction boss, Bangsund, then start back. Blake's hand closed on the tiny, one-shot dart gun in his pocket. But Warford stopped, changed direction, and went to the temporary toilet and closed the door.

Blake immediately selected one of the alternatives he had devised, and walked quickly over to Bangsund.

"There's been a change," he said. At Bangsund's expression he smiled a tight, confidential smile. "Not really. Just an option that Mr. Voss is exercising, something he has been thinking about." Before the construction boss could ask questions, Blake continued: "Warford isn't going. *I* am."

Bangsund's thick eyebrows shot up, but Blake hurried on.

"Just between us, Warford failed a last-minute test and . . . well, Jean-Michel doesn't trust anyone who isn't one-hundred-percent ready and eager." Blake looked around conspiratorially. "He thinks maybe—just maybe, mind you—that Warford is in the pay of the Raeburn bunch. Voss wants you to . . . detain Warford. I think you can appreciate that the boss wants only the most trusted and loyal people with him."

"Aye," Bangsund said, looking alert. Without another question he gestured toward two of his strongest-looking men.

"Good," Blake said. "I'm certain Jean-Michel will appreciate your discretion in this matter just as he has appreciated your discretion in the entire construction job."

"I'm not paid to gossip," Bangsund said stoutly.

"Right." Blake started back, then stopped to say, "Remember, let the medical team get a good distance away before you blow." He added a bit of mystery by saying, "Double-check your own men. You can never tell about that Raeburn bunch. They've fouled up things before."

Bangsund looked faintly offended, but then the toilet door opened and Warford came out. Bangsund and his men started toward Warford as Blake hurried back into the chamber.

He paused outside the inner lock and looked in. Voss's lid was closed and sealed, as was everyone's but Vogel's and Warford's empty cases. He heard Vogel's voice, sleepily asking, "But what about Johnny?"

"He'll be here in a moment and we'll get him fixed up," Engelson said smoothly. "Don't you worry."

In a moment the lid clicked shut and Sabra Wood said, "Why did he have to go out? Now we'll have to re-sanitize him and—"

She looked up, expecting to see Warford, but saw the environmentalist-designer. She looked past him, saw no one else, and looked hard at Blake.

Blake tried to look confident. To Engelson's surprised look he said, "Change of plan."

Engelson looked past him, then back to his face. "What's wrong?"

"Nothing now." He spoke briskly and with assurance. "Security matter that Jean-Michel entrusted to me. He was suspicious of Warford for some time, and he betrayed himself outside."

Blake started taking off his clothes as the two doctors exchanged looks. He didn't give them much chance to think. He walked purposefully to the portable sanitizer and removed the rest of his clothing.

"Let's go! Sorry you have to sanitize someone else, but it couldn't be helped. But it's getting dark outside and they want as much light as possible when they blow the mountain."

Dr. Wood snapped on the machine as Blake stepped into it. There was a scale in the base.

"There's a difference in body weight," Engelson muttered. "We'll have to adjust for that." He stepped to the portable terminal link and did some computations, then went to the base of Warford's sarcophagus and made the adjustments that would make it Blake's.

Dr. Wood finished a run of her instruments over his body, then tossed him a tunic of inert fabric. "It's *your* funeral," she said grimly. "Maybe literally."

Tugging the garment on, Blake climbed into the big white coffin and lay down. Wood and Engelson exchanged looks, shrugged, and began attaching sensors to his body. He grimaced as they fitted tubes to his penis and anus. "All waste matter will be evacuated this way, but certain nutrients will be dripped in through this one here," Engelson said.

"He really hasn't been properly prepared," Dr. Wood complained.

"There isn't time. I'll take my chances," Blake said. He was acting braver than he felt.

Engelson gave him an injection.

Sleep came slowly. The sight of the open lid, the ceiling, the busy doctors slowly blurred. There was only a slight moment of panic as he saw Engelson reach for the lid. The doctor paused.

"Good-bye," he said.

Blake found he could not reply, so he closed his eyes. He heard, dimly and far away, the lid click shut. There was suddenly complete silence and complete darkness, then he heard his heart beating.

Rio . . .

His mind drifted—fragmented images skipping and slipping through his awareness, distorted and fractured thoughts rising and falling. He was floating on a sea of light, with a sky of darkness over him, and pain pricks of stars forming and dissolving . . . Then there was more pain, and then still more, the level rising until Blake wanted to scream: his whole body was filled with needles, lancing into his bones, tearing at his flesh with tiny swords . . . *It wasn't suppose to hurt,* Blake thought.

Suddenly the sky ripped open, splitting down the center and flooding flame into his eyes. He screamed, and pain seared his throat. *Fire!* His eyes seemed stuck together, but the pain in them was driving into his brain. He tried to move his hand but found he couldn't. He moaned and then he heard some noises.

Someone was speaking to him. Harsh, loud words were driving nails into his ears, screaming at him in his tomb of silence.

"You son of a bitch!" Voss said.

Blake opened his eyes.

Voss stood looking down at him. He was thinner, but looking good.

Suddenly Rio looked over the edge of the sarcophagus and Blake thought her hair was very long and unusually unkempt. "Welcome to the future," she said.

Blake sat weakly on the floor by the sarcophagus, leaning back against its sleek side. Voss and Rio had helped him from the cryogenic vault, but the financier had walked away almost at once. Rio was now across the room attending to Doreen, who looked much thinner. The chamber looked about the same, yet somehow different, but Blake could not pin what the difference was.

Blake turned when Vogel entered, and felt a chill as the tough-looking mercenary looked down at him.

"You suckered Warford." It was a statement, not a question.

The bodyguard knelt on one knee and put a hand on Blake's shoulder. Although the pressure was not much, the pain streaked out from his tortured flesh and Blake could not suppress a startled gasp.

"I'll get you for that," Vogel said softly. "The boss says no for now, but I'll get you."

The pain passed and Blake's eyes cleared. He looked into Vogel's dark eyes and found implacable hatred. It startled and confused him. He had never done anything to Vogel, and Warford was long gone in the irretrievable past. Then he saw the hatred as something basic to the man: he *hated*. That was what he did best. He hated everything, and perhaps only Warford had been close to him. In the dirty business of guarding bodies, some men had learned the need for trusting a partner. Warford had been that partner and Blake Mason had taken a part of Vogel away.

Vogel let Blake see the hatred in his eyes, then he rose without a word and left the Inner Chamber.

Blake felt exhausted, not only from the effects of cryogenic time travel but from the intensity of Vogel's hatred. He sighed deeply and watched Rio feed some broth to a very weak Doreen. He felt the first stirrings of hunger himself and was grateful when Rio brought him a bowl and helped him eat.

He felt strength returning, and at last tried to speak. His voice was a croak and his throat hurt, but he managed to get his question out. "Did everyone make it all right?"

Rio shook her head. "Not Flower. I don't know what went wrong, whether it was the equipment or the conditioning or what. We . . . we opened the crypt and found her rotting."

Blake tried to speak again, but Rio stopped him with a spoonful of soup. "Don't. Everyone else made it—except, of course, Warford." Her mouth formed a smile, but she did not comment any further on that matter. "Granville is outside. Now that we're all awake, Jean-Michel wants to leave." She hesitated. "He's very angry at your coming. He needs Vogel, and Vogel needs backup. I think Vogel and Warford were very close. No, don't try and talk."

Rio put down the bowl and got up. "Come on, I think you can go into the outer chamber now. You'll be more comfortable there."

Blake let her help him up, swaying dizzily as he rose and grasping the edge of the cryogenic vault to steady himself. Next to his sarcophagus was a closed one, and he shuddered.

Rio helped Blake pass through the lock and into the sumptuous outer chamber, and as they did so Blake recognized what had disturbed him: the Inner Chamber had been a sterile place, in what only seemed like one sleep ago. Now it was finished, its mission had been completed. The room was dead.

Blake sank into a luxurious but musty Life-style chair and it crossed his mind to wonder what sort of furniture was in style now. He smiled faintly, for he had unconsciously shifted his *now* almost a hundred years ahead in time.

After a time, Rio helped Doreen into the room, and she lay weakly on a nearby couch. Rio opened a Cantillon cabinet and brought out a sealed metal chest. She put it down, and Blake could see Doreen's name in faded letters on a strip of tape fastened to the lid. Rio broke the seal, opened it, took out a hypodermic gun, and shot the contents into Doreen's arm with a muffled hiss. Rio also gave her some pills, and a tube of sterile water to wash them down.

Blake watched dully, still weakened by his ordeal. As Rio reached into the cabinet for a second metal chest, he croaked, coughed, then asked, "How long has it been?"

Rio smiled. "I thought the first words were always 'Where am I?' "

"I know *where* I am," Blake said in a creaky voice, "but not *when*."

Rio sat down next to him, opened the small chest, and took out the hypogun. "You are one hundred and seven years, eight months, and two days older." She put the hypogun to his arm, and he felt the chill of the spray as it hissed through his skin. "I woke up first. It took me hours to get out of the damned coffin," she said as she put away the hypodermic. "I unsealed the lock and crawled out here to get these chests. Engelson put them out here to give us a little time to adjust. Then I waited three *weeks* before Granville thawed out. For a while there I thought I would be the only one."

Blake touched her arm. Awakening more than one hundred years into an unknown future was bad enough, but alone ...

"Jean-Michel awoke fourteen days later, and Vogel about a week or so after that. Then they blasted the entrance open and looked around outside and sort of got things ready. Granville read the hardcopy on Flower and ... we opened her ... her coffin. That was two days ago. Then today the monitors flipped green and we uncorked both you and Doreen. Granny says a seven- or eight-week span when you're over a hundred years is practically zero perfect, even if the estimate for all of us was off nineteen, almost twenty, years."

"Are ... are we all going to ... to make it?"

Rio smiled. "Sure. We'll all live four hundred years at least. Our youth and middle age will be indefinitely prolonged, maybe in excess of three hundred years, three fifty." She smiled wanly. "We'll have fifty years of old age, and maybe a couple of decades of senility, but what's the difference? There are black pills and high dives and laser pistols."

"You sound gloomy," Blake said. He felt his strength returning, and when he glanced at Doreen he saw the color back in her cheeks. She was struggling to sit up.

Rio stood up. "Vogel hates you. He says he is going to kill you. Voss hates you, too, but he hasn't said anything."

Blake nodded. "I know. But I couldn't help it. I couldn't lose you." He looked up at her and was pleased with her smile.

"It was flattering," she said. "But dangerous."

Blake sighed wearily. "I know. I didn't think much about what I did, I just did it. It's not like I killed Warford or anything. I don't feel guilty about that. I could have ended up like Flower. The cryogenic program was calculated for Warford's weight and metabolism, not for mine. Engelson's alterations could have been too hasty . . ."

Rio touched his shoulder. "You look a lot better now. Want to come look at the outside?"

Blake nodded and rose carefully to his feet.

"Come on, Doreen," Rio said. "What about you?"

Doreen made a croaking sound and grasped her throat and made a face, but she got to her feet and followed Rio and Blake as they crossed into and through the big, luxurious outer chamber and passed through the open lock.

The mountains were the same. It was spring, and fleecy white clouds were heading southeast with perceptible movement. There were flowers around the edges of the small clearing. The hidden explosive packages triggered by Voss and Vogel had blown away the tumble of earth and rock that had covered the tomb entrance. The raw earth and split rock was ugly on the green grass of the hillside, but the entrance was clear. One large rock had been lasered into pieces and shoved aside.

Blake noticed a pine tree quite close to the entrance, shading the lockport, but he remembered no tree nearby when they had gone in—yesterday.

He looked out over the forest below and thought there must be differences, but he could detect none. Trees must have grown into maturity, died, were burnt by fire or blasted by lightning. In other areas they would have been logged off and new growth planted, but here was still virginal land.

Blake looked to the right, where Vogel and Jean-Michel were assembling the aircar. It was an eight-passenger Aeroford with an oversized fusion engine, the very latest design. *One hundred years ago,* Blake thought.

Voss turned to Rio after a glance at Blake and at Doreen, who had sat down upon a rock. "We can take off tomorrow. I think everyone will be in shape by then."

Rio nodded and asked, "Where's Granville?"

Voss pointed down the mountainside. "He went to look for some detectors he planted. There he is now!"

Blake looked and saw the tiny figure come out of the trees and start up the slope. The trees were just beginning to thin here at the tomb site and the view over the mountains was gorgeous.

"It feels good to be alive," Doreen said with a raspy voice, and Blake turned to her.

"Yes, it does. Can I do anything for you?"

Doreen smiled weakly. "No, I'll be all right." She indicated the aircar with a tilt of her head. "That thing going to be all right after a century of sitting like a lump?"

Blake blinked *There is something about the phrase "a century" that is more staggering than "one hundred years."* He smiled at himself and told Doreen, "Probably. It was double-sealed and first-grade workmanship."

Doreen squinted at the machine. "I don't know. It could have been sabotaged. Not everyone is . . . uh, was . . . a fan of Jean-Michel Voss, you know."

Blake was a little surprised but made no comment. He patted Doreen's knee, then looked down at himself. He plucked at the thin woven plastic garment. "Care to slip into something more comfortable?" he asked.

Doreen smiled and took his hand to rise. "Anything I have is now a costume, not clothes. But lead on."

Doreen and Blake re-entered the tomb. Blake paused for a second at the lip of the lock and looked back. Vogel was looking after them with an expressionless face. Blake shivered.

Doreen and Blake took showers in adjoining sonic stalls, but the sight of her nude body did nothing for him. It crossed his mind that after a hundred years he should be quite eager. *Maybe my body has ignored the signals for so long that nothing is functioning anymore.* That gave him a moment of pause. *Three or four hundred years of life is an exciting prospect, but not if there will be no sex, not if I've somehow become impotent!*

They dried off and found garments in a Vuitton cabinet. Warford's clothes fitted Blake moderately well, though he found the bodyguard's taste somewhat somber.

Doreen chose what was, for her, almost chaste coverings even though the garment exposed much of her ample bosom. She was combing out her hair before a mirror when Rio approached them.

"You look good, both of you. Come and eat. Granville is back and interpreting the detector records."

Doreen and Blake walked around the wall of the Inner Chamber to the dining area, where Rio had laid out an attractive meal from hermetically sealed dried foods.

Granville was there, eating with one hand as his other shuffled rectangles of hardcopy. He looked up and smiled at Blake. "Welcome to Tomorrowland, Mr. Mason." He waved a fistful of thin plastic cards. "No great rise in radiation. About, um, forty-nine years after we hibernated there was a blip, probably just one bomb somewhere. But for the rest of the time the level has been moderate. Slight rise over norm—norm for our time, that is. So . . . no atomic wars, no mutations, no big trouble." He looked at Jean-Michel and Vogel as they sat down. "I checked, and it still holds. No radiation rise of any importance. Civilization is probably still out there."

"We saw a contrail," Vogel said. "Going north."

"Polar route," Granville said, nodding. "Good! Good!"

"We leave at dawn tomorrow," Voss said. He looked around the table. "All of us."

Blake raised a fork of something dark and grainy to his mouth and Rio caught his eye. She was bent over a second food package, turned away from the group, but Blake could see her biting her lower lip.

Later, Blake lay on a couch trying to sleep. The lights in the outer chamber were turned low. He could hear Vogel's snore, Voss's heavy breathing, and Granville's soft, sighing wheezes. He couldn't understand how they could sleep. *They have traveled in time! A one-way trip, sure, but they're in the future!*

Blake wondered what had happened to the world in the nearly eleven decades they had been sleeping like Barbarossas in a mountain. Man didn't seem to have killed himself off in a war. *But he just may have starved to death*, Blake thought. *And my business, my unfinished projects . . . what happened to them?*

Blake hoped his letter had been posted. A trust should have been established. Elaine, Sebastian, and Aaron had been given the business. Blake had no close relatives, or none he liked, and his parents were dead. *There should be money in a trust, maybe quite a bit, if we can get to Los Angeles . . .*

He stared at the dimly lit ceiling and his thoughts were jagged and chaotic. *Maybe I shouldn't have come . . . No! I had to. Don't have any second thoughts now! For one thing, it's too late.*

Either they accepted the papers and a trust had been established, or not. With the money that Voss's companies would have paid for my end of the tomb deal, plus what I had, plus anything the company might have earned . . . for a hundred years at six percent . . . Not bad. Maybe things weren't so bad. They knew where I was. I wasn't legally dead. There might have been some legal problems, but Elaine would have fought for me. I'll have enough money to take care of Rio. I'll start another company. I'll be hopelessly outdated as an environmentalist, unless there's a nostalgia fad going on—or I can start one.

On the other hand, he realized he might have been declared legally dead, his estate settled, and he would be a dead man without even a tombstone.

Blake sighed, and turned onto his side. *Tomorrow we find out,* he thought. Around the outside curve of the Inner Chamber he could hear the rustle of someone moving. *Rio or Doreen, perhaps just as sleeplessly contemplating the future.*

The future doesn't lie ahead, it's here.

He closed his eyes, and for the second time in more than a hundred years Blake Mason went to sleep.

□

The aircar rose slowly, the helicopter blades kicking up dust from the earthen terrace. Blake looked down at the tree they had felled to hide the entrance to the tomb. Vogel banked away and the tomb was lost to sight.

They headed straight south, angling over the Bitterroot Range and climbing to ten thousand meters. The first town marked on the map was Salmon, but they couldn't make out anything from that height. The rugged Salmon River Mountains were beneath them for kilometers, then the Sawtooth Mountains and the Snake River plain.

"Want me to go lower?" Vogel asked his boss.

"No, keep on. These are the provinces."

The bodyguard shrugged, and the aircar bore steadily south. They could see some evidence of civilization at Minidoka, but it could have been either ruins or a bustling city. Both the height and clouds obscured their vision.

They crossed over into Utah and saw smoke over Logan and definite signs of life at Brigham City. As they approached Ogden, Voss ordered them lower. The Great Salt Lake sparkled off to the west and Blake averted his eyes from the glare, looking again at the gold bars that covered the floor around the base of the seats. They were only a fraction of Voss's cache and that mountain of gold was only a small part of his immense fortune placed in Swiss and other banks, and in trusts and foundations.

Just a little pocket money, Blake thought.

Ogden was a multiple-domed cluster stretching for kilometers. It looked like a soap-bubble blob at the edge of Salt Lake's basin. The domes were white or gray, with hundreds of projections: antennae, landing platforms, observation blisters, radar towers, cargo

114

waldoes, hatches, locks, service catwalks, and here and there a statue.

"They've put it all under a dome," Rio said. "The whole city."

"It's an alternative to the arcology concept," Voss said, "as long as your population is low, or controlled."

"Do we land?" Vogel asked.

"No, go on to Salt Lake City."

The clusters of domes thinned and grew smaller as they flew south, then multiplied again, never quite forming a distinction between the cities. Green, bountiful fields stretched in every direction, and the long half-cylinders of hydroponics housing looked like seams.

Suddenly four jets dropped out of the sky ahead of them, rocketing by at terrifying speeds, flanking the aircar on every side, top and bottom. Their passage rocked the Aeroford, and Vogel struggled to right it, swearing at the jets in vehement curses.

In a few seconds they returned, their speed slowed to match the aircar, and dangerously slow for the military craft.

Blake stared at the odd markings. "What does LDSAF mean?"

"Could it be Latter-Day Saints Air Force?" Doreen said with a nervous laugh.

Vogel snorted in disgust, but Jean-Michel looked at the planes thoughtfully.

"Beautiful," he said, almost to himself. "About as advanced as *air* craft can get. They're motioning us down."

"I don't hear anything on the radio," Vogel said, twisting channels. "They must be using—"

"*—identified aircraft, repeat, unidentified aircraft, you will proceed to Ezekiel Field and land. Further instructions will follow. Acknowledge.*" There was a pause before Vogel picked up the mike. "*Unidentified aircraft, unident—*"

"This is Voss Electronics 7TR640, acknowledging landing instructions."

"*Very well, 7TR640. Keep this channel open.*"

"Verify, uh, LDSAF flight. What is this about, anyway?"

"Land as instructed, 7TR640."

Vogel shrugged, looked at Voss, then put the mike to his lips again. "Uh, LDSAF, where is this landing field?"

"Continue south fifteen kilometers, make ten-degree turn, and descend to one thousand meters. Escorting aircraft will rendezvous."

The jets started climbing, increasing their speed, and circling back.

Voss peered at them through the canopy. "They'll be watching us. Do as they say."

Small, fast aircars rose to meet them, with several on each side and two more high up and to the rear. The pilots peered at them with some interest, but no hostile moves were made. Each helicraft bore the LDSAF logo, and all appeared heavily armed.

Ezekiel was a large airport, fringed with service structures, and packed thickly beyond were larger and larger domes. Beyond them were a number of arcologs, massive buildings a half-kilometer high. Toward the center of the city an immense low dome spanned at least ten kilometers of downtown Salt Lake City, using the arcologs almost as posts around the outer perimeter.

"Look, almost every building seems to have gun domes and radar disks," Rio said.

"They're armed for something," Voss said.

"Have we arrived in the middle of a war?" Doreen asked.

"No damage," Vogel said, looking down.

The LDSAF aircars landed smoothly as Vogel set the ship down. The military ships ringed Voss's, all heading inward, their weapons pointing at the invader.

"What do we do now?" Vogel asked.

"Wait."

"Unidentified aircraft, you will disembark," a new voice said. *"Stand clear of your ship with your hands on your heads. Do not move once you have achieved stationary status. Execute orders immediately."*

"Come on," Voss said.

Granville was the first out of the plane. He had been

silent throughout the flight, carefully checking his radiation detectors and the other devices, checking ground features with a map, and keeping a sharp eye out. He left the ship almost eagerly, his head turning one way and another as he looked at the ships and the approaching file of armed men.

"Come on," he said encouragingly to the others.

Blake found it strangely annoying that the officer the ship. The file of visored soldiers kept efficient-looking rifles trained on the newcomers while a small group of officers inspected the aircar.

One officer walked over to the group, inspected them briefly, and spoke to Voss. "Are you the leader?" Voss nodded. "What is the meaning of invading our air space in *that?*" he said, pointing at the Aeroford. "Why reproduce an antique aircraft? Who are you?"

"I am Jean-Michel Voss. That is not a reproduction, but an original. My crew and I have been in a cryogenic vault for one hundred years, and—"

"One hundred seven years, eight months, two days," Granville said, and the officer gave him a lightning glance, then returned his attention to Voss.

Blake found it strangely annoying that the officer would automatically assume that Voss was the leader, but it did not surprise him. Voss had that kind of bearing.

Voss smiled faintly. "Correction noted, Mr. Franklin." To the officer he said, "I am the director of Voss Electronics, Voss Investments, Voss Oil, Voss Marine—"

"Stop," the officer said without much agitation, but Voss stopped his litany, calculated to impress everyone, even the unimpressionable. He looked annoyed. He had been interrupted twice in one explanation. *That must be a first,* Blake thought with some amusement.

"Your papers, please," the officer said, holding out his hand. With his other he indicated that all of them should present identification. He took Voss's wallet, handed it to an aide without looking at it, and passed on the others' IDs also without examining them.

"What is your explanation of the illegal gold we

found on your ship? Are you smugglers for the Guardians?"

Blake looked at Voss, and Jean-Michel looked at Granville Franklin.

"No, we're just out of cryogenic sleep," Granville said.

"We've just traveled to the future," Voss said. "Our future, your present . . . and now our present. What is going on?"

"The Archangels? Skypilots? Any of the Orders?" The officer's eyes narrowed. "You aren't believers in any of the *old* faiths, are you? Catholics? Hebrews? Baptists?"

At those words Blake saw the hands of the soldiers tighten on their weapons. Rio drew close to him, looking at him around the curve of her arms as they rested folded on her head.

"No, no, of course not," Voss said. "We have no such affiliation."

The officer's eyes narrowed warningly. *"No* affiliation?" he said softly.

"If anything, I'm an atheist," Granville said, and the soldier recoiled.

"Arrest them!" he said sharply.

The soldiers crowded about closely, and over Voss's protests they were driven across the field to a waiting armored van. The steel door clanged behind them, and Blake joined the others sitting on the metal benches lining each side.

"I think you said the wrong thing," Rio told Granville with a smile.

The generalist shrugged. "A peculiar reaction. They seem to be very religious, or at least militantly partisan. Most peculiar for Mormons."

"Are they Mormons?" Voss asked.

"LDS, Latter-Day Saints, Salt Lake City," Granville said, gesturing around him. "Their own air force and army. Most peculiar."

"A church with an army?" Doreen asked incredulously.

"It's happened before," Granville said. "The armies of the Old Testament, the Crusaders, the armies of the

Borgia and the Medici popes, of many of the Hindus and Muslims. Any land where church and state are one. The Saracens, Spain of the Inquisition, the old armies of the emperors of China and Japan."

"Enough!" Voss said quietly. "We get the point. Now how do we get out of here?"

"The gold," Vogel said.

"It's back at the ship," Rio reminded them. "But if we can convince them we are not smugglers, it will be ours again."

Voss was deep in thought. Blake examined the van as it rumbled along. Solid steel painted dark gray. A guardport at the cab end, through which a guard could be seen watching them. Near Doreen's head on the opposite side of the van someone had scratched "The Lord giveth and the Lord taketh away."

No one had any contributions, so they fell silent. After a while the sounds around them closed in and echoed. "We're inside something," Vogel said. The van continued with undiminished speed.

"A dome?" Rio asked.

Voss and Blake nodded.

After a time, the van stopped and the rear door clanged open. They were inside a large room. Huge metal grilles closed passages at both ends, and beyond them were solid doors. Gun and gas ports were everywhere, looking down at them.

Visored soldiers directed the prisoners into a corridor, then put each one of them into a separate room.

Blake looked around. He was not handcuffed, or even searched. They must be supremely confident, he thought. Then the door opened and in walked a soldier with the traditional staff of Hermes—the caduceus—upon his collar. He ordered Blake to strip behind a screen and to hand out his clothes, which he did. He expected a rectal search but instead was given a loose gray jumper to put on. Then he was instructed to stand before an opalescent panel higher than his head. *An X-ray of some sort,* Blake thought.

Satisfied, the medic departed with all of Blake's clothes, and he was left alone for almost an hour. Then a burly officer entered and politely asked Blake to sit in the room's only chair.

"Now keep your hands flat upon the arms," he said amiably. *A polygraph!* "My name is Colonel Calkins, of the LDS Intelligence Service. Your name, please?"

"Mason. Blake Paul Mason."

"Paul, that's a Biblical name. What is your affiliation?"

"You mean what church do I go to? What difference does that make?"

The colonel shrugged. "Just a casual question, Mr. Mason. But your attitude surprises me. Are you an atheist?" The last question was more firmly and suspiciously put.

"No." The questions seemed to have a deeper meaning than Blake was able to discern. The officer on the landing field had been much more agitated over the answers he had received, but Calkins seemed to be a more skilled interrogator. "I have no religious affiliation." Blake felt that a further response was needed, for Calkins just looked at him. "I—we've—been in the cryogenic vaults for over a hundred years. Churches, religions could change. We would have to look around, I'm sure."

Calkins did not change expression. "Tell me the whole story from the beginning," he said, leaning back against the wall and crossing his arms.

Blake told it as quickly as he could, from Voss's original commission to the approach of the jet planes.

Calkins seemed lost in thought. "We will check on that. Your friend Voss seems reluctant to disclose the coordinates of the cryogenic tomb, but Sister Meaker will be back from a testimony at the Capitol Reef Congregation this evening. She is our expert in interrogation."

Blake shivered. Delivered even casually, his words still had a terrifying effect. *Our interrogation expert.* To Blake that title smacked of the ancient Gestapo and the female torturers of the Indian tribes, or perhaps one of the Mongol interrogators used by the old Russian Communist countries.

"It's not easy to describe where the tomb is exactly,"

Blake said. "I couldn't give you the exact location, myself." *Voss is keeping all that gold safe,* he thought. *Goody for him, but what about us?* "Look, Colonel, I don't know what any of this is about. I've told you why Mr. Voss decided to do what he did. What's wrong with that? He is, er, *was,* a very powerful man in our time. I'm sure he still is, or will be, once he takes control of all his various trusts and funds and things."

"Yes," Calkins said, "I'm sure he would be. Except research and experiments into longevity are forbidden for the good of the state."

"But we were up in Idaho, not here in Utah. You can't—"

"It is illegal everywhere. All over the globe. Even in the territory controlled by the Church of Converted Avatars, even in the land of the cursed Host of the Angels of the Earth."

"But why? Scientific research is—"

"It is forbidden." For the first time the colonel looked disturbed. "Surely even an unenlightened one from the past, such as you, can see the problem? You had large population problems even back then. If we extended the life span of even a tiny fraction of the population it would be disastrous! There are *sixteen billion people* on Earth today! We can barely keep ahead in food and other production. That's the only reason we allow the Circus. It reduces tensions; it's not to reduce the population, as the blasphemous Catholics say, not at all. An insignificant number perish in the Games. No, it is to give our millions a release for their emotions. Even the Ministers of the Will of God see that. The Believers in the Fundamental Bible have just opened their own arena, in United Kansas, and they were the last holdouts. But now even they have recognized the value."

Colonel Calkins inhaled deeply and regained his composure. To another man the subject would have been almost nothing; but Blake thought that for the colonel this must be a strong emotional issue.

"But we didn't know that! We did it years, *a hundred years,* before any law was passed against it! It was legal in our time!"

"We will take that under consideration. But there is still the matter of the gold, unauthorized flight in an unlicensed aircraft, indecorous clothing—"

"But how could we license a ship when we were ... Uh ... indecorous clothing?"

"One of your group, Sister Doreen O'Shea, was clothed in a fashion long prohibited by both custom and law. A serious offense."

"A low neckline is *illegal?*" Blake was incredulous. "But how were we to know of your nudity taboos?"

"The Elders will take that into consideration. Meanwhile, you may rejoin the others."

Abruptly the colonel left, and in a few minutes a soldier escorted Blake to a room where everyone but Granville was gathered.

Quickly they each told the story of their interrogations, and with minor discrepancies they matched.

"We had no time to think up a cover story," Rio said, "and a good thing, too. Those polygraph chairs were pretty efficient." She didn't explain how she knew, but Blake imagined she had been caught in a lie.

"Let us pool what we know," Voss said. "They want the location of the tomb. They have some expert coming in tonight to question me."

Blake and Voss exchanged looks, and Voss shrugged.

"They are religious fanatics," Voss continued. "Much more so than the Mormons of our time."

"I think they are under great pressure," Rio said. "The air force, the guns, the suspicion ... There seem to be a number of religious factions or groups that control areas, or influence politics, or something. It's pretty vague."

"There's something called the Swords of St. Michael," Vogel said in his rough voice. "I think they're cops. Calkins asked me if I was registered with them. He called them Defenders of the Faith, too, but I think they're something like the Federal Bureau of Intelligence back in our time."

"I'm sorry about my clothes," Doreen said apologetically. "My God, I thought these were pretty conservative, too!"

Rio patted her arm. "Don't worry. I almost wore something just as revealing. They don't seem to like sensuality very much, do they?"

Doreen shook her head, her fingers holding closed the front of her dress. Voss began to pace the floor, and Vogel looked nervous.

"Where's Franklin?" the bodyguard asked Voss.

"I don't know. They seemed distressed that he was an atheist."

"Thank God, I'm not an atheist," Doreen said, and they all looked at her. Her smile melted away and she hung her head.

"They mentioned several religions or sects, or what I *thought* were religions," Rio said. "Quite a few, in fact. Guardians of the Throne of God. Archangels of the God Triumphant. The Congregation of the Most Faithful Minions of the Lord, or something like that."

"Calkins mentioned some to me, too," Blake said. "Church of the Converted Avatars, Host of the Angels of the Earth ... something called the Believers in the Fundamental Bible, too. *They* just built a Circus."

Vogel spoke again. "He mentioned Minions of Gabriel to me. But it didn't sound like a church, the way he said it. An army maybe, or some kind of force."

"He asked me about some of those, too," Doreen said, her head still down. "Skypilots, Incorporated ... Shapers of the Coming Truth of the Crucified Christ."

"All Christian churches," Voss said. "That's significant."

"Calkins didn't think much of the Catholics," Blake said.

"Splinter groups, dissidents, secessionists. Like the Roman Church from the Hebrew, like the Protestants, like the schismatic orders that split off from the Catholics. All Christians but all fighting."

"Holy wars," Blake said. *Oh, Jesus!*

"Those were always the worst," Voss confirmed. "How many burning saints can dance on the point of a pin? Brother against brother, heresy and the Inquisition."

The words cast a gloom over the group and they sat or stood mutely for some time.

Then Rio said, "We've got to get away!"

"Where?" Doreen asked, looking up. "It sounds as if it is the same all over."

"I must get to Switzerland, or at least New York. There I can activate my contacts," Voss asserted.

"What about Los Angeles or San Francisco?" Vogel said. "We might make that."

"How?" Blake said, gesturing around at the prison walls.

"This is not the first jail I've been in."

I bet! thought Blake.

Vogel looked up at Jean-Michel. "How much of the gold can I use to bribe?"

"All of it, if you need to. Just get me out of here."

Blake noted the "me" bleakly. *Here it comes,* he told himself.

Vogel rose and took Voss to a corner, where they conferred for several minutes. A little later the door opened and a prisoner in gray wheeled in a cart with food. He would not talk, and left quickly.

The food was delicious, but a few odd tastes stumped their minds. Almost the moment they were finished, the door opened again and the same prisoner took out the cart. Vogel attempted to engage the guard in conversation but it didn't work.

An hour later, Granville Franklin came in. He seemed unhurt and almost cheerful. They pelted him with questions, but he held up his hands. "Easy, easy, now! The world is run by a number of large militant religious organizations, you found that out? All right. It looks as if the pendulum has swung the opposite way from our time." He looked at Doreen. "Did they discipline you? No? They will. Your public indecency is almost as bad as smuggling. Maybe worse, to some."

Doreen hung her head again. "I'm sorry, I'm sorry."

"It is a sexually oppressive world. But get this!" He gestured around him. "*This* is supposed to be an island of enlightenment in a dark world. Yes! The Mormons were always independent and they still are. But ... they, too, are influenced by social pressures."

"I've got to get to New York or Zürich," Voss said determinedly.

Granville looked doubtful. "Yes, well, perhaps. Travel is pretty much controlled, too, and you have to have passports to go from state to state here in America."

"How did you learn all this?" Rio asked.

Granville smiled. "If you keep yourself calm, you can learn much from the questions an interrogator asks. And I asked a few, too, for background in which to frame my answers."

"What about Washington, or some sort of central government?" Rio asked.

"I'm not certain there is any," Granville answered. "The government seems to be a group of corporations, sometimes church-owned and sometimes church-controlled, but certainly church-influenced. The governmental services they need seem to be established mostly on a franchise basis—a direction the police departments back in our time were heading in. Instead of the election of a new political party, bringing reorganization and political plums, there are regular contracts—like those with garbage collectors or building contractors. Contracts up for renewal are put out for bids from qualified security-service companies."

Granville chewed at the inside of his mouth. "But with these strong regional governments, the central government seems to be rather weak. I'll learn more if I can talk to someone who really understands the situation. Or get to a Total Information System terminal."

Rio whispered to Blake, "See why Jean-Michel brought him?"

Blake nodded, whispering back, "How can we get away?"

Granville heard him and said, "With difficulty, I think. We are on Level E of a thirty-eight-floor dome with nine levels below ground. We are five levels below the surface. I don't think we'll *bust* out."

"Buy out?" Voss asked quickly.

"Probably the best way to try. But they have the gold."

"They don't have all of it," Vogel said.

"Are you going to try to take us all out with you?" Blake asked Voss.

There was the smallest of hesitations, then Voss said, "Of course. Even you, Mr. Mason, the stowaway in time."

"Very poetic, Jean-Michel," Blake said, not fooled for an instant.

"The Grand Inquisitor, or whatever he is, is coming tonight," Voss said. "We'll have to work fast. I don't know what sort of methods or drugs they have now."

Granville nodded. "Have you tried talking to the guards?"

Vogel nodded. "Nothing."

"Calkins?" asked Granville.

"You think you can bribe *him?*" Rio asked.

"It is all in knowing the price a man will accept," Voss said.

"Cynically but sadly true," Granville said, giving Voss a cryptic look. "How are we going to go about it?"

"The first one who gets him alone will offer him the location of the tomb," Voss said. "Providing we all go along."

"Why should we go along?" Granville looked worried. "Only one is needed. He might get suspicious."

"Tell him it takes four of us to open the vault, but not which four," said Rio quickly.

"Have you people even thought about this place being bugged?" Vogel asked.

Granville shrugged. "We have nothing to lose." He gave each of them a significant look. "It takes four of us, each with a part of the combination to open the vault where the gold is stored, do you understand me?" Everyone nodded. "The hypnotic implants are triggered only by symbols on the site. Not even we know which four. Got that?"

"Pretty good," Vogel said, then fell silent as Granville shot him a black look.

"There are ... um ... how many millions in gold there, Jean-Michel?"

"Ten. No, twenty-two. By the values of a hundred years ago."

"It matters little," Granville said. "Even with the fusion torches refining our refuse and cleaning sea water, the world's gold supply is not increased very much.

That stack of bars would be worth a fortune—or several fortunes—in any era of Earth's history.

"Bait," said Voss.

"How many soldiers can they take with us?" Vogel said.

"Enough, perhaps," Blake said.

It was Voss himself who got Calkins alone a half-hour later. He came back into the room to the others, barely suppressing his delight. For the benefit of any possible hidden microphones Voss said, "Well, I had to tell him. He could see that if Sister Meaker got the information from me, it wouldn't help him. And after Sister Meaker worked me over, I might not be in the proper serene mental attitude to open the vault. He figured, correctly, that I had to be one of the four. We leave in an hour or so," Voss said, looking pleased.

"North to the tomb," Vogel said.

"Yes," Voss answered with a look of anticipation. "I also discovered that west of here—from the Shoshone Mountains to the Sierras—is the province of the White Kingdom of Light. All across northern Nevada. The lower part—down to Vegas, Death Valley, and east over the Grand Canyon and almost down to Phoenix— is controlled by the Eye of the Mystery of Eternal Life."

"What about California, over to San Francisco?" Blake asked.

"I'm not certain. It's either the Order of the Celestial Hierarchy, or something called Guardians of the Throne of God."

"They sure have some names," Doreen said. "My mother used to go to the Church of the Redeemed Son of God, and I thought *that* was some name."

"Notice that the names are often rather specific," Granville interjected, "as though they outlined, or specified a certain *aspect,* and not a broad, general faith. Maybe we can use that theory in some way."

"I don't see how," Doreen said. "It sounds as if the whole damn world has gotten religion." She looked suddenly tired. "It just isn't what I expected. I—I expected . . . more."

"More?" asked Rio.

"More of what we had. More fun, more excitement, more . . . uh . . . *more*. Bigger pleasure domes, maybe quicker and easier ways to get to Mars, or something like that. Just, uh, *more*."

"Yes, I'm certain we all expected something different from this," Granville said, "but this is what we've got."

"For four hundred years," Vogel added.

"My God!" Doreen exclaimed. "I'd forgotten." She looked at Voss. "I . . . didn't really think it would happen—or if it did happen, we wouldn't *really* live *hundreds* of years."

"Maybe we won't," Vogel said gloomily. "Or else they'll give us life."

"Oh, dear," Doreen sighed. To Rio she said, "I thought it was kind of like, you know, going along to *Triton* for a week, or maybe a weekend sub party out of Brisbane. I didn't . . ." Her voice trailed off and the voluptuous young beauty looked lost.

"What's Calkins's plan?" Vogel asked.

"I don't know," Voss answered. "We don't know how they'll transport us. We may be in separate ships, or in holding cells in some kind of airborne version of what they brought us in with. But we have to watch for an opportunity."

Vogel made a cupping gesture with his hand around his ear, and pointed at the walls. The financier nodded, paused, then said quietly, "Don't jump at the first chance. Consider all possibilities. Try to alert the others." In a slightly louder voice he continued, "We don't know what the triggering mechanisms are for the hypnotic suggestion. We don't want to mess up our opportunity to get all that gold out of the vault."

To Blake the words were nonsense, but he saw how they fitted roughly into the idea Voss and Granville Franklin had planted in Calkins's mind.

Blake asked Granville, "Did you deduce anything else?"

"No, not much. I think they are down on sex because sex is the cause of pregnancy and pregnancies are the cause of overpopulation. I wouldn't be surprised if they licensed pregnancies. If not here, then somewhere, or maybe everywhere."

"Why do you think the Catholics and Jews are on the shit list around here?" Vogel asked.

"I don't know. I don't have enough information yet. Perhaps because they are older religions. There are older ones, of course—like the worship of Ishtar, the Olympian gods, or various Egyptian gods and goddesses or those found in Slavic and Norse myths—but some of those religions died out or were insignificant even back in our time. Perhaps even 'immortal' gods lose their power or potency when people stop believing in them."

Granville rubbed a hand across his face, massaging it hard. He took a deep breath and continued, "But the Hebrew religion is old, very old and well entrenched. Of course, there have been purges. Orthodox Christianity is also well established, especially in the Roman Catholic Church. Perhaps all these *new* religions didn't want to be compared, or reminded, or something . . . I just don't know yet."

They waited, impatiently and with growing nervousness. So much could happen to thwart them.

Finally, Voss said, "We will try to fly west to San Francisco. Los Angeles will be our second target, if we are diverted or blocked. I think I can contact my factors there. There should be some office of *something* here. Or a secure line to New York or Zürich."

A little while later, Blake spoke to the room at large: "A hundred years. One-oh-seven plus. We thought it was going to be ninety." He looked at the ceiling thoughtfully. "You know, I thought the future was somehow going to be different. You know, *different* different—airy crystal cities and creatures of pure energy, fairyland parks with strange and wonderful devices to amuse us."

"Or a ruined, blasted land," Granville added.

"No, I thought we would find something really fine," Blake said. "A hundred years, maybe that's not enough. A thousand, three thousand maybe."

"More like a quarter-million, I'd say," Granville insisted. "Or more. A million. 'Creatures of pure energy' take time to evolve." The generalist turned to Vogel, who was next to him. "What did you think the future would be like?"

"I didn't think much about it," he said. "Like home maybe, only more so: more people, tougher."

"Then why did you come? Was it money?"

Vogel glanced at Jean-Michel Voss. "I was paid well."

"Is that the only reason?" Granville asked.

Vogel shook his head and took his time answering. "When times are tough, they need people like me." He didn't want to continue, and Blake saw Vogel's eyes swing to give him a hard look.

Granville turned to Rio. "And you, my dear, why did you come?"

She shrugged. "I was needed. And . . . it was an adventure."

Granville snorted, then laughed. "Yes, indeed, it *is* that. And I suppose I must ask myself that same question, in all fairness. I came because it was a challenge! I had made certain public predictions, and I wanted to see . . ." He smiled around at the others. "We all wanted to see, I think. Man has always wanted to see what was on the other side. The other side of the time hill has proven to be most interesting."

"You think this is *interesting?*" Doreen asked incredulously.

"Oh, most interesting, my lovely lady, most interesting. It's less than a hundred and eight years, true, but the hundred years from, say, the end of the American Civil War to 1965 was a fantastic hundred years! Everything had accelerated tremendously! That's why I became a generalist—because the specialists were having such a hard time even keeping up with their own disciplines. Things were happening too fast, and had been, ever since way back in World War II. My specialty is generality: seeing the bridges between specialties, the connections between isolated discoveries or theories, the spots where paths are sure to have crossed. I can also eliminate duplication of effort: often people in the same field go on making the same mistakes others have made because the field is so complex, and moving so fast, that they can't keep up, much less know what others have done."

Granville beamed at his fellow prisoners. "So I came

to see what God had wrought with what Voss had bought."

Granville looked wryly now at Blake. "And you, our stowaway, why did you come? Was it just the semi-immortality?"

Blake hesitated. "No, I didn't really think about that at all. Did you?"

"Yes, a little. I thought it would be nice to have doubled or tripled my life span. I could study much more that way."

Blake looked at Doreen. "Did you think about the longevity benefits?"

"No." She brushed her hair back with both hands. "Not really. If I did, I guess I expected ... well ... a sort of very long youth. I came because ... I guess because Jean-Michel invited me." She gave the billionaire a quick look, but he was not paying her any attention.

"You haven't answered my question," Granville reminded Blake. "Why did you come?"

"Because of *her*," Blake said, looking at Rio.

Granville sighed. "Forgive us, Hernando! Forgive us *Señor* de Gama! Forgive us Captain Hudson! Forgive us, Sir Francis! Forgive us Cristoforo! We came not for gold, but *with* gold!" Granville laughed loudly. "We came for immortality. For the invitation. Because we needed. Because of love ... And because it was possible." He laughed again. "Forgive us, Magellan, for we have sinned on the explorer's code! Forgive us, Lewis and Clark! Forgive us Admiral Peary! Forgive us, Leif!" Granville chuckled again. "Neil, Marco, Sir Edmund, forgive us! We are petty explorers, without noble dreams. What would Darwin or Cook think of us, hey?" He slapped Vogel's knee in delight.

"Shut up," Vogel grumbled, but the generalist only laughed again.

They fell silent, with only an occasional rumble of quiet, wry laughter from Granville Franklin.

At last the door opened and Colonel Calkins entered. He went straight to Voss. "The gold. You can get it from the vault with no trouble?" Voss nodded. "Good. The congregation will be pleased. It will surely count on your record."

And yours, Blake thought. *Or will the congregation ever know?*

They walked out single file, down the corridor, and were put into a security elevator while Calkins and several soldiers rode in a second elevator with television and gas controls. They rose to a twenty-fourth-floor landing deck and were checked out by the colonel himself.

The aircar was big, but Blake was glad to see there was only one. The six of them climbed in, followed by Colonel Calkins and six soldiers, joining four crew members who were already inside.

The crew was in a sealed chamber forward, and Blake's heart sank. The new arrivals were put in seats and strapped in. Blake looked down and saw that the seat-belt harness was in reality an electronic alarm device that could only be unlocked by the crew's central control. *Only a professional escape artist could wiggle out of this one,* he thought darkly. Their fine plans of hijacking the aircar began to dissolve.

It rose swiftly and headed north.

Blake didn't have a good view, but the vehicle seemed to be moving very fast. After a half-hour it suddenly took a dive, and through a window Blake saw mountains rising around them. He heard Voss ask Calkins what was going on.

"Going below the Skypilots' radar sensors. We will fly just off the surface until we reach our destination."

Blake groaned. The surface from Salt Lake to the Sawtooth Mountains in Idaho was not too rough, but the Sawtooths ascended to the Bitteroot Range, which became the Rockies, and it was all up and down. Blake settled down for a rough ride.

The aircar swooped and fell, rose and plummeted for nearly four hundred miles—all at high speeds—with sudden, jolting azimuth turns as well, as they traversed canyons and valleys. Time after time Blake saw treetops and cliffs flash by right outside their windows. Rio, Doreen, and Granville became airsick, and he himself was on the verge. He looked at Vogel and Jean-Michel, who didn't seem particularly discomforted by the stomach-turning flying. Four of the soldiers had vomited all over themselves and were swaying weakly in their harnesses. One of the other two looked green.

The aircar suddenly lurched uncommonly hard, and Blake's head banged Rio's sharply. Sitting next to him, she was pale, with a greasy sort of sweat coating her face.

She smiled weakly at him and raised a feeble hand to pat his cheek. "Poor darling," she said.

Then the ship slowed and leveled, and there was a sigh from everyone. It descended, then touched down, and the rotors whispered to a silence. Several of the soldiers were ordered out, and they went, looking quite unmilitary.

After the "beachhead" had been secured, the prisoners heard and felt the seat locks click. Then they rose and exited from the aircraft, followed by Calkins and the rest of the squad; the four crew members exited, too, to stretch their legs, and walked off, chatting, away from the aircar.

The terrace was much as they remembered it.

Voss pointed out the lock entrance. "You had better let me go first, Colonel, as there are certain, ah, booby traps."

" 'Booby traps'? Oh, you mean suckertricks. All right, but we'll be right behind you. Kroeg! Hayes! Cover him!"

Attempting to distract the colonel, Rio said, "My goodness, Colonel, was it necessary to make the trip that rough?" She looked sick and swayed on her feet.

Blake didn't know if she was faking or not.

"You people were quite lucky getting down to Salt Lake. We picked you up early, up near the Snake, but you just happened to come down the channel with the lightest radar coverage of the whole Skypilot state."

His eyes never left Voss, who was climbing over the debris and around the branches of the fallen tree. Blake could hear Voss direct the soldiers not to step on a perfectly harmless rock. They looked warily at it and edged around carefully.

He's setting them up nicely, Blake thought. *He has them doing exactly what he wants them to do, like a salesman asked the kind of questions that generate a lot*

*of "yes" answers. But we must generate our own
schemes, in case his fails.*

Blake decided to back Rio's ploy. "You look pretty
sick," he said to her. He edged toward her consolingly,
watching the laser rifles of the soldiers but not appearing to do so.

Voss and the soldiers, meanwhile, disappeared into
the tomb.

After a few moments, Voss reappeared and called to
the colonel. "All right, send everyone up."

Blake gave Vogel a look and they each took the
elbows of one of the girls and started on ahead, without
waiting for the colonel's order. Granville started angling
slightly to the right, as if choosing an easier path.

"Get ready," Blake whispered to Rio. "I think he
is—"

"Down!" Voss's cry from the lip of the air lock sent
Blake and Vogel into the rubble, pulling the girls down
next to them.

At the same moment the hiss of the laser rifle from
the air lock burned the air over their heads.

Alert as they were, the unexpected move caught most
of the soldiers by surprise. Several fired at the mouth of
the air lock but the full sweep of Voss's stolen laser
ripped into the flesh of the guards. A blast from a
falling soldier flashed off a rock near Rio and another
sliced into the clumps of dirt at Blake's side, but neither
of them was hit. All was silent for a moment, then there
was a clatter behind them and Blake heard a man
moan. The laser hissed again from the air lock and
there was a gurgle, then silence.

Blake twisted his head around and looked back at the
soldiers and crew members. Two had been cut down flat
by the heavy military weapon and another lay against
the skid of the aircar with both legs gone and a pool of
blood glistening around the stumps. He was alive, but
stunned and unmoving. Colonel Calkins lay close behind Blake, his eyes staring open and a deep slash from
shoulder to chest all the way through his body. Blood
and bits of viscera were seeping slowly from the wide
wound. He was dead.

"Are you all right?" Voss called.

"All right," Vogel answered, getting up.

He reached over, took the laser pistol from Calkins's hand and walked back to the legless soldier, who did not look up. His hands were twitching, and his eyes were open, but he didn't move. Vogel shot him expertly through the heart and the man died at once.

Now me! Blake thought suddenly. He thrust himself to his feet, and jumped a small rock to seize a laser rifle from a soldier with a blood smear where his head should have been. Blake hadn't the faintest idea how to use it, but presumed it would not have been on safety. He aimed it roughly in Vogel's direction and watched as the man turned.

Vogel's eyes went to the gun and he stopped. He looked up at Blake and a slow, evil grin crept across his face. "Smart," he said, and thrust the laser weapon into his belt. He started up the hillside to Voss without looking further at Blake.

A percentage player, Blake thought. *The percentages were not in his favor, so why risk it?*

"My God, my God!" said Doreen, sitting up and looking at the carnage.

Rio rose and dusted herself off. She seemed neither elated nor distraught at the bloodshed. Blake felt sick, but under control. He moved on up the hill to the air lock.

Voss's first furious firing had exhausted and partially fused the delicate laser, and he now held Kroeg, the other soldier's, weapon in his hand. His face started to twitch into a smile as he looked at Blake.

"Thank you for saving Rio," he said.

Blake noted the singular "object." *The rest of us are spear carriers in your life, aren't we? Even Rio is only a character actress. An expendable bit player.*

"They're both dead," Vogel told Voss, coming back out of the air lock.

Voss raised his eyebrows, and Blake had the uncomfortable impression the two soldiers had been alive when the financier had taken their weapons. "Of course," Voss said. "Drag their bodies out of here. Put them all in the aircar."

"Why not just bury them?" Blake asked.

"We're going to dump them in some lake so there will be no trace. The aircar, too. But first we'll have to find some other transportation. Mason, get down there and pull as many good uniforms off those men as you can. Clean 'em up. *Move!*"

Blake obeyed, a sinking feeling in his stomach. *If low-necklines are trouble, what is multiple murder?*

But as he went down to the aircar Blake argued with himself. *What else could Voss have done? It was certain we were headed for prison, perhaps even for execution. Voss could have called out for the men to surrender, but would they have done so? They had five hostages right in front of them. What would Jean-Michel have done if they had put a gun to my head and ordered him to surrender?*

Blake shook his head sadly. He knew what Voss would have done.

They hovered over the Salmon River and shoved the mutilated and nearly nude bodies out of the ship. The bloody corpses fell forty meters into the stream below and trailed a bit of pink as they were swept toward a stretch of rapids further downstream. Vogel twisted the aircar, whose controls were not basically different from those of one hundred years before, taking it up to cliff height and over, toward the Snake River to the west.

Blake, Vogel, and Voss all wore uniforms of the Latter-Day Saints Air Force. It seemed to annoy Jean-Michel that the officer's uniform fitted Blake best.

"A gentleman at last," he sneered.

They flew quickly and close to the surface, frightening a few deer and not a few cows. They caused a beetle-shaped vehicle to swerve off the road as they came through a small valley.

"Keep going!" Voss ordered. "Perhaps he won't report it."

"But we're in the White Kingdom of Light," Rio said. "Are they going to shoot at us?"

"I'm not certain of their relationship with the Mormons," Granville said, "but I would imagine they are not too friendly. The Mormons were always considered a bit odd by other Christian sects. I wouldn't count on any friendly waves, not as long as we're in an LDS aircraft."

"Aircraft ahead," Vogel said, and everyone tried to see through the windscreen at once. "There!" he said, pointing.

"It's going west, too, almost," Voss noted. "Keep it in sight, but keep it just a dot. That way they won't be able to read our markings."

"Won't the Mormons be after us?" Rio asked.

"Not up here," Granville said. "At least I don't think

137

so. There is probably no extradition treaty between these groups—that is, if all the country is as feudal as it seems to be, with each church or sect or order controlling its own little turf."

"Besides," Blake said, "if I read Calkins right he didn't file too careful a flight plan."

"He was trying to score points over this Sister Meaker," Rio suggested. "So nobody will miss them right away."

"Let's hope not." Granville peered out a side window. "If and when anyone finds those bodies after a few miles in the rapids they won't be able to tell how they were killed, much less who they were."

"But what do we do now?" Doreen asked, looking sick again from the dipping and lurching of the aircar as it hurtled into the growing darkness of late afternoon.

"We have to switch aircars, or disguise this one," Voss said.

"It might be safer to disguise this one," Granville suggested.

"We could turn southeast, get back into Mormon country, but west of Salt Lake," Blake suggested. "Then these uniforms might do us some good. If we are caught in these, we might be shot as spies by the White Lighters, or whatever they call themselves."

Voss thought a moment. "That's not a bad idea. Then no disguise would be necessary on the ship. Vogel, go south, toward Boise, but east of it."

Vogel leaned forward and traced a route on an illuminated map with an electric stylus. The ship turned gracefully and headed south by southeast.

"I'm hungry," Doreen announced.

"I'll get something from the supplies here," Granville said.

"I'll help," Doreen volunteered.

Rio sat next to Blake and ran her finger along the thick tubular barrel of the laser lying in his lap. She looked very solemn as she murmured over the noise of the jet blades, "I'm sorry I got you into this."

Blake raised her chin and smiled. "Hey, I'm a volunteer, lady. Maybe I didn't know I would be getting into the middle of some kind of nutty holy war, but I volunteered. You did everything to discourage me." Blake glanced up into the cockpit, where Voss was examining some maps by the light from the instruments. "Jean-Michel wants you. I want you. You are grateful to him and feel needed by him. Perhaps you are even flattered that the great Voss chose you, I don't know. But I *love* you."

Rio's eyes grew large and shiny. Blake grinned crookedly and said, "I hadn't planned to tell you that again under such romantic conditions, but I've been thinking: maybe we won't have any other chance. I have no regrets about coming, Rio. None. Not if I can be with you. No, don't say anything, don't protest! I'm with you now. I'll be with you as long as you will let me."

Blake put his hand over hers, lying on the crystal chamber of the laser. "Back there, when Voss was going to shoot past us at the soldiers, I thought—all in a flash, an instant—I thought, *Oh, God, don't let him hit Rio!* I was angry at Voss for endangering you, but I don't know what else he could have done. I'm sorry those men died, but I'm not sorry we lived. And I'm very glad *you* lived."

Blake looked down at her hand and stroked the fine-boned back of it. "I love you, Rio, and . . . and I'll kill for you if I must." He looked up at her. "I won't like it, but I will if I have to."

Rio's face was soft and wondering. Again, Blake stopped her words with a gesture. "You don't have to say anything. No promises, no lies, no words. I don't know what we are in for, or that will happen to us, but I love you. Know that. Rely on it. Use it. Make your own decisions. Don't feel guilty about me, or about Voss. You came along, into the future, into . . . this. That cancels out any obligation. You are free, Rio. You can't even let Voss make your decisions for you any-more."

Rio's eyes wavered and dropped. She was breathing shallowly and she bit at her lip. She started to say some-thing, then stopped as Doreen and Granville came for-ward with small trays of emergency rations. Doreen handed two up to Voss and Vogel, then went back for her own.

Blake nodded a thanks at Granville and took two trays, passing one to Rio. They ate without further talk, and Blake found it difficult to swallow.

They went down the state along the Snake, skirted Boise, and were just starting out over the Snake River plain, when a single military jet streaked by. There was a white cross on the side, with thin red rays radiating from it. The plane came so close that the turbulence almost upset the helicopter, and Vogel fought the controls, cursing fluently.

Voss picked up the radio mike and said sharply, *"Overflight, overflight, this is Brother Jean-Michel Smith of the CDY. We are on a Code Ten intelligence flight with a top-security clearance. You are endangering our cargo of Almanite Nine. Unless you want the Snake River contaminated with radioactivity for the next three hundred years I suggest you stand clear. Over."*

Blake raised his eyebrows at Voss, who gave a twitch of his lips.

"LDS flight, this is White Force One-Sixteen," came the reply. *"you are unauthorized to cruise at this altitude in improperly marked aircraft. You will turn one-eighty and set down at Brotherhood Field."*

"One-Sixteen, this is CDY, repeat, CDY, on a Code Ten, repeat, Code Ten. Our cargo is Almanite Nine, repeat Almanite Nine. We are under security. Our authorization is . . ." Voss hesitated a moment, then continued, *". . . from the Brotherhood Central itself."*

"LDS, this is White Force One-Sixteen. You mean Brotherhood Temple One?"

"Affirmative, One-Sixteen. From the Central Control of Brotherhood Temple One. Over."

"Continue on your course, LDS flight, while I confirm on Seven-Niner Alpha. White Force One-Sixteen on standby."

"CDY copies. Out."

Voss turned to the others with a thin grin, and Rio gasped. "How did you know what to say?"

"I made it up. Throw in lots of letters and numbers

and some kind of priority status and make it their responsibility if things go wrong. Some of Hannibal's elephant handlers probably did the same thing."

"What is he doing?" Granville asked.

"Circling," said Vogel. "But falling behind."

"In that jet he could catch up quickly," Granville grumbled.

"We'll be into northeastern Nevada by the time they get the red tape worked out," Voss said. "We'll still be in their territory, but . . ." He shrugged.

"The night won't help us," Vogel said, gesturing at the control panel. "If they're like this one, they have radar, sonar, infrared—and something called 'spot-all.' "

"Whatever that is," Doreen commented.

"Fascinating," Granville said.

"What was the outfit that controlled *lower* Nevada?" Blake asked Granville.

"Um . . . the Eye of the Mystery of Eternal Life."

"Sounds ominous," said Doreen. "The Eye sees all, knows all."

"We've got to think up some sort of pitch for *them,* too" Blake said.

"Could we be defectors?" Rio suggested.

"I don't know," Voss said. "That could get us into more trouble. I knew we'd be out of place, of course, *today,* and would need to feel our way. But this is troublesome.

Blake had to smile. *Pursued as outlaws, we are temporal castaways whose only assets seem to be our wits.*

The warplane dropped further and further behind and they eventually lost sight of it. The situation kept them on edge, but no pursuit was detected.

"We may have crossed some kind of border," Granville suggested. "I only hope no one has called ahead."

"Turn the plane southwest—gently does it—Vogel. I've changed my mind about going back to Utah. But our escape has been a little too easy," Voss said thoughtfully.

Blake wondered how many dead soldiers there would have to be for Voss to consider their position "difficult."

"But maybe there isn't much cooperation between states . . ." Voss added.

No one had anything to say.

They crossed northwestern Nevada without incident, keeping so low they sometimes frightened animals. They were heading into the eastern flanks of the Sierra Nevadas when Granville Franklin spoke up.

"The defector idea isn't bad. Depends on whether or not whatever cult controls the area we find ourselves in is friendly toward the Mormons. At least they would listen to us."

"Before they shoot us, you mean?" Doreen said sarcastically.

"How do we explain the dead bodies and this LDS aircar?" Rio asked.

"They won't find the bodies right away," Voss said, "and I have a hunch that Calkins didn't exactly broadcast his destination or purpose. We may have more time than we think."

"Unless Sister Meaker expected to find us ready for her," Blake said.

"Just keep going," Rio said. "What other choice do we have?"

"Oh, we have lots of choices," Granville said with a wide grin. "It's just that most of them are unpleasant."

They crossed the Sierras, taking the Feather River route, flying low and between the cliffs. Blake wasn't too happy about leaving his life in the hands of a man who hadn't flown this particular type aircraft before and whose flying license expired a hundred years before. *And who hates me!* he thought. But he had little choice.

They came out into the lush green of the Sacramento Valley and saw a dramatic increase in air traffic and signs of civilization. To appear less conspicuous they rose to the south-bound air-traffic lane, crossing high above Sacramento and curving toward San Francisco.

"So far so good," Granville said with a smile.

"You certainly are cheerful," Rio said to him.

"Why not? It's all so fascinating. It's a marvelous adventure."

Blake looked at him with raised eyebrows. "You've never done anything like this before, have you?"

"No," the older man grinned. "Have any of us?"

Blake looked at Rio and shrugged. "Watch him. I think he has delusions of heroism."

Granville grinned widely at them and returned to his avid perusal of the ground and sky.

Civilization began to thicken below, and less and less land was visible. Long before they reached the widening of the river that preceded the entrance to San Francisco Bay, the hills were covered with rows upon rows of multiple dwellings, then bigger and bigger structures, until San Francisco appeared ahead of them, across the bay. It seemed to be one large building, bisected by the Golden Gate, with the bay as a kind of glorified pool in the patio. The eastern edge of the bay, from Contra Costa County to Santa Clara, seemed one huge factory and storage area, broken only by the architectural complex of the University of California, thrusting up from the plain of steel and concrete with a series of imaginative towers, domes, and spires.

"Is that what I think it is?" Doreen said, pointing to a light in the sky over the city.

They all peered at the light and Voss snorted. "An electric angel."

It was a huge figure, perhaps a hundred meters in wingspread, that sailed and soared on the breezes. Even in the daylight it glowed and the golden trumpet in its hands glittered.

"Lightweight animatronic robot," Blake analyzed. "Maybe solar-powered, maybe some sort of lightweight fusion power plant."

"And one hell of a billboard," Rio said.

"Where do we set down, boss?" Vogel interrupted.

"Might as well head for the site of the old San Francisco Airport, but don't be surprised if it isn't there. Go into anything that looks good—and legal."

"I wonder why they haven't spotted us." Blake asked.

"Maybe they have," Rio suggested, "and are just waiting. Or we might have slipped in as part of the regular air traffic."

"Look!" Doreen cried. She pointed out the window at a black-and-white aircar with some kind of official-looking seal on the side.

Everyone tensed up, but the police aircar did not seem to notice them, continuing along in the same airlane.

"How do I get down?" Vogel asked everyone at large. "I'm a little afraid to ask for instructions, and with this much traffic they must have some kind of automated control."

Voss searched the control panel and studied the map panel. He used two illuminated cross hairs to get a fix on the old location of the airport, where a winged symbol appeared. Then he punched the green button at the screen edge, and the aircar made a slight course correction.

"We're on automatic, I think," Jean-Michel said. To Vogel he added, "Just stay alert, and if it looks like we're coming to an airport, let it handle itself. Unless we start landing on a police car."

Vogel nodded and the others watched in fascination as they flew down the center of the bay. Both old bridges were gone and the buildings had encroached on the waters considerably. There were several ships in the bay, one a beautiful sailship whose tall metal vane sails were multicolored and graceful. Another was a low, wide plankton skimmer with a damaged bow, towed by two sturdy tugs. Two of the ships were surfaced submarines—one a fat cargo sub and the other a gaily painted pleasure sub with dozens of observation blisters.

"Isn't that where Alcatraz used to be?" Blake asked, pointing at a small but highly fanciful arcolog.

Granville nodded agreement. "No bridge, no boats. They must get there by aircar or tunnel."

"Looks like a pleasure ark," Doreen said. "I bet it lights up like a lighthouse in the fog."

"We're coming down," Vogel announced, and everyone moved to his seat.

Looking ahead, Blake saw the airport. Three long runways crossed at angles, but between them and in a massive bank to the western edge were hundreds of circular landing pads. Each was numbered and had various symbols painted boldly upon it.

Blake gave one last look at San Francisco's massive skyline and wondered briefly how they had handled the earthquake problem. Then the ship was settling down onto pad number 625. Two pads over—on 623— there was a landing decorated with a broad red line bisecting a six-pointed star. In the middle of the star sat a large black-and-white aircar that had several gun turrets.

Vogel killed the rotors and Voss said quickly, "Let's get the hell out of here!"

"Just don't look too scared or run too fast!" Granville cautioned. "Let's act like a group late for an appointment."

The air was fresh and brisk and smelled of salt.

Blake helped Rio down and they followed the others across the pad and down the stairs at its perimeter. Under the pads was a large area of steel posts, repair shops, service bays, junk-food dispensers, telebooths, and entrances to a lower level of slidewalks.

"We've got to get out of these uniforms," Voss said, eyeing a passing group of monks in amber robes accompanied by a stately priest in white.

A little further on they saw a large group of uniformed men and women, garbed in pale blue with black belts and berets. Several of them nodded politely to Voss and his crew as they passed. Voss pulled them to a stop by a drink dispenser, and they crowded close for a conference.

"Did you see the symbols on their caps?" Rio asked. "An angel over a book, and she's holding up a fistful of lightning."

" 'It,' not 'she,' " Granville corrected. "Despite their male names, angels were neuter."

"Never mind that," Voss cut in. "The point is, we've seen perhaps three different sects, and unless they are different orders of the same church, something is very odd."

"I could go ask one," Doreen said. "I'll just play dumb and——"

"And you could be asking a deadly enemy of the LDS who he represented," Voss warned. "No, ask a civilian." He inclined his head toward a plump man standing by a dispenser, looking nearsightedly over the offerings.

Doreen nodded and casually wandered over to him.

They spoke for a minute, and the man looked very nervous throughout.

Then Doreen returned and said, "He was sure funny. I did the usual, you know, and it made him very edgy." She looked back at the man, who had hurried off without a drink. "I hope I didn't do anything wrong," she said.

"Tell us what he said!" Voss snapped.

"Uh ... Oh, he said the ones in blue were members of the Congregation of the Most Faithful Minions of the Lord. Those monks we saw were Brothers of the Wardens of Life Eternal. He said he was a faithful member of the Church of the Seventh Heaven." Doreen looked puzzled. "I don't understand him. He took one look at my chest and just never looked again. That just isn't like a man. I mean, a normal man."

"Lots of different faiths here," Granville said. "Living together without trouble. I wonder if they are allies, or what. No one seems troubled by our uniforms."

"I have an idea," Rio said. "Anyone have any change?"

"They felt through their pockets, but only Blake came up with anything from his officer's uniform pockets. "Will a change-card do? It's for Salt Lake City, though."

Rio examined the card closely. "It says 'Valid in all sovereign states of the republic.' " She shrugged. "Well, let's see." With Blake, she walked briskly to a visionphone booth and put the card in the slot. She looked over the small instruction panel, then punched for Information. A face appeared on the screen that was so neuter in appearance that Blake couldn't decide if it was an animatronic robot or not.

"Computer simulation, I'll bet," Granville said, walking over and peering at the screen. "Unisex designation."

"A listing, please, for every major religious center in San Francisco." Rio was saying.

"Clarification, please. San Francisco City or County or both?"

"County."

"Clarification, please. Religious embassies, consulates, corporate offices, meditation centers, or trade missions?"

Rio looked at Voss, then back at Blake. He shrugged. "Corporate offices."

"Corporate offices," Rio said.

"Verbal or hardcopy? There are one hundred and sixteen listed."

"Uh . . . Never mind. Cancel."

The screen went blank and the time travelers looked at each other.

"Maybe San Francisco is some kind of neutral zone, like Switzerland," Granville suggested. "Try for, um, a definition of the neutral zone, Rio."

Rio punched again for Information, and the same unisex figure appeared.

"Visually define the San Francisco neutral zone, please."

"Clarification, please. Do you desire the physical limits of the neutral zone of the Treaty of Jerusalem or the physical limits of the Western Republics Neutral Trading Port Treaty as regards the City and County of San Francisco?"

"Uh, whichever is the most recent," Rio said.

"Thank you. That would be the Treaty of Jerusalem."

A map of the peninsula appeared on the screen. It seemed to cover a hundred-kilometer circle with the center at the Golden Gate.

"Information?" Rio said.

"May I help you?"

"Yes. Can you define the terms of the Treaty of Jerusalem? In brief, that is."

"The Treaty of Jerusalem defines the physical limits and laws governing the establishment of neutral trading zones throughout the world. This includes seaports, airports, ground terminals, sea vessels, non-attached arcological structures, and other such areas as are designated by the Celestial Council of United Faiths. Commonly referred to as Free Ports, no such established neutral zone shall inhibit the passage of any citizen of any republic, save those engaged in criminal or other proscribed procedures as designated by International Law.

The treaty was subscribed to by the Republics of—"

"Never mind," Rio said.

The face on the screen stopped talking, and waited, patiently.

"Now what?" she asked the others.

"Free ports! That explains it," Granville said.

"Ask him—uh, it—to recommend a good hotel," Doreen said.

"No, ask for the address of the Voss Investment Corporation," Jean-Michel said.

Rio asked the question, and the information face said promptly, "No such listing is recorded. Could it be listed under any other name?"

Rio looked at Voss, shrugged, and pulled out the change-card. The screen blanked and they all looked at each other.

"We could try calling New York or Switzerland," Rio said.

Voss shook his head. "I'm not certain how much that card can be stretched. Let's think." To Granville he said, "Do you think the card could cover hotel rooms for us? And new clothes?"

The generalist shrugged with his eyebrows. "I don't know. We ought to get out of sight and think our plans all through."

"Come on," Voss said, starting down a corridor.

"Wait, boss," Vogel said. "What about the aircar?" He gestured with his thumb back toward the pad where they had landed. "Won't they get suspicious if we just leave it there?"

"You're right." Voss thought a moment, then spoke decisively. "Rio, get the number of this booth and give a copy to Mason." He looked at Blake with a wicked grin. "Now, *Colonel* Mason, you go back, put that thing in a repair shop. Break something on it first. Tell them you are in no hurry for it, that you'll phone in with your hotel number as soon as you are settled. Have them bill *you*, not the LDSAF. Tell them it was your fault and that you want to keep it quiet. Let them overcharge you, which they will if they think you are in a spot."

Voss gave him a triumphant look. "Rank hath privileges, Colonel. They'll take it from a colonel, so throw that rank around. Give him the number, Rio. Wait here for our call, then meet us at the hotel."

Blake gave Rio a look, and she smiled at him and touched his arm. "Don't worry," she said, then hurried off after the others.

Blake went back, opened the cowling of the aircar and did damage to the fusion generator. Then he walked to the below-pad area and found a mechanic with a shop name on his jumper. The mechanic called his boss, who came with a tow truck; then they brought down the pad and towed away the aircar.

As Blake watched the vehicle being hauled off through the forest of pad supports, he suddenly realized he had no money or even a change-card to get him to whatever hotel they picked.

Blake smiled bitterly. *Voss a billionaire and me— hopefully—with a fat trust fund. And I don't have the money to make a phone call!* He walked quickly back to the visionphone booth, glancing at his stolen watch. It was slightly less than an hour since they had left him. Blake thought about ways he might make a call to Los Angeles, but then realized he wouldn't know who to call until he did some research on what bank might have his trust fund.

Blake stood impatiently in the vicinity of the booth for several minutes, then saw someone about to enter. He quickly stepped in the way, smiled brightly at the frustrated citizen, and pulled the booth door shut. He sat there for several more minutes, but the confines of the booth depressed him. *I wonder if I got an induced claustrophobia after a hundred and nine years in a steel box?*

Blake flicked the *"Out of Order"* signal and stepped out for some air.

For a while he watched robed and uniformed figures walk by. Some gave his LDS uniform a scowl, but took no other notice of him. Blake glanced at his watch: almost two hours.

Then the soft buzz of the visionphone summoned him. Rio's face filled the screen.

She smiled warmly at Blake and said, "We're at the New St. Francis."

"I don't have any money to get there. Can you pick me up in a taxi?"

Rio pursed her lips, then leaned out of range of the pickup to speak to someone. She looked nervous when she came back into view. To someone off-camera, undoubtedly Voss, she said, "Well, he has no other way to get here. I'll have to go get him."

"There's probably a taxi pad up here somewhere," Blake told her. I'll be at the one on the southern end, if there is more than one. Or on the western end, if they run that way. All right?"

Rio nodded, looking angrily off camera for a second. "I'll be there as soon as I can, Blake. I promise."

They punched out, and Blake walked quickly toward an airport map he had seen earlier. He located the taxi pads, memorized the way there and started walking briskly. He was startled by the salute of two young LDS troopers, and returned it belatedly, much to their surprise. Nervous and anxious to get out of sight, he walked as quickly as he could to the southern pad. He did not expect Rio so soon, but he wanted to scout the area.

Blake picked up a brochure for Bibleland, the General Animatronics religious amusement park. He was pretending to look through it when he spotted the black uniforms of two strolling policemen. He turned toward a kiosk stocked with pamphlets, picked out two more, and was deep in an appraisal of the two communities of Bethlehem II and The Promised Land in the reclaimed Sahara when the two policemen walked by. He made the mistake of glancing up to find one set of hard, shrewd eyes on him.

"Colonel," the policeman said politely, making a half-salute with the neurobaton he held like a sword.

Blake nodded back and returned his eyes to the glories of a religious community on the shores of Lake Sahara, until he sensed the policemen had departed. He then crossed a mall and went partway up the stairs until his eyes were on a level with the landing pad. He could see the fog coming in over South San Francisco, filtering through the big arcological mountains, graying the world.

Something seemed familar about the unfamilar sky-line, but it took Blake a few moments to recognize what it was. The once bright-surfaced arcolog of *Hexahedron West*—where several friends had once lived and which once dominated the South San Francisco skyline, almost blotting out the sight of San Francisco itself, over the big hill—was now all but hidden in the towering structures around it.

The scale of the newer buildings was staggering. They were all twice as big as most of the arcologs of his time, each one thrusting up through the fog almost three-fourths of a kilometer or better. The stream of air-cars that flowed out through a canyon-like passage between arks toward the airport were just dots against the vast concrete-and-steel pale beyond. Lights were already going on as the fog moved in, and more than one structure bore fanciful variations on crosses as the topmost symbol of the building. Aircars going the other way were wavering red dots and the traffic flow seemed endless.

An aircar taxi now landed on the pad and two thin young men jumped out, followed by a woman. Their yellow robes whipped and roiled in the wind coming across the bay and their shaved heads made Blake feel colder. They hurried toward the stairs, then hesitated when they saw Blake.

"What is it, Member Timothy?" the woman asked.

"Nothing," the man said, hurrying past Blake, down the stairs.

The woman then saw Blake and gasped, halted, then hurried past with nervous energy, careful not to look at him.

Out of sight on the curving steps, but still within hearing, one of the men said to the woman, "Member Jennifer, this is a neutral zone. You must remember that. You'll not be harmed."

Blake scanned the sky for any approaching taxi as the one that had delivered the robed trio departed.

His eyes kept returning to the great impressive mass of the city. Once he understood the new scale of the spacescrapers, he quickly located *Barbarytowers* and the little ark whose name he could not recall: the one where

Liz Zachary used to have her strange little parties. The arks seemed shrunken and disguised with added floors and modifications. The city seemed drab, without the gay character it had once had.

When a taxi dropped out of the overhead traffic and Blake could see Rio's face in the window, he was at the hatch before the skids touched the pad. The taxi was up and away while he was still buckling the seat belt and trying to kiss Rio at the same time. This was almost the first time they had been alone since coming from the tomb and the only time they were certain Voss would not walk in on them.

After a few moments Rio pushed him back and said, "Let me tell you what we've found out. Those computer terminals are excellent, much better than the Total Information Service we had back . . . back then. We hit some areas where the damn thing would just blink and say 'Proscribed . . . Proscribed' and we were afraid that would trigger some kind of alarm. But nothing happened."

"Never mind that, kiss me," Blake said.

"No, Blake, please. Things are happening too fast. Voss is afraid his money is gone! Cryogenic work is proscribed, and he has the feeling that he was declared a criminal and his money confiscated because of it." Blake kissed his own trust fund good-bye.

"All of us were declared criminals?" he asked.

"He's not certain. It's difficult to find out anything without tipping someone off. He's trying. He thinks it happened about fifty years ago, more or less, when all these religions came to power after the Flash War."

"That must have been the radiation Granville found on his sensors," Blake said.

"I guess so. So much information really requires prior knowledge, an understanding of the culture. We tried getting a history of the last hundred years, but it was so filled with religious propaganda that it was almost useless."

"Can Voss contact any of his people?"

"He's trying. Switzerland seemed vague, with promises to check as soon as the offices open in the morning. Doesn't that sound odd? Even in our time, corporations that did business in multiple time zones had a skeletal staff at night."

Rio looked worried, then smiled slightly and continued: "The religions seem to dominate everything, especially here in the Western Hemisphere and in Europe. Not so much in Asia and Africa, I think. But with trade and religion and government all mixed together, it is pretty difficult to get it straight. The atmosphere is repressive in social and governmental areas," she went on, even as she looked out the window at the city. "Especially regarding sex. Just walking past a group of nuns in the hotel lobby, you would have thought Doreen and I were stark naked. Even in our drab uniforms!"

Rio sighed. "Jean-Michel says the religious taboos seem to have caused a freeze on society and on business. Only one child per person is allowed, just as in our time, but now they've put some real teeth in the law. A third child is a hell of a tax burden and a fourth child would just about ruin an average family, not to mention causing mandatory sterilization. But get this: there is no birth control. None. No pills, no abortions. That would be against the word of God."

Blake groaned. "So that's why sexual attractiveness and sex itself are so proscribed. Beauty leads to sex and sex leads to pregnancy and pregnancy leads to overpopulation." He looked down at San Francisco as they passed over a huge stadium and into the busy air passages between the massive towers. "Some glorious, shining future world *this* is! Where are all the creatures of shining light?"

"Oh, that reminds me. Jean-Michel found out what happened to Theta. She died about thirty years ago in the Abbey of St. Anne of the Skies—a *nun!* Not only a nun, but the Chief Abbess."

Blake shook his head in wonderment.

"Voss is in contact with some lawyers," Rio said, "and he's—"

"Never mind him." Blake reached for her, and they were still kissing when they set down on the landing pad atop the arcolog that held the St. Francis.

□

The rooms were expensive. Jean-Michel explained it as hiding where they could not be seen. Then he and Granville left to make calls from other visionphones and to try and obtain some different clothes. They had been gone about two hours when the door was unlocked.

Blake turned, expecting to see Voss. Instead, he saw a drably dressed civilian holding a magnetic key in his hand step back out of the way. Then the police charged in.

Blake stared dumbly into the pinpoint muzzle of a police laser, his heart sinking and his stomach twisting itself in knots. Feeling foolish and helpless, he looked at Rio.

She was wan and pale, as was Doreen, who stood in the bathroom doorway holding up a towel, which covered very little.

The officer in charge was a brutal-looking man with a depilated head and face. He angrily ordered Doreen to get dressed. Then he waved his weapon at Blake and Rio. "All right, you accursed heretics! Now the judgment of God is upon you!"

□

Blake was put in a small, clean cell that was spartanly functional, with a narrow folding bed and a low toilet. The clothes that replaced his stolen uniform had metal fibers woven into them that the guard boasted were trackable for a hundred kilometers.

They had fixed a narrow metal band around his neck, and Blake went over to the small mirror near the toilet to look at it. It was comfortable, but heavy, and engraved upon the dull blue metal were words. Reading them backward, Blake made out PENAL SECURITY CORP., LEAVENWORTH, KANSAS, PARISH 29, MINIONS OF GABRIEL. Below, in red, was the warning, DANGEROUS WITHIN TEN METERS. DEACTIVATION AUTHORIZED ONLY BY ORDER OF WARDEN.

Blake stared at the reversed words he had painstakingly decoded. *It'll blow my head off!*

He sat down suddenly, fingering the neckband gingerly. There was a depression for a mag key next to the seam, but no other markings.

What have they done with Rio? Blake thought angrily. *Maybe I could tell them I dragged her along against her will.*

An hour went by, then another. He could hear movement, and some distant, muffled talk, but nothing happened. Another hour crept by. He lay on the narrow, hard bunk, glaring at the protected lens of the television security camera, thinking of ways to escape and creating lurid scenarios for what was going to happen to him and to the others. He cautiously fingered the explosive band around his neck, and his mood became gloomier by the minute. And with the gloom came anger.

His captors arrived at last, the tough young Swords of St. Michael, Defender of the Faith. They were dressed in black-and-silver uniforms, ornately handled nerve

155

whips at their belts and dark-visioned helmets set square on their heads. Blake went with them without resistance.

Blake expected a court and found himself in a court. But it was an ecclesiastical court, with white-robed figures on a high bench and a large cross on the wall behind. The cross was banded with triple rows of soft neon and it seemed to quiver faintly.

The judges were old, with pale skins and pale eyes, their faces set in one expression: disapproval.

"Blake Paul Mason, come forth," a red-robed bailiff said.

Another robed figure from a tier of robed figures to the right read aloud the accusations. "The accused is charged with temporal transportation, longevity research, unlawful flight, grand larceny aircraft, unlawful possession of dangerous weapons, impersonation of an officer of a friendly state, possession of cryogenic equipment and processes, illegal entry, illegal exit, no visible means of support, suspicion of blasphemy, unlawful cohabitation, suspicion of proscribed sexual acts, and violation of the fugitive act."

"I want a lawyer," Blake said.

"Quiet!" said the bailiff.

"I want a lawyer!" Blake said loudly.

One of the judges looked up from a readout screen and glowered at Blake. "Young man, this is not a court of law. This is a court of enquiry."

"It looks like a court to me," Blake said, his anger obvious.

The old man merely looked at him and then gestured toward the bailiff.

"Do you desire a Bible?" the bailiff asked. "What version? Celestial Council? Authorized Kingdom of God? Guardian? Archangel? Blessed Revised? Skypilots Easyread?" The bailiff paused and looked suspiciously at Blake. "You don't want one of the *old* ones, do you?"

"I want a lawyer."

"You don't need a lawyer. The court will see that you are fairly handled," the bailiff said sternly.

It took about ten minutes. Blake was not given a chance to ask questions or to make a statement. The only thing he said was, "Not guilty, and you don't un-derstand that—"

"The decision of this court is that you be mandated to a court of law and there be tried for offenses against the State. You are judged guilty of all charges against the Church and automatically excommunicated from its protection. Bailiff!"

Blake looked at the old men on the bench, his teeth pressed tightly together and his muscles bunching. They appeared oblivious to him and the next case was called.

He spent more hours in his cell, then was transported to another jail and another cell and waited still more hours. Finally he was taken to another courtroom and put in a clear-plastic booth three meters square.

The courtroom was almost empty, only a few disin-terested spectators lounging in the rows of seats. Blake saw screens, and quickly realized that both judge and prosecutor were there only on television—safe from the violence of the courtroom and detached from those they judged. It angered Blake still further to be handled like a piece of meat, without even the dignity of meeting his accusers face to face.

They brought in Doreen after a few minutes, and then Rio. Both women were wearing the same sort of drab gray uniforms that Blake wore, but not even those shapeless garments could hide their figures. They, too, wore neckbands.

All quietly compared notes, and they found that they each had been tried in the ecclesiastical court, and that their charges had been the same—except for an addi-tional charge of "unlawful garments" that had been added to the women's accusations.

A plump young man approached and was admitted to the booth. He introduced himself as Ben Richards and announced that he had been appointed their law-yer.

"Where were you when we were in the goddamn church court?" Blake growled.

Richards looked shocked. "Please, don't make it worse by blaspheming."

"What? What the hell kind of lawyer are you, any-way?"

"A devout one. There is no use your protesting the findings of the ecclesiastical court. It is out of our jurisdiction. I'm only here to defend you in the criminal action in state court. My advice to you is to plead guilty and throw yourself on the mercy of the court."

"But we're innocent!" Rio said. "We didn't know about your laws—how could we?"

"Cryogenics were legal in our time," Doreen protested.

"Please. You know your guilt. The ecclesiastical court established that. Plead guilty and recant, take your penance and give thanks to God."

"Some lawyer!" Doreen groaned. She moved close to Richards and her voice dropped seductively, "Listen, honey, get us off and . . ."

The lawyer paled and moved to the other bench quickly, dropping some papers from his briefcase.

Doreen looked at Blake and Rio and shrugged. "Funny world," she said. "That used to work pretty well."

Richards went before the judge's lens and announced he had been appointed defense lawyer. He thrust some papers under a reprofax, then came back to the defense booth.

"What have you decided?" he asked nervously.

"To get another lawyer," Rio said.

Richards shook his head. "No, I'm it. You're lucky to get me. I'm only here because my clients in an airtaxi suit got into another dispute on the way here and they're in Mother of Angels right now. The controller caught me on the way out."

"Then get us off," Doreen said.

"I can't. You're guilty."

"But that's your job—getting us off," Doreen said.

"But I know you're guilty," Richards complained.

"What's that got to do with it?" Rio asked sharply. "Are you a lawyer or not?"

"I know a guilty client when I see one." Richards glowered. "I didn't want this case on my record. I tried to get off, I really did. But that Ruffner, he's had it in for me ever since I beat him on the *Fitzgerald* versus *Boers* case. He's assignment proctor today and—"

"Listen," Blake said, grabbing his arm. "Defend us! We admit we are here by cryogenic methods, but that wasn't illegal in our time, so how could we know? Now get up there and tell them!"

The lawyer sighed. "See? You admit your guilt." He sighed again, elaborately.

A soft bell rang. The screens lit up and a panel of three judges appeared. On another screen, a bailiff read the accusations and added that all three of the defendants had been found guilty in Ecclesiastical Court Fifty-Six, Parish of St. Randall the Extreme, Division Twenty-One.

"How do you plead?" the center judge asked in a bored voice.

"Guilty to all counts, your honor," Richards said.

"Hey!" Doreen said, making a grab for Richards.

Blake seized her, and Richards dodged around her, leaving the booth without much dignity.

Their trial was over in less than a minute: the judge must have had the computers already programmed. Hardcopy slithered out of a slot, and a court marshal read the verdict aloud.

"The defendants have pleaded guilty and are sentenced to one year's assignment to the staff of the San Francisco City and County Recreation Department."

Blake stared at the television screen. It seemed such a trivial sentence for such serious crimes. This world would never cease to amaze him!

He turned to look at Rio and Doreen. Confusion replaced the fear on their faces.

Richards spoke to them through a grille in the wall. "I'm sorry. It's not so bad, though. You could have gotten thirty days. The court must have considered your, you know, unique situation."

The three defendants looked at each other, puzzled and confused.

The lawyer looked around, then said quietly, "See, on a thirty-day sentence they hit you with the really bad acts right away. But on a year's sentence you get *some* training so you won't embarrass the cadre. They'll put you in the parades and maybe into some of the easy acts, like the clowns. Unless they really need you in the, um, heavy acts. Or if you antagonize someone. Sometimes the projected rate of disability increases unexpectedly and . . . well, you understand . . . in that case they . . ."

Richards shrugged and left the sentence unfinished. "Of course, along about the tenth month they start listing you for . . . well, bigger draws. You know." He gave them a sad smile and reshuffled some papers in his briefcase.

Blake, Rio, and Doreen just looked at him, not knowing what to say. "Well, look, I wish I had more time to talk to you folks, I really do," Richards said. "That must have been pretty exciting, living back there in the old days. But I'm afraid a—" he paused to look around again—"a heresy monitor might see me and . . . Well, it doesn't do much good to be seen with known heretics, does it?" Richards smiled a sick smile, closed his untidy briefcase, and started to leave. He stopped, looked back, and added: "Nothing personal." Then, to a nearby trio of marshals he said, "All right, they're all yours."

Rio, Doreen, and Blake stared at each other.

"Where the hell is Voss?" Rio asked.

"Blake," Doreen asked, "did I hear that right? We *are* being sent to the Circus, aren't we?" Blake nodded. "Jesus. Say, isn't that cruel and unusual punishment?"

"It's probably not unusual around here," he answered.

Then the marshals took them away to separate cells.

□

The police airbus dropped directly into the compound, down past the guard towers and high walls into a rather small landing space. Blake had not been able to see any of the vast Caligula Sports Arena, for the ship had no windows. He was still wearing the neckband, as were the other four passengers, and they were all chained together.

As they filed out on command, Blake smelled the sea. He wanted to ask where they were, but conversation had been forbidden.

As the five prisoners marched into the tunnel, Blake kept his eyes open for Rio and Doreen. Sneering guards had told them that since they were notorious they would be processed quickly. Blake took that to mean they would all be put directly into the games while their novelty value was still high. But he did not see either of the women and he wondered again, for the thousandth time: *Where is Voss?*

Their file tapes were passed over to a beribboned lieutenant, the crossed swords of his order glittering on his cap device.

The officer scanned the hardcopy, and snapped orders to the sergeant in command. "Weissman, Linford, and Rampton are to go to the armory. Mason, come with me!"

The sergeant used his mag key to free Blake from the common chain, and Blake followed the officer to a heavy-duty lock. Two of the laser-bearing soldiers followed.

The officer keyed another lock and they walked a few meters to his office. Blake stood before a desk as the lieutenant sat down behind it.

On the wall behind, a huge map of the arena showing six underground decks was dotted with colored symbols.

On the wall to his right, Blake saw a collection of framed plaques, tridee photos of the officer with various people, and four large, shiny trophies. On the left-hand wall was a collection of ancient Roman gladiator armor, swords, and helmets—all dented reproductions. He also noticed the scratched and ruined arm of a fighting robot, with wires still trailing from the shoulder; it had been lovingly mounted on a wooden plaque, and there was a shiny metal panel with engraving that Blake could not read.

"Mason, Blake, Two-dash-One Two-Five-Three point Two-Two-Three. Sentence of the court: twelve-month duty with this command." The officer looked up from the hardcopy readout and his eyes were stern. "We've had a lot of men and women sent to us for disposal, Mason, but you and your perverted friends are the worst. You have offended our whole society. You are disgusting, an offense to every right-thinking Christian."

The officer leaned forward and his face folded into the caricature of a smile. "You will die here, heretic. You will die, but it will not be an easy death." He leaned back. "Frankly, I'm sorry we don't still have the stake as a legal method of execution. I always thought it was an excellent deterrent. Nice, crisp close-ups going into every schoolroom in the parish would soon set those little imps on the right path. They would never be heretics, they would be believers!"

The Christians are throwing the pagans to the lions, Blake thought.

"Why are you smiling, Mason?"

Blake was genuinely surprised. He didn't feel much like smiling, now that he thought of it. Hearing a judge pronounce a rather oblique death sentence in a courtroom had not really penetrated. Hearing the man who seemed to be the one who would implement that death sentence was another matter. The trouble was that Blake suddenly found the reversal of the traditional historical roles quite ludicrous.

But he did not want to let his sense of humor, even gallows humor, obscure his objective: escape. "I'm sorry, sir, I guess it was just a nervous reaction."

The lieutenant looked at him narrowly, and Blake stared steadily at a point just below the officer's hairline. He felt no desire to exhibit a bravado that would put him in some dark cell until he was trotted out to meet the "lions"—probably some horrible robotic version of an updated gladiator.

The officer seemed slightly mollified and he continued: "My name is Lieutenant Cady. The commandant is Colonel K. A. Ozanne. The adjutant is Major Miller. Your section sergeant will be White. You will start training immediately, not that it will do you much good. But the crowd likes a good fight. They become restless when someone commits suicide in the ring. So learn as much as you can in the time you have left." Cady let a crooked smile crawl across his face, and Blake felt the hair on the back of his neck rise. "From birthdate to deathdate, you will be the oldest man we've processed here. But make no mistake—you will be processed!"

Blake said nothing. What was there to say, except some melodramatic statement that would only lead to physical pain. He was no larger-than-life hero from the television dramas.

"Dismissed!"

The guards led him out to a fortified elevator, in which they dropped into the depths of the arena complex. The guards seemed studiously watchful.

Blake stepped out into mass confusion. The sheer volume of the noise startled him.

The elevators were in an alcove, beyond which a five-meter-high passage came from the left and disappeared to the right. The unbelievable confusion was caused by a steady stream—in both directions—of as motley a group of people, animals, robots, props, and assorted oddities as Blake had ever seen.

From the right came a procession of bloody and broken bodies, both wounded and dead. Some of them walked, or limped, and several fell as Blake watched; others were carried by robot one-place ambulances with stretchers and life-support systems as part of their bodies.

Blood, warmed to the proper body temperature and matched perfectly to the victim's blood type, was being piped into their bodies from inner recesses of the robot's carriage. Tiny waldoes administered oxygen and pain killers as other sensors monitored the life functions. Blake saw one ambulance stop as lights flickered, then reverse direction and disappear down a side passage as the lights blinked red. The waldoes retracted into the machine, and the blood needles returned to their niches.

Blake gave it a quick salute with two fingers. *We who are about to die, salute you.*

Seeing a break in the stream of arena warriors, Blake's guards shoved him forward into the crowd.

Many robots were returning from the fray. Most were anthropoid and only a few were injured in any way. Some looked like centaurs—gleaming metallic animals whose fierce mask-like faces were made to resemble ancient statuary. A few were quite small, hardly more than shiny silver beetles bristling with teeth and tiny claws, weaving their way expertly through the crowd in long lines of thirty or forty—a miniature death swarm. More than one had tiny gobbets of flesh still hanging from their claws. Some of the robots were hulking monsters, with one and two sets of powerful arms and thick armor.

Blake saw guard posts set into the wall at intervals and protected by television monitors everywhere. *They are taking no chances,* he thought.

Going in the opposite direction, toward what Blake assumed to be the Arena gates, were examples of what he could only think of as fresh meat. Some walked bravely, with grim faces and narrowed eyes. Some were pushed by burly guards with nervelashes. A few of the prisoners, who were catatonic or shivering with uncontrollable fear, were carried in little electric carts driven by brutal-faced men in black. Not even such paralyzing fear was going to prevent the condemned from appearing on the execution dock. Not one of the men or women was armed, and Blake presumed they would be issued weapons at the gate.

The guard behind Blake shoved at him with the butt of his laser and gestured to the left.

Blake merged with the traffic and found himself walking next to a young man who had an unbandaged head wound. The youth was staggering but still moving. He fell against Blake for a moment, who supported him until the guard grunted and knocked his arm down.

The wounded man looked up at him wearily. "You seem to be in one piece. What did they do, match you with a gone-under?"

"No, I just arrived."

The injured gladiator flashed a smile, then grimaced with pain. "*Ow!* Damn." He tried the smile again, but it was a little ragged. "Welcome aboard, as they say. Let me give you some advice: Don't make friends here. They'll ... they'll be certain to match you up against him." Tears welled up in the young man's eyes. "Or her. They rely on your sense of self-preservation." He closed his eyes, another wave of pain torturing his features.

The blood-splattered warrior staggered and fell against the wall. He was jostled roughly by a three-meter robot. The big, clanking machine had a smear of blood running down his side from a red mess jammed into where his saber-tipped arm joined the trunk of his silvery body. The robot swayed, then righted itself with a whir of gears and strode on without looking back. After a few steps, he turned down a passage marked ROBOT REPAIR, BAY SIX. Blake looked back as the guard pushed him on, but the injured young man was already lost in the hurrying crowd.

The guards stopped Blake and directed him down a passage. He walked down a ramp that was relatively free of pedestrians, except for an old man leading a docile grizzly bear. The bear had a metal plate set into the fur of his skull, and the old man carried a black control box clipped to his belt.

They emerged into a two-story hall. Cells lined both levels. Some had solid doors but most were barred. In the center was a long table with a scarred top. Against one wall was an enormous weapons rack, with locked and shatterproof plastic doors. Inside were swords, spears, tridents, axes, maces, and morningstars.

At the far end of the room were a large wallscreen and a door. The door opened and a tough, well-muscled man in a dark-gray uniform entered. His shaved head was scarred. He eyed Blake without expression as he took the hardcopy orders from the guards.

The hard-faced trainer thumbprinted the orders and handed them back. "All right, he's mine." He hooked his thumbs into his belt and gave Blake a searching look that lasted until the guards had disappeared back up the ramp.

"I'm Sergeant White. You will learn to hate me, but most of all you will fear me." Without warning, he struck Blake in the stomach.

As he doubled over with pain, Blake had the feeling he was either going to rupture or to vomit, possibly both. Then White hit him on the side of the head, crashing him to the concrete floor. Blake gasped with pain. The room blurred, and he felt as if something had broken, somewhere.

"Get up," the sergeant said conversationally.

Blake expected a kick, but none came. Using the wall, he pulled himself upright. He had a hard time focusing on the bare-chested sergeant, and swayed on his feet. He still felt as if he were going to vomit. The taste of bile was in his mouth and that alone was almost enough.

"You will fear me, but you will obey me. I may be the one that sends you out to die, but if you don't go, I will see that you find it less attractive to stay here."

The sergeant turned to one of the solid doors and opened it. He looked back at Blake and gestured him forward.

Blake started toward the door, but veered off to the left. He stopped, corrected, and made the entrance to the cell. He thought he was being put away, but what he saw within shocked him.

Two figures in dirty tunics hung from the ceiling. One was a woman and one was a man. As Blake watched, their fists clenched in the irons and their entire bodies stiffened into twisted and tortured positions. The man screamed, but the woman made no sound, even though the cords of her neck stood out plainly and her mouth was distorted. Then, just as suddenly, their bodies went limp and they hung there by their wrists, their feet a few inches from the floor.

"Nerve shock," the sergeant said casually. "Ten hours' discipline. *She* refused to go up against her old priest, and *he* tried to escape." The sergeant reached up and roughly pulled the woman's face toward him. Her eyes were open and she was quite mad.

The sergeant turned and walked from the cell. Blake followed, eager to be out of sight of the two prisoners. He had no desire to help them, for they were beyond help. The crude lesson the sergeant had given him was all too clear.

Blake realized that the sergeant was looking at him, still without expression. Finally White grunted, as if in satisfaction. He sat on the corner of the table and said, still quite conversationally, "I guess you degenerates back in the old days saw plenty of action, huh? I read some of the old books. I saw some of the tapes when I was a kid—before they burned them all. Great big Games with lots of bare tit and plenty of splash. I guess you ate that up, huh?" He waited for an answer, leaning forward expectantly.

"Yes, they were quite popular."

"Yes, *sir!*"

"Yes, sir. We had some big Circuses then, too. They called *them* degenerate then, too. But they were nothing like this."

The sergeant laughed in a surprisingly high voice. "Yeah, some of those short-swords call *us* degenerates, too. Imagine that? We who perform such important public services. We give good solid entertainment—*real* entertainment, not that acting stuff—to the millions. And we purge society of the heretics and malcontents and criminals in a way that is honest and that gives them a sporting chance."

How much chance does a girl have against a robot? Blake thought angrily.

"We're here to serve a greater purpose," the sergeant said. He leaned forward, his eyes bulging. "We serve *God* here! We are the purging arm of a score of faiths! We take the scum and filth and we shape it into something fit enough to die with dignity. What do you think of that, huh?"

Blake was wary. The soldier seemed half mad, at least, and the power of life and death that he held was awesome. "Well, you certainly seem to do your job, Sergeant," Blake answered.

"I'm just as much a prisoner here as you are, civilian. The only reason I'm not out there on the sand is that somebody has to run these cadres. So I'm going to do the best job I know how, and keep my ass clear. You sync with me, clean-boot? I do what I have to, understand?"

Blake nodded. "Yes, sir."

White seemed to relax a little. "What faith are you, anyway?"

"I'm . . ." He didn't know what to answer. Anything might be proscribed, or out of favor. "Well, Sergeant, the church I attended back in . . . in my time seems to have disappeared. So I guess I'm just looking around. You know, seeing what looks good."

"Ever try the Church of the Celestial Angel-Princes?"

"No. Is that your faith?"

"Well, I ain't saying, but you might look up the Vicar-Baron Jardine. You can find him around the Arena two, three days a week looking for converts."

"Yes, sir, I'll keep that name in mind. It might give me, uh, peace."

"Okay, I hear them coming back . . . They were out in the gym, working out."

The sergeant got up and faced the ramp entrance as a large group of men and women stumbled in. Some were obviously bone-weary and others were visibly excited by the workout.

A short, bulky soldier in leather was hurrying them along. "All right, you rippers, get in the showers. Bennett, you unlock."

The soldier tossed a long-haired young man a mag key and he unlocked the barred door to a short passage that led to the showers.

With much concern for privacy, the various men and women went into their cells, undressed, put on long robes, and came out holding towels. The soldier watched until everyone had gone into the bath, then he relocked the door.

White gestured for Blake to follow, and they walked along the cell block until they came to an empty cell.

"This is yours. You'll get to be just like those others soon. You won't give a damn. You'll go up there and they'll match you against some woman. She knows she'll live another day, another week, if she slices your gut. So she'll try. And you'll slice hers to stop it."

White shook his head. "Once in a while you'll get a good fight. I mean, one with some skill about it, you know? But most of them are just hackers. Can't teach 'em a thing. I even tried hypnosleep, but I guess that's something you can't stuff in later. Either you got it or you don't. In the original specs, I mean." He gave Blake a slow grin. "Always remember this, Mason: this cadre will be run *my* way, because if my people don't score well out there, I'll be dodging the robbies myself." He gave Blake a mean look and walked away.

He stopped by the central table and looked back. "Mason?"

"Yes, sir?"

"They got a lousy union here." Then the sergeant laughed, loud and hearty. He repeated himself several times as he went to the other end of the room and through the door. The soldier who had brought the novice gladiators back was still lounging against the wall. He looked at Blake as if he were a delicious dinner.

Blake shivered and moved into his barren cell. Sitting on the padded bench that served as a bed, he put his face into his hands. *Where is Rio? Where is Voss? What about Vogel and Granville? Did I come a hundred years to die miserably, as entertainment?*

After a while Blake's fellow gladiators came back from the shower. He saw two women walk into the cell across the passage and finish drying their hair. Their robes clung here and there to their damp skin. One of them noticed Blake watching, and turned away angrily. A couple of men went into a cell on the top tier, still toweling their wet heads. A woman entered the cell next to them. She was in her early thirties and seemed very vulnerable, not at all like a hardened criminal who was sentenced to death. Blake heard others moving about. Someone started to sing a popular song, then let it die away. He heard a man cursing the powers that had put him there.

They haven't stamped it all out, Blake mused, *not even in here. But maybe they have nothing to lose once they are here. What more could this odd, unfeeling society do—give you to a hungrier lion?* Then Blake thought of the two people hanging in the discipline room, and he shuddered.

The light was blocked for a moment and Blake looked up. The long-haired young man who had opened the bath door stood there toweling his thick hair.

"Hello," he said pleasantly. "I'm Gali Bennett."

"Blake Mason."

They shook hands.

"You're the time traveler," Bennett said.

"I don't think of it that way. That always reminds me of crystal devices with lots of piping and dials and things. I just went to sleep and woke up here."

"Rip Van Mason, huh?"

"Something like that. Look, can you tell me what is going to happen?"

Bennett nodded. "Yeah, just a minute." He started to leave, then stopped. "No, come on. Might as well meet the others."

Mason followed him as he went out of the cell and crossed to another on the opposite side. Two men and two women were inside. They were all dressed in shapeless gray uniforms. Bennett introduced Blake as the time traveler, which caused some raised eyebrows. The men he introduced as Rob and Narmada, and the women as Neva and Marta.

Blake spoke without hesitation. "Look, I don't know what your crimes are around here, but my crime was time-traveling and longevity research. What were yours? I mean, if it's all right to ask?"

"Oh, we have no taboos against talking about that," Narmada said. "I got here because I am a Hindu. Not that being a Hindu is a crime—not really—but they aren't about to overlook anything if you step out of line, either. They found me with a copy of the *Kama Sutra* during an ordinary student dorm search."

Rob spoke next. He was a strong, sturdy, plain-faced man. "I'm here on nothing so fancy as Nar's. I was down in the Nation of Sinners Redeemed, down in old Georgia. I just didn't go to church enough to suit the Elders, so they brought me before the Lord President and sentenced me to a year in the swamps—which I did, and I have the scars to prove it. Afterward I went back, found those two Elders and bashed them with a shovel and headed west. I got triggered down in San Luis Obispo and—"

"Saint Florian of the Park. Remember? They changed it." Neva said.

"Oh, yeah. I keep forgetting. Why don't they leave things alone? Anyway, they pokied me for being a vag, and one thing led to another and here I am."

"He slammed a deputy deacon through a window." Neva grinned.

Rob smiled shyly. "That I did, that I did."

Blake looked at Neva, who shrugged and said, "I had this patriarch down in Modesto. That's Guardian country." She looked closely at Blake and then added, "Guardians of the Throne of God?" Blake nodded recognition, and she continued. "He wanted me to do a little sinning with him. He had some pretty fancy ideas, too, for a country parson. But I wasn't interested, so I spurned him, as they say. I guess I didn't know what an ego that minister had. He turned me in as a heretic and sent me to summer camp." She gestured around her with a lopsided smile.

"Innocent, every one of you," Marta said. "All framed." She looked at Blake and said, "That the right term? 'Framed'? I never knew what it meant, until I was. I became pregnant. Don't ask me how. I guess I'm in the outer edges of the bell curve on statistical possibilities. I was taking the shot every year, even if they are illegal. But they said, because I already had the legal limit of children, that I was a criminal." She looked suddenly very sad as her knees came up and she hugged them soulfully.

"Desperate criminals, every one of you," Blake said,

trying for humor. "I've fallen among thieves!" He nodded at them all as Neva stroked Marta's hair. "Where are the pickpockets and axe murderers?" he asked. "Where are the wife beaters, the stickup hards, the computer thieves?"

"They don't *all* get sent to the Circus," Narmada said. "There are regular jails, work parties in the ark foundations, psychosurgery—all that. But the really desperate criminals are sent here."

"We're the ones who are really threatening society," Bennett explained. "Thieves they can cope with. They just cut off one hand the first time, the other on the second conviction, and give him the torch on the third."

"If thy hand offend thee," Blake said softly. The others gave him a quick, surprised look.

"The murderers get sent here most of the time, especially the violent ones. But computer thieves are seldom caught, and if they do they are usually subdeacons or lieutenant bishops or something. And the wife beaters are given to some Women Corps patrol for a while."

There was a silence, then Blake asked Bennett, "Why are you here?"

"Well, it's not because I'm homosexual. That used to be a pretty radical charge, but not anymore. They even encourage it in some parishes. No, I was having an affair with this Angel of Punishment and—" He saw Blake's expression, and smiled. "That's the law-enforcement branch of Children of God, Incorporated. Anyway, he and I had a fight over the silliest thing and I took his laser to all his clothes and uniforms. I accidently sliced his mother's holo, the only one he had. They put me in prison; then I was sold to a dealer and he sold me here."

"Sold?" Blake was startled.

"Oh, yes. You didn't have that in the Circus back in your time? We've had it as long as I can remember. Condemned prisoners can be bought for the term of their sentences. Not political prisoners, but many."

Suddenly Blake had hope. *Voss! Voss could buy us out! Maybe he wouldn't buy me, but surely he'd buy Rio!*

"Tell me more about this buying process," he urged Bennett.

"It happens all the time. I read somewhere that the origins of the custom come from the American Civil War—the first one—when men drafted into the military could buy their way out or pay other men to serve for them. Then some prison officials, or even county or parish officials, used to rent out prisoners as laborers. Then around the beginning of the twenty-first century there were labor contracts that were much like slavery, really."

"Yes, I remember that," Blake said, thinking of Sundance and Theta Voss.

"The reason I know about this is that I have—or had—certain friends who I thought might buy me out of here." Bennett looked sad for a moment, then continued with his explanation: "It became quasi-legal about thirty years ago, then a regular policy throughout all the parishes. However, certain categories are unavailable for buy-out."

"How long do you have to be in before you can be bought out?"

"Anytime after sentencing. Lots of rich ones never see the inside of a jail, much less the luxurious confines of a Circus training center," Bennett said wearily. "I thought I had friends, but . . ."

Blake wondered if Voss knew about this. At least Rio and Doreen could be saved. "Is there any way to get word to the outside?" he asked.

"Oh, of course," Neva said. "Words but not bodies." She laughed. "Who do you want to contact?"

Blake realized that he did not know where Voss was. *If he is still free, he might be anyplace. Why do I assume he will stay out of jail? Blake asked himself. Just because he is billionaire Jean-Michel Voss? In this world he is no better off than anyone else, at least out of touch with his money. You can't take it with you, Voss!*

"Tell us about yourself," Neva asked.

Briefly, Blake related their adventures, but left out the killing of the Mormon guards, saying only that they escaped.

Neva shook her head sadly. "If only Venus had found you first. The points they could make with you."

The others nodded agreement.

"Venus? We have colonies on Venus?"

"No, not that Venus. Venus, the goddess of Love. Aphrodite." Neva whispered the words, and all of them looked around nervously.

"Don't be so careless with those words," Rob muttered.

"Why? What's wrong?" Blake asked.

"Gali," Neva said, and the slim young man stepped to the cell door and lounged there casually. After a moment he nodded. "Venus, the Venus," she continued. "They're . . . a sort of underground movement."

"Revolutionaries?"

"No, not exactly. Well, yes, perhaps. They are opposed to all the sexual repression. They want sexual freedom and are willing to fight for it."

Sexual freedom fighters. Blake could not explain why he felt like smiling. It seemed so silly, coming from his time. *The world has come full circle,* he thought. *But we never outlawed those who sought a return to religion or who wanted to reduce the blatant sexuality. We laughed at them. Now they are getting the last laugh.*

"How did the world get into this mess?" he asked the group.

"It's a legacy from your time," Narmada said. "When the pendulum swings as far as it can one way, it has only one way to go: back."

"It seems to me that the pendulum has gone as far as it could the other way now," Blake said. He looked at the faces around him. "Can it be made to reverse again, toward freedom?"

They all looked doubtful. "Perhaps," Narmada said slowly. *"You* would have a better perspective on that than we do."

"Venus could really use him," Neva said, almost to herself. "A man from the free past, thrown into prison, sentenced to a terrible death just because he walked through time."

"I slept through it."

"No matter. Sleeping implies no action at all. 'Leapt through time.' That would be even better."

"Well, how do I get in touch with this Venus?"

Everyone suddenly found something else interesting to look at. Blake was frustrated.

From the door Bennett said, "That's right, Mason, we don't know that you *aren't* a Sword or one of the Glorius Cherubs."

"He could even be one of the Friends of the God of Abraham," Rob said. "Or an Archon of the Almighty God."

"Or an Angel of Punishment." Marta shivered.

"Yeah, or from the Lightning Bolts of the Terrifying God of Heaven, or a Temple Virgin of Mary Magdalene," Narmada said nastily. "We have no way of knowing." He looked at Blake. "One thing, though: if they kill you out in the arena, we'll know you were straight."

"Thanks a lot!" Blake said. "Posthumous vindication." He looked around at the other prisoners. "So you think I'm a spy." He shrugged. "All right. I understand. But look, I was arrested with two women from my time, Rio and Doreen. Rio is beautiful—well, both of them are beautiful—and she has long dark hair and a kind of golden skin and . . . a very good figure. Doreen has a big chest and, well, she looks like a Doreen. Is there any way I can find out where they are?"

There was a short silence, then Neva spoke. "If they are beautiful, I mean *beautiful,* they are probably in Troop Nine. That's the special group that gets solo executions."

Blake's heart sank again. "Oh, God . . . *Why?*"

Rob inhaled deeply and then said, "Because the churches are against physical beauty."

"Why? They never were before. They built fancy, glorious churches and altars and temples . . ."

"You're thinking of the *old* churches: the Roman Catholic and the Episcopalian, those of the Hebrew faith and the Eastern religions. But even back in your time I'm certain there were some that didn't fancy themselves up."

"Yes, but neither did they execute people for being beautiful!"

"You don't understand," Neva said. "They—and you—were sentenced because of your special crimes. They will give your friends special solo executions because of their beauty, that's all. Torn apart by a robot, or—"

"There's some talk of bringing back those *big* robots they used to use," Bennett interrupted, distaste and fear on his face.

Blake looked at Neva in shock. "They do that sort of thing here? My God, I thought they were Christians—people of God, religious people!"

"Exactly," Narmada said. "More blood has been spilled in the name of Christ than in the name of anything else—Christian against pagan; Christian against Christian; Christian against witches, unbelievers, Jews, heretics, anyone who opposed them. Your Christianity has devoured whole peoples, and gods as well! Whenever the Christians moved into a region, if the local pagan gods could be absorbed, they were—Saint Patrick, for one. They became saints or angels or other aspects of God. But when they could not be absorbed, they were outlawed, declared evil, made part of Lucifer, banished, exorcised. Their idols were smashed, precious art and history destroyed. The Aztec Coda was burned and—" Narmada stopped abruptly, breathing heavily.

There was a silence, then Blake sighed. "It's not *my* Christianity . . ."

"Your Rio, your Doreen," Narmada said, "will meet degrading, horrible deaths, much worse than anything Neva or Marta or the other women here have to face. At least our women face death with trident or sword, and will have a fighting chance, even if the odds are against them. If you face one fighter, you may vanquish him; but, of course, after you've faced a hundred, two hundred, the odds eventually work against you. If you look as if you are going to be able to defeat all comers—which is very rare—they change the rules on you, put you up against twice as many, against a totally new robot you know nothing about, against something you can't handle. Your women will not even have that chance. They'll undergo a few preliminaries, like being put in a drama or a spectacular, but then they will be staked out for the robot ants or—"

"Nar, stop it!" Neva said. She was hugging Marta and they were swaying. "Nar, we know all that, and if you want to tell Mason your grisly details, please do it some other time."

"I'm sorry, Neva, I forgot. I get so angry, though!"

Blake felt sick. Neva stood and pulled Marta to her feet, then they left the cell. Narmada moved to the bunk and sat down. Rob picked at the raveled edge of his sleeve.

"They had the Circus back in my time," Blake said. "It was bloody, all right; but there was some kind of professionalism to it. They just didn't dump in meat— human meat. Everyone watched it, everyone knew it was the ultimate entertainment, real-life drama, life and death."

"The Romans knew it, too," Bennett said. "Bread and circuses. Keep the citizens happy, keep them occupied. When there's no work, at least give them some entertainment. It was the same in your time and it's the same now, only worse."

"People haven't always had Circuses, have they?" Rob asked Blake.

"No, not really. People used to go to hangings, bringing along their children and lunch. Then there was the Mardi Gras, a kind of religious orgy."

"We still have that," Narmada said.

"Then we had a lot of professional and semi-professional contests. Football, baseball, soccer, boxing, roller derbies."

"What about robot fighters?" Rob asked. "Did they have them back then?"

"No. Not way, way back. They had automobile races." He looked at their faces and tried to explain. "Automobiles were vehicles, like aircars. Only they went on the ground. Some of them were very fast and people would race them."

"I remember reading about those things," Rob said. "They caused the air to be unusable, isn't that so?"

"They were one cause, yes. But they started having

contests to see who could smash up the other's car first. Dozens of people would try at once. They had airplane races, too. They were like aircars. Then along in my time they started having the first robot fighters and robot cars. They used to put fake things on the robots to get knocked off and squirt fluid, just to make the contest look rougher than it was. Then they started matching up men and women against robots. At first, the humans usually won, because they were more agile and could think faster; but the robots improved and—"

"Yeah, that's how it is now," Rob said. "Except now, the robots are like tanks, with flame guns and rockets; and they really fight. There are robot swarms, too— little bastards with teeth that come at you in bunches." Rob shivered and looked at the opposite wall.

"But *why? Why?*" Blake asked angrily. "Are they getting revenge for the Christian martyrs thrown to the lions? Don't they realize they are making the same mistake?"

No one had an answer, and after a few silent moments Bennett said, "I want to get to sleep. It's a long day tomorrow."

Rob and Narmada stood up and left. Blake was slower, and Bennett stopped him.

"I'll get word out. Maybe we can find out where your friends are."

Blake nodded his thanks and walked away.

What am I doing here . . . ? he asked himself.

The wallscreen showed two fighters in the Arena. One was a retiarius: a slim girl who wore no armor—just a leather-like uniform and sandals—and carried a trident and net. The net was edge-weighted for better control, and she circled the bigger opponent warily, keeping her trident up and the net moving.

"Notice how she keeps the net in motion so that there will be no betraying gesture to show she is about to cast it." Sergeant White stood at the edge of the screen, holding a long pointer. "See how she keeps the trident at the ready. It keeps the secutor at bay, and she can use it to advantage at any time."

The secutor was a broad-shouldered African whom Neva said had been captured while attempting to smuggle some blacks out of the annexed state of Baja California. He wore a helmet, smooth and round, without any decoration that would catch on a net. He had on a breastplate, but no backplate. He wore a greave only on his left leg and his right arm was protected by a flexible armor. He held a small round shield against the jabs of the girl's trident and carried a short, heavy sword in his armored right hand. Blake felt as if he were watching a historical drama.

"The statistics say that if a secutor and a retiarius of equal skill are matched, the retiarius will win 86 percent of the time. But watch this."

The girl cast her net in a smooth overhand motion, using her trident to capture her opponent's sword at the same moment, holding it away from his body just long enough for the net to settle. The big Negro twisted away, entangling himself in the net. The girl released his sword and drew back her arm for a violent thrust of the spear. But the secutor threw himself toward her—net and all—instead of trying to avoid her trident. The three-pointed spear missed him and he swung the sword against her unprotected torso. It cut deeply, and blood gushed. She staggered back, her face in shock, and fell to one knee. She kept the trident up and pointed at the big man as he tore away the net. Contemptuously, he knocked aside her spear. The back of the trident hit the girl in the side and she fell onto one hand. She looked up at the secutor to see the sword falling. He cut through her neck in one slice and the head fell. The secutor, placed one foot on her back and raised his sword to the crowd.

Blake did not feel he was watching a historical drama anymore. The tape was silent, but he could imagine the roar of the crowd.

The screen went blank abruptly and Sergeant White started asking questions. "Neva, what did she do wrong?"

"She wasn't prepared for an unorthodox move. She should have been, because getting in past the spearpoint is the best defense-offense."

"Bennett, did the secutor make any mistakes?"

"Well, he won, so he made fewer mistakes than she did. But he should have moved faster at the start, to take advantage of her nervousness on seeing such a strong opponent. Then, in the middle, he allowed her to get the sun in his eyes—something he could have corrected by moving to the right." Bennett stopped to think for a moment, then added, "Finally, she always moved her hand back a little, with a sort of jerk, before she really threw the net. He should have recognized the pattern and been ready."

"Mason, did he kill her properly?"

"Dead is dead, Sergeant. She probably felt pain only for a little while."

Sergeant White looked disgusted. Then he sneered. "All right, now we'll look at the new Attila robot."

The screen flashed into life, and once again Blake was observing the Arena from eye level. Three-meter robots were lined up, four of them against eight humans, who looked pitiful in their archaic armor of breastplates and helmets and their primitive swords against the gleaming steel might of the huge anthropoid robots.

"Sweet mother, look at the size of those robbies!" a man near Blake said. "They're bigger than the Madman series!"

"These are the Attila, Mark VI," Sergeant White said. "They are by General Robotics, which means they probably have more speed than maneuverability in the upper arms. Remember, the Genghis Khan series was weak in the rear right quarter, upper vector."

"If you can jump that high!" a man in front said.

"Remember the trip techniques you've been taught. Get the iron down and then hit the weak spots. Now watch these pieces of scrap in action."

The battle was one-sided. Only one robot was toppled, and at the cost of one human. But before the other human could attack the fallen robot, it lashed out with a taloned arm and tore the leg right off the charging man. The battle was over in less than two minutes. Dismembered and torn bodies lay all around as the robots methodically grouped together, saluted the bishop's box, and left the field. Their only signs of battle were spurts of human blood drying on their sleek metallic flanks.

The crowd of novices was silent when the picture ended. Sergeant White said, "Don't worry, we'll study all the tapes. We'll find the weaknesses. There will be at least six or eight troops going up against them before you do." No one spoke. "All right, the exercise arena. Mason, you stay."

The others left the room quickly, and Mason followed the sergeant, who took him to a room filled with padded seats equipped with tie-down straps. Blake stared about doubtfully.

The sergeant said, "Don't worry, this is to protect you. Sit down and let me fasten you in." Seeing no alternative, Blake sat and in moments was virtually immobile. The sergeant picked up a headset that hung on the back of the seat, and Blake recognized the induction pickups of a sensory recorder.

Such things had been popular with certain types in his time, especially those who preferred their sex vicariously. The recorders were also superb trainers for certain jobs, and Blake had learned to ski from one. Once he had felt the flex and balance of an expert skier in his own body-mind, the actuality of learning came much faster. Doctors had used them to examine a patient, recording every bit of sensory input that went through the sensory cortex, separating the various impressions, and making playback possible. After an examination, the doctor would play back the tape and then could determine exact areas of pain or distress and more quickly diagnose the illness. Lovers could use the recordings to enter the body, but not the mind or thoughts, of one another; feeling what it was like to be of the opposite sex, they might become much better lovers. Homosexuals found certain heterosexual tapes very popular. With instant replay, two lovers could each know, within milliseconds, exactly what the other felt. "Becoming one" had indeed approached reality. Masochists used certain tapes to achieve unusual effects without a mark on them. Cripples could dive into the depths of the ocean, or sail within the body of a hawk. The old could once again feel the throb of youth, providing their doctors approved. Pornography was the natural medium of the sensory recorder, and an entire industry had been producing sexual epics in Blake's day.

"This'll show you how it is out there," the sergeant said. "The straps are to prevent your sympathetic reactions from getting carried away. They've filtered the pain levels so you'll feel it, but it won't knock you out."

The shaven head of the burly soldier glistened under the lights as he looked through a fistful of recording rectangles. He selected one, stuck it into the back of Blake's chair until it clicked, then said, "By the way, you get killed in this one. But don't worry, they'll pull you out of it before you synchronize." His thumb pressed a button, and the Arena appeared around Blake.

Like a double exposure, he could still see the room full of padded chairs and Sergeant White walking away; but the dominant image was the Arena surrounding him, the steep wall going up five or six meters to the first row of seats. He could see the miters of bishops and the skull caps of priests in the first rows, as well as richly dressed civilians. In the wall he also saw windows and gates, and in some of the windows were television cameras. The noise of the crowd was almost deafening, and several flowers landed on the combed sand near his sandaled foot. He moved and there was a pain along his side—an old pain, like a recent wound not quite healed.

Blake wanted to look down at himself, to get his bearings, but the recording did not let him do that. He was a passenger in the gladiator's body; he did not control it, and he could not sense any of the man's thoughts, but his mind felt whatever the doomed gladiator's body felt, or what it did.

I'm going to die, Blake thought. *With sensory recorders, a brave man can die as often as a coward . . .*

A gate opened in the far wall and out came a magnificent figure of a man, broad-shouldered, well-muscled, obviously confident, and well-coordinated. He wore a breastplate and a helmet that covered his head, had an armored right arm and two greaves. His weapon was not the traditional short sword but a wicked-looking mace. He brandished the weapon and Blake felt his own arm rise to return the arrogance; for the first time he saw that he held a sword, the usual broad, blunt Roman sword.

Why are they such traditionalists? Blake asked himself. *I'd love a good Colt Two-Millimeter laser right now.*

Blake started moving in on his opponent much sooner than he really wanted, but, trapped in the gladiator's body, he had no choice. The overlay of sensation from the room full of padded chairs dimmed and was gone as the more powerful and more immediate sensation of the Arena took over. Blake felt the grit of sand under his feet and the sun on his skin. The crowd's roar seemed to dim, too, as he concentrated more and more on the impressive figure of the advancing warrior.

They now grew quite close to one another, though neither one was yet in a defensive posture.

Blake was beginning to feel real fear. *Is this some ghastly joke, on the sergeant's part? Is the body I'm in a suicide? Or is he so inept that he stands no chance against the other man? My host body is going to die,*

*probably from a savage blow. Will it be quick or slow?
Will I feel much pain?*

The fatalism of his situation overcame him. There
was nothing he could do. If the body he was vicariously
visiting was mortally wounded, he knew he would be
saved only by the technicians, who supposedly had
monitored and reduced the pain input in the recording.
His own body would be untouched, but many deaths
back in his own time had been attributed to sympathetic
reactions while using a sensory recording.

The two gladiators came within weapon's length of
each other, stopped, and turned. They stood in the
middle of the Arena, toward the side of the bishop's
box.

As the enemy gladiator raised his head and mace for
the salute, Blake saw the stands were filled and the
bishop's box held many mitered and robed figures. A
lavish, ornamented awning shaded them. Darkly robed
figures stood in attendance on every side, heavy lasers
holstered at their hips and their eyes roaming everywhere but in the Arena.

Blake felt his lungs fill and a great shout go out from
his mouth, spoken in unison with his fellow gladiator.
*"Hail, Lord Bishop! We who are about to die salute
you!"*

There was the flutter of a hand from the center figure, a frail-looking old man. A flourish of trumpets
sounded, and Blake and his opponent backed away a
few steps from each other.

They began to circle one another, each trying to get
the sun in the other's eyes. Like an unwilling passenger
on a runaway train, Blake felt his muscles tense, his
strong legs flex and his body leap forward, his sword
slashing and cutting at the other warrior. Metal clashed
on metal, and he could distinctly hear the grunt and
breathing of the other man—even over the shouts of the
crowd.

They fought, it seemed to Blake, for hours. His
sword arm was weary and his legs ached, but still the
man he was inhabiting drove on. His shield arm was
bruised from catching the hard-driving blows of the
other warrior, and his head rang from a glancing blow

off his helmet. He parried and thrust, parried and thrust, hacking and reversing directions with a speed that dazzled him. The thrusts were made and over before Blake was really aware of them. *If this is the skill I must obtain, I'll be dead in the first minute!*

With a suddenness that startled Blake and disoriented him, his host body dodged a blow and dove at the sand, hitting and rolling, his sword cutting at the other's legs in a vicious swipe. His blow, aimed at the junction of greave and sandal, missed by a fraction of an inch, glancing off the metal with a loud clang. Blake's host-gladiator then reversed his swing and cut at the back of the other's leg, behind the greave. The sword struck flesh, but the leg was moving away. Blake dodged a blow, then caught another off his shield as he scrambled to his feet.

Blood gushed from a deep wound in the other man's calf, but his leg was not hamstrung. He pressed his attack with a vengeance that frightened Blake. *He needs to win, before the loss of blood weakens him!*

The attacker jumped close, his mace yanking down at the shield that protected Blake. Blake's sword arm swung hard at the too-close head, glancing off the side protectors of the helmet and cutting shallowly into the neck muscles. For a brief moment the two men were locked together, each fending off the other's weapon with his shield. Blake looked into the slits of the helmet and saw two dark, glittering eyes.

Then they leaped apart. But by that time, his opponent had hooked an ankle behind him, and he tripped and fell. Blake's host crashed to the ground and pain flooded his right side, for his sword and sword arm were under him. He raised his shield to ward off the rain of blows from above, and kicked out at the legs of the other man. Sweat ran into his eyes and blinded him, and he could smell blood and death.

He jerked his arm out from under him, but a mace blow drove the sword from his hand. A foot struck at his shield, forcing it back to the sand. Blake reached for the foot with his sword hand, grabbing the ankle and twisting, but it was too late. He saw the blow coming, a savage stabbing down at his unprotected stomach.

Blake felt a sudden, fantastic puncturing of pain in his buckling body. Then the agony lessened. He felt the mace strike, then the rip upward through his flesh, but it was far away.

He now looked down and saw the mace buried in him, just below the breastplate. He felt it twist against the armor as he squirmed. He heaved at the leg on his shield arm and the other warrior was thrown back, stumbling to gain his balance, ripping the mace from Blake's intestines.

Blake lurched to a sitting position, reaching for his lost sword. It was at a hand's width from the tips of his fingers but he could not grasp it. A great numbing was spreading throughout his body. He looked again and saw a handful of gray-blue intestines coiling out from his belt line, smeared with blood and pulsating oddly.

He stared at the inside of his body sliding out and into the sand in this slow, sinuous movement. He stared a long time; then he fell back, his helmeted head thudding into the sand, followed by another flood of distant pain. He lay in the sand, looking up into the blue sky. Tiny black dots swam across his vision, dots with trailing lines and wiggly black lines that floated. He blinked, and the dots and lines changed direction.

I'm dying . . .

The other gladiator came up into view. He looked down, seemingly impassive behind his helmet. Then slowly the man removed the helmet and Blake saw that he was crying.

The sky grew dark and Blake felt his throat trying to form words, but only a croak emerged. Everything seemed to slide away, melt away . . . Pain, feeling, vision, all melted and ran. The sky grew blacker, closing in at the edges, and he felt as if he were sinking into a deep hole in the sand, sinking backward into darkness.

There was now only a thread of pain. Then there was nothing. Nothing at all . . .

The room began to reappear. The nothingness had seemed to last for a very long time. Gratefully, Blake felt the restraining straps and the cushioning seat. He saw the room, the white walls, and the gray seats. A little bit distant was a scrap of paper on the floor. Blake stared at this one disrupting element in the whole room, and it seemed oddly significant, as if *he* were that scrap—a discard among piles of garbage, but incredibly glad to be alive.

In a few moments Sergeant White reappeared. He did not speak, but unfastened the straps. Blake found that his body was sweating, a cold, frightened sweat, and he felt too weak to stand. The sergeant leaned against the back of a nearby seat and looked at him a moment.

"You were Jim De Santiago, one of the best fighters this Arena has seen. The other man was Lloyd Berman, Interparish Children of God champion from Los Angeles. That tape is fifteen months old. Berman went down two months ago, in Denver, to Philippe Huppé, of the Lord of Light of the Fantastic Truth, out of their Paris mission."

"I hope I never meet any of them."

"They are all professionals. They fight for money and glory, and they rarely meet a condemned criminal in combat. Most of them think it is beneath their professional ethics to execute for the State."

"Then why did you have me go through that?"

"To see how the best work. Very few of the condemned get as good as the pros. Some do, and those are the ones the pros will fight. But it takes a certain aptitude, a certain killer instinct, and a lot of dedication. Few of the prisoners get to spend that much time at practice."

"Then why are you doing this to all of us?" Blake asked angrily.

"All of us, *sir!*"

"All of us, sir."

"Because you must not just be led in for a slaughter. You'd grate on the sensitive feelings of the crowd if they thought you were just throwing your life away, a suicide like one of those protestors. You must put on a show, a life-and-death circus, something real, something that at least looks equal, even if it isn't fair. Something so that the bishops and the parishioners don't feel guilty about sending you in to die."

Sergeant White rubbed his face, then looked at Blake

through narrowed eyes. "And you *will* learn one end of a sword from the other. Also the net, the flame spear, the robot tank, and anything else I show you. If you go out there and just get slaughtered, they come down on me. There is no way I am going out there myself. I will do anything I have to in order to prevent that. Even if every man, woman, and child they send me gets killed. You understand that, Mason?"

Blake sighed. "Yes, Sergeant, I understand it." *Self-preservation dies hard in all of us.*

"All right. Now get into the locker room and draw some equipment. Get Gimp to show you what you need. Then go right on out to the exercise room. Snap it!"

Blake threw up his shield to ward off the blow of Kapuki's sword and thrust his own plastic weapon at her blindly. He felt a sharp pain in his side and jerked down the shield to catch another stinging blow on the side of his neck.

"Stop!" Sergeant White's voice was angry. "Blessed be the saints in Heaven, Mason, but don't you *ever* recognize a feint?"

Blake looked wearily at the slim Kapuki, who now was resting, leaning on the blunt tip of her practice sword, grinning at him. "All right, Sergeant, I'll try, just for you."

Blake put up his shield again and stood in the stance he had been practicing. There was a sudden movement behind him and a blinding blow to his head, and he pitched forward to crumple in the sand of the practice arena. He twisted around, spitting sand, blinded by the ceiling lights and his own blurred vision. Sergeant White stood over him.

"Don't get loose-mouthed with me, Mason. I don't care how much of a novelty you are!" He kicked Blake painfully in the thigh. "Get up! Take your position! Kapuki, you slam the sass out of this dumb toad!" When Blake did not get up fast enough, White added, "Starting right now!"

Kapuki's sword kicked up sand as she brought it up in a swift movement, grabbing it with two hands and bringing it down with all the force she had on Blake's unprotected back. He yelled in pain and struck back at her with a wild blow.

Kapuki easily evaded it and jumped in to stab at him again, giving him a bruise on the already painful side. Blake angrily came up on one knee and knocked her

189

sword aside with his shield, stabbing back at her with his own blunted weapon.

"That's it!" Sergeant White said happily. "That's it!"

Blake made several rather wild strikes at the slender oriental girl as he rose. She parried one and he missed getting a blow across the face only by a millimeter or two.

On his feet now, Blake pressed the attack, using shield, sword, and fast footwork to drive Kapuki back several steps. She got in one more blow to his hip, a glancing hit that opened her up for a brutal thrust to her midsection. She gasped, gagged, and fell back, sucking noisily for air, and Blake moved in fast. He hit her shield so hard she lost it, and he battered her with his until she fell, still gasping. He raised his sword for the kill, then suddenly stopped.

He looked around. Several of the others had stopped their practice to watch. Sergeant White was smiling, leaning with folded arms against a much-patched robot practice gladiator.

Blake glared at the instructor. "You made me do this." Blake flung the sword away, followed by the shield in the other direction. "I won't kill her, not even in practice." Blake felt himself trembling with anger and almost in tears from his frustration.

Sergeant White kept on smiling. "But for a second there . . ." he said softly. He shoved himself away from the robot and sauntered toward Blake, nodding his head and looking from side to side with a smile. "You'll go out there, all right," he said casually. "You'll kill or you will be killed. But you won't go out there and throw your life away. *I* won't kill you, but you might wish I had."

He stopped, facing Blake, who was still quivering with anger. Without warning, the sergeant's hard fist came out and hit Blake on the side of the head, sending him once again into the sand. The arena lurched, and the sounds of the others still practicing at the far end were sharp and clear, but somehow slow. He looked up at White and saw him looming in a distorted way. The gladiator trainer snorted in disgust and walked away.

Narmada and Bennett helped Blake to his feet and

over to a bench. Blake sat there a moment with his head in his hands, then raised it. He looked for and found Kapuki nearby, rubbing at a large bruise. "Kapuki, I'm sorry, I didn't mean—"

"You *better* mean!" she said. "The only way you are going to survive out there is if you are good. If you and I meet, with real weapons, I'll kill you—but not because of *this*. Just because I want to live!"

Startled by her angry words, Blake stared at her. The slim young oriental girl looked at him with hard eyes. "Soft, stupid fool! If they were all like you back then, no wonder we are in such a mess!" She turned and walked away toward the medical robot.

Blake looked at Bennett, then Narmada. "I just wanted to apologize for hitting her like that."

Narmada looked disgusted. "Apologize? Are you going to forgive her or do you want her to forgive you? She's right. No wonder we're in such a goddamn mess now!"

Neva moved closer and peered at Blake through the slits in her padded practice helmet. "You all right?"

Blake nodded and watched the others move away and resume practice.

Neva watched them go and then said softly, "They're right. Going out there and fighting is playing their game, I'll admit. But going out and just giving up, letting yourself be slaughtered, is playing their game, too, on a different level. If you give up, especially *you*, then it proves men are sheep, it proves that those in power do know what is right for us."

Blake didn't speak for a long time. His side hurt and he knew there would be a terrible bruise. Then he said, "Why especially me?"

"Because you're a symbol. I know you don't think of yourself that way, but you are. All of you are. All of you who came here the way you did—anachronisms in the flesh. You *are* that romantic past, that time of freedom and love!"

"What have you been reading about my time? Freedom, yes. But it was hardly a utopia. We, too, had overpopulation, food problems, sociological turmoil—"

"But it was different. Then there was religious

freedom, not religious chaos. There was sexual freedom and—" She stopped talking, as if she had gone too far. "You're a symbol of that, Blake Mason, whether you want to be or not." Neva looked around, then stood up. "Go fix your cuts. We'll . . . we'll talk of this later."

Blake watched her go back to pick up her sword and shield. She seemed lost in the heavy padded breastplate and helmet, a child playing at some deadly game. Blake shivered in a sudden uncontrollable spasm.

Why did I come to the future? One foolish moment and I threw my life away. Rio is lost to me, perhaps forever, perhaps even dead. The two or three or even four hundred years of life he supposedly had coming to him now were fool's gold, meaningless—even dangerous.

The world was full of beautiful women, he thought. *Why did I have to pick Rio?* Her picture came into his mind, surprisingly not the beautifully gowned Rio he had seen at Voss's dining table, but Rio as he had first seen her at the top of the stairs at Casa Emperador— more than a century before. He recalled clearly that shock of recognition that had gripped him then. *She's the one,* he had told himself then. *She's the one,* he told himself now.

I have to save Rio, he thought.

He looked at his sword, partially covered by the sand where he had thrown it. *Those who live by the sword, die by the sword.* He got up and walked over to it. His side was stiffening up, and he grunted when he bent down to pick it up. *But maybe they can live by the sword for a while.*

He looked at the others, hacking and thrusting, and heard the clang and thud of their blows. He limped over, picked up his shield and fitted it to his left arm, feeling the solid grip in his hand. He hefted the sword and started toward Kars, who everyone said was the best of the class.

Kars was fighting with Rob, and Rob was losing.

"May I cut in?" Blake said.

Rob looked at him in amazement, then stepped back. Kars looked from Rob to Blake, then shrugged and began the attack.

□

Blake lay on his bunk. His bruises had faded and he had not gotten any new ones in over a week. Kars was nursing the first bruise he had received from anyone but Sergeant White, and that made Blake smile.

Tomorrow they were getting real swords.

Blake closed his eyes and tried to sleep. *Where are you, Rio?* He shifted on the bunk, feeling the newfound muscles flex. He ached a little all the time, but Neva said that was standard.

Tomorrow they were getting real weapons.

□

Blake walked into the cell room wearily, followed by
Kapuki. They had both just spent four hours in the sensory recorder chairs, running an orientation tape on
handling the big twenty-foot, human-controlled killer
machines, and they were both exhausted. The different
Arenas around the country had different attractions,
and the Caligula Arena was thinking of importing some
of the Magnabots from the Alamo Arena in Houston.
Knowing there was a man inside one of the flame-
throwing, metal-clawed monsters was proving to be
more exciting than just watching animated piles of metal
and computer parts fight it out.

"We gotta keep up with the times," Sergeant White
had said.

Blake asked Kapuki to share some of his hoarded
watered wine, and she agreed.

Neva suddenly appeared at the door of his cell, and
Blake offered her a thick ceramic mug filled with the
sweet wine. She took it, leaned against the wall of his
cell, and started to say something. But she stopped and
took a gulp of the wine.

"Go on," Kapuki said, smiling at Neva's hesitation.

Neva took a deep breath and looked out the cell
door. "How would you like to get out of here?" she
asked softly.

"I'm *going* out. Up a few levels and out onto the
sand."

"No, I mean *out* out."

Blake looked at her, her hair dark and damp. "*Out*
out?" She nodded. He smiled thinly. "I'd say 'Whom do
I kill?' but I guess we know the answer. Each other!"

Neva bit her lip, then started talking in a fast, low
voice. "Blake, remember our talk about you being a
symbol? Well, the committee agrees with me."

194

"What committee?"

"The committee for this area of . . ." She hesitated, then said it quickly. "The committee of the New Day." Blake raised his eyebrows in a questioning gesture. "The People for a New Day. It's a . . . revolutionary group. I . . . I was one of the committee before I turned down that minister. I've communicated with them about you. They agree you could be a unifying force and—"

"Wait a minute! I'm no revolutionary. In my day I was considered practically a reactionary!"

"One century's reactionary is another century's radical," Kapuki said quietly.

"You're a symbol. Not much of one, I admit, but you're all we have." Neva leaned close to him, her bare breasts brushing his arm, distracting him. "We're going to overthrow these sanctimonious bastards, Blake! We're going to break their hold on the people! And you are the only one who can help!"

Blake couldn't resist a smile. "The only man in the universe who can help, huh? The *only* one? 'Only you can stop the invasion of the blue crabs from outer space, Captain Laser!' 'Only you can stop the dread nine-meter stainless-steel worms, Blake Mason, only you!' "

Neva and Kapuki looked blankly at him.

Mason shook his head. "Never mind me," he said. "Go on, tell me how I'm the only one that can save the world from God."

"Not from God," Neva said. "From religion. Our rulers have perverted religion! The religions are corporations, not faiths. These people don't preach the word of God—any god—they quibble over it! They are not religious, they are *ir*religious! Calling yourself a Guardian of the Throne of God doesn't make you one!"

"Wait a minute," Blake interrupted. "How do I fit in? I'm just a glorified interior decorator more than a hundred years out of his time. I'm no symbol, and I'm certainly not a craggy-jawed hero with rippling muscles."

Kapuki reached up and caressed his bicep. "Better than you were a short time ago," she said.

"Hey, those guys use lasers and microwaves and have

big armored aircars and things that go zap in the night! I'm only one man."

Neva whispered, "There are more revolutionaries than you think! It's a whole underground! Sure, some of them are on the lunatic fringe, some are floaters just having a dream, some are blast-poppers and Eroticenes. But most are serious, dedicated people who are going to *do* it! With you as an example, maybe they can unify different factions and get things rolling!"

"Maybe even the Catholics," Kapuki suggested.

"What do you mean, maybe the Catholics? That's a church, too, isn't it? Or did they sell the franchise?"

Neva looked quickly into the room outside the cell. "The Catholics are outlaws, just as they were two thousand years ago. Ragnar is one, and . . . one or two others. The pope is in exile somewhere, probably in Italy or in New America—um, the South America of your time, I think. Yes."

"The Hebrews have fractionalized and gone underground as well," Kapuki muttered. "The old religions were driven out of business by these new ones. The old ways didn't work—or so the people thought. They were sick of the excesses, and some of the new cults seemed to promise them peace and quiet. Once the new ones got to be a majority here in America, they outlawed the Catholics and some of the Eastern religions. Later on, these were outlawed in Europe, too, and elsewhere. The pope has been in hiding for years. He was . . . What was his name, Neva?"

"I'm not certain. There were about five popes in two years. They kept killing them off, assassinating them."

"Assassinating them?" Blake was startled. Somehow the idea was shocking, even more shocking than the reports he had heard of the hundred million dead in India during the First Famine.

Neva nodded. "I think the last I heard, it was Clement XV."

Kapuki disagreed. "No, they blew up his bunker in the Vatican, remember? No, the pope must be Urban IX, unless they got him, too. But I think they would have announced that his death came while resisting lawful arrest, if they had: they love that sort of thing. No, I think it is still Urban."

"It doesn't matter," Blake said. "Our problem will be in getting me out of here."

Kapuki patted his leg and said, "It's very difficult to get out, unless you get bought out. Of course, people have managed to become so popular as gladiators that they were moved into training cadres, but that doesn't happen often. Sylvia Component was unique. Flynn was made director of—"

"Component? What kind of name is that?" Blake asked.

Kapuki looked blank. "Just a name. Oh, is it—I mean, was it—a name from your time?"

"No, it's just . . . not like a name."

Neva spoke up. "What does Taylor or Weaver mean? Wheelwright? Turner? Smith, Tinker, Hunter? Bell, Blood, Sheppard, Glass, Short, or Sawyer? Names are built, or appropriated, to fit the user. We now have Elecktron, Urbotower, Foundation, Acolyte, Angelman, Host, Faithman, Minion, Component, Zapfax, Kingdom, Airburst . . . um, and Skylord. Did you have those names in your time?"

Blake shook his head. "I understand. I have so much to learn." He took a deep breath and let it out slowly. "You know, in my time I guess I was considered rather sophisticated. But here . . ." He looked at their odd expressions and asked, "What's wrong?"

"That word," Neva said. "Sophisticated. What does it mean? 'A follower of Sappho'?"

"No," Blake smiled. "Sophisticated means . . . worldly . . . um, experienced."

"Oh, I remember that word," Kapuki said. She closed her eyes and recited. " 'Sophisticated: deprived of original simplicity, made artificial, or, more narrowly, highly complicated, refined' . . ."

"Huh?" Neva said. "That doesn't sound too good." She looked at Blake with an expression of mild disgust. "That's what you were?"

Blake shrugged. "Maybe I was. It seems far away now, much farther than just the years. Another age, another world." He snorted. "They would have called what I've got 'culture shock' back in my time."

"They call it 'death sentence' here," Kapuki said.

They were silent for a time, then Blake asked the oriental girl, "Would you really kill me if we were sent into the Arena together?"

Without hesitation Kapuki answered. "Yes. I would not like to, but I would if I could." She smiled. "One time I could have succeeded, but now I do not know. You have a natural aptitude for combat."

"The reluctant warrior . . ." Neva said. "As long as you still have that reluctance, you will be defeated by the more determined, the more desperate, the ones more eager to survive."

"I can't help it," Blake said. "I'm still not ready to— to kill." He looked at the ceiling of the cell. "Maybe it still seems like a game to me, I don't know. I can't quite believe it is for real."

"Better get over that. Lieutenant Cady is coming tomorrow, for an inspection," Neva said.

"Hooray!" Blake groaned.

□

They stood at attention in the practice arena, each in the uniform of his specialty. Blake stood with the secutors and was directly opposite Neva in the ranks of the retiarii, who were mostly females. Kapuki was somewhere farther back in the ranks behind Blake, almost hidden by her full practice padded armor.

Lieutenant Cady was approaching, down the line, followed by Sergeant White and another sergeant whom Blake did not know. The inspection seemed perfunctory, and Blake was starting to relax when the arrogant officer stopped in front of him.

"Ah, the famous time traveler!" His words were an insult, but Blake kept his face expressionless. "The *infamous* time traveler, in fact. And how are you getting on, Prisoner Blake?"

"Fine, sir."

White was looking at him steadily from behind Cady's shoulder.

"Fine, sir? Indeed. You like it here, then?"

"No, sir."

The officer's face slid into a wicked grin. "Oh? Sergeant White, this notorious criminal does not like it here. Have you been treating him badly?"

"No, sir. Standard training procedures."

"You see, Mason? But perhaps you think you should be treated in some *special* way, just because you come to us from the decadent, godless past?"

Blake had been staring about five meters beyond Cady's head. Now he focused on his eyes. "No, sir."

Cady's face hardened, and he spoke sharply to Sergeant White. "See that Prisoner Mason receives some special treatment, Sergeant. But I want him to go into the Arena as soon as possible."

"We have another week on the training cycle, sir.

Then there is the special training for the novelty acts."

"Never mind that!" Cady's tongue slid out and wet his lips. "Give this prisoner an early call, as early as can be arranged; and notify my office. I don't want to miss his first and last appearance in the Arena."

"Yes, sir."

Cady and the noncoms moved down the line, and Blake let out a long breath.

Special treatment. Early call . . .

Back in the cell room after the inspection, White crooked a finger at Blake and walked toward the cell where Blake had seen the man and woman getting the electric shock. He stiffened but didn't move. He had seen the two of them since, two automatons, half mad, half comatose, going through their training in a blundering fashion, a near-living warning to the others.

Blake was not going to have that happen to him. He had his sword, even if it was only a plastic practice sword, and his armor. He would fight and die right here, rather than be turned into a vegetable. He set his feet and tensed up, watching White.

The sergeant looked at him, blew his cheeks out, and walked over to him heavily.

He did not seem threatening, but Blake was waiting now for the sergeant's sudden, treacherous blow.

White stopped, his head down, his hands on the weapons belt around his waist. "Look, Mason, I have my orders. But the Lieutenant didn't say how *long* you were to have special treatment, did he?" He looked up at Blake and there was a faint smile on his face. "Trust me."

Blake felt the anger go out of him, at least anger toward Sergeant White. He followed White to the cell and the sergeant closed the door behind them. At White's order, Blake dropped his armor and weapons and put his wrists in the metallic bonds.

White pressed a button and raised the metal handcuffs on their cord until Blake stood straight, hands over his head. His mouth felt bitter and there was a fluttering in his stomach that felt like a twanged nerve. He watched the burly sergeant set a dial to the minimum setting, then a timer the same way.

He looked at Blake, his finger poised over a red button. "You know," he said, "if they could read minds, I'd be in here myself." Then he pressed the button.

The electricity hit Blake like a lightning bolt. He didn't even scream, for his entire body was paralyzed. His flesh seemed to be made of wood—burning wood—and his brain exploding. It lasted only a fraction of a second and then it was over, but Blake was left trembling, unable to control the involuntary nervous twitches of his limbs.

White lowered the wristlocks and Blake fell awkwardly to his knees, banging them on the floor. He gasped in pain, for it seemed as if his dry, wooden body had been bent and broken, shattering splinters into his brain. The vision of the man and woman he had seen hanging in the cell, their bodies jerking and writhing, came back to him. *How did they live through it?*

Blake tried to rise, but his trembling legs refused to cooperate.

Sergeant White reached down and pulled him up and kept him up until Blake felt steady. "All right?" he asked. Blake nodded. "So, go lie down a while. We're having some more tapes to look at after the meal."

Blake walked shakily to his cell. He waved off Neva and Bennett, who wanted to help, then lay down wearily on his bunk.

How did they live through it? That explains their being semi-vegetables. Blake felt the trembles still in his arms and legs, but they lessened now. *Some church, some religion!* he thought, *that can do this to an individual, even a condemned criminal. I wonder how they square that with their Christianity? Do they think of the Circus as retribution for what the Romans did over two millennia ago? These people may have their church, but they certainly aren't religious.*

After the evening meal, the novice gladiators gathered again in the main room and the wallscreen lit up.

"This is the Mark III Berserker," Sergeant White said, pointing at the swiftly moving beetle-like robot.

The monster on the screen came to a stop, sand spurting under its treads. The turret of the black metal tank whirled around several times, firing flaming darts in every direction. The expenditure of ammunition seemed foolish, as there were no opponents in the Arena.

"The Alexander Company likes flash," White continued. "If you remember, the El Cid fighter had flamethrowers even though they were forbidden in combat. They used to blast around the ring in a fancy show before the fight, just to make a big splash. This Berserker is much the same, with the same blind spots in programming. Zamparelli, in the Caesar last year, knocked out two of them in one fight, all by himself. Notice how deep the treadmarks are? These babies are heavy with all that extra shit on them, so even though they have the standard Fifty power plant, they are a touch slower—even if they do put up a lot of flim-splash."

The lecture droned on, and Blake was only paying a tiny bit of attention to it.

Bennett slipped out of his seat and moved to sit by Blake. "Enjoying yourself?" he asked.

"I can't wait for the cartoon," Blake replied.

"We are going to take you out," he whispered. "The People for a New Day." He grinned, his teeth white in the light from the wallscreen. "For me they'd never take the risk, but for you . . ."

"Bennett! Why does the Berserker favor a right turn to rear?" Sergeant White's voice cut into their awareness.

Without hesitation Bennett answered loudly, "Because the wear mode is to the right, because of the placement of the firedart feeder line from ammo stores, sir!"

"But reactions are randomized for efficient fighting modes."

"Yes, sir, but the wear factor is greater to the right after eight hours of operation, due to the monitor heat from the feeder chute, sir. An advantage of 8 percent is estimated, sir."

"Correct, Bennett. So you can see you have a plus 8 percent chance of the Berserker turning to the right on a one-eighty to rear."

The sergeant's voice droned on, but Bennett continued to whisper into Blake's ear.

"It'll happen soon, hopefully before your first combat assignment. Keep yourself alert. You'll know when it is happening." Bennett moved away, then leaned back to add, "Unless you *like* it here . . ."

The People for a New Day. Underground revolutionaries against a worldwide religious cartel. Blake chewed on the inside of his right cheek. *Anything would be better than this,* he thought. *Or would it?*

□

Several days passed, but Blake had received no folded notes, no whispered code words, and no encouragement. He only spoke of it once to Bennett. "Are they taking us all out, or just me?"

Bennett shrugged. "I don't know. One is easier to hide, but then again, they would gain a few trained soldiers if they took all of us."

Blake waited impatiently. Where is Rio?

A few days later, they were sent out on parade, in full armor and weapons. Blake could not help but notice the guard bunkers all along the wall, small recessed forts with heavy lasers and monitoring television cameras.

It was Blake's first visit to the floor of the Arena where he could look around as he cared to, rather than seeing it while restricted to the movements of the sensory recorder. The real thing offered much more than the recorder had given him. A thousand small details had been lost in the transfers of brain to tape and tape to new brain, almost an avalanche of information. Music, waving pennants, bright colors, roars, cries, screams, a steady undulating hum, the echoing roars of beasts still caged, the creak of armor, the crunch of sand, the clink of metal, the low-voiced commands of the officers, the erotic moans of the women aroused by the sight, the trumpets, the booming broadcast blessings by the archbishop, and the blessing by a visiting French prelate.

They marched around, their pseudo-Roman costumes gleaming, their legs moving in perfect unison. Circling the Arena, they went out again.

Blake pulled off his helmet and wiped his sweating forehead as they paused a short way down the large ten-meter-wide corridor to watch the first act move by.

204

The Tamerlane robots were brightly painted but obsolete, and were up against a band of New American Protestants who had defeated a mammoth Darius Tiger the week before. The muscular Protestants walked along next to the Tamerlanes without so much as a glance at them. They carried their only weapons—long spears—in their right hands, moving easily and loosely. Their eyes scanned the mixture of prisoners, robots, and guards that lined the corridor. They had the eyes of trapped animals that had learned patience.

Blake was not to see the outcome. Sergeant White sent them back to their cells, down a long ramp and into a bank of elevators.

When he stepped out, a short, dark man in the uniform of an accountant stood waiting for the elevator to empty. As Blake passed, their eyes met and the man nodded. Blake walked on down the passage to their cell complex, wondering if the nod had been a signal or not.

My life depends on this, and I'm not even sure of the signals!

They watched the rest of the day's games on the wallscreen, Sergeant White pointing out mistakes and good work by both sides. Afterward, he put a sheet of reprofax on the board and went off to his room.

"Blake," Rob said, "you better read this."

Mason, Blake, 8420-2925-M-14, 10/19: Main arena, #17, it said.

"You're the seventeenth act tomorrow," Rob explained.

"What am I up against?" Blake asked.

"I don't know. None of *us*—or at least we aren't posted."

"Then . . . tomorrow is it."

Blake felt very hollow and not one bit brave. Suddenly all his expertise at swordplay and robot-kill simulation seemed as nothing. All his hours and days of physical training, of hard work and bruises, all his efforts, seemed futile. *How can I, a displaced person in the time stream, a novice gladiator, hope to overcome killer robots designed by several generations of trained technicians?*

Blake went to his cell and tried to get some sleep.

Where is Rio? Where the hell is Voss? Is this "underground" really going to try and take me out?

Blake turned his face to the wall and attempted to put it all away from him, back into the fantasyland from which it had come.

□

The wait seemed endless. First, marching with his companions in the parade, seeing the thousands awaiting his death, smelling the heat and sweat, sensing the bloodletting mood of the crowd. Then, the long stand in the corridors, shuffling forward and waiting.

Ahead of him were small, slim young men and women, possibly from Southeast Asia, sitting astride mechanical mounts, grotesque spindly-legged robots something like ostriches. One-half of the humans rode green birds and the other half sat on red ones. They carried short spears and didn't look at one another. Behind him squatted the act that would follow him into the Arena, or at least one-half of it: an outsized gorilla with a steel hemisphere where the top of his skull used to be.

Electronically controlled? Blake wondered. At first he had thought the monstrous gorilla was to be his antagonist, but the ringmaster's list showed it to be Number 18. Blake knew that often opposing members of a combat entered from different corridors to the ring, so he still had no idea whom—or what—he was to fight.

The line started moving forward again. In a few minutes, medics came out bearing the gutted bodies of two women and a man, all wearing costumes patterned after World War I uniforms. Behind them rolled a red machine, its scalloped wings folded back against the body of the ship, and large Maltese crosses painted on the wings and tail. In the cockpit sat an animatronic mannikin formed to look like a mustached, begoggled German officer, complete with leather-like flying helmet, black leather coat, and a flowing white scarf. There was a bullet hole where the pilot's right eye should have been; but the animatronic Red Baron still flashed his teeth and looked pertly over the side. The propeller was bent, and turned spastically, with a wrenching squeak.

Suddenly the ringmaster was at his side. "Get ready, Number Seventeen, you'll go on soon."

A number. Not Blake Mason, but Number Seventeen.

Blake turned, expecting to receive the order to go on, but it did not come. He looked inquisitively at the ringmaster, who was gazing into a small screen at the side of the gate and pressing his earphones to his ears. He glanced at Blake and held up his hand. *Not yet.*

The big gate closed and Blake looked out through a port. Men and robots were setting up something in the center. There was a flash of something white between the figures, then the men were moving away and the utility robot was lumbering off. They left behind them a three-meter post firmly implanted in the center of the ring. It was garlanded with flowers, and tied to it was a woman dressed in flowing white. Blake could not see her face because of the fall of dark hair, but his senses began sending him messages. He pressed to the viewport, staring at her.

A roar came from the crowd and a movement from one of the other gates. Blake looked to see a monstrous anthropoid robot move ponderously out onto the sand. It stopped at the edge of the Arena shadow, and Blake saw it was a three-meter-high Attila. The crowd shouted its approval.

As the noise brought the head of the bound girl up, Blake cried out: *"Rio!"*

He pressed against the gate, but it was unyielding. He ripped his sword from its scabbard and pounded on the viewport with the hilt. The gorilla behind him snarled and pressed back against the retiarius, who jabbed at it with his trident. The crashcars raced their engines and a lion roared somewhere.

The ringmaster grabbed at Blake's arm. "Bless you!" he snarled. "Not yet! You'll get out there!"

"Let me out now!" Blake shouted.

He fought the ringmaster and shoved him away. He leaped across to the control desk and reached for the door control, but the ringmaster knocked him back with a stinging blow from his nervelash.

"Bless you, *not yet!*"

Blake jumped to a viewport in the gate and looked out. The Attila was circling the helpless Rio, and the crowd laughed as it swung one of its four arms near her face. Blake pounded again at the port and the ringmaster struck at him again with his nervelash, causing Blake to double up with pain. But he fought the agony and lunged back to the port.

"Let me out!" he cried once more.

The huge Attila was reaching out. Blake uttered a raw cry of rage. Almost delicately, the robot's claw slipped under the shoulder opening of the dress, then with a wide vicious sweep of his arm he ripped the dress. The crowd gasped with shock, and nervous laughter followed. Blake could see them leaning forward, eyes staring at the bare shoulder of the captive girl, lasciviously taking in every detail while they commented on her obvious guilt.

The ringmaster grunted, watching the screens over his control desk. "Bless me, they are programming those tin cans to be positively obscene." He shook his head. "We don't have to put on a dirty show to draw the crowds."

Rio's initial shock had worn off and she stood straight and bravely, looking at the Arena wall rather than at the circling robot.

The mob started shouting encouragement to the robot executioner, and more than a few wanted him to tear more of her dress.

"All right, Seventeen!" the ringmaster said.

Blake looked hard at him, then at the guards behind the gunports, with their lasers and stunners aimed at him. The ringmaster pressed the button and the gates started to rumble open. Blake was ready. He threw himself at the narrow opening and forced himself through as the gate widened.

Sword in hand he raced out into the sunlight and across the sand. He had only a metal sword to use against the awesome height and skill and weight of the Attila, but he had to try. The crowd screamed approval.

Rio looked at him.

He could see her mouth move, but he could not hear her words, which were drowned by the crowd's strident cries. Blake raced toward her, hoping to cut away her bindings in order to give them both mobility. He had no real hope of winning, but at least they could die together, on their feet and fighting.

The Attila moved to cut him off, blocking his way. Blake changed direction, trying to outflank it. The armored robot waved its four threatening fighting arms and blocked him again.

Blake now stopped, breathing heavily, and forced calm upon himself. *Anger gives strength,* he told himself, *but it can more easily betray you.* Sergeant White's words were coming back to him: "The Attila is fast, but has limited use of its upper arms. General Robotics' robbies are usually weak in the upper-right rear quadrant."

Blake started walking toward the huge cybernetic killer in a slow and deliberate way. The crowd fell silent, with only an occasional yell.

He stopped just out of waldo range and looked up at the automaton half again as tall as he was and ten times heavier. If it had been human, Blake would have used some kind of psychological trick. He stared at the grim Attila, knowing it was going to kill him. Then he looked at Rio, and a mood of fatalism overcame him. Its effect was a surprising one, even to Blake.

"Your mother was a trash heap," he said to the robot. "Your father was an ingot." He laughed at himself and waved his sword at the assembly. "They *want* you to fail, Attila the Ashcan! I am human and you are a machine!"

Blake felt suddenly foolish and moved to the side to be able to see Rio. But the robot did not move, except for its stereo lenses. This non-reaction puzzled Blake, and he frantically tried to remember what he'd been taught about robot reaction programming. "They have only a limited number of self-initiated programs," Sergeant White had said. "Mostly they react to you, to your attacks or retreats. If you were to do nothing at all, they would initiate standard kill programming, and get it over with. But remember, 75 percent of the time their reactions are just that—reactions."

Blake began walking up and down before the robot,

keeping an eye on its feet. They would provide the clues to a coming attack.

He started to berate the robot. "Your waldoes are ugly, your skin is made of recycled oil drums." Blake was neither attacking, retreating, nor standing still, frozen into immobility by fear. "Your eyes are from an old Napoleon, and everyone knows what miserable fighters they were! You have third-rate drip in your gears, you smell like something is burning inside you. Checked your interior alarms lately? Nothing? Aha! But I can smell you burning! You'll go in a minute, and they'll scrap you; they won't even recycle your parts. They won't put your program in another body. No, sir; they'll just dump it in the torch and reclaim the elements. Oblivion, Attila baby, nothingness, complete unawareness."

Blake still walked back and forth, but on each turn he went a step or two nearer.

The crowd was restless, annoyed by this unconventional fight. The mikes were probably picking up his words for the television audience, but the shouting throng in the stands couldn't hear, and they were restless.

Blake could see Rio struggling to get free, but so far she was unsuccessful. He continued his verbal attack without stopping.

"Or maybe they will just dump your program into some box somewhere and let it set. Awareness of nothingness, Attila, my beauty! No input, no exterior senses, nothing but your own dull thought, reliving old fights just to have something to do."

The robot stayed motionless, except for the tracking lenses, with a stillness a human being was unable to match.

"You're going to lose today, Attila. Everyone loses someday, even you! You've seen others lose, haven't you? A nice shiny Genghis Khan comes tumbling down. A good-old experienced Black Prince gets his. A Kublai Khan mysteriously fails. A Saladin One Hundred blows up; an Eisenhower stops for no reason. You've seen it happen, Attila, my pigeon, you've seen it happen."

Then its right foot moved, and Blake threw himself

down and forward as the big robot attacked. The lower set of arms both swung at him, but Blake was on the sand, rolling, and getting to the safe area just around the robot's feet. The huge feet kicked at him awkwardly, but Blake was already climbing the robot's back.

The sea of faces in the stands screamed approval as Blake gained the head of the metal giant. The upper set of arms clawed back at him, but Blake struck at them with his sword, bending several claws with hard-flung blows.

Blake climbed higher and reached around to jab at the lenses of the face with the butt of his sword. He smashed one lens; then a claw ripped at his left arm, gashing him deeply in the back of the bicep. Blake cried out and grabbed the waldo and bent it in a surge of strength. The bent arm lashed at him but only managed to get in the way of the lower waldoes, which were trying to get at him. The other upper arm clawed at him, but Blake sent a savage blow into one of the elbows, partially severing the limb and cutting the connections. The lower part of the arm went dead and hung loosely while the upper part still tried to reach him.

He now smashed the other lens and took a cut on the shoulder, then the loose waldo became entangled in the claws of the lower arms. Thinking it had found Blake, the lower limb savaged the arm, pulling it out and throwing it away. But by then Blake had driven his swordpoint into the joining of the upper-right back plate. The swordpoint broke, but Blake savagely forced in the rest of the blade, using it as a pry bar to break the connections. The rear quadrant plate fell away, and Blake plunged his ruined sword into the complex interior mechanisms.

The robot jerked, went rigid, then began a spastic dance that flung Blake off. He fell heavily to the sand and almost blacked out.

In a moment, Blake looked up to see smoke coming from around the sword still buried in the spasming robot. The four clawed waldoes fought at each other and the robot lurched toward the Arena wall. It hit with a crash and stood there, its feet still trying to force it on, sparks and smoke pouring from its back. Then it stopped moving and the sparks ceased, and slowly ... very slowly ... it began to fall over. The waldoes made a series of scratches on the wall as the robot fell. The metal monster finally toppled sideways to crash with the sound of dropped trash.

The shouting of the multitude deafened Blake as he rose wearily from the sand. Some of the people were screaming in rage, but most were shouting in praise. It was seldom that a human defeated a robot, and the novelty was exciting. The robot had stopped moving completely, and only a thin line of smoke came from it.

Limping, and with blood running down his left arm and right shoulder, Blake went over to Rio. He saw that her bindings had magnetic clips and freed her easily.

Rio flung her arms around him, kissing him all over his face, laughing and crying at the same time. He saw blood on her hands and body when she pulled back, but she was smiling. She repeated his name over and over as if she couldn't believe it.

"Those goddam sneaking bastards!" he cried. "They planned this whole thing!"

Angrily, he tore away from Rio and started toward the bishop's box. He knew he could not get up the wall, or over the electric fence, but he was mad enough to try.

Rio ran after him, grabbed his arm, and pleaded, "Don't, Blake! Not now!" She pressed her mouth to his ear and tried to keep up with his angry stride. "They are going to get us out! They told me today! The New Day people! They are going to do it *today*!"

He stopped. He looked at Rio, and for the first time felt the pain in his arm. At that moment the medic team arrived on the scene, and the lead doctor hit him with a hypospray. As Blake fell back into the arms of the stretcher bearers, he said, "Today ..."

The hypospray reduced his pains to distant hurts, and Rio walked beside him as they bore him out of the Arena. Blake saw the secutor and the retiarius pass him and heard the thunder of the crashcars as they moved up, revving their engines noisily. Blake, Rio, and the medics went past the long line of cars, past the patient cleanup robots, and down the corridor to the medical station.

Rio stood by Blake as the human and robotic attendants cleansed his wounds, sealed his cuts together with a sonic needle, and sprayed on bandages.

The ringmaster entered and congratulated Blake. "You'll be a big draw here, Seventeen, er, Mason. They are already editing the tape for national distribution tonight. By tomorrow, you'll be the celebrity of the week. The ringmaster looked pleased. He beamed at Rio, saying, "You were perfect, perfect! They'll probably want to use you again. I've already spoken to the circusmaster and we'll get an island for you—water all around, some electrosnakes and animatronic alligators in the water—and Blake—" He stopped and laughed. "We'll work it out. Don't want to give it away, huh?" He slapped Rio on the shoulder, then said, "Take care of yourself, Mason. You're going to raise the San Francisco rating at least three points!"

Blake stared at the departing man blankly. "He sent us out there to be killed and now he thanks us for raising the ratings!"

Rio looked around, and helped Blake off the medical-examination table. "Come on."

At that moment, a group of television newsmen came bursting into the room. Their lights went on and in a few seconds Blake was surrounded by inquiries.

"How does it feel to be the first man to kill an Attila in three years?"

"Are you going to protest the decisions of the Ecclesiastical court?"

"Do you employ any particular spells in your defense?"

Blake looked blankly at the last questioner. "Spells?" he asked.

"Yes, are you a member of any of the outlawed covens?"

"I—"

"You can speak freely, you are already condemned."

"No, I—"

"Is there any truth to the rumor that you are a Catholic and that the pope aided you with special outlawed prayers?"

"No, no, nothing like that," Blake said. *Covens? The pope?*

"All right, that's enough!" Sergeant White's voice cut through the babble. "Leave him alone, he's mine. Let me through, let me through." The sergeant grinned broadly at Blake. "Bless your bones," he said, smiling. He turned toward the news reporters. "One of my best gladiators. Reminds me of myself when I was younger. I fought a pair of Nebuchadnezzars in the Romulus Arena in '42—me and my mate—and we knocked them both out!" Behind his back, White was gesturing to Blake to get away.

White jumped up on a chair. "You'll want to know how I train my people for the ring. Well, I use pyschology and . . ."

Blake and Rio slipped out of the door quietly. Only one reporter saw them, and followed.

"An exclusive, gladiator? I can get you some special food down here, I promise you that. Maybe even a chunk of real meat, how about that?"

The reporter followed them down the corridor to the elevator. "Mingus Arcoman, *Peninsula Seven*. Come on, we'll just go down here away from the others, and you can tell me all about it."

Blake looked past the newsman and saw the short, dark accountant again, the one who had mysteriously nodded to him earlier. The accountant was looking at him, but so were several passing gladiators and others.

Blake steered the newsman further along the passageway. "Yes, yes, you are probably wondering about how I, a mere novice, and a stranger to your time, could conquer a mighty fighting machine like the dread Atilla. Well, it was this way . . ."

Blake moved Rio in close to the accountant and kept up his stream of words to the newsman. He saw Rio and the other man exchange a few words, but his attention was on the story he was giving the reporter. ". . . You see, the men of my time have it all over your people here. We lived close to the soil then, and draw our strength from it. And I was but the lowest of warriors fighting for his faith, a mere beginner in the art of robot slaying . . ."

Rio looked at Blake and gestured with her head.

"So you see, Mr. Arcoman, that I will make a very good drawing card for whatever Circus holds my contract."

"Contract? I thought you were a condemned criminal? What's a 'drawing card'? You use such ancient terms that I—"

"Later, Mr. Arcoman, later. I must go. Orders, you know. I don't want to be late for my meditations." Rio drew him toward the elevator, and Blake smiled back at the reporter. "Mason, Blake Mason. M-a-s-o-n. Thank you, thank you . . ."

The door closed and Blake fell silent. He put a hand to his arm, which throbbed alarmingly, but the nu-skin was smooth. He looked at Rio, then at the others—a dull-looking minister bearing an autographed greave and a janitor with a can of something. Rio shook her head slightly and Blake kept his mouth shut.

They got out at Blake's cell-complex level and he pulled Rio aside. "Well? Was he the contact?"

She nodded. "He said to go to your cell and wait."

"What about you? Are they going to miss you?"

Rio smiled wanly. "They didn't really expect me back, anyway, but I guess they'll start looking soon." She pressed herself against Blake's arm. "But by then it will be too late—you'll be out!"

"Me? What about you?"

"They're just taking you."

"Oh, no! Either we both go, or no deal!"

"But—"

Blake grabbed her arm and pulled her along toward his cell section. "That's the way it is," he said firmly.

Bennett, Neva, Rob, Narmada, Kapuki, and several others greeted Blake noisily.

"We saw it on the screen!" Bennett shouted. "You were fantastic!"

"A tiger!" Kapuki said.

"And this is the girl . . ." Neva said, looking Rio over in one sweeping glance.

"This is Rio," Blake said.

As the others continued to congratulate him, he pulled Bennett aside. "They want to take me out today—but only me. I'm taking Rio, or I don't go. You tell that to . . . to whoever. *Both* of us, understand."

Bennett nodded, his eyes on Rio. "Not bad," he said, "if you like the type."

"Mason, Blake!" came the sharp words from the entrance.

Mason looked over to see four black-clad Swords of St. Michael standing arrogantly in the doorway. *Are these the ones?*

"Mason, Blake!" one of them said sharply.

"I'm Mason. What do you want . . . sir?"

"You. Come with us. The Bishop of San Francisco wants to see you."

"All right. Rio." He reached out for her, but the Sword put up a hand.

"Just you, Mason. We don't need any fallen women." He studiously avoided looking at Rio's ripped dress.

"I think the Bishop would like to see both of us, sir." He tugged at Rio's hand and forced her to his side.

The Sword looked around, and Blake thought his eyes stopped on Bennett's face. But he could not be certain. The black-clad man shrugged and gestured them on.

The soldiers formed a box around the two of them and walked briskly to the intersection.

This was the moment of truth. If they turned left, they would be going toward the bank of elevators reserved for high officers and the higher echelons of the clergy. If they turned right, they would be heading toward the service elevators and cargo lifts. They turned right.

Blake squeezed Rio's hand. He thought about Neva and Kapuki, Bennett and the rest, but his elation did not make him feel guilty. *I'll come back for you!* he vowed.

They took one elevator down several levels, crossed through an animal-containment area, then up to a robot-repair shop, walked up a flight, stepped out into an accounting sector, and went down a hall. It was quiet here, with only a little choral music from the wall speakers. The hall might have been in any office building anywhere, and not the business offices for a Roman-style arena.

They stopped before a door marked DEACON J. JACKS, PROVISIONAL ACCOUNTING, and a Sword gestured them through. Before the door was closed, the four men were walking briskly away.

There was an outer office and a smiling, dark-haired woman behind a desk. She stood up, opened an inner door, and said, "Please. And hurry!"

Inside, the short, dark man was getting up from his desk; and he was also smiling. "Congratulations, Mason. I see you insisted upon bringing your rescued damsel. Very romantic. We can use that, I think." He looked her over with a certain lust in his eyes. "Very nice. Why they would want to destroy such a lovely object, I'll never know." He turned toward his desk, saying, "Christians! I'll never understand them. Never!"

Jacks reached into a drawer and took out a small device that Blake recognized as the kind of magnetic key to the explosive neckband they both wore. Blake's unspoken fear had been that the Arena police would trigger the neckpieces and kill them both.

Jacks pressed the end of the mag key to the side of Rio's neck and then to Blake's. The explosive bands fell off.

Blake threw his in the wastebasket, but Jacks retrieved it and took both of the prison devices out the door. In a few moments he returned. "If they set it off now, they will be quite surprised where it goes bang. Now, for clothing."

He took a key from his pocket and opened a side door. Inside was some clothing. In a few moments Blake was dressed as a robot technician and Rio was wearing the tunic and brassard of a novice medic. They returned to the hall, where Jacks was waiting.

They followed him at a distance. He went into one elevator, holding three fingers pointed down. Rio and Blake waited for another cage, then dropped three floors. They picked him up again and followed him several hundred meters around the curve of the Arena, through several training sections, and into another elevator. Up five levels, they followed him through an unmarked door. A gaunt, harassed woman inside gave them new identification papers after she had taken their photographs. Blake and Rio then followed Jacks for several more level changes.

They finally stopped in a secluded niche, and Jacks said, "They should be catching on by now."

"What do we do?" Blake asked.

"Go to that elevator there. It will lead you to the service exit. Just walk out as if nothing were wrong—but not together. Oh, here!" Jacks dug into his pocket and handed them each a Unicard. "Use these. They're stolen, but I don't expect the alarm for several hours yet, so the alarms won't go off. Take the Two-Fifteen to downtown and get off at *Sutter Towers*. Don't go in the front; use the service entrance. Go to condo Six-Oh-One. That's on the Gold Dust level. Don't be frightened by the way it looks. Just act like you are on call."

"What then?" Blake queried nervously.

"You'll be met. You'll be asked about something in your past, Mr. Mason. Don't worry, you'll be among friends."

Blake nodded. He knew that this group, whatever it was and whatever it stood for, planned to use him in some way; but he didn't mind, not as long as they got him and Rio out.

"Come on," he said to Rio, and they walked quickly toward the elevator bank.

□

Blake took the service elevator to the Gold Dust level. The escape from the Circus had been easier than he'd expected, although they were standing on the monorail platform when they heard an alarm go off. But now, buried safely in the giant arcological complex that was San Francisco, he began to relax. Rio was a few minutes behind him, coming up another elevator.

Blake's elevator door opened and he found himself in the rear service passage. The walls were studded with readout dials, bolted access panels, barred rear exits from the condos, tube terminals, and an occasional television monitor. As Blake walked towards the 600 series, he passed an occasional repairman whose head was buried in a panel or who worried over a plug-in unit with intermittent cutout. They ignored him or nodded casually.

He found the 600 series and stopped at the rear door of number 601. Trying not to look around to see if anyone was watching, he knocked sharply on the door. In a few moments he sensed a darkening of the peep-eye and then heard a voice coming through a cheap speaker.

"Yes?"

"I'm here to repair your robbie."

"Where did you say you were from?"

"Uh . . ." Blake glanced down at the small toolkit Jacks had given him. "Uh, General Robotics . . ."

There was a pause, and Blake could not resist looking up and down the service corridor. Then the speaker squawked again.

"When were you born?"

"What does that . . . ? Uh . . . October 24th . . . uh . . ." He had started to give the year, and his near-slip disturbed him. *I'll have to be more careful!*

No answer came, but in a few seconds he heard the

220

mag locks snap open; then the door slid back. A small brown man stood inside; he was dressed in a plain tunic. He was balding and appeared very clean, as old men often did.

He smiled and gestured Blake in, and closed the door behind him. "This way," he said.

Blake hefted his tool kit and followed. *What if I have to really repair some robot? I'll fake it and get out as fast as possible.*

Blake knew he would have to work quickly and find out what was going on, because Rio was due in less than five minutes. He had not wanted her to come with him, in case there was danger. Unless a code word was given, she was to pretend she had the wrong condo and leave.

The condo was plain, and hardly looked lived in. It had standard furniture, the usual GE wallscreen, and a few copies of newsfax. Blake swept the room in one quick scan and watched the other doors alertly.

The old man stopped, and said, "Let me introduce myself. I am Emelio Radiodifundir. Would you like a drink, *Señor*?"

Blake's eyes flicked again over the apartment. It was too clean, too impersonal! Either no one lived here, or it was a trap. He began edging toward the rear door again. "No. No, thank you. Where is the robbie you wanted fixed?"

The old man smiled and sat down. "Don't be alarmed, *Señor* Mason. You are quite safe. Is *Señorita* Volas coming up the front or the back?"

Blake's tenseness drained out of him. They either already had him, or he was safe. "The back." He gestured around him. "Who lives here?"

"No one. Or I should say, no one permanently. It is merely a convenience address for our organization."

"The People for a New Day?"

The old man smiled and nodded. "Among others. Are you certain you would not like a drink? We have some passable Rugan Viñon from Napa and a rather good *juntamente vino* from the Brothers."

Blake shook his head. He was listening for sounds in the condo, and for the sounds of Rio at the rear door. He still stood, and was still not completely satisfied.

The old man seemed to sense this, and said, "Please, *Señor* Mason, you are quite safe here. Please, not to worry." He smiled again. "Perhaps it would put you at ease to know who I am." He held up his hand. "Oh, I am Emelio Radiodifundir. all right, *sí*, even though my papers say I am Paul Mendoza. You might know me better as Urban IX, the bishop of Rome."

Blake stared, disbelieving this little brown man in the rather shabby tunic and ill-fitting trousers.

The man smiled wryly. "Ah, yes, I know. The robes, the miter, the jewels, the incense, the acolytes—I know." He sighed deeply. "I never knew them. I have seen pictures, of course, and a few relics and some lovely crucifixes people have hidden. But all that was before my time."

"But you are supposed to be in New America or somewhere down south," Blake said.

The little man nodded, his bald head gleaming. He smiled with a sort of childish glee as he said, "Yes, yes, good! It is good you think so. Perhaps *they* shall, too. The outlaw pope." He looked up at the ceiling. "It has a certain romantic air, does it not?" He looked with quick concern at Blake. "Not an *anti*-pope, you understand. Bless me, no! The Church has had enough of those, dear me, yes. Even one Urban, who was not my idea of a good prelate, I'm afraid—not an anti-pope, that Prignani, a rather savage little man, but then I suppose they were all a bit that way in the fourteenth century. Ah, but I digress. My apologies, my son."

The little man's spout of words had given Blake a few seconds to think. *An outlawed pope . . . A revolutionary underground . . . Escaped time travelers?* He had to smile, and was still smiling when he opened the rear door to Rio's knock.

"It's all right," he said, giving her the code word he and she had agreed upon. "Come, I want you to meet a pope."

The little Spaniard was both gallant and regal as he met Rio. Blake saw her accept him at face value, and that settled it for him. Once again they were given a change of clothing, this time a figure-concealing dress and cloak for Rio and a severely cut drab suit for Blake. They changed clothes, then sat down to eat some food.

Urban talked as they ate. "I am but one link in your underground route. Next, you will go to Venus." He smiled at their expressions. "No, Venus the organization. They will guide you to the New Day people."

"It sounds as if there are many dissident groups," Rio said.

"There are a few, yes," Urban said, nodding. "But they are not very effective. They have their own internecine battles. The People for a New Day are political. We Catholics are, of course, religious. Venus is . . . um, rather pagan in its beliefs. The Lutherans are different still, and the Mormons were always independent. But those two groups appear to conform."

The old man shook his head. "Mankind was never *one,* but it has rarely been so militantly fractionalized. Each group develops its own plans, ignores the others. Each is too weak to do anything itself, so nothing gets done."

The thin pope leaned forward to emphasize his words. "This is why *you* are so important. The timing of your arrival was superb! The New Day people finally had three plans approved by the majority of factions— which is the first step. But no one has agreed on the date, nor on what to do afterward. Everyone is afraid we will lose what gains we make in the in-fighting after it is over."

"Why do they need me, or us?" Blake asked.

Pope Urban leaned back. "Let me give you an idea of what we have done. First, the religious oppression is such that no one is happy with it, not even many of the churches. They maintain armies and do what they must do because they are afraid of being overrun by other religions."

"Holy wars . . ." Rio said.

Urban nodded. "Worse. Civil wars are always the most vicious. But this fractionalizing among the religions—if you can call some of them that . . . forgive the chauvinism, my dear—has broken down communications between countries, between the people in the middle, between philosophies. But the plans the New

Day people have made seem feasible. The best plan was given a 64.2 percent chance of succeeding, given certain factors. You are one of those factors, and a major one."

"How can one or two people make any difference?" Rio asked.

The prelate smiled. "Psychological. A sign from a more liberal time. A neutral factor, not aligned with any of the dissident groups—one they can all rally around. Let me tell you about revolutions."

The old man poured himself a glass of wine and sat back. "Revolutions succeed when, and only when, governments have become rotten or soft, or have disappeared or abdicated their duties, or are just too distant to enforce the laws and/or are too busy doing something else. Revolutions succeed in power vaccuums. How?" He held up his hand, a finger in the air. "One, revolution depends upon organization and communication. We are organized into cells, with each of us knowing only one above and one in the organization below. We communicate mainly through the Total Information System net, on sealed circuits. We have enough people in the TIS to be reasonably sure we will not be tapped."

He held up another finger. "Two, there are always betrayals. Three, it is easier to get people to hate than to love, and the whole oppressive church system is helping us there. Four, revolutions are won by a few who have been trained for it. Five, revolutions are not won by the masses. *They* only provide the foundation, an atmosphere in which to work. If the masses are not basically on your side, they must at least not be on the side of the opposition. Six, revolutions succeed only when they take place at the proper moment. Too soon, too late, and they don't work. We have decided that *now* is the time. If we do it right, there will be a minimum of bloodshed. If we do it wrong . . ."

The old man shrugged.

"But," he continued, raising his hand, "I think this is the time. Lurid, programmed events like the Arena slaughters can only entertain the people for so long. Likewise, the television dramas, the staged miracles, the pageantry, all the propaganda slop the people have been getting, telling them no one ever had it so good . . ." His lined face was grim. "These ... 'churches' have ruled unwisely. They proscribed too much, limited life too much, though those at the top live a different life entirely. You haven't been here long enough, or traveled enough, to hear the grumbling, the frustration. The people are rebellious and ready. Ready for a leader."

He paused, then went on. "Remember," he said, "revolutions never work in the midst of happiness. They start as conspiracies of dissidents, then build to a ground swell, but succeed only if properly managed. You must use only those elements that are necessary, and no others. For example, we never accept anyone as a member just because he wants to join up. That would be the grossest breach of security."

Blake grinned. "But you take people who don't even want to join."

"Speak for yourself," Rio said. "*I* want to join."

"I'm not yet convinced it is going to work," Blake said. "Bomb-throwing anarchists, outlaw popes, reckless hedonists, gladiators, time travelers—hah!"

"We have done our homework," Urban insisted. "For instance, despite the fact that there are so many different churches and that they fight, they do align themselves in groups. These groups are serviced by master computers, which we have people ready to sabotage or to control. Centrality increases vulnerability, but decentralization and parallel, fail-safe systems cost money— so brother-churches share computer systems. No modern complex system can get along these days without some kind of computer facility. People are basically lazy, and they tend to let machines do more and more of the drudge work. As a result, most of the logistics, bookkeeping, simple storehousing, and a hundred other things are done by computers. Sometimes only the master computermen can read the programs correctly. Forty-eight percent of those computermen are our people."

"Your Holiness," Rio said, "when does a revolution have the *right* to succeed?"

"When its philosophies and goals truly reflect the majority opinion. And when it has the guns," he added with a grin. "But we have developed alternate plans and organizations you need not know about."

"The less we know, the less we can tell," Blake said.

"There is always that chance of capture, yes," Urban said. "Speaking of that . . ." He dug into his tunic and took out some papers. He sighed, then smiled at them. "Now, on your way! Here are your identification documents. You are Noble and Dyami Youngblood, of the Sparrowhawks . . . the Crows, that is. Indians. You are on your way to fetch a dead chief and bring him back to the tribal burying grounds. Take the seven-o'clock shuttle to Los Angeles, to the Palmdale Airport. Call the number on this slip of paper. Identify yourselves as Metatron—he is the 'chancellor of heaven'—and as Batna." He smiled at Rio. "One of the names of Lilith, my dear. I hope you don't mind."

Rio shook her head and smiled faintly. Urban concluded, telling them they would then get furthur instructions.

"Will we see you again?" Rio asked softly.

Urban shrugged. "Only God knows, my child."

Blake spoke. "May I ask you a question?"

Urban smiled at Rio and said, "I have never understood why people say that, do you? I usually say 'No,' but they ask anyway. Go on, *Señor* Mason, ask your question."

"You are a Christian, all these weird churches and cults or whatever they are say *they* are Christian. Yet you are hiding? Why is that?"

The little wiry Spaniard nodded. "Yes, I know. But why did the Church punish deviations? Why condemn any form of worship of God? It is a mystery, indeed. How easy it would be to say that God works in mysterious ways. I've always thought that idea was a deterrent to rational and logical thinking; you can say that, perhaps, when your meager efforts have failed. But you should *try* and not give up *too* soon, yes? Now, in answer to your question: I would say that I do not know. There were political reasons, ethnic reasons, geographic reasons, reasons that were said to be temporary and others that were said to be necessary, but I have never really understood why. We all worship God, whether we call him the Great Spirit, Supreme Being, Brahma, First Cause, the Infinite, Allah, Yahweh, Jehovah—or you make up a name. The Holy Roman Church believes that its path is the true path, but perhaps all paths lead to Him." The old man smiled softly. "Perhaps His ways *are* mysterious."

He pursed his lips, then said, "I have lived a sheltered life until a few years ago. I am learning . . . It is good not to be isolated from the people—no leader should be. So I am learning. I learned that greed is a powerful motivation, and that men saw power and wealth in religion and organized it with computer research and motivational analysis, finding out the fears of men and playing upon them. That is nothing new, but they brought it quickly to a fine art, playing on the reactions to . . . to your licentious time."

"It was a free time, though," Blake argued.

"Perhaps too free."

Blake felt a sudden anger. "You can't be *too* free."

The aged pontiff nodded. "Perhaps . . . you are right. Perhaps I should have said your age required more self-discipline. Would you agree?"

"That's different. With that I would agree."

"Come on," Rio said. "I don't care to argue theology now. We've got to move."

"Go with God!" said the Holy Father.

"And with haste," Rio added.

"Thank you," Blake said, and the little brown man made the Sign of the Cross in the air.

Rio and Blake walked out the front door and went quickly toward the drop elevators.

"He seemed so alone," Rio said.

"I never thought I'd meet a pope."

Blake slipped his stolen change-card into the slot on the pay pictophone in the echoing mall of the huge Palmdale Airport. He looked at the number on the paper and punched it out.

The screen cleared almost at once, revealing a pretty woman in a plain blue dress. Behind her was a veneer wall with a large commercial logo. "Proteinettes, good afternoon!"

Blake didn't know what to do. It seemed unlikely his contact was a switchboard operator or a receptionist. Perhaps he had mispunched. "Is this two thirteen, four sixty-five, sixty-six forty-four, fifty-six ninety?"

"Yes, it is, sir. How may we help you?"

"Well, I'm Mr. Metatron and—"

"Ah, yes, sir! Is your wife with you?"

"Yes, uh . . . Batna is here."

"Very good, sir. Would you please take the monorail to St. Timothy's Gate, *Casmaran*. You will be met by a representative of this office."

Blake repeated the destination and the connection was broken. He looked at Rio. They both shrugged and started walking.

"Do you feel like a pawn?" she asked.

"All too often," he said.

The monorails rose like silver spaghetti from the airport terminal, and branched out in every direction toward arcologs. Overhead, swift aircars moved on invisible wires in steady streams. Rio saw a moon shuttle coming down and pointed it out to Blake, but he was too busy looking over the other passengers and trying to decide if any of them were tails.

The monorail skimmed over the mountains, past small arcologs and then bigger and bigger ones, as they neared Los Angeles. None of them was familiar to

Blake or to Rio, although they thought one of the smaller arks might be *Mojave* and another was perhaps the old *Sahara*. They stared out of the windows at the passengers at every stop and even at the advertisements on the wallscreens at each station.

About a third of the ads were for soya foods and algae products. Rugged, handsome men in rough-weather gear were manning improbable algae boats and urging that you buy Seawheat or Oceanein or Protein-A. Handsome, chaste-looking women suggested you use Soyall or Soyasea, and there were tridees of beautiful, healthy children smiling as they emptied bowls of Proteinums. Another third were religious-oriented, offering the addresses of main temples, advisory services, heresy teams, rehabilitation centers, seminaries, hospitals, and the like. The final third were advertisements for Circus bills, Arena trainers, personal medicines, new and used transportation sellers, arcolog rentals, and a few television shows.

Casmaran was a large ark on the eastern edge of what Blake figured was the San Fernando Valley. As they stood waiting for the representative, they read a large sign that said *Casmaran* was the name for "summer" and that the different main levels were Tubiel, Gargatel, Gaviel, and Tariel. It was built and operated by the Potent Lord Construction and Realty Corporation, which also operated *Talvi, Ardarcel,* and *Farlas,* the other three "seasons."

Bored with waiting, Blake and Rio discussed their probable futures and Blake thought of asking Rio where Voss and the others were.

"I don't know," she said. "I heard a rumor that someone was trying to buy me out, but I never knew who it was. It could have been anyone who, you know, saw me in a parade and . . ."

Blake nodded. "He's somewhere. Do you think he made it to Switzerland?"

Rio shrugged. "I don't know. Oh, Blake, this world is so different from what I expected, from what Jean-Michel expected! Why did we come here?"

"In pursuit of immortality," he said wryly. "Maybe

in two or three hundred years it will change and we'll still have two hundred or so to live in peace."

She looked at him sadly. "I'm sorry you came, Blake. I've condemned you to—to this."

"No, I'm a volunteer. Besides, if I hadn't come, I would have been dead decades ago! I'm alive and well and living in the future."

"Some future!"

"Mr. Metatron?" The voice was at their elbow and soft.

Blake stood in the window with his arm around Rio and looked out at the megalopolis of Los Angeles. It was even larger than when Blake lived on the other side of the Hollywood Hills. It seemed to be just one enormous building now, and even the spaces between the arcologs were filled thirty or forty stories deep at their shallowest. The arks were bigger than any of those of his time, and Blake counted several times the number that he remembered.

They had stopped at a transfer terrace on the escalator trip up the outer facet of *Casmaran,* and Rio had marveled at the horizon-to-horizon supercity. "It's bigger than San Francisco," she said.

"It always was," Maya Higgins said, unimpressed. "It's a monument to stupidity. Forty-one million miserable souls, and climbing daily."

"Forty-one million?" Blake asked. "In Los Angeles?"

Maya nodded, directing them to the next escalator. "It's the second-largest city in the world now. Tokyo has forty-six point two, London has thirty-nine something, Shanghai has about forty. So do Moscow and São Paulo. Bombay, New Delhi, and Calcutta dropped, of course, since the famines. I think they were quite large in your time. Cairo, Rio, and Peking are catching up, though. But Los Angeles had such good a climate and all that desert to grow into!"

Blake thought about the hordes that now, he was told, bulged every ancient city site across the world, plus all the new cities, the floating arks, the underwater cities, and even the populous Arctic metropolises. *Sixteen billion . . . !*

He held Rio closer and they watched night overtake the huge city. Lights burned deep in the canyons and clefts long before the sun had left the faceted towers of

231

the tall buildings. Unceasing streams of aircars wove intricate multilevel patterns in the air, hopping from the landing pads of one structure to another, dropping, rising, weaving, and never hitting each other.

Maya now escorted them into a beautifully decorated apartment. Rio and Blake turned to her. "New clothes, new ident, a new life," the short, voluptuous woman said. She gestured at the clothes she had put on a wide bed-lounge. "Your new wardrobe."

Blake started unzipping his tunic. Maya got an odd, uncomfortable look on her face and turned her back to him. Blake ignored her.

"We're being handed from one secret hideout to another," he said to her, "but where are we going? The New Day people? Venus?"

"Oh, we're Venus. Didn't they tell you? Everyone wants you, you know. Just everyone! You are real prizes, people we can all identify with. A genuine pair of time travelers from the era of true freedom—*and* famous in the Arena. You might be the catalysts that bring all the different groups together at last."

"How many are there?" Rio asked as she, too, changed clothes. "Besides Venus and New Day?"

"Oh, let's see. There are the Angels of Liberation, the American Patriots, the Iconoclasts, a few really odd religious groups that don't mesh with the Christians. The anarchists, naturally, but they are quite spread out and disorganized. The Thomas Paine Society, the Termites, and what's left of the Congress, the Catholics, and the Orthodox Jews."

"The Congress? Of the United States? That's an underground group?" Blake stared blankly at Maya. The status of the pope had surprised him, but an outlaw congress seemed truly fantastic.

"Oh, didn't you know? No, I guess you couldn't have. Once the different churches became powerful they started lobbying, of course, and electing their own men and women. Eventually, it caused quite a few fights, and it came to a head with the election of Joan Hillary to the House. They refused to seat her, then others who they said were 'unfit.' By that they meant un-Christian. The whole episode grew into quite a fight. Just paralyzed Washington for months. The church people had the numbers and the rules. Then someone tried to assassinate President Canfield, and all hell broke loose. Congress declared about forty congressmen and senators wanted criminals and ... well, they finally disbanded Congress by acclamation, returning power to the states. The elected members went around for years as a government-in-exile, but most of them were eventually captured, killed, or betrayed ... Oh, Rio, that looks marvelous on you!"

Rio now wore a dress that covered her completely to the neck but still managed to show off her figure. Blake had on tights and a severely cut jacket. Maya handed them both dark cloaks.

"You can wear these to the party," she said.

"Party?" Blake asked. He felt constantly foolish, always asking inane questions about what was obviously commonly accepted practices, but he had little alternative if they were going to learn anything.

"Yes, Venus is giving a party in your honor."

"Is that *safe?*"

"Oh, yes, quite safe. We've never had a raid of that sort in this ark—not one. That's why we brought you here. Everyone is dying to meet you!"

Blake looked at Rio.

"It might be good relaxation," she said.

"It seems so dangerous for two fugitives to ... Oh, well, let's do it."

Maya smiled brightly and took their hands. "Good! Follow me!"

The party was in the big, rambling condo of Walter Robinson, the majority stockholder of Proteinettes. The robot butler let them in after identifying them visually, but the foyer seemed like a tomb. Rio and Blake looked at each other, their expressions saying, "A party?"

Then the robot keyed an electric door with his radio, and it slid open. The room beyond was quite dark, and Blake saw some movement. But there was no sound whatever.

Maya stepped forward, gesturing them to follow. As they passed through the door, noise flooded over them in a sudden, shocking wave. First, the hard pulsebeat of music, which almost drowned out everything else; then, filtering through, a few grunts and cries.

"Ohh!" said Maya, her eyes bright as she turned back toward Blake and Rio, who stood just inside the acoustical curtain. "Isn't it deliciously exciting?"

Blake and Rio peered into the darkness beyond the wedge of dim light cast through the electric foyer door. They caught glimpses of movement, flicks of light on metal or jewelry, the gleam of eyes, the faint sheen of sweaty flesh. But nothing definite. Then the door closed silently behind them and the room was almost pitch black.

Maya took their hands and whispered, "This way."

They followed her on a weaving course through the big room, sometimes stumbling over an unseen soft object. Soon they approached a faintly glowing ball, which illuminated a few steps, and carefully ascended them, emerging into a short hall.

Maya led them through a curtain of fabric and another acoustical curtain, into a room more brightly lit. Here the music was quieter, less strident, and more erotic. A man and woman detached themselves from a group of softly laughing people and ambled toward them.

In the dim light Blake was not sure if he would recognize these people on the street. He was introduced to Walter Robinson, a man in his fifties, with an air of power and authority about him, and to Ramona Nelson, a slender dark woman. They shook hands, and Blake was immediately annoyed at the possessive manner Robinson adopted toward Rio. He was also aware that Ramona's eyes had never left his face or body.

"Greeting, wayfarers," Robinson said with a dramatic voice. "Welcome to my humble abode." He gestured around him, into the semi-darkness where others were heard laughing or talking. "Everything you see is yours."

Ramona closed in on Blake with half-lidded eyes. "You must come with me, Blake. We are all eagerly awaiting your reactions to our little group here."

The woman tugged at Blake's arm but he did not

want to be parted from Rio. He held Rio's hand tightly and she signaled back with her grip. Robinson and Ramona were persistent, but unsuccessful.

"Aren't you all afraid of being arrested?" Rio asked. "I thought this sort of thing would be—"

Robinson laughed. "Oh, no! The level monitor is one of us, and the floor monitor is sympathetic. The sounds never penetrate outside, and my people are careful."

"This is Venus?" Blake queried.

A sudden burst of laughter rang out in a dark corner and Robinson looked that way with a tolerant smile. "Part of it," he said. "There are thousands like us, just waiting for the time when we can overthrow the shackles of oppression," he said proudly.

Blake glanced again at Rio. The man seemed sincere, but to Blake this underground attempt at an orgy was ludicrous. *Liberty is never won by hiding away and pretending one's lusts are revolutionary. Liberty is only won by deeds. Robinson's guests and their pitiful attempts at striking back at their society's sex taboos are sad. There has to be more to Venus than this,* Blake thought; and he could see by Rio's face that she was hopeful, too.

Robinson was still pressing Rio to go into another dark room with him, just as Ramona was tugging at Blake.

We're prizes, not people, Blake told himself. He turned quickly to Maya. "Look, we're tired. This party is very nice, very much like the very best sort of parties in our time, but we'd like some sleep. It's been a long time, and—"

"Don't go," Ramona said, coming close.

"You're going?" Robinson said incredulously.

Maya was also surprised, and she protested.

Blake was adamant, however. "Some other time," he said soothingly. He gestured around him and told Robinson, "Very nice, very nice. Wish we could stay, but really, we're bushed."

" 'Bushed'?" Ramona asked curiously.

"Tired. Worn out."

Blake let Robinson and Ramona follow them back to the front door, acknowledging a few introductions to dim figures on cushions and couches, then told his hosts good night. He gently but firmly refused the offer of their company, then followed Maya back to their hideout.

Maya became more and more excited as they neared the apartment. Obviously the now bubbling, eager Maya was expecting a triple—something she could brag about for the rest of her life—and Blake hated to disappoint her. But he and Rio both made it obvious they were looking forward to rest. Finally she took the hint.

"This is your room," she said to Rio, then pointed at another door. "That's yours."

Blake and Rio looked at each other in surprise. Somehow they had expected to finally share a bed. But Maya looked firm. "That's right. One may . . . may *do* things together, but unmarried people just don't sleep together."

"All right, my little revolutionary," Blake said. He smiled at Rio. "I'm tired. Things have been happening so fast. I'm tired of running."

"I'm so weary," Rio agreed. Her eyes lingered on Blake, then she went into her room.

Blake said good night to Maya and fell into bed. He lay awake for a few moments, thinking over the long day, wondering what lay ahead for them. Tomorrow, Maya had said, they would be sent to the New Day people.

Pawns. Prizes. Targets.

But you must keep moving, Blake thought sleepily. The idea of giving up never occurred to him.

□

Rio and Blake had insisted on sleeping late and spending the afternoon talking with a now sober Walter Robinson. It was after six p.m. when, with Maya, they left Venus.

Maya stood on the public mall and pointed over the edge of the railing at the arcolog next to them. It was like pointing across a canyon to an adjacent mountain. "There, that pinkish dome, the one by the blue pyramid? That's Level Ninety. Go in there and ask for Linda Muirwood."

Blake took her hand and thanked her for all her help. She looked sad, but smiled anyway. "Maybe next time," she said.

Blake wished he had something to give her, but he had nothing that she had not given him. So he kissed her.

She started as if struck by lightning, and jumped back, blushing furiously. She looked around in fear, saying, "Don't, please! Oh, dear . . ."

Rio tugged at Blake, and they went down the escalator nearby, then took a drop elevator to an interark slideway and went over to the other arcolog.

"That wasn't too shrewd a move," she said as they slid between the man-made mountains. "But I know why you did it."

"I keep forgetting the way they feel around here," Blake said. "It just seems so foolish to deny perfectly natural feelings."

Rio nodded, her eyes on the upper levels of the arcolog they were approaching. "What next . . . ?" she wondered aloud.

Blake's eyes were on a black-clad policeman standing just inside the slideway entrance to the arcolog. He was scanning the passing throng, and then his eyes lit on Blake and Rio and he didn't look away.

"Pretend you don't know me," Blake said quietly. "The blackcoat at the entrance—"

"I see him," Rio said in a whisper.

"You go left, I'll go right. If he follows me I'll lose him. If he follows you, I'll—I'll follow him."

"Blake . . ."

"You forget, I'm the terror of the Caligula Arena." Blake shifted his weight away from her and moved to get off the slideway first. He stepped off fairly close to the policeman and paused as if to get his bearings, then strode off purposefully to the right. Rio went the other way, down the mall, and Blake glanced around casually and saw the officer speak into a communicator. Blake started to walk faster, and the black-suited officer started after him.

I've got to do this quickly, he thought. Blake rounded a corner and saw the entrance to a working-class saloon ahead. *I can't just lose him, I've got to stop him!*

Blake slowed and turned into the saloon just as the policeman came around the corner.

Blake quickly took stock of the bar. It was neither as dark nor as disreputable as he would have liked, but it was all he had. He walked quickly toward a passage marked WASH ROOMS, smiling confidently at the bartender. The few customers paid no attention.

Without hesitation Blake stepped through the door marked WOMEN. No one was inside. He held the door open a crack and heard a rough voice say something and another voice grunt. Then the policeman was in the passageway. He passed the women's wash room as Blake hoped he would, holding a stubby black weapon in his hand. A jewel-like light pulsed steadily at the back of it.

Blake stepped out.

The policeman started to turn, but Blake hit him hard on the side of the neck. Two more blows and the blacksuit folded, his weapon tinkling to the floor. Blake grabbed his feet and tugged him through the door into the women's wash room and set him in a booth. He found the weapon was fastened to the man's locked belt by a thin but tough line.

Blake gave up trying to get it loose, and shut the booth door and walked swiftly out. The bartender looked up from a visionphone and Blake smiled.

The bartender watched him leave with expressionless eyes.

Blake took a direct elevator to Level Ninety and walked along until he found the pinkish dome Maya had described. He lingered near a food dispenser and looked for Rio. He found her near a pillar, and walked over to her. She acted as if they had never met.

"Were you followed?" Blake asked, scratching his face to hide it.

"No. What happened to you?"

"Tell you later." Blake looked around. "Come on, pawn of fate," he said. "Nothing looks suspicious around here."

"Do you think you'd know what *was* suspicious in this crazy world?"

"So I haven't had much experience being a fugitive. You wait behind. Look in those windows over there. No use both of us getting caught. If I don't come out, or if the forces of law and order come charging in, then go back to Maya and see what they can do."

Rio nodded, squeezing his hand in a quick gesture as she walked away.

Blake went along the mall, dodging a whispering electrocart filled with boxes, then stopped before the dome entrance. Scores of semi-autonomous domes fringed the arcolog on several levels, giving the illusion of being separate houses instead of being part of the massive, immovable ark mountain. The pink dome, a five-eighths globe, housed a retail store that sold religious artifacts. The name "Muirwood's" was scrawled across the curve of the dome in a glowing cerise line.

Blake went inside, walking between larger-than-life statues of saints, some with symbols that Blake found odd indeed. He also noticed figures that had a demon-like quality, something like gargoyles—fierce-faced and horned, fear-making statues designed to be impressive. Blake wondered what kind of religion needed to frighten its believers, but then he remembered that that wasn't so unusual in history, after all.

The dome opened up into several balconies overlooking the main floor, and everywhere there were robed figures shopping. Some were in black, some in gray, a few in blue and scarlet. Several of the uniforms made Blake accountably nervous, but no one seemed to pay any attention to him or to his conventional dress.

He walked through aisles displaying dozens of different bibles, crucifixes, statuettes, and animatronic Christs that blessed, turned, smiled, and glowed. Blake saw a door marked OFFICE and headed for it through a covey of green-clad nuns with sour faces.

Linda Muirwood was slim and blond, with pale white skin and large blue eyes. She looked at Blake across an ancient carved desk, now black with use, gleaming from polish. "You are Blake Mason," she said, making it a statement. She looked past him and raised her eyebrows.

"She's nearby."

Blake gave the room a quick look. Shelves covered two walls and overflowed with objets d'art. A Byzantine mosaic fragment sat next to an early-twentieth-century soft-drink tray. A child's skull, covered with small polished stones, was between a battered plastic object that looked like a peanut made in the shape of a man and a bell jar containing a child's doll with plastic hair and the look of a prostitute, wearing a lamé dress. Across the room was a shelf holding old paperbound books, a small sensatron repro cube of a Caruthers landscape, several framed and faded bank checks, a jar of late-twentieth-century pennies, and dozens of odd plastic objects that Blake could not identify. There were boxes and chests, plastic stasis containers, jars of dark glass, and several very old soft-drink bottles on small wooden bases. A portrait of Linda Muirwood hung on the wall behind the desk—a spot Blake thought inappropriate, since the painting and the subject just below it were markedly different: the painting was the more alive of the two.

Blake took his time examining the room and the woman. She wore a curious pendant that looked something like an animal's head with horns and a long neck; it was wrought in metal. She fingered it as she inspected Blake in turn.

"So," she said with finality. "Are you satisfied?"

Blake shrugged. He was tired of running and of being sent from hither to yon. "I'll get her," he said, and went back outside.

"Is everything all right?" Rio asked.

"I suppose so. If this is some kind of trap, they already have us. If it isn't, then we are only taking one more step."

"Where are they sending us now?" Rio asked anxiously.

"To where they think we will do the most good . . . for them." He smiled reassuringly at Rio. "Fear not, all will be well."

Rio shivered, and hugged Blake's arm as a wind swept through the mall, which was open to the sky along one side. "Where is Jean-Michel . . . ?"

Blake had no answer. He took her arm and they entered the Muirwood dome.

Linda gave Rio an even closer examination with her eyes than she had given Blake. As she did, she fingered a silver bracelet set with large blue-green turquoise stones. Abruptly she said, "We will have a reading." She reached into a drawer of her desk and withdrew a deck of large tarot cards.

"We don't have time for that," Blake said. "Please pass us on to the next step, or whatever it is you are supposed to do with us."

Linda Muirwood gave him a steady gaze, her face expressionless, but Blake sensed anger or possibly hatred. "Very well," she said at last, and put the deck back. She rose. "Follow me."

She went into the shop, down between display cabinets of robes both ancient and modern, past trays of rings and racks of ornamental swords. Blake and Rio followed her briskly walking figure, trying not to look nervous. Linda passed between counters of embossed silver trays and ceremonial cups and on into a storeroom.

Here the dome curved down and the walls were

stacked high with boxes and shelves of merchandise. Several stock clerks noticed her passing, but gave Blake and Rio only a cursory look. Linda took a stairway down and the two fugitives followed. They came into a lower deck, below the surface of the mall, where the air-conditioning ducts and the various pipes, tubes, and conduits were located. Linda was still walking briskly, following a path that was twisting and turning.

Blake knew they were well past the mall and into the outer wall of the arcolog, but he was beginning to lose his sense of direction. They went through fire doors, utility access hatches, company ports, and anonymous arches until he was completely lost.

"Where are we?" he called ahead to Linda.

"Sector six, quadrant two, level three-four-seven, sublevel B."

"Thanks," Blake said. "I should have recognized it right away."

A few moments later, Linda took utility stairs up one level and stopped at a locked door. She produced a key from her clothing and pressed it to the lock panel. The door clicked open and the three of them entered and closed it after them. They were in the technical-services hall to a series of condominiums.

Linda walked quickly to the third of several doors and pressed another key to a blank spot on the wall near the door.

She paused, and looked at Blake and Rio. "A moment," she said.

They heard a noise, and Linda stepped onto the ident panel before the door. A few seconds later the door slid back and Linda walked through quickly. Blake and Rio hurried after her.

The condo was large and dark, except for candles. The person who opened the door was robed in black. Blake observed the figure putting a laser gun into a pocket of his robe, then all Blake could see was the gleam of eyes in the darkness of the cowl. *What have we fallen into* this *time,* he wondered.

The air was heavy with incense and the steady chant of a number of people. Blake came up behind Rio as she stood at the entrance to the main room. Linda had disappeared into the dimness and Blake sought her in the crowd of kneeling figures, but could not find her. Some of the figures wore black masks, and there were about as many of one sex as another. Against one wall an altar stood on a section of flooring raised up a few steps. The altar was made of some dark, polished stone and the candles on it were of black wax and were set in ancient holders of ornate silver. Before the altar stood a black man, in a black robe, speaking in a sonorous tone, reading from a heavy and ancient book. The language was unintelligible.

"It's black magic!" Rio said in a whisper.

Blake gripped her arm and gave the passing figure of the one who had opened the door a quick look. The man passed on across the room, and Blake saw him kneel with another small group of robed figures who were all but invisible in a corner. They seem to be praying, and all held candles.

"Perhaps it is *white* magic," he told Rio. He felt her shiver and he murmured reassuringly in her ear, "It's just another religion. If it were a black mass, they'd have an inverted stolen crucifix and would be reading the Mass backward. At least, I think that's what they do."

"We serve in a way far older than that," said a voice at their elbow. Startled, Blake and Rio turned to see Linda standing next to them. "Those who mock the Christian service with their blasphemies are but upstarts. We here follow a far more ancient form of worship. Listen!"

Blake and Rio listened, but all they heard was the chant of the group of kneeling people who were following the man before the altar.

The whole ceremony seemed to have significance to Linda. "Watch," she whispered. "Constantine is about to make a woman his slave."

The man at the altar stopped his chant and put away the book. He took a piece of parchment given him by one of the women and drew three large concentric circles upon it with a quill pen. Then the acolyte offered him a small pot, which seemed to be filled with ashes.

He dipped his quill into the pot and wrote something in the center of the circles.

"Her name," Linda whispered.

They watched as he pricked his left thumb with a needle. With his own blood he drew seven five-pointed stars within the circle where he had written the woman's name. After squeezing more blood from his thumb, he drew seven open eyes in the next ring, and in the outer ring seven quarter-moons. He then folded the parchment in half, then in half again. He knelt on the floor before the altar and an acolyte handed him a horseshoe and a black candle.

As he was lighting the candle, Linda whispered, "Bloody hard to find iron horseshoes these days. One of the reasons I'm in the antique business."

The black man held the paper to the candle flame, and the horseshoe in his left hand. Then he began to speak, this time in English:

> "Lord of the Night, of the Moon, the Stars,
> All-seeing Eye,
> Hear me.
> Great Lucifer, Beazelbuth,
> And all the fallen of the realm,
> Hear me.
> I command that you come here to this place
> And listen to me.
> Get this woman, Christine Tsitrian,
> And bring her to me,
> Drive her to me,
> Take her soul and give it to me.
> Lord of the Night, Great Lucifer,
> Do as I command
> Or I will curse you with angels
> And the eternal light of Heaven."

The man began to repeat the incantation, using some of the ashes from the burnt parchment to draw a cross over his heart. He placed the horseshoe and the candle flat on the floor and drew a piece of black cloth over them. Then he rose and, apparently lost in thought, left the room.

"I was waiting for her to appear," Rio said.

"She will. In time. A day, two days."

"Does he know her or is it someone he has merely seen?" Blake asked.

"He has met her, yes." Linda looked at Blake, her eyes unreadable in the dim candlelight. "You believe?"

"In witchcraft? No, I'm sorry, I don't. Look at his spell. He was intimidating Satan: Do this or I'll make you sorry! A very powerful Devil would hardly bow to a little chant like that."

"It has worked," Linda said.

"How many times? And how many times has it not? Do you follow the scientific method here, or do you just remember the winners? I'm sorry if I am insulting your beliefs, but you asked me."

Linda nodded. "People turn to magic during times of great uncertainty, when the importance of the individual seems to be slipping away and life becomes cheap. Surely life was never cheaper than now? Biblical Jews turned to Moses, who was a great sorcerer, to save them from the Egyptians. It is quite possible that early Christians believed that the magic of the Christ was greater than that of other magicians, Roman or Hebrew."

"But we will never know, will we?" Blake said.

"Perhaps," Linda conceded. "There are many paths." She turned and walked away. "Come."

As they circled the group of kneeling worshippers— who were now chanting something to the Lord God of the Heavens—Linda seemed to disappear into blackness. But Blake and Rio moved ahead and found a parting in the black curtains. They emerged into a hall-way hung with cryptic drawings and discovered her waiting by a door.

"This way," she said patiently, and they followed her.

The room was expensively decorated. *But it's likely no different,* Blake imagined, *than any of a hundred like it in the arcolog.* It was the study of a rich man, with no more evil touches than a stuffed Angora cat on a shelf. The music tape cassettes filled a huge rack and the wallscreen was tuned to a muted abstraction channel. There were comfortable chairs and subdued lighting.

The man who had been at the altar was now clad in

a dressing gown of a rich, velvety fabric. He looked up from selecting a music tape and smiled at Blake and Rio. "Ah, our distinguished visitors from the past!"

He came forward and took Blake's hand in a firm grip, and then bowed over Rio's hand in a curious way. As he smiled at her, Blake knew whose name was going to be on the next parchment.

"I am Constantine Dahomey." He made it sound as if the letters of his name were set in neon. "But perhaps you would like a drink? Something of your time, or perhaps something you might not have tasted? A nicola? Itano? Burgundy? Chablis? A brandy, perhaps?"

Rio asked for brandy and Blake agreed. As they sank gratefully into the comfortable furniture, Blake was struck by the swift transition he had made from a gladiator's barracks cell to a rich man's study. Then he smiled to himself. *Or from a nice comfortable job to a fugitive in one easy sleep.*

Linda disappeared and Constantine sat down, giving Blake a little time to study the big, strong, black-skinned man. He was attractive, powerfully built, and had an assurance that told of quiet arrogance. Blake had not liked him to begin with and nothing new had changed his mind. Constantine was obviously playing a game of his own, and everyone else was either pawn or opponent.

Settling into his chair, Constantine's eyes were on Rio, who seemed to be somewhat disconcerted by his attention. This struck Blake as odd, since she undoubtedly had been the target of hundreds of attractive men when she was with Voss. The possibility that she was attracted to Constantine occurred to Blake, and it made him edgy.

"I thought black masses and so on were conducted in the nude," he said, to divert Constantine's attention.

"We consider that both old-fashioned and rude," the black man said, not looking away from Rio. "One shouldn't appear naked before his god. We don't need to do that sort of thing anymore. Our magic is more sophisticated these days."

Before Blake could comment, Constantine struck the arm of his chair. "Enough of that! You must tell me of your adventures!" He spoke with enthusiasm, turning from Rio to Blake.

Reluctantly, Blake gave him a capsule version. Constantine kept interrupting to turn and ask Rio's feelings about each event, and his smile never wavered as he looked at her.

When Blake had finished, he said, "But what do they want of us, these People for a New Day? Where are they?"

Constantine waved a manicured hand. "We are the People, all that you have met are of the People for a New Day." He smiled again at Rio. "An uneasy alliance, yes, but an alliance nevertheless. We have plans for you. You will be useful."

"Pawns?" Rio asked.

"But no!" Constantine reached out and took her hands, looking into her eyes and still smiling. "Not pawns! *Catalysts*! One so beautiful would never be a pawn. A *queen*, yes, but not a pawn. No, never!"

Blake broke in. "Do you know of Jean-Michel Voss?"

For the first time, Constantine Dahomey stopped smiling. He looked narrowly at Blake. "Yes, I have heard of him. He was one of you, was he not?"

"Do you know where he is?" Rio asked.

"Not exactly, but generally. Why do you want to know?" His smile to Rio had returned, but with less voltage than before.

"He can help us. He is powerful and rich and . . . one of us."

Constantine shook his head. "I think not. Perhaps once. Jean-Michel Voss is now Special Adviser to the Grand Council of the Archangels of God the Triumphant."

Blake and Rio stared at him. "You mean, he's on the other side?" Rio asked.

Constantine nodded.

"Where is he?" Blake asked.

"At the Temple. The main temple, in San Diego. If you are looking for him to help, I'm afraid you might be disappointed. He issued a warrant for your arrest through the cooperating councils. Even those who fight among themselves will often cooperate in apprehending criminals of your type."

"Perhaps he is just trying to find us in order to help us," Rio said.

Constantine raised his brows. "I think not. The order has 'Shoot if resistance is given' written all over it."

"How do you know this much?" Blake asked.

Constantine's smile was broad. "I am district commander of the Seraphim of the Sanctified Host. Church cop, if you will."

"But—" Rio said.

"Yes, I know. But it makes a good cover, and I can help my people. The position also pays very well. You'd be surprised how many people prefer to pay a quite heavy tribute to avoid prosecution."

"Blackmail?" Blake asked.

Constantine looked puzzled. "I do not know the word. Some argot or sliptalk of your time? It does not matter. Well, you must be tired. May I show you to your rooms?"

Blake and Rio exchanged looks of longing. He nodded, resigned to accept the obviously strong taboos of this strange new society. *Someday!* he thought. *Someday!*

They exchanged a few words in the hall outside their rooms. "Jean-Michel was always a survivor," Rio said quietly.

"So are we. Maybe *he* picked the wrong side," Blake said.

"Maybe *we* did."

They sighed, and kissed, and parted.

Blake lay awake in his bed, thinking of Walter Robinson, of Venus, and of Constantine Dahomey, finding them much alike and neither of them much different from Voss. All three were powerful and arrogant, their contempt for others masked in politeness and distance. They were *users*. They all desired Rio—although Voss seemed willing enough to sacrifice her if doing so meant his own safety.

Only the elderly pope had been different, much different from Blake's conventional concept of a Holy Father. *Urban is an outlaw—as many popes have* been—but Robinson and Dahomey are not. *They are secure behind their money and position. Then why are they involved with illegal and revolutionary movements? More Power? More wealth? Voss has found a niche of safety and perhaps power, probably buying it with his hidden wealth and securing it with his devious mind.*

Blake turned restlessly in the bed. *Three hundred years to go. Perhaps four hundred. Surely no underground can shuttle us safely back and forth for that long, no matter what sort of symbols we are.* All the semi-immortality that he and Rio had achieved now seemed to be more of a burden than a prize.

How long can such a restrictive society last? Blake wondered. He thought with gloom of the thirty- and forty-year reigns of difficult kings and vengeful popes, of the dynasties of China, of the dictatorships and presidents-for-life, of the hundred-year dominance of elitists in what was now New America. *Even Napoleon and Hitler ruled for a decade and a half. But no one man caused an empire to exist, and no one man can cause it to fall. And there is now no one despotic king to battle in mortal combat,* he thought. *No single master computer, no cabal to outwit, and bring this monolithic society to ruins. Only the people can change it, not some fortune hunter, some freebooter or fugitive from a cryogenic time machine.*

Blake thought that he and Rio might do better than blindly follow the secret plans of the New Day people. *What if they are bungling amateurs or head-in-the-sand types like Venus, who live to play at revolt? Suppose their plan is to make us dead martyrs? Causes love martyrs—they always have, they probably always will. The early Christians had them; Hitler had Horst Wessel; all the undergrounds have had their dead heroes to whip up enthusiasms for dangerous games.*

Blake turned over again, punching up his pillow. *Why don't we just head for the Sierras, or the Superstitions, or back up to the Rockies? We could find or build a cabin, and just live out our lives in the snow and summer grass, away from everyone, away from corruptions of religion, away from the crazies—far, far away?*

The memory of Neva and Bennett came back to him. Marta, Rob, Kapuki, Narmada, and all the others came back to haunt him. *Damn it, where is Granville? What have they done to Doreen in revenge? Is Voss going to think only of himself?* Frustration fed the rage in him. *Who did those religious bastards think they were, condemning us to death?* The terrible, painful, humiliating public execution they had planned for Rio in the Arena was vivid in Blake's memory. *They do not deserve their power,* he thought angrily. *They do not deserve the name "religion."*

In that moment Blake's resolve was forged: *Destroy them. Destroy them before they destroy us. Destroy them—or die trying.*

Sleep came hard, and Blake's bed was lonely.

□

Constantine had left them at breakfast, saying the condo was theirs, but suggested they stay inside. "Tonight the leaders will meet and we will decide how best to utilize you."

"Will we be there?" Rio asked.

Constantine shook his head. "That won't be necessary. There are some you should not know, so you could not inadvertently betray them."

He left, smiling, and Rio and Blake looked at each other. "Big Brother knows best," Rio said.

They looked over the big condo and found the room that had been filled with witches and warlocks was bright and sunny, with one window opening toward the south. The black drapes turned out to be dark blue, were tied off in twos, making the room appear lavishly decorated, but not bizarre. The altar was now a bar, the shelves under the back filled with bottles bearing labels with which Blake was not familiar.

Blake and Rio settled into a couch and decided to find out more of their world by looking at television. The big wallscreen lit up and showed an expanse of ocean, deep purple and whitecapped, a vast plain of undulating water. Near the camera was a wide, low plankton skimmer, and the narrator was speaking of the majesty of the sea and the ripe harvests gained from it. On the horizon was the graceful and colorful shape of a sailship, the sun flashing off the metal vane sails set in ranks up three tall metal masts.

The camera now sank beneath the waves, and Rio and Blake saw the great suction mouths that drank in the seawater, pumping it through the filters, extracting the plankton and other forms of food. The camera dropped further into the sea, and a small submarine passed by. They could see a fat cargo sub in the murky distance, then another cruising closer. The first dome tops began to appear at a hundred fathoms, and more circling subs of various sizes. The camera passed over the domes, looking down, then curved around and passed by on one side of the cluster. The narrator spoke in reverent tones about the bravery of the aquanauts that had established this research station so deep in the ocean.

Blake and Rio could see through some thick ports at the interior of the domes. Men and women were at work and robots loaded cargo subs. The narrator launched into a long, boring speech about life under the sea. Rio changed the channel.

A church service was in progress in a vast cathedral of crystal and chrome, a glittering temple of reflections and light. A woman in a richly ornamented robe was raising high a jeweled cross, and Blake noticed that the bottom arm of the cross was pointed and sharpened, like a short, thick sword.

"Enough of that," he said, and pressed another stud.

The screen showed a slow camera pan around the Grand Hall—that magnificent, cryptic ruin on Mars. It was near sunset and the weak, red light brought out the worn nature of the stones, the carvings on the walls blurred by more than two hundred centuries of blowing sand. "Christ walked upon these sands in the years before his ministry, reading the ancient writings and contemplating his glorious future," the narrator said unctuously. "All the mysteries of the ancient Martians were revealed to our Lord and—"

Blake cut the sound and made a rude noise. "They have yet to decipher anything because nothing readable is left!"

The screen now cut to the incredible Star Palace—that mountain-sized mass of organic crystals arranged in tiers, balconies, caves, passages, domes, spires, and a million other beautiful shapes.

Blake cut the sound back in.

"— here in the Crypt of the Holy Virgin Mother, she lay for seven times seven years before ascending to Heaven. No resting place on Earth was sufficiently—"

"Do-it-yourself religion," Blake muttered as he changed channels.

The next channel was showing a commercial for Freezedri Foods: "The best in the western parishes!" This was followed by another commercial for an arcolog called *Kaniel* on the Adriatic Sea. One of the features stressed was a temple on every floor. Then the screen switched to a nighttime view of a Circus arena. "Welcome back to the highlights of last night's games at Augustus Arena in Florence, Italy. This is Chick Porter at arena side." The screen cut from a high-angle shot showing the thousands of spectators to a ground-level camera. A man and two youths, possibly his sons, were in the center. A metal snake slithered in.

Blake cut the wallscreen off. After a long moment, he looked at Rio. "Death as entertainment. And they called *us* corrupt and decadent."

"People died in the Arena in our time, too," Rio reminded him.

"But it was more professional and . . ." He stopped. "But that was how the *first* Roman Games started, isn't it?" He got up and went to the window. "We shouldn't have come, any of us."

"But we did and we must make the best of it."

"I know, but . . ." He turned toward her. "When I saw you in the Arena I went crazy. I would have killed anyone to save you. When I think of the way they—!"

Rio rose and went to him, holding him close. "It will turn out all right," she said.

"Have faith? Trust in God?" Blake snorted.

"Yes," Rio said. "Maybe not the god they seem to revere around here, but some kind of god."

"I've never been one that was very religious," Blake said, smiling wryly. "I wasn't even interested enough to find out if I was an atheist or an agnostic."

"Or a believer?" Rio asked softly.

Blake was silent. After several moments, he said, "Yes . . . or a believer."

□

Constantine came home late, bringing Linda Muirwood with him. They were smiling. The black man instantly went to the bar and poured drinks all around of a potent dark liquid called St. Vitus.

He raised his glass and said, "A toast!"

Blake and Rio looked at Constantine warily.

"To what?" she asked.

"To victory! To the triumph of magic! To a new day!"

"I'll drink to some of that," Blake said, and did.

"Sit down," Linda suggested, her eyes sparkling. "Let us tell you what the leaders decided."

"Here it comes," Rio said softly.

Constantine paced back and forth, and his enthusiasm was infectious. "They were all there. Robinson, Urban, Craddock, Dr. Constance, Colonel Hope, the Abbess of St. Mary's, Brother Ziehm, even Judy Johnson from New America and Milliard from Canada. Some were on security null-circuits—but they were all there."

"What happened?" Rio asked impatiently.

"We have decided to attack!" He smiled widely and took a big swallow of his drink.

"And the honor is ours!" Linda Muirwood said. "*This* area, I mean.

"New Day's responsibility, of course, will be to cast spells, supply talismans, and make charms."

"Just what every revolution needs," Blake commented.

"And a revolution it is!" Constantine exclaimed. "What a day! What a day! And you, the two of you, will have the fantastic honor of leading the revolt!"

Blake looked at him for a long moment, then he glanced at Rio.

254

"Oh?" he said to Constantine. "How nice for us. Why don't you just cut our throats now, dump us off the ark, and claim the Swords did it. That will be just as good in the publicity line."

Constantine sighed, his smile dying slowly. "No," he said. "You must lead! You must be *seen* leading the revolt. We will put everything on tape until we seize Network A, when we'll put it on the air. From then on, the coverage will be live."

"And what will the forces of righteousness be doing while we are doing that? They have an *army*!" Blake exclaimed.

"But it is not a robot army, my dear Mason, not even in our ever so advanced time. It is an army composed of *humans*, men and women and even cyborgs who grew up in this society, who have seen what it does to people. One survey showed that 82 percent of the citizenry have had a relative or a friend get in trouble with church law. Forty-four percent have had someone they knew sent to the Circus. That's a lot of people. Up until now, they have not been united. There was just no common bond. Look at us! How could we, in good conscience, cooperate with the Roman church? They have persecuted us for over two thousand years! How could Venus expect the stricter disciplines to help *them* out? Even coalitions like the People for a New Day needed a focus, a catalyst. And you are it!"

Constantine spread his hands wide. "They were here, all of them—unhappy, discontent, angry, oppressed, and just waiting. *You* didn't create them, nor did I. The various churches did, by the way they did things, by their We-know-best-for-you attitude, by their arbitrariness, by their arrogance and corruption. We are the tinder, Blake Mason, and you are the flame!"

He smiled brightly at both Blake and Rio, but they did not seem to respond with the enthusiasm he wanted.

"What an adventure," Constantine continued. "What an incredible adventure! The anarchists are ready, naturally, and the Lutheran League, the First Amendmenters, the Congressionalists, the outlawed political parties, the opportunists, the Order of St. Michael—"

"Who are they?" Rio asked. "They sound like one of those orders the other side has, the 'Swords' . . ."

"They're fighters who have been trained in secret by certain, um, interests. *Their* flaming swords are pretty powerful lasers. They were recruited from quite a few different factions, and are a rather motley collection. They sometimes call themselves a 'Foreign Legion,' whatever that means."

"How did they keep all their military preparations secret?"

"They didn't—at least not for too long. The first training group of the order was massacred by the Imps of Solomon the King. A portion of the second group of volunteers was hit by the Warriors of the Purest God, the fighting arm of the Eye of the Mystery of Eternal Life."

"Oh, god, those *names!*" Blake groaned.

"We have had our losses," Constantine said. "We have been betrayed, penetrated, killed, captured, pursued. But we could only exist if the people wanted us—not a majority, perhaps, but enough. We think an attack like this one will swing enough to our side to make the difference."

"You said 'attack.' That doesn't sound like a victory. A sacrifice, perhaps, but not an operation you think is going to win." He looked Constantine over carefully. "It's a diversion, isn't it? Something with a lot of splash and noise, with two dummies volunteering to be dead martyrs? No thank you! We won't play."

Constantine's ever-ready smile faded. He glanced at Linda, who bit her lip.

"That's too bad," he said quietly. "Then we *will* cut your throats and dump you, and you'll be dead martyrs without ever even being able to fight for a chance."

Blake's body became tense and his eyes bore into Constantine. "You'll lose a lot of troops trying this attack."

Constantine smiled faintly. "Yes, no doubt. But you help us more as dead martyrs than as live but invisible fugitives."

"Blake," Rio said, "I think he *would* kill us."

"Of course, I can think of many more pleasant alternatives," Constantine said, looking at Rio. "Many. But I have a higher duty."

"It's amazing," Blake said, "how many people excuse their crimes on the basis of political expediency and in the name of some god or other." He looked levelly at Constantine, whose mouth continued to smile but whose eyes had stopped.

"My dear Mason, we need not quarrel. We will give you every opportunity to succeed. We *want* you to succeed! We will give you some of the best fighters we have."

"Could I get the gladiators out of the San Francisco Circus?"

Constantine pursed his lips. "I don't know. That's a large order. However, we have the option of striking here, at the Forum or City Center, or in San Francisco. That was left up to us, organizers on tactical grounds. I *suppose* we could hit there, and recruit your precious gladiators. It might have a comforting publicity angle: Spartacus and his men, that sort of thing. They held the whole Roman army off for a couple of years, didn't they?"

"Several armies. But are you running a publicity campaign or a revolt?" Blake asked.

"Ah, my dear fellow, every revolution needs publicity! The common people must know what is happening and why, or at least they must know what we want them to know. That is why we are hitting Network A: if we plan it right, we will take over right at the top of the ratings, right at the height of the Centurion Classic, the year's biggest event. Millions will be watching! Lofflin estimates that close to *three billion people* will be watching! It is perfect for us!"

Constantine leaned closer to Blake. "That is why the man from the past and the woman out of time must appear, in person! You are symbols. Pete Fields is writing you a speech. Ted Tuckahoe is going to need a run-through, then he'll score it with some stirring music. Too bad we can't use Alpha projectors through the television. We'd have them screaming for blood in seconds!"

"Is that what you want, blood?" Rio asked.

"They won't give up and step aside because we ask, you know," Constantine answered. "There will be fighting, there will be dying. On both sides. If it takes blood to get us free, then, yes, I do want blood. But we must win. This is the biggest coordinated revolt in history. There's been nothing like it. It will be worldwide. Craddock, from *Dubeers Towers* in Capetown is in on it. Colonel Hope of the North American Defense Command. Dr. Constance over on *Novanoah,* Jack Barrow's group in *Empire Tower* back in Buffalo. Goldstone at *Nepenthe* up in Alaska. Willis is ready at *Castlekeep* in Devonshire, and Curlind in London, Berry and Hughes in Florida, Eric at *Cloudcastle* in Austria, Milliard from Toronto's *Diamondtowers.* Even some of the churches—yes, they have joined in. The smaller ones, of course, and some rather odd cults, too. We'll have a hell of a time getting things straight afterward, but first we must *win."*

"And you can't do it without us," Blake said dubiously.

"We can do it *better* with you. But they all know about you now, that's the important thing. If you died in the next half-hour it wouldn't stop the revolt. We'd just keep it quiet. We might use doubles. But it would be better if you were there."

Blake took a deep breath. He looked at Rio. "Can it be just *me*? No need for Rio to go. If . . . if I should fail, you'd still have her in reserve, for the next time."

"There won't be another time, at least not for a long, long time, Mason. Not for a *very* long time. If we try and fail, they'll hunt us down. They would have more evidence than before, more faces, more bodies, more lines of investigation. It might take fifty years to get another such force together: people would be too afraid. It would only consolidate the power of the churches if we tried and failed."

"It's now or never," Linda Muirwood said intensely. For a moment she looked more like the portrait in her office.

Blake sighed. "All right." He took Rio's hand. "The two of us. When does it happen?"

"Three days from now. Fields will have the speech in

the morning. Tape it, and we'll get a copy to the musicians. You'll do it live, of course, when the time comes, right from the Arena. That would be better than the studio, for the Circus is a symbol. People hearing our capture of it would be good symbology. Yes, you'll give the speech from the Arena."

Blake nodded, and squeezed Rio's hand. "I hope making a speech is *all* I have to do," he said.

Blake stepped off the escalator and joined the crowd of excited citizens heading toward the gates of the Caligula Arena.

His nearness to the huge structure again made him nervous and he was unable to resist checking the attitudes of the black-clad police who stood along the mall. There didn't seem to be any more than usual, although the usual number was quite large, due to the reactions the Arena crowd exhibited from time to time. Certain acts and certain types of acts were popular, some were not. Certain gladiators were in favor, others were not. The police often had to quell small riots with nerve-lashes, gas, and weighted batons.

The crowd was moving slowly but steadily. Blake was in no hurry. It was still half an hour before the opening parade. He mingled with one group of boisterous citizens and hoped to be accepted by them. Rio was somewhere behind him, with a pair of strong young warlocks supplied by Constantine. Linda was with Constantine, and they would make their entrance much later. The coven leader had separated Blake and Rio, and both were disguised to make them less conspicuous. Rio's long black hair was hidden under a fashionable hat, though a few strands peeked out. Blake wore a workingman's tunic with MARIN COUNTY RENTFORCE across the back. It was Blake's hope that any cop might think a second before he cut down a member of a brother franchised police force, even if he were only a janitor or mechanic.

"Say, I heard they're having a Black Prince go up against an Eisenhower today," a man at Blake's elbow said.

One of the others spoke up. "Naw, they stopped doing that ages ago, Miller, you ought ta know that." The man in front spoke back over his shoulder. "Them big companies got together and said it was bad for a Robotics to fight a General Animators. Bad image, y'know. Fight a human, much better."

"Yeah, but I used to like those fights. They were really somethin', y'know? Remember the Titans? That was a robot team, huh?"

"What I heard," said a man behind Blake, "was that there was going to be an execution today. You know, one of *them* kind."

Several men gave leering laughs, then looked around quickly. The man walking next to Blake said to the man behind, "Aw, now, Schroeder, you know we ain't supposed to take no pleasure in the righteous execution of no heretic. Serves 'em right, though, huh?" He swung an elbow into Blake's arm. "How about that, huh? Serves those scuzzy unbelievers right, huh?"

Blake nodded and made a small, rather sick grin. "What else is on today?"

"There's a race between the Greens and Blues today," the man behind said. "If Blanchard can keep her chariot on the track, that is." The men laughed at this. "There's the usual retiarii and secutors, the regional crashcar championships, some sweets ripping each other—you know."

"I heard they was bringing back old Kong," one of the other men said.

"No kidding? I thought they retired those big robbies as being too expensive to run. Except in the religious festivals and things. What about Bunyon, Zeus, Octobot, ol' Godzilla, that bunch?"

"Don't know. Just heard about ol' Kong. He's been de-mothballed down the peninsula someplace, I think. Anyway, that's the word I heard."

"They don't give us no shows like that no more, bless 'em," another man said.

They were still talking as they went through the ticket takers and on up into the Arena. Blake stayed with them, not so close that they would feel he was intruding, but close enough so that any casual police observation would include him in the garrulous group. He saw the television monitors up on poles and on the walls of the

passages through the Arena to the seats. They settled
into padded seats, and Blake saw that the dome sections
had been retracted so that they were open to the sky.
He could feel the salt air off the bay, even if he couldn't
see the water.

Blake looked around him cautiously, trying to spot
both police and the revolutionaries he knew by sight.
Police he saw, but not anyone else he knew. He then
concentrated on the Arena itself.

Blake had been in the Circus before, recently, but
now he had a whole new perspective. Sitting in the
stands, he saw the workings of the Arena in a whole
new light. The sand had been combed into an intricate
Ando design which he now realized was a secret good-
luck symbol. The huge doors at the "base" of the oval
ring had considerable activity around them, and Blake
looked at the smaller entrances to the Arena. The one
on the left was the one through which he had charged to
save Rio. The bishop's box was to Blake's left, and he
could see the minor officials arriving, preparing the
throne-like chairs for the archbishop's arrival. From this
angle he could also see several television screens around
the base of the box so that His Excellency could see the
close-ups.

A flair of trumpets sounded, and everyone came to
his feet. Blake saw the reason for the fanfare: a line of
robed figures had emerged from a private entrance and
went among waving citizens to the bishop's box. The
column was led by several high-ranking clergymen and
clergywomen. They were followed by the San Francisco
archbishop and two or three bishops, who blessed the
crowd to either side. The robes of their various clergy
identified them as members of two different sects, but
Blake was not interested in their political gestures. His
eyes found and held a single figure at the base of the
box, standing in rigid salute. Lieutenant Cady was
someone Blake was not likely to forget.

The prelates were soon in their seats and Blake saw
Cady speak into a communicator. Almost at once, another flurry of trumpets sounded and the gate on the left
rolled open, the first figures in the parade emerging. The
honor guard, in exact replicas of Praetorian Guard uni-

forms came out, flags flying, banners rippling, symbols glittering. These were followed by the honorary grand marshal (an aging vidstar) and then a troop of mixed retiarii and secutors. Blake tried to recognize faces in the troop of gladiators, but the distance and the helmets prevented him.

As the honor guard passed the bishop's box, they saluted and dipped their colors. The grand marshal gave a regal bow from atop his magnificent stallion. The officer leading the gladiators saluted smartly, then passed on.

Each unit that passed offered some sort of salute. The crashcars slammed their clawed waldoes into a straight-armed vertical salute. The slim, tanned group of wire walkers did flips and a bow before the box. Lumbering flamefighters in their stiff white protectors held the deadly flameguns over their heads with both hands. Graceful maidens riding animatronic centaurs waved as the metal beasts rose on their hind legs and shot flaming arrows into the air, which became colorful bursts of fireworks. Each group and type made its salute, and the parade curved around and disappeared into the far exit.

Blake noticed that Lieutenant Cady had disappeared, then spotted him near the private bishop's entrance, talking to someone. The officer moved slightly and Blake went rigid.

Voss!

The lean, saturnine man wore a severe black costume with a red Maltese cross on his left breast. Even in the plain uniform he had authority, and Cady was obviously being servile to him. Another officer joined them—a man of high rank—followed by several subordinates. Voss gestured them toward the bishop's box in a gracious invitational bow, and the men walked past and on up under the crimson awning.

Blake watched Voss narrowly as he spoke to several more subordinates, then walked briskly up the steps and disappeared among the exalted group.

Blake's anger tore at him. *Traitor! Turncoat! You abandoned us! You left Rio to die!* Only an effort of will prevented him from running down the steps and attacking Voss. He looked quickly around and caught a glimpse of Rio not far away. He watched until her searching eyes found him, and they smiled, briefly.

More trumpets sounded the beginning of the games, and at once ports opened and two armored tanks thundered at each other. Their treads tore up the carefully combed sand in roostertail spurts and the sun glinted brightly from the long lances that protruded from their steel noses. Both lances caromed off the tanks' sleek sides; one lance bent and the other broke. The tanks screamed with protesting metal as they spun into turns. The broken lance was ejected with a click, falling and rolling to the side. The other tank kept its lance, the turret swinging sideways as they charged at each other again. The first tank sprayed out a thick white fluid from the lance socket, covering the other tank in an instant. But the sidewise swipe of the other's bent lance struck the turret of the spewing tank and knocked it off course. Fluid extruded from nozzles all over the wetted tank, washing away the white fluid, but the acid was already doing its work—eating away at the surfaces.

The acid-covered tank now ejected its bent lance with a click, and from the same port came another metal protuberance: the stubby snout of a flamethrower. The tanks spun again in the sand, maneuvering for position, and the acid-covered tank got behind the other one. A ragged bit of metal dropped off the flank of the charging tank, however, then another. The pieces lay steaming in the sand, slowing dissolving. But, the dying tank rammed into the rear of the other tank and, at the same moment, the object sticking out of the port spewed fire; waldoes popped up from concealed panels and seized the treads of the other tank and began to push it over.

Spumes of sand from racing treads hid the action for a moment, then the first tank toppled on its side. Instantly, the other's waldoes wrenched at a bottom access panel and ripped it loose. The flamethrower depressed and fired a long, fiery blast into the interior of the tank. But the acid-covered tank was dropping more and more bits as it started to back away. Nevertheless, it suddenly gave a jerk, lurched forward, and hit the overturned tank, which was burning furiously. It spun the flaming wreckage around and ran on jerkily for several meters, stopped, shuddered, and stood motionless as more bits and pieces fell off it.

"Why don't they get out?" Blake asked.

The man next to him gave him a disgusted look. "They're cyborgs, chief."

Blake sank into his seat. He stared with sick fascination at the biers of the entombed brains until the cleanup robots wheeled out and scooped them up. One robot sprayed flame retardant on the burning tank and the other cleanup machine gushed a neutralizer over the pitted tank. Smaller cleanup robbies snatched up the steaming pieces just ahead of a wide, low sandcomber. In seconds the arena was almost the same as it had been before. Only the faint odor of burnt metal, acid, and the acrid smell of burned flesh remained.

Blake was not certain that the odor of burned flesh was real. *It could be my imagination. A brain is not very much tissue to cremate,* he thought. *Not enough to spread the smell over this whole arena. I wouldn't put it past them to add a little scent now and again.*

The next act entered at once—a fast chariot race, followed by a traditional secutor and retiarius combat. Blake could not identify either gladiator.

He looked at the clock above the stone eagle on the memorial tower to the east. *Almost time. The strike force must be in position by now.*

Blake looked around for Constantine and Linda. They were still not in sight. He exchanged glances with Rio and saw her pale and worried.

Someone stepped in front of Blake and squeezed past him, then sat down next to him. Blake gave him a cursory glance and was startled.

"Hello," said Pope Urban, smiling. He was wearing a nondescript brown tunic and carrying what appeared to be a box lunch packaged by someone named Mother Lovinghands.

"What are you doing here?" Blake asked. He gave a quick look around, but no one was paying any attention. A troop of Amazonettes had marched onto the field.

"I wouldn't miss the Centurion Classic for anything,"

Urban said with a serene smile. He lifted the box lunch and let part of it rest on Blake's thigh.

It was heavier than any box lunch Blake had encountered. He looked up at the old man, whose smile widened.

Urban nodded and said, "I'll be doing penance the rest of my life for what I must do today."

Blake reached to feel the flat GE.2 laser stuck in his tunic pocket as he rechecked the immediate vicinity. "Get away," he said in a fierce whisper, "you're too old for this!"

"You are never too old to fight for liberty and religious freedom," the old man said. "Nor too young. Go on, top that."

Blake shook his head. "No. You are probably just as much a victim of the times as I am. We're both here because we really have no other place to go. But let me give you a tip: Don't stay close to me. I figure I've got to be a high-casualty-rate area, all by myself."

Urban smiled, and Blake felt his finger move against his thigh beneath the box lunch. The old man drew a cross on his leg, and his lips formed a silent "God bless you."

"How did you know I was here?" Blake asked.

The pope shrugged and pulled the box lunch back into his lap, closing his arms around it protectively. "I was told. They wanted me here, too, and some of the other leaders. I brought some of the cardinals, too."

Blake's eyes jerked across the crowd below. He ignored the noisy battle of the Amazonettes and the Daughters of Bilitis below as he sought to find a scarlet cape or skullcap. "Where?"

Urban IX, Bishop of Rome, Vicar of Christ on Earth, pointed at a nearby middle-aged fat man who looked drunk and who was cheering and booing enthusiastically. "His Eminence, Wesley Cardinal Parsons." Urban indicated a sour-faced man staring gloomily at the Arena. "His Eminence, Gregory Clement. And that underfed stork at the end of the third row down is Cardinal George Crowe of Boston. I've lost track of His Eminence Marcello Orsini, but he's around here somewhere."

Blake closed his eyes a moment and sighed. "All or nothing, huh?" He looked at Urban, who nodded.

The old man had ceased to smile, and he leaned closer to Blake to speak. "I deplore the blood that will be shed today. I have prayed over this for days, seeking guidance. But not to fight for freedom seems also a sin. It is very preplexing. Not all of my advisers feel the same as I do and I'm afraid the days when a pope's word was law are long gone." He pursed his lips, his eyes narrowing as he looked at the slaughter in the arena. "Perhaps that is best. Not every man in my position has made the best possible decisions every time." He smiled wanly. "The doctrine of infallibility put us in a corner, I'm afraid. Ah, Pius was a Ninth, just as I am. He confirmed that albatross in 1848. Paul the Sixth started the Second Great Schism, you know, with his bull on contraceptives, back in the twentieth; and Benedict the Sixteenth made it worse in the twenty-first." Urban stared at the bloodied sand below, but did not see it. "You inherit what you inherit, and you do your best."

They sat in silence for a few moments while the survivors were taken off. The sandcombers raced around, sucking up bloodied sand and spraying out fresh.

The old man looked at the clock on the tower at the end of the stadium. "It's almost time," he said.

Blake looked back at Rio, then at the bishop's box, where he saw Voss chatting amiably with a bishop and with a man in an expensively cut suit. His fingers crept toward the laser beneath his tunic.

A port in the Arena wall opened and a single girl in a simple white dress emerged. Something about her was familiar. Her head was down as she walked out into the center, her red hair bright against the beige sand.

The crowd stirred restlessly.

"What's this?" snarled a man near Blake. "Not one of them blessed cultural readings, I hope."

The lone figure stopped in the center of the arena. She did nothing for a moment, then she raised her head.

Doreen!

Blake looked quickly back at Rio and saw that she had recognized their fellow traveler in time. Rio looked at Blake with a plea in her eyes. Blake shot a glance at the clock. *Too soon to start now. Everyone's timing would be off.*

Suddenly there was screaming from high up in the stands, around the top rim of the stands. People were standing, pointing south and crying out. Many started to run down and some fell.

Blake stood, as did thousands of others. His hand was on his laser, and he looked frantically around for Constantine.

"Blessed Mother of God!" Urban said, and crossed himself.

His outlawed gesture went unseen as thousands of San Franciscans stared in horror at what appeared over the lip of the open air arena.

First it was a black, furry dome, then a thick brow ridge and beady bright eyes. Finally a black hand grasped the edge of the wall. Concrete broke as the monster heaved itself up.

"Kong!" the mob screamed.

The gorilla robot was almost eight stories high. It stood on the Arena wall on bowed legs—black, hairy, and an incredible symbol of primitive strength. It raised its long arms and beat on its chest in thunderous thumps as it screamed out a savage cry. People fainted and fell, others ran, some sat petrified.

"King Kong!"

Kong lumbered down, stepped over the wall and into the Arena floor, five meters below. Doreen stared at him and all life seemed drained from her.

The great robot ape's feet made deep depressions in the sand as he waddled toward her. He reached down and seemed about to touch her, then stopped. He bent closer, seemed to sniff at the solitary figure; then sniffed again, closer. Doreen was swaying on her feet.

Even if she knows the script, Blake thought, *the sight must be paralyzing!*

An idea came to him at that moment, and again he searched for Constantine in the excited, standing crowd. Some cheered now and the cries of fear had almost ceased, although some men and women were still sobbing from their initial shock. Individuals were starting to shout out suggestions.

"Eat her, Kong!"

"Step on her, she's a heretic. Step on her!"

"Pick her up!"

Blake looked back up the aisle and saw Constantine coming down. He stepped around two men and grabbed the leader of the witchcraft cult.

"Let's go now!" Blake said loudly, to carry above the din.

"Too early," Constantine shouted in his ear. He pointed at the clock.

Blake pulled him closer. "I know that girl out there! She came with us! I must save her!"

Constantine shook his head and tapped his wrist. "Not yet, not yet." He broke away from Blake, cut through the audience—now shrieking with excitement—and headed toward the bishop's box.

"Screw you!" Blake said and turned back to the pope. He grabbed the old man's thin arm. "We're going *now!*"

In the Arena, Kong had picked up Doreen, who was futilely fighting his grasp. The great beast stood and brought her close to his face to examine.

"We're too early," Urban protested.

"That's Doreen!" Blake shouted, pointing up at the eight-story robot's prisoner.

Blake ran down the aisle, twisting and turning around excited spectators. The guard at the base was facing the Arena, and Blake gave him a savage blow on the side of the neck. He squeezed between the spear-point fence guarding the edge, then leaped into the Arena.

The five-meter drop shook him up. He jumped from his ungraceful sprawl and raced across the sand.

Bring down the iron, Sergeant White always said. But bring it down without hurting Doreen.

Blake tugged his laser from beneath his tunic as he ran. He knew his small hand weapon was not powerful enough to slice the legs from the enormous robot, but he had to try something.

Hamstring it. Cut the motor wires. Bring it down!

Blake ran to the legs. He sprang back as one of the more than two-meter-long feet shifted. Oblivious to the cries of the mob in the stands, he leveled his weapon at the right ankle. He fired, but little happened, except for a small, smoldering fire that started in the thick fake fur.

Blake ran closer, aimed again, then stopped. The fire had burned away some of the imitation gorilla hide around the ankle, and Blake saw a hinge. *A door! An access panel to the robot's interior.*

He ran now to the foot and jumped up on the instep just as the sand bubbled and turned to steaming glass a few inches away. Another long gash appeared in the sand near Kong's foot and ran up into the side of the foot, where the great metal monster absorbed the energy of a laser being fired from the stands.

The foot lifted, carrying Blake several meters into the air. He clung to the fur as he sought to find the outline of the access panel. The foot came down, jarring him loose; but he caught on before the foot moved again. Just above his head the fur started smoking in a pinpoint patch, and he heard Kong's roar.

Sensor circuits, Blake thought as he groped wildly for the door. Seeing several figures running out from the Arena wall, he redoubled his search. Suddenly he felt a lump, and lifted a patch of thick black fur to grasp a handle. He turned it, and almost at once a door swung out. He scampered in, scraping his shins, and jerked the door closed behind him. He was in a tube about two meters in diameter, with a ladder up one side, and labeled access panels all around. Blake put his laser to the lock, held it on target as Kong's leg moved, and fused the door shut.

Next, he stuck his laser in his tunic and grasped the ladder, climbing as quickly as he could. He had to get to the control room, which he assumed was in either the head or the chest, and he had to get there quickly! He navigated the knee joint with more luck than skill, and then climbed steadily up the interior of Kong's thigh.

The pandemonium of the multitude was now muffled, but Blake could hear the squeak and thump of the ponderously moving robot clearly. He heard relays open and close and selsyn motors whine into usefulness; he smelled lubricating oil and heated metal. As he climbed, Blake kept looking up—and that saved his life. For as he neared the hip, he saw in the socket opening the flash of a green-clad arm and a hand briefly seizing a hold as Kong lurched.

Blake swung away from the ladder, holding on with only one hand and one foot, and pulled the laser from his tunic. The green-clad woman who stuck her closely-cropped head over the hipjoint opening had a big laser in her hand and was already pointing it down the ladder. Before she could correct for Blake's unexpected position, he fired.

The ruby beam sliced into the side of her face, through her brain, and nicked the upper edge of the opening. She fell limply across the opening, the laser dropping from her fingers and tumbling down the interior of the thigh with a metallic clatter.

Blake quickly ran up the last of the ladder rungs, his weapon at the ready, but he found no one else.

The ape's pelvic area was wide and empty, except for a heavy-duty fusion engine and many black boxes. Blake ran toward the ladder at the center of the space, which continued all the way up the torso. He peered up the ladder well suspiciously, waiting for another green-clad protector, but none appeared. Blake grabbed the laser in his teeth and started up the ladder, past some kind of big tanks and twin gyroscopes.

Poking his head up cautiously, he came onto another floor in what he guessed was the chest area. He had found the control room.

In the center was a clear-plastic inertial-guidance sphere, three meters in diameter, which rotated in gimbals to stay always level. A man stood on the rock-steady stable platform within the sphere. Sensors were attached to his arms, legs, and head. Before him was a big screen, and on it Blake could see Doreen clearly, as she was held by a giant black hand. On either side of the screen were smaller screens that showed different views of the ground around Kong's feet. Blake could see a small crowd of angry police trying to force the door in the leg. A man was bulling through the cops with a meter-long laser.

On another screen—evidently carrying a picture taken by some camera in the stands—Blake could see the full length of Kong. Looking at the man in the sphere, Blake saw that he was in the exact same position as Kong.

Blake approached the sphere and pointed his laser at the man. "Get us out of here. Don't drop the girl or you die."

The man did not move, only stared wide-eyed at the intruder. Blake raised the gun and pointed it at the man's face.

"Do as I say, or die. Then I'll attach the sensors and do it myself."

"Uh . . . I . . ." The man seemed frightened but his two weak syllables were translated into a booming Kong-voice.

Blake took a step closer, his weapon pointed right into the man's face. The controller of the huge robot nodded, and on the full-length screen Kong nodded.

Kong, at Blake's bidding, raised his foot, and several men fell from the instep. Blake turned a bit so he could watch the screen, but kept his gun on the man in the sphere. In the screen he saw Kong walking in a perfectly normal ape-like manner toward the spot in the Arena wall at which he had entered. The sphere remained balanced, but the man looked quite frightened. Then he jerked, twitching as if someone had stuck a pin in his back. He jerked again, and Blake saw that they were firing at Kong's back.

"Cut the sensor circuits!" Blake shouted to the man.

"Uh!" The man pointed at one control panel in a series around the outer circumference of the sphere, and on the full-length screen Kong pointed.

Blake ran around and found the panel labeled EX-TERIOR SKIN SENSORS and turned it off. The man nodded gratefully, then his eyes grew big.

Blake's gaze snapped to the big front screen. He had forgotten about the other part of the re-enactment of the King Kong legend. Fragile, rickety planes were coming in, zooming over the Circus, their guns blazing. Blake ducked, then realized he had neither heard nor felt any bullets strike.

Blanks, of course!

Blake got up from his defensive crouch. "Ignore them!" he called to the Kong-controller. "Keep going! Over the edge!"

Blake watched in the lurching control room as Kong climbed the Arena wall, and lumbered up the empty section of crushed seats. He heard the planes coming in again and saw the fear in Doreen's face.

"Hold her close to your chest!" he ordered. "But don't crush her, or you're a dead man!"

The planes flew past, guns noisily blasting Kong, who was now poised on the top edge of the stands. Blake saw the man trying to see his footing in the screen for the difficult task of getting down. Blake saw several crushed groundcars in a small parking lot, and a long section of wire fence that Kong had snagged earlier and dragged along.

Suddenly Kong roared, and Blake looked at the big screen. One of the planes was heading directly for them, and evidently one had just tried to ram the robot.

Blake cursed. *Robot ships!* "Get it!"

Kong's mighty hand struck out. The ship was half crushed and fell like a rock.

Another plane was coming in from the rear; Blake saw it on a screen. "Behind you!"

Kong turned, but not quickly. The plane struck its shoulder and Blake was thrown across the control room. He heard the plane falling down the outside of the gorilla-robot as he pulled himself erect.

"Put the girl down!" he yelled. "Gently! Put her down gently!"

He held on as the control room tilted and on the big screen he saw Kong put the redhead down on the upper tier of the seats. She started to run, fell, got up and ran again.

Blake turned his attention to the bishop's box. He could see that though most of the religious executives had left, several figures still stood amid the overturned chairs and discarded programs.

"There!" he shouted, pointing at the screen that had the image. "Step on them!"

The Kong-controller looked stricken. "But—but that's the—"

"*Step on them!*"

Kong lurched toward the raised VIP box just as Blake recognized one of the figures as Voss. "Get out of there!" he muttered to himself. Although he disliked Voss for joining the "enemy," he had not yet heard Jean-Michel's side of it. But he did not stop the immense Kong robot from crunching his way down toward the box.

A flicker of color stood out on the edge of the screen. It was Doreen, her dress in tatters, scrambling over seats and through clots of people now running for cover.

"She's going to Voss!" *No, no!* "Watch out, Doreen!"

Blake saw Voss catch sight of her and step away from the cringing remnants of the San Francisco archbishop's party. Deliberately, Voss raised a weapon and pointed it at Doreen. She froze. Voss ran to her, grabbing her arm and putting the laser to her head. Blake saw him look up at Kong, holding Doreen as he backed away.

As rage engulfed him, Blake shouted at the big screen. "You goddamn son of a bitch!" He turned to the frightened man controlling the hairy colossus. "Turn! Don't step on the box!"

The man looked grateful as he turned away from the seat of power. He teetered a moment, caught his balance, then started upward again.

"Now get those goddamn planes!"

Kong rose to full height and roared. Blake was surprised until he realized the controller was starting a well-rehearsed scene.

"Goddamm it, don't play with them, *get them!*" Blake screamed over the sound of the dive-bombing planes.

Kong roared again and a plane crunched, then exploded in his fist. On a side screen, Blake saw thousands of people trying to get out of the Arena. Police and revolutionists fought across the stands and the hundreds of still, broken figures. *Not Rio, please, not Rio . . .*

I'm trapped here, Blake thought. *If I leave him, this controller will tell them. If I stay, they'll get me.*

Blake moved close to the sphere, which rolled and rocked—or rather, it was Blake that rocked and the sphere stood level. "They'll kill you now, unless you kill them first," he said to the man. "Knock them down, then run like hell! You can always say I made you do it."

The man touched a button on a neckband and spoke. His voice did not now boom out as Kong's. "They'll kill me, anyway, just for not stopping you."

He looked sad, but Blake shrugged. "Sorry, but I'm not just a troublemaker, really."

"I know who you are." The man stopped talking to make a futile swipe at another plane. "This beast won't hold together much longer, but . . . go do what you have to. I'll get the rest of these bugs and lead them off."

Blake looked at him. The only thing that came to mind was the old cliché "Go on without me, it's only a flesh wound."

Blake waved at the nameless controller and ducked down the ladder. He was banged up as the great robot lurched about, but he made it to the right leg and scampered down the ladder. At the bottom he saw a communicator inside the door. He snatched up the mike and said, "Put your right foot near the bishop's box and hold it there for ten seconds. That's all I ask. And good luck!"

Blake dropped the mike and braced himself for the bone-crushing thump of the huge leg. After a few moments, the foot came down with a teeth-smashing slam and Blake fused open the door and leaped out. He dived off the foot and rolled as they had taught him, but came up hard against a fastened-down seat.

There was noise and confusion everywhere. The bishop's tented box was in ruins, even one side of the laser-proof glass that had risen swiftly at the first signs of trouble was smashed in. Inside were several bodies and one gibbering man in robes embroidered to depict an atomic explosion.

Blake looked around for Voss or Doreen, but found

no sign of them. Most of the bishops, clergy, and police had gone, leaving only bodies and wreckage.

A man, his face splattered with blood, came up to Blake and tugged at his tunic. With difficulty Blake recognized him as one of the outlawed cardinals Urban had pointed out. "Oh, it's terrible, it's terrible!" he moaned.

"Where's Rio? Where is Doreen?" Blake realized the man was half out of his mind. "Where's Urban?"

The cardinal crossed himself and pointed. A cluster of people surrounded several bodies sprawled between the rows of seats. Blake ran over and saw that Urban lay in a pool of his own blood. His lunch box and shattered laser was close by two of the bodies, which were brutal-faced police. The old man's head lay in Rio's lap. Blake looked at her and she shook her head.

"Mason . . ." Urban acknowledged his presence with a weak smile, "God . . . bless you, Blake Mason!" A bloodied hand tried to make the sign of the cross, but it was too weak. "Have we won?"

Blake looked around. It looked more like a riot than a victory, but he could see fresh police arriving by an entrance on the far side. Kong had gone over the wall and there was the sound of falling wreckage and screams coming from that direction.

"I don't think so," Blake said, "but we've hurt them."

"That's . . . not enough. We must *win*. George . . . George?"

One of the men kneeling at Urban's side took his hand. "Yes, Your Holiness?"

"We must win this one. You are too old, George. We are . . . we are all too old now. The leader must be young . . . and strong. He . . . may have to fight for years."

"Don't try to talk, Your Holiness," the cardinal said.

The old man smiled bleakly. "I must. I don't . . . have much time." He looked at Blake. "You. You . . . are the one. You must become pope."

Several people gasped, and Cardinal Crowe made a sound of protest.

"I'm not even a Catholic, Father . . . uh, Your Holiness."

"You are . . . the one. You have the strength. The people will . . . follow you as they would never follow me. My time is passed . . ."

"Your Holiness, uh, I have a woman . . ." Blake and Rio exchanged looks and she smiled faintly.

The dying old man smiled again, weariness heavy on his features. "You . . . you would not be the first. Those Borgias, those Medicis . . . Oh, what a trial they put upon us! But that . . . doesn't matter now. Later . . . later . . . you can resign, when this is over . . ."

"Holy Father, do not strain yourself," Rio said.

"You must do it." The old man reached out and grasped Blake's sleeve. "You *must*. Lead them . . . my son. They . . . are afraid."

"What do you think *I* am, Father?" Blake said. "I'm scared to death!"

"But you always do what . . . you must, even though you are frightened. You . . . are the one—" The old man fell back, gasping. After a moment, he opened his eyes and looked at the circle around him. "He must be . . . the new pope. Do you see why . . . you must elect him?"

Several men nodded, but more looked at Blake with suspicion and fear.

"I'm not a Catholic, I don't know the rules, I don't know anything about your church!"

"You . . . you don't have to . . . to know how to do anything . . . but win." The old man looked again at those surrounding him. "You must. He . . ." His gaze shifted and he stopped speaking. A smile began, and he died in the middle of forming it.

Finish it in Heaven, Blake thought, and rose.

"Wait!" Cardinal Crowe said. He rose and pulled Blake away from the others. "You must do it! You know you must."

Blake looked down at the fragile body of the old man, and at Rio's bowed head. They were praying over him, fingering hidden rosaries and muttering prayers unheard a few feet away.

Blake looked around, hoping their forbidden practices were unseen, but he only saw the confusion of the

Arena. Many small groups clustered around broken bodies.

"Why should I?" Blake said. "Because he asked me? Don't be silly. I don't owe him anything. He was a nice old man, but——"

"Not for him," the skinny cardinal said, "but because he was right. You *can* lead us." He waved his hand around the ruined Arena. "All these people have heard of you, many believe in you, believe that you are a cleansing force sent to us. They fought today, here and all over the world—did you know that?—because of you. Some died because of you."

"They didn't fight because of *me*, they fought because of themselves, their families, their beliefs, their desire for freedom. Don't sentimentalize it, *padre*. I am just a convenient figurehead. Dead or alive, it doesn't make any difference. I was a convenient nonpartisan whom all sides could agree on without losing face."

Blake stepped closer and grabbed the cardinal's tunic. "Listen, no one does anything except in his own self-interest. If people fought today, if people died today, it was because they thought they were doing the right thing. That goes for both sides. The moment one side thinks it is not doing right, they quit, they change. Even the baddies think they are doing what is right for them; they either don't think they are doing anything wrong, or they justify it to themselves as necessary to their survival, or survival of the status quo. People kill to survive. Though sometimes that survival is only for their image of themselves, and not for their actual physical survival."

"Is that why you went to the rescue of the girl in the ring?" the cardinal asked.

Blake hesitated. "No. We came here together. She was . . . helpless. Someone had to do something."

"Was risking your life something you did in your own self-interest?" The cardinal was smiling now, a faint, knowing smile that annoyed Blake.

"I—I don't know. I had to do it, that's all."

"You have to do this, too. You must do it because you know it will help."

"I'll resign as soon as this is over," Blake said.

The cardinal smiled slightly and said, "You must be elected by the College of Cardinals, my son. The office of the Holy Father is not given out like some political plum. But, in the interests of the Church and of God, I think we will agree to your leadership."

"My figureheadship, you mean," Blake grumbled.

"We can work out the legalities and precedents later. If there *is* a later."

"Pessimist," Blake said with a smile.

"We are all in God's hands, my son." He pulled away from Blake, and was suddenly all business. He spoke to the men praying around the dead body of Urban. They gathered up the remains and headed for the exit.

Rio came to Blake's side. "He was a nice, brave old man," she said.

Blake nodded, looking around. The Arena had taken on a new feeling. Police aircars were overhead, and loudspeakers were ordering everyone to leave the Arena in an orderly manner.

Blake took Rio's hand and started running for the concrete passage that would take them out, following the cardinals and the other men. Partway down the passage, one of the cardinals opened a service door and they went into a drab concrete corridor, down several stairs, through some unused storage rooms, sprinted across a public hall filled with crying, nervous citizens, and into a maze of more passages. They halted at last in a storeroom, and several people began to prepare Urban's body.

Cardinal Crowe came up to Blake. "We will do it now."

"Here?"

"Here. We know these passages well." He smiled. "The catacombs of our time," he said. "What name will you take?"

"What?"

"Your name? The name you will use during your reign as pope."

"I hadn't thought about it. What's wrong with Blake?" Before the cardinal could answer, Blake shook his head. "You're right. Pope Blake just doesn't sound right."

"May I suggest something?" Rio said. "Pope Urban was well known as a fighter for liberty, wasn't he?" Cardinal Crowe nodded emphatically. "Why not use his name? He was the Ninth, you could be the Tenth."

"I still don't believe all this," Blake said, squeezing Rio's hand. "All right, fine. So I'm Urban the Tenth. That's X, isn't it?" The cardinal nodded, and Blake grinned. "Urban the X, the first X-rated pope. Urban and his band of merry outlaws! All right, let's get on with it."

To Rio, Blake said, "Voss used Doreen to keep me from getting to the bishops. I don't know where he is, but it sure as hell isn't our side. See if you can find out if he dumped her someplace. I think he went into the passage that all of the clergy used."

Rio's face grew dark and angry. "I'll find her."

"Watch yourself. I don't think Voss is playing around." As Rio started to go, he added, "And find out where the hell our magical friend Constantine is."

As Rio went through the door, Blake shouted after her. "Don't try to take Voss yourself!" Several faces tightened at the sound of the name.

"Voss is the one who ordered those men to kill His Holiness," one of them said.

"Are you with Constantine Dahomey?" one of the others asked Blake, who nodded.

More faces grew taut and two men crossed themselves.

Blake turned to Cardinal Crowe. "Tell me what to do."

"God will do that, Your Holiness."

"Don't count on it. He might not be as happy with your new pope as you are. We've never been on very good speaking terms."

The cardinal smiled softly. "He's heard you even when you didn't speak."

Blake made a face. "Don't say 'God works in mysterious ways,' for God's sake."

"You are certainly evidence of that," the older man said.

"All right, let's get this over with."

□

Rio re-entered the concrete storeroom followed by Constantine.

"Where were you?" Blake asked him.

The head of the witchcraft cult stopped, causing Linda Muirwood and several others behind him to bump together. The big black man looked over the group, his eyes not missing the wrapped form of the dead pope and the several men kneeling in prayer around it.

"I was doing what I was supposed to do—cast spells."

Blake made a growling sound. "Spells! We needed swords and lasers, not spells."

Constantine's smile was slow and his face formed an expression of tired superiority. "Perhaps our magic did more than your swords, my friend."

"His Holiness wanted to know—" began Cardinal Parsons.

"His Holiness?" Constantine's expression changed to one of mild surprise and disbelief.

"Yes," Blake said curtly, somewhat embarrassed by the title and the terms of address. "I am pope." He ignored Linda's quick arcane gesture of protection. "We must rally at once and strike again."

"Pope?" Constantine said softly, his eyes narrowing and his body becoming more tense. "Pope Blake."

"Urban the Tenth. Now what is the situation? What have you seen?"

Constantine moved into the room in his long black cloak. His followers filled the doorway and stood warily inside. "There is rebellion everywhere, or almost everywhere. No country—not even this one—has enough police to put down a really popular revolt. The only time revolts fail is when they don't have enough popular support, or their leaders are betrayed, or—and this is the greatest cause—when they don't have weapons, or when the opposition has more weapons and greater skills."

"Thank you for the lecture, Constantine," Blake said, "but what is the situation?"

"Revolt, my holy friend, revolt! The Tiberian Arena in Verona and the Darius in Baghdad are just starting the night games and things are happening. But already the Garibaldi in Milan, the Hadrian in Venice, and the Marcus Aurelius in Palermo are in our control. They beat us in Tehran, at Theodora's Circus in Istanbul, and at the Circus of Constantine the Great in Turkey."

"What about here?" Blake asked.

Constantine smiled. "Nero, down in L.A., is ours. The Romulus in New York is still undecided. We are winning all around in the Jim Bowie in Dallas, and in Houston they blew up the whole damn Alamo Arena. We have the Borgia in Atlanta, but I've lost contact with Detroit."

Linda spoke up. "They broke out of the Horatio Nelson Marine Arena in Liverpool in amphibious tanks and are raising hell there."

"Do you know anything about Plaza Montezuma in Mexico City?" Cardinal Crowe asked. "My brother is the chaplain there."

Linda shook her head. "Things are so mixed up. Things are happening so fast—"

"Where are we losing?" Blake demanded.

"The Custer in Chicago. They nerve-gassed the whole Arena. The Hannibal in Naples is a complete wreck. The King Feisal in Mecca was lasered to rubble by the army—people, Prince Hassim, and all. But I have hopes for the MacArthur Arena in Manila. We have some good people there."

"But the people are all *bottled up* in the arenas," Blake said. "Get them out, get them into the streets, up in the arks knocking out the police, capturing the television stations, moving—!"

"It is happening where people are allowed to concentrate, you know that," Constantine admonished. "We *have* captured the majority of stations, but we get cut off, too. That's why we have to get the network here, if it isn't too late."

"I saw them setting up some big fuckin' lasers, all around the studio," one of the men behind Constantine said. "That one is going to be a bitch to take."

"Isn't there some way we can negotiate?" Cardinal Crowe asked.

Both Blake and Constantine gave him disgusted looks.

"I think that time is past," Constantine said. "We tried for years, but they just kept arresting the negotiators." He pulled a laser from his cloak and held it up. "This is what will give us liberty!"

Blake put his hand on the cardinal's shoulder. "Every generation fights for its own liberty in its own way. I'm afraid this is the only way left to us. Those in power never give up easily. They never have, they probably never will."

Blake now looked at Rio. "Doreen?"

"No trace. One woman said she saw them leaving the Arena together, but was not sure where they were going."

Constantine said, "Your friend Franklin is all right, by the way."

"Granville?" Rio said eagerly. "Where is he?"

"He was recruited by a Mensa cell just after you were arrested. When your friend Voss started working with the bishops, Franklin went underground."

"Voss is working with the churches?" Rio asked, her face sad.

"Went right up into the hierarchy. Birds of a feather, I should say. He is probably holing up with the archbishop at Riot Central."

"Where's Granville now?" Blake asked.

Constantine grinned wickedly. "He has been working on Operation Sword, for the Order of St. Michael, to drive the wicked from the Garden of Eden. It's a strike plan to hit Riot Central."

"Why didn't you tell us Granville was working with us?" Rio asked.

"You had no need to know, my dark-haired wench. The Mensa cell went to considerable trouble to make it look as if your friend Franklin had been dropped in the chute to the torch."

"Why?" Blake looked surprised.

"Because your friend Voss had him on the 'Shoot on sight' list, that's why. But these old arks have a lot of warrens the blackshirts don't know about. He was well hidden."

"Thank God!" Rio said, and Constantine arched an eyebrow at her.

"First things first," Blake said. "We must secure the whole network operation." He gestured to Rio, Constantine, and Linda. "Let's go look at this network studio."

A few minutes later the four crouched behind a pile of concrete rubble, a result of one of Kong's giant footsteps.

The network roof had been broken and Blake could see the sky. Columns of smoke rose here and there, and quite a few military aircars were flying around. The mall before the network was filled with dead bodies, trash, a crying child, rubble, and, at the end, a barricade of unbreakable metal mirrors.

Constantine swore. "Those damn mirrors will turn a laser, at least *these* lasers. But see those muzzles? Those are .5 GE Jupiters. Probably tied into the main circuit, too, or at least into the station's emergency fusion engine. They can outshoot us and outwit us, both. And the soldiers must be on their way by now."

Blake and Constantine turned to sit down below the edge of the rubble.

"If we could have hit fast enough . . . Damn . . . !" Constantine's face was angry and brutal-looking as he pondered the problem. "I'm not certain a curse would work under these conditions," he said.

"GE Jupiters," Blake mused. "Jupiter. Zeus. Isn't there another one of those big monster robots like the Kong—a Zeus?"

"Yes, there used to be. They haven't used any of those things for several years. Scared the hell out of people and used to cause more damage than they were worth in production value." He stopped talking and looked at Blake. "I'll be damned . . ."

"Yes, you probably will. Where are those things now? There were others, the . . . uh . . ."

"The Octobot; a big cowboy one; some kind of legendary dinosaur; a big ape—Kong, they called him— and Zeus. There were *several* dinosaurs, though, and some big snakes. Symbols of evil they called them— which shows you how people really know about symbology . . . or evil . . . or opposing forces." Constantine sneered and shook his head in disgust. "But let me see, where were they put?" His face brightened and he sat up, grabbing at Blake's arm. "*Here!* There's a dinosaur here, in San Francisco!"

"Where? The dinosaur must be Godzilla."

"Let's see . . . They were going to have the ape and the dinosaur fight and wreck the old Oakland Bay Bridge; but before they could get all the clearances, some church official committed suicide by ramming an airbus into it. Zongos had been doing that for years; they used to jump off, too. But after they closed it and built cheap condominiums across it, that stopped."

"Never mind that. What happened to Godzilla, the dinosaur robot?"

"They were going to have the fight, anyway, out in the Bay; but about that time some Indian magnabot, Kali, I think, dumped on the Siva Arena in Bombay. Killing a few thousand Indians was no big thing, but the American ambassador and some church people got wiped out. So they called off the fight here, tore down what was left of the bridge; and that was pretty much the end of the big robots. That was what was such a big surprise when the ape appeared."

The warlock pursed his lips and shut his eyes. "Let me think. I seem to remember they stored him in some warehouse along the Bay. I seem to remember a picture of the two of them standing in a big warehouse somewhere in . . . South San Francisco!" Constantine opened his eyes. "Yes, I think I know where that is. Right between *St. Thomas* and *Iconium,* yes, that's it. They store a huge Christ there, too, something they use in religious parades, and some rather big angels that they fly around hung from aircars."

"Let's go get the damn thing and stomp this town down!" Blake said.

"Is that the way a pope should talk?" Rio grinned.

"That's the way *this* pope talks. Come on!"

"A pagan pope, that's what you are, a pagan pope." She shook her head.

They started running back the way they had come, and Blake's heart was pounding.

They paused long enough to give orders that the various factions continue the fighting, whenever possible, in the streets and throughout the arcologs. Constantine sent Linda off to meet with their coven and continue the spell-making, then he guided Blake and Rio down the passage that lead to the heliport at the south side of the Arena.

A sudden shout was heard, and the sound of pounding feet. Then a mob of bloodied men and women came out of a side passage waving weapons. Some of them wore full gladiator armor, others had only bits and pieces, and some were in motley civilian clothing. The man in front threw up his muscular arm in a sudden, violent gesture, waving his sword and giving a fierce shout of joy and recognition.

"Blake!"

Through the blood and dirt on his face Blake recognized Bennett, his fellow gladiator. Marta and Kapuki ran forward, too, and they all embraced.

"How did you get free?" Blake asked.

"A member of the cell assigned to freeing us slipped us a laser as we were coming out of the Arena yesterday. We started cutting our way out when we heard the fun starting," Bennett said.

Blake looked around at the group of twenty or so gladiators and others. Some he recognized as being in his training group and others he did not know. "Where's Neva? Rob? Where's—"

"Dead," Marta said. "Rob and Narmada got it two days ago, going up against an old Madman modification. Neva . . . was hit an hour ago."

Blake held Marta close.

Kapuki said fiercely, "But Sergeant White got the sons of bitches that did it!"

Blake looked up from Marta's hair. "What?"

"Sergeant White jumped right in there and got every one of those bastards," the slim oriental girl snapped.

"*Sergeant White?*"

Bennett nodded. "Once the fun started, he joined us. If he hadn't, I don't think we would have gotten out of the cells."

"Where is he?" Blake asked.

"Come on, Blake," Constantine urged.

"He got hit just a few minutes ago," Marta said. "Back there. He was leading, and . . . we came up against some blackshirts with heavy lasers."

"*Blake!*" Constantine tugged at his arm.

"Rio, this is the bunch of fumble-footed zongos I was training with. Look, you children of fate, Rio and Constantine and I have something to do. I can't take any more time to explain, but I need your help and it's important."

Bennett grinned through the blood on his face as he turned to the others. "Come on, you zongos, let's get this revolution on the road!"

□

Constantine set the stolen Department of Recreation aircar down next to a large warehouse close to the water's edge. Two massive arcologs rose close by, putting the warehouse in shadows. Between the two arks and off to the north, toward the city, the buildings became larger and larger, filling in all the spaces between the arcological structures, but here most of the buildings were only five or six stories high. The ten-story warehouse was the biggest structure in the immediate vicinity and had a wide ramp up from the Bay.

"They must bring them in on barges," Kapuki said.

"No guards," Bennett said, fingering the laser they had taken from a dead policeman.

"Electronic alarms, surely," Constantine warned.

"The blackshirt cops would be too busy right now," Blake said.

The group spread out, lasers and arena swords at the ready. The warehouse door was huge, almost as high as the building and twenty meters wide, but next to it was a smaller door. They lasered this one open. Ignoring the alarms that rang furiously, they cut their way through two additional doors and into the huge main room.

"My God!" Marta said.

"In a sense, yes," Blake said, looking at the massive Christ figure.

Three figures stood in the room. The largest was the twenty-seven-meter Godzilla, a huge mythological beast that looked vaguely like a *Tyrannosaurus rex* but with spines. It stood with open jaws, its face enclosed by a safety grid that was part of a ceiling-hung service device. A massive arm had been detached and lay on the floor, partly dismantled.

"Goddamn!" Constantine groaned. "It's not working."

288

"Maybe we can fix it," Rio said as they crossed the big room.

"No time," Bennett said. "What about that one?" He pointed to the smallest of the three figures, a seventeen-meter Japanese samurai warrior.

"Yeah," said Kapuki eagerly.

They looked toward Blake and found him gazing with a bemused expression at the third figure, standing by itself past the spot where Kong must have stood. The twenty-meter Christ was very realistic, wearing a white floor-length tunic and a deep-red robe. It had shoulder-length medium-brown hair, a short but full beard, and was the epitome of the Anglo-Saxon Christ—blue-eyed and fair, with serene features and delicate hands. They had all followed Blake's gaze.

"Oh, no!" Constantine said.

"You can't fight with that," Kapuki insisted.

"It would be blasphemous ..." Bennett said, "I think."

"It only took two to run Kong," Blake said. "We could use both."

Kapuki was running toward the samurai. Before the rest got there, she had opened the greave shinplate to reveal the passage upward, and had disappeared into the samurai's leg. Bennett jumped in after her and climbed the ladder.

"Better get back," Constantine said. "These are likely to be a little awkward at first."

"Do they know how to run it?" Blake asked.

"Everyone does. These huge robots were very popular at one time and they ran lots of vidspecials on them. I wish we had the Octobot, though. That was a terror—eight arms, all kinds of weapons as standard, about forty meters high."

Blake looked up at the big, fierce-looking samurai. "Pageant. Bread and circuses. Shows and executions presented as entertainment. Manufactured excitement. Kill a pagan for Christ!" He shook his head. "I'll never understand human beings. Or gods, for that matter."

Constantine spoke softly. "You'll make a wonderful pope, I can see that."

"That's only for—"

A screech interrupted Blake, and one arm of the samurai jerked upward. Unfortunately, it was the arm that held the eight-meter sword. The weapon slashed into and through the roof. Bits and pieces of metal and roofing material showered down upon Blake, Rio, Marta, and Constantine, who ducked away hurriedly.

"Sorry," boomed the samurai. His other arm moved more smoothly; then the sword was pulled from the roof with a loud, ripping sound.

"Get back against the wall, all of you," Blake ordered.

The samurai suddenly made a short hop out into the center of the cleared space. It made a loud growl and the sword swept across the air two meters over the heads of the crouching revolutionaries.

"Hey!" Marta shouted. "Watch it!"

The samurai stopped moving, and its voice boomed out. "I've got it licked," said Kapuki. "I just need a little practice."

"Not in here!" Blake shouted up at her.

"I'll get the door," Rio said.

"Don't do anything in here!" Constantine shouted.

"All right. But hurry up!" Kapuki boomed. "I'm anxious."

The door moved aside with a rumbling like thunder and Kapuki guided the samurai carefully outside. Almost at once, Blake heard her using her sword, cutting slashes into walls and severing a few poles.

Blake and Constantine ducked under the hanging robe of the Christ figure and began prying open the locked access hatch in the ankle. Marta and Rio lifted the robe edge and stepped in as they popped the door open. Constantine climbed in, followed by Blake. They climbed quickly up through the shin, the thigh, and into the pelvic compartment.

The magnacreature was a scaled-down version of Kong, as far as its interior went. Blake grabbed the ladder in the center and climbed into the chest-cavity control room.

The arrangement of control panels was very similar to Kong's, and the central sphere was exactly the same. Constantine was turning on equipment, and looked up as Blake opened the sphere door and stepped in. For a second he looked angry, then he snorted amiably.

"No, I guess I would be inappropriate in this," he said, waving around him. "Whereas Christ in you, your Holiness, would be more appropriate."

Marta looked from one man to the other, and Blake said, "Later. I'll explain later."

"Your dear friend from the gladiator days is now head of the Roman Catholic Church," Constantine told her. He seemed wryly amused by this. "Pope Blake the First."

"Don't mind him," Blake said to Marta. "Help me."

Marta and Rio helped him attach the many sensors to his body while Constantine came over and thumbed through a manual he found.

"I think you can do almost anything in this," the warlock said. "Sit, run, bend over—though it recommends you squat rather than bend over. I think they don't want you to run, though, as they had a governor on that control. But I took it off. We are on green, with a functioning fusion engine, and the last maintenance was less than three weeks ago. They must keep this thing ready for religious functions, though I can't remember when they used it last." He laughed. "But then, those aren't my biggest interests. The churches have been trying everything in the last few years: big spectacles, bigger and bloodier arena events, holograms a kilometer high of Biblical nonsense, these big brutes here. They weren't above staging a few phoney miracles, either."

Constantine backed away from the sphere and started to fiddle with more of the controls. "This isn't my field, you know. Lucky they made these things fairly simple."

"I had some training tapes on big robots, but nothing like this," Blake said.

"There, that's the last one!" Rio said, stepping back.

"Better get out of the sphere," Blake advised.

The boom of his voice startled him. Constantine made a gesture at his throat, and Blake cut the exterior speakers.

"No use everything we say being broadcast."

"All right, let's try it." Blake spoke with no great enthusiasm.

"The board is green," Constantine reported.

"Hold on!" Blake said, leaning forward. "Activate."

Constantine pushed a button and the control room lurched violently. "Goddammit, Mason, will you stand like the *figure* should stand, to start? That adjustment is a killer!"

"Sorry. Okay, screens on."

The big screen in front showed the other side of the warehouse. The side screens showed views both beneath the robe and immediately outside it. Blake had no full-length shot of the whole figure he'd had inside the Kong.

"Hold on, here we go!" The Christ turned and walked toward the big door. A treadmill beneath Blake's feet kept him walking naturally; it seemed to be connected to sensors in his hips.

Outside, Kapuki and Bennett had devastated the exterior of the warehouse with a multitude of long horizontal slashes and a few vertical ones. The samurai stood a little distance off, and when the Christ figure came into view the Japanese bowed formally.

Blake switched on the exterior speakers. "Let's go!"

The samurai swung about, and the two enormous robots incongruously matched and controlled by an even more improbable group, started toward the center of San Francisco.

□

Blake-Christ walked slowly along an avenue reserved for outgoing trucks; he had gotten used to the odd way of walking, at the cost of bumping into a few buildings. He had chosen the outgoing one-way street so that he could see the approaching vehicles. Most of the ground-car traffic pulled to the side, and the drivers stared as he went past. Occasionally Blake would make the Sign of the Cross in the air, though mostly he just kept walking. But not even a six-story Christ figure stopped some truckers, and from time to time he accidently knocked over a truck or stepped on one that had tried to get by. Luckily, the twenty-five-metric-ton weight of the mammoth robot crushed the trucks flat without causing Blake to become unsteady.

The smaller, samurai robot walked about fifty meters behind the Christ, and Kapuki was having fun waving her sword and jumping about. Blake regretted that there seemed to be no communication facilities available between them, or none that his inexperienced crew could find.

"Well, well, Lucifer Supreme," Constantine said happily. He waved the operational manual at Blake as he held on with one hand. "They have quite a few surprises built into this thing! Integrated miracles, you might call them." He pointed at a diagram. "Your right hand has a couple of nice gadgets built in. The tip of your middle finger can fire a lightning bolt, or at least a hundred-thousand-volt charge. Your index finger exudes charged gas particles that will glow, even in bright sunlight, so you can make a Sign of the Cross that just hangs there, burning, until the winds drift it away." The warlock chuckled. "You could shoot loaves of bread out your left hand, if you had any. Bless the demon, these charlatans will do anything for a laugh!"

Blake stepped over a pile of wreckage caused by the exodus of excited citizens, and kept on walking. "Can I walk on water?"

"No, but it says here you can glow in the dark. There are millions of filaments in the robe and imbedded in the outer skin."

The steel-and-concrete canyons through which Blake moved grew higher and higher around him as the buildings became forty and fifty stories high. It was like walking through a structure with narrow corridors and no ceiling. At one intersection a number of police waited, but they stared stupidly at the passing Christ figure and did nothing. They were more animated about the samurai robot, but still did nothing.

"They think we're on their side," Marta said, looking into a screen.

"We have to make a choice," Blake said. "We're coming up to where we must either go right to the Caligula or straight ahead to the city."

"Go straight," Constantine urged. "Let the others handle the Circus."

"We could head for the main Network A offices on Montgomery Street," Marta suggested.

"Marta, you and Rio come here and let me show you how this all works. When we get to the network, I'll go in," Constantine said.

Blake walked up onto a wide freeway that curved around a hill between mountain-sized arcologs. "There it is," he said.

San Francisco was a massive mound of faceted buildings that went from Pacific to the Bay and was three-fourths of a kilometer deep. It was broken only in a few places by the deep slashes of streets that separated the reinforced-concrete behemoths. But most of the streets were simply tunnels that went from building to building.

Blake was now finding it difficult to walk, and he looked at the screens that showed the ground. He stopped. "I'm too heavy for the elevated highway," he said. "We're punching holes right through."

The screens showed a freeway with long, ragged rips

where the twenty-five-ton robot had punched its way through.

"Get over onto the streets, the ones on the ground," Rio said.

"I can't. There are too many wires, overpasses, bridges from building to building . . ." Blake said. "I'll guess I'll have to keep going on this."

Groundcars and trucks leaving the besieged city were piling up as the first vehicles stopped at the ragged edges of the footsteps. This quickly became too dangerous for Blake, so he stepped over onto the incoming lanes and walked along next to the lines of outgoing staring, frightened citizens. Then he and the samurai came onto a section of freeway that was supported more strongly, and he found they could walk much more quickly.

"Oh-oh!" Rio said, looking into a screen. "Police aircar on the right."

A large black aircar with the San Francisco Police logo flew slowly along, pacing them. Blake raised his hand and made a glowing Sign of the Cross, then left it hanging there as he strode steadily onward.

"They're still following, but they're not doing anything," Rio reported.

"Keep an eye on them. If they look like they have figured us out, tell me," Blake said. "What are Kapuki and Bennett doing?"

"Still behind, but they had a much rougher time getting over to this lane. They're about a kilometer behind us."

"Watch them, too."

Blake simply stepped over several police barricades, and none of them did anything. Marta guided him through the narrow canyons until they could go no further.

"It's through there," she said, pointing at the enormous barricade formed by the joined lower sections of several arcological structures.

Blake looked at the great wall, rising up more than three hundred meters before it separated into the different towers that rose another four or five hundred. "Strap yourself in," he said. "We're going up."

He turned, looked back at the samurai figure, which was catching up. He pointed at himself, then up the arcolog wall. He pointed at Kapuki's robot and signaled that they should raise what hell they could.

Even before Blake could start up the wall, a troop of police came down a side street. They pointed at the figure of Christ and started toward it. Blake made ready to defend himself, then he saw the samurai robot come up behind the black-clad police and start in on them with its huge sword.

Lasers flashed, but they were no match for the big armored robot, which crushed under its feet what was not destroyed by the swift sword. Over its shoulder, Kapuki gestured for Blake to start climbing. Then she turned to wait for the next danger.

Climbing the cliff-like face of the man-made mountain was difficult. It was no question of power or strength—they had plenty of that. But climbing was vastly different than walking: the robot was in a different position entirely, and Blake had to be careful about each hand and foothold, grasping and placing the hands and feet carefully. His progress was slow, but luckily there were open-air malls at different levels, or enclosed malls where he could break the windows and use the frames as handholds. Many of the malls broke under his weight, and several times he almost lost control and fell backward into the street.

Constantine muttered spells constantly, but it was Rio who watched the screens and warned of dangers and Marta who helped monitor the functions of the huge robot.

The side of the arcowall was in ruins by the time Blake got to the top. He stood at last on the roof, knee-deep in broken floors. His legs, the cameras reported, were in tatters, the synthetic flesh ripped away and some of the metal plates dented and gashed.

"Carefully," Rio said. "We don't want to hurt people."

Blake grunted, and very slowly began to walk across the roof, shattering hundreds of solar-energy panels as he waded. His feet caught on unseen girders and parts of his tunic and robe were torn away. When he reached the far edge of the structure, Marta pointed across the narrow canyon.

"There, where that big 'A' sign is!"

Constantine stopped mumbling spells and looked at the screen. "You can't jump, you'd go right through it. Climbing down and up again would take too long." He unbuckled his safety belt and rose from his bucket seat. "I'm going up. There's a hatch at the back of the neck, too, under the hair. Reach over, punch a hole through the wall, then reach back and I'll climb on your hand and you can put me across. With you looking in their window they will probably not want to argue." He flashed a wicked smile at Blake. "Ingrained superstitious nonsense has its uses."

Constantine vanished up the ladder to the head, and Blake moved ponderously into position.

Suddenly Rio cried a warning, and Blake turned just in time to see two police aircars coming straight at him. His skin sensors told him of laser beams making jiggly lines across his chest, and his response was swift. He pointed his right hand at one of the aircars and hit it with a hundred-thousand-volt blast. The other aircar veered off; Blake hit it, too, but on the second try.

"That will bring them!" Blake said.

Quickly he reached across the deep canyon and stuck his left index finger through the wall right next to the big "A," then rotated it to make a bigger hole. Then he reached back and plucked Constantine from his neck and put him into the opening. With the skin sensors he had a keen sense of touch or he might have crushed the black man. Then he looked around for more aircars.

"I think I'm getting the commercial channel on this little screen here," Rio told him.

Blake looked and saw himself from an odd angle, standing in the wreckage of the top of the arcolog. Peering around at the angle, he saw a crimson Network A aircar hanging nearby and made another fiery Sign of the Cross, even as he noticed the wreckage of the two zapped police vehicles.

"You know," he said to Rio, "I feel a little like Goliath waiting for David and his slingshot. I feel vulnerable!"

"You don't *look* vulnerable, though, and that is important."

The screen suddenly changed to a montage of scenes around the Caligula Arena, then more shots throughout the city. Constantine's image came onto the screen.

"Citizens of San Francisco! Citizens of the World! Rise up! Throw off the chains of religious oppression! The day has come! Fight for your liberty! Fight for freedom! No longer must the decadent heel of oppression grind into the neck of the common man! Rise up! Smite the evil minions of repression!"

"Turn him down," Blake said. "I feel as if I've heard all that before."

"Oh, my God, oh, my God, oh, my God!" Marta cried.

"What's wrong?"

Marta was pointing into a side screen, and Blake turned in the same direction so that what she saw went onto the big screen.

A crimson-skinned Devil was floating through the air at them. Its forked tail switched back and forth and its taloned hands clenched and unclenched. The figure was the archetypal Satan, horned and forked-bearded, bright scarlet and naked, but neuter. It sailed through the air straight toward them.

Blake looked above the swiftly approaching Lucifer and saw that the figure was born on cables by four huge aircars with the logos of one of the churches. The aircars lowered the crimson robot onto the ark roof and it, too, plunged knee-deep into the structure. The cables dropped away, the aircars lifted, and the furiously scowling devil started stalking toward Blake.

"What is it?" Marta said.

"Another religious metaphor," Blake said.

He saw that combat was inevitable and, as Sergeant White had taught him, he began to size up his opponent. They appeared to be about the same height and probably were similar in weight. But the demon had claws, and Blake's Christ had only normal human-shaped hands.

That forked tail may be more of a liability than an

asset, he thought. *Probably a separate person is controlling it.*

"This looks like the classic confrontation," Blake said, "but I wish I weren't here right now."

Blake pointed his right hand at the demon-figure, who ducked at once. *He knows my capabilities!* Instead of firing his electrical charge, Blake made another fiery Sign of the Cross. This caused the Devil to snarl and start forward. A part of the roof collapsed and the crimson robot sank to his hips, but he quickly pulled himself out. *Made to be very agile, probably to ape the scamperings of an imp*, Blake thought.

"Strap yourself in," he said to the women, glancing at the commercial channel to see Constantine still talking. Then he gave his full attention to the coming battle.

Lucifer charged, confidently flexing his taloned hands, his wide-toothed mouth grinning widely.

Blake did not move until the scarlet robot was within arm's reach. He ducked under the thrust, grabbing the demon's wrist and elbow and throwing the monster robot in a clean hip toss. He whirled to see the robotic image of the Prince of Darkness rupture a wide section of the roof.

Swiftly the red-skinned adversary climbed from the wreckage and came at Blake's robot with a great roar. His taloned feet punched raw holes through two floors as he lunged at the Christ.

Blake aimed his lightning bolt and fired, but Mephisto dodged. Before he could correct, Blake was seized and flung to the roof. The balanced sphere kept Blake level, but the big screen was now far over his head. He rolled around but it only made it worse. Now the screen was behind him and upside down.

Blake struck out blindly, hit something, missed with the other fist, then grappled with something that felt like a leg. Something began whipping at his face, and Blake ducked and clutched at the Devil's tail. The two figures rolled over twice, and all at once Blake got his orientation as the big screen appeared before him again.

"What was the matter with those designers? Why didn't they put the screens in the sphere?"

"They probably didn't expect a wrestling match," Marta said.

Satan was on his knees, rising fast, looming over Blake, his fist swinging down to crush. Blake blocked the blow, striking at the legs of the devilish figure. They broke apart and Blake rose shakily to his feet. But something somewhere in the bowels of the big Christ robot was broken and made an increasing screeching sound.

The crimson Lucifer was charging again, when an abrupt collapse of a section of roof made him falter. He stopped, raised his talons high above his head, and uttered a fierce scream. Blake aimed his lightning bolt finger and fired . . . but nothing happened.

"Something is wrong with the goddamn lightning-bolt mechanism," he yelled angrily. He covered by making another glowing Sign of the Cross.

The figure of Beelzebub gave another mad scream and charged again.

Blake ducked under the outstretched arms and flipped Satan over on his back once again. This time an even larger section of roof fell in and the crimson Devil's scramble out was slower. Blake saw him reach into the wreckage with his claws, tug, tug harder, and then pull loose a large bent girder. Bits of metal and other objects were still attached to it as the Prince of Darkness came up swinging the huge steel club.

Blake jumped back to avoid a blow and the girder scarified a section of solar panels, collapsing a large energy collector in a great clatter and crash.

The Devil swung again and missed, but caught Blake on the return swing. The Christ was knocked back and only kept from falling by coming up against a geodesic dome.

Old Nick swung again, shattering the dome as Blake dodged away.

"Look out, we're at the edge!" Rio cried.

Satan charged, swinging his titanic weapon viciously. Blake ducked under the blow, seized an arm and a leg, and used the momentum of the robot's charge to flip him over.

Marta screamed, and Blake whirled to see the crimson robot go over the edge of the arcolog. They heard the bellowing cry echoing in the concrete canyon.

Blake carefully peered over the edge. His crimson adversary was still falling, bouncing off the arcolog walls and disintegrating raggedly. It was a long fall, and Blake turned away before the figure smashed into the street. But he heard the massive crunch.

Sickened, Blake looked at his various television screens. An airborne camera was zooming in on the shattered wreckage of the demon robot far down in the street, and he looked away.

"I smell something burning," Marta said.

"I think we'd better get out of here. The sensor overloads have cut in twice. I'm hurting someplace, but I'm not certain where." Blake moved to stand conspicuously near the edge of the arcolog, raised his right hand in a gesture of blessing, and ordered Marta to cut power.

He stripped off the sensors and they scrambled down the ladders to the feet. Breathing heavily, they paused by the hatch.

"I hope it isn't blocked by wreckage," Rio said. "We're almost knee-deep in this stuff."

A girder had fallen nearby, but the door could be opened. Blake and the women scrambled out and down over the pulverized remains of a once fashionable complex of condominiums. Marta seized Blake's hand and said, "This way!"

"Wait!" Blake pulled some clothing from a ruined condo closet. "Get rid of those Arena things and put some of these on."

Blake watched nervously as Marta changed. In a couple of minutes, they were running down an unruined corridor toward the elevators. A disheveled couple staggered from a door and the woman cried out, "What's going on?"

"Revolution," Rio answered.

The samurai robot was still standing in the street where they had left it. Laser cuts were all over the armored body, but the pile of bodies and equipment that littered the street was impressive.

Blake shouted up to Kapuki and Bennett, and after a few moments the ponderous robot put a foot down near them. Blake opened the hatch and shoved Rio and Marta inside.

When the three stuck their heads up into the control room in the chest cavity, Bennett gave them a shout of glee.

"Constantine is all over the net! Someone hooked him into the satellite system and he's broadcasting all over the world! They played an old tape of you in that ape machine and they have just finished sending out a repeat on your fight with Satan!" Bennett clapped Blake on the back. "Hey, you were paying attention in training, after all!"

"Everybody, sit down and strap in," Blake ordered. "Kapuki, take us to Riot Central, wherever that is."

"City Hall," she answered. She stood in the middle of the three-meter sphere, grinning at him. "When in doubt, attack!" she said.

"I'm in doubt, all right," Blake admitted, "but I think we should strike while the iron is hot, hit 'em where it hurts, and lop off the head." He looked at Rio. "Did I miss anything?"

"An apple a day keeps the robot away."

"I'll have you excommunicated for that," he said.

He saw Bennett's curious look and quickly explained about becoming pope.

Kapuki laughed, carefully stepping over the wreckage of two Riotmaster robots. "They told me it took all kinds to make a revolution, but I never thought it might take a pope like you."

"Just watch where you are going, lotus flower, and don't let any of those baddies hamstring us," Blake said to her.

An aircar dropped down into the narrow canyon between the huge arks and Kapuki swung her sword at it. It dodged, but caromed off a building and fell a dozen floors to crash in the street. A roadblock had been set up a block further on, but Kapuki insolently swept it aside.

"Uh-oh," Bennett said, peering into a screen. He ran up the magnification and groaned. "Trouble ahead. There's a barrier up ahead and I think that's a Jupiter they have. They'll hurt us with that one."

"Turn left here," Blake said.

"That's Powell," Kapuki said. "It dead-ends into the old *Francis Drake*. We can't squeeze through where the street goes into it!"

"We're not going in. Put down the sword a moment and rip out a chunk of that wall. Then step out quickly and throw it at the barrier."

Kapuki grinned and set down the surrogate sword she used within the sphere. She stepped to the side of the nearest arcolog, plunged her armored hands right into the walls. She gripped the reinforced wall and tugged. There was a terrible rending sound, an ascending groan, then a snap. The samurai robot staggered back, holding a massive block of concrete with a broken window near the center.

"It must weigh five tons," the oriental girl gasped as she waddled toward the corner. She raised it over her head, stepped out suddenly, and heaved the huge missile toward the next intersection.

The police laser was firing, swinging toward the middle of the seventeen-meter robot. Just as the Jupiter's ruby beam touched the samurai armor it swung violently away, slicing into the side of a building, jiggling upward, carving a deep gash in the ferroconcrete, then lancing through windows and slicing the side of the ark open. It stopped abruptly, and Blake could hear distant screams.

"Your sword!" Bennett snapped, and Kapuki stepped back to retrieve it.

They backed out, then ran as fast as the samurai robot could move, rupturing the street with heavy footfalls. At the street barricade, they saw the police and their big Riotmaster robbies crushed beneath the huge concrete block. Kapuki struck at an undamaged robot, spitting it on her sword and raising it into the air. She threw it at a small oncoming tank with the snout of a massive laser pointed at them, overturning it and causing it to explode.

"City Hall this way!" Marta said, and Kapuki swung the big robot around and headed up the street.

A police aircar dropped some gas grenades but they were too high in the robot's chest for the gas to get to them. Another aircar tried a laser on the head and chest of the samurai but was too far away. It caused disfiguring gouges but no structural damage.

"We certainly are obvious," Rio said.

Blake thought for a moment, then spoke. "Kapuki, stop in front of City Hall, if you can. Rio, Marta, and I will get out and go see what hell we can raise."

"Hey, what about me?" Bennett said. "I've been copilot long enough."

"I'll stay," Marta said. "I know how to run this machine. They are all mostly alike."

"All right," Blake said. "Kapuki, don't hang around. Drop us, then keep on going. Do what damage you can."

"You don't want me to wait for you?" she asked.

Blake shook his head. "No. If we are successful, there will be no need. If we're not . . ." He looked at Rio and saw her gaze on him. "Well, in that case there is no reason to tie you down for target practice. Keep moving, keep fighting!"

"City Hall is just straight ahead," Marta said.

"Get down in the feet and be ready to disembark," Blake ordered. "Let's not make them stand still and be targets."

Bennett dropped down the ladder, followed by Rio.

Marta stopped Blake with a gesture. "Your blessing?" she asked.

"Oh, come on, Marta, I . . ." He stopped, looking at the expression on her face. Then he raised his hand and made the Sign of the Cross. "Bless you both," he said solemnly. Then he dropped down the ladder.

He joined Rio and Bennett in the right foot, and held on desperately as the huge thing thumped and swayed, each step a jolting shock much more jarring than any they had felt in the cushioned control room. Finally the foot was still, and Bennett sprung the door and leaped out. Rio followed, then Blake.

They were on some wide steps leading up from a plaza. The huge structure loomed over them, capped by an enormous dome so high they could only see it reflected in the glass front of a building across the square. Bennett was already taking the steps three at a time, sword in one hand, laser in the other. Rio and Blake followed, jumping the remnants of a police crowd control fence.

A single black-shirted policeman ran out and Bennett's laser was bearing down on him when the man shouted, "No, no! Don't shoot!" His hands were in the air, his laser in its holster.

Bennett ran up to him, disarmed him, and tossed the weapon to Rio.

"Don't· kill me," the policeman said shakily. He looked in awe at the departing figure of the samurai robot, now lumbering across the plaza, scattering pigeons and benches. "Look, I'm on your side!"

"Sure you are," Bennett sneered, dragging the man up the steps into the protection of the entrance.

"No, I am, I am! Not all the police are against you! They rebelled over in Greater Berkeley, and the Oakland boys haven't been straight since '49." He looked at Bennett's laser with apprehension. "Really, it's true."

"Don't kill him," Blake ordered. "Remember, it takes all kinds." He grabbed the policeman and fired questions at him. "Where are the defense forces here? Is Riot Control upstairs? Is the Army coming in?"

The black-clad officer answered quickly. "The ones that were left ran when they saw that coming in," he said, pointing at the samurai, which had just thrown a Riotmaster through the glass wall of a building. "The others, they went down Montgomery to some big fight that was going on. Yeah, yeah, Control is up there, and they have lots of protection."

"What about the Army?" Bennett insisted.

"I don't know. I heard there was trouble down in Fort Fremont and over in the Presidio. Riots and things. Some said one of the commanders turned out to be a Jew, or perhaps a Catholic. Something like that. I don't think the Army will be much help, or much hindrance either."

"Have you seen a lean man in black? He may have a redhead with him in a torn dress?" Blake asked.

"Yeah, he was here, but he left. I remember, because he was one of the first bigshots to run, and the girl didn't look like she wanted to go with him. He . . . uh . . . he killed her."

Blake felt sick and Rio's eyes filled without her uttering a sound.

"Where's the body?" Blake demanded.

The guard pointed toward the entrance. "Uh, I don't think you want to look at it, sir. She hit the guy pretty good and started to run, and he . . . well, he kept cutting her up even after it wasn't necessary, if you know what I mean."

"Which way did he go?" Blake asked angrily.

Before the policeman could answer, a large group of revolutionaries came running out of a nearby slidewalk exit. They shouted when they saw the group on the City Hall steps. Someone fired at the four, but the shot was off-target. When Bennett stepped forward, they stopped, seeing his gladiator costume. He waved them forward, and they came, shouting gleefully.

Blake grabbed the policeman and shook him. "Where did he go?"

"Bibleland, I think. At least that's what it sounded like when he gave the order to the aircar driver."

Bennett tugged at Blake's arm. "Look, I'll take these zongos up and knock out the Control. You go rescue your friend." Then he grinned at Blake. "Hero!" he said, and laughed.

"I'm coming, too," Rio said.

Blake started to protest, when a flight of aircars came

over the nearby arktops and settled into the plaza. More revolutionaries piled out and Bennett stood high on the steps and waved, shouting. As the surge of people spread out, Blake saw Granville Franklin, wearing a jumpsuit and looking fit. Blake waved at him and grabbed Rio's arm to point him out.

Granville ran up the steps to them and hugged them both. "Ah, my reluctant hero, my ravishing heroine! Together again!" He waved his hand at the growing numbers of men and women forming up for battle. "Isn't this fascinating? And they said 'You can't fight City Hall.' " He snorted. "Most interesting, watching humans exchange one oppressor for another."

"Granville!" Rio cried. "Surely you think we're going to get rid of these holy dictators?"

"Oh, yes, yes," he said with irritation. "Their minds have stagnated. They didn't want science—or anything else—to advance, unless discoveries were made they could use. Why, do you know they have virtually stopped any sort of basic research? For that alone I could destroy them."

Granville made a face and blew out a long sigh. "Well, I had best get on with it. I was working on some very interesting data that suggested we have experienced interstellar contact when Voss decided to get rid of me. It seemed I asked the wrong sort of questions and said the wrong sort of things to be a friend of one in high places. I was an embarrassment to him. I got out fast."

Granville squinted up at the buildings around him. "I want to get back to that as soon as I can. Some interesting discoveries have been made by scientists working on the physical way we think, too. Then there is some black-hole data I want to look over." He bared his teeth in a savage grin up at the building in front of him. "Mr. Voss, here I come!"

"Voss isn't up there," Blake explained.

Granville grunted in annoyance. "Damn! And I was looking forward to meeting him again: I wanted to thank him in person for making me go underground. But do you know there isn't a safe computer terminal in all of *Yerba Buena?* I was having the most delicious time playing chess with a computer in Huntsville until Voss turned my name in."

Bennett ran up to Blake, breathing hard. "He's definitely gone. We'd better go after him. He could make a lot of trouble. I'll get an aircar."

Blake stopped him. "Voss is my business. They can probably use you here." He hesitated, then said, "Besides, you know he killed Doreen."

"You're going after Voss?" Granville asked, his eyes bright.

"Yes, but you'd better stay here. Isn't *this* operation yours?"

Granville looked annoyed once again. "Yes, dammit. This *is* more important. 'Seize control centers as soon as possible' is the motto. We can get dear Jean-Michel anytime. Too bad, though. I had the idea of dropping him down one of those waste chutes and letting a little of him wear off against the sides."

Rio took Blake's arm as Granville moved off. "Blake, he's dangerous. Let him go. Don't risk it."

Blake's face was grim as he said, "No. I must. He's caused us a lot of pain, endangered your life. No. He doesn't care about us, about anyone. He stuck us into that Arena jungle. He's feeling invulnerable now, kind of sacred and superior. He knows that somewhere down here people die and are tortured and in pain, but he doesn't care. He thinks the blood won't splatter on him, that no one can really get to him because he's the great, immortal Jean-Michel Voss. I want to show that bastard he's not as untouchable as he thinks."

"And you want to kill him?" Rio said, her eyes luminous.

Blake took a deep breath. "I don't know. I really don't know." He looked deep into Rio's eyes. "If I have to . . . I won't hesitate, I won't regret it."

They looked at each other a long time, then Rio said, "Do you want to remove him from . . . from between *us?*"

Blake took another deep breath. "Probably. I can't say I like the way he has treated you, just abandoning you because it might be politically too delicate to save your life. And there's the matter of Doreen."

Rio looked satisfied, and took Blake's hand. They pushed through the mob as they ran to where the aircars were parked. Most were empty, but they found one with a driver nursing a bloody arm in a sling.

"Take us to Bibleland!" Blake ordered.

"Can you fly this machine?" Rio asked, pointing at the man's arm.

The pilot nodded and they jumped in. When the ship rose straight up, Blake caught a glimpse of the samurai robot standing in the middle of a street nearby, blocking it with its bulk and with its long, slashing sword. In front of the fighting robot lay several wrecked Riotmasters, a litter of body parts, and a police personnel aircar on its side.

□

Bibleland park was on the other side of the Oakland hills, past the biggest of the arcologs and not far from one of the faults of the San Andreas, now rendered relatively safe by forced water lubrication—one of the methods used by modern seismologists. The park took up the entire roof of the highest arcolog in the area, a building more than half a kilometer square, and its most obvious landmark was a huge revolving, illuminated cross atop an artificial hill.

"It's deserted," Rio said, looking down.

"Everyone probably ran for cover when this started," the pilot said. "Where do you want to sit down? Landing pads? St. Carol's Square?" He looked back at Blake quizzically.

Blake studied the park and pointed down. "There, by that patch of green."

"That's the 'Garden of Eden,' " the pilot said. " 'The Creation' is right next door, in that building there. Quite a show, too. Starts out in black with this deep voice, and you see everything taking place. Damn near makes a believer out of you—except I heard the same actor do a commercial."

"Come back for us in an hour," Blake said.

The aircar set down on a grassy lawn near a waterfall. Timid animatronic deer sipped water warily, and after the aircar had lifted away, Blake and Rio could hear birds.

"So peaceful," Rio sighed.

"It's all phoney," Blake said, fingering a green plastic leaf.

There was motion beyond some bushes, and Blake pulled Rio down. They crouched warily. Blake's laser was aimed at the flicker of movement.

Out walked an almost nude man and woman, flanked

310

by a lion, rubbing his mane against Adam's thigh, and a unicorn, prancing prettily next to Eve. The two humanoids wore fig leaves, and Eve's long blond hair concealed her breasts.

Blake made a snort of disgust as he and Rio moved on, the quartet of robots paying them no attention at all as they strolled happily through the garden. Blake and Rio walked by a towering tree in which a glittering snake moved sinuously, his forked tongue slithering in and out. He hissed absently at them as he waited.

"Let's not go out the main gate to the garden," Blake said, pulling Rio toward a side exit.

They pushed open the door marked NO ADMITTANCE and walked past a fierce-looking St. Michael standing with blackened sword just behind an opening. Blake could see tiny holes in the sword that emitted the gas. The fine wires that held the archangel figure off the ground had not been camouflaged in this instance.

Blake and Rio passed through another door and emerged cautiously into the public street. Across it was what seemed to be the entrance to an ancient city. They could hear music and shouts of laughter coming from it, so they ran, crouched, across the street and flattened themselves against the wall, then peered in through an arch.

The street inside was twisted and narrow, with many branches. Blake could see animatronic robots hanging out of the windows and standing beneath arches. They were all human figures, so gross and overstated as to border on the unrealistic. The men were coarse and lecherous-looking, the women overendowed and bawdy. They all had one expression: a leer. The costumes were vaguely Biblical, the jewelry heavy and barbaric. The music was throbbingly suggestive.

"Where's Lot?" Rio asked.

They moved into the tiny city-within-a-city cautiously, hoping to find a real human in the midst of the hundreds of fakes who populated the reconstructed Sodom. They caught glimpses of people through small arches and windows, but no actual orgy scenes. Everything was hinted at but not graphic. But the figures were so real as to give Blake and Rio the jumps whenever one happened to look anything like Voss.

"Why do you think Voss switched sides?" Blake asked Rio as they exited the electronically controlled pageant.

"He didn't. He was always on that side, the side of power. He simply went where the power structure was." She touched Blake's arm. "He was unconventional, but never a revolutionary. He simply chose to make the best of it within the existing power structure."

Blake nodded as they moved toward the entrance of a big building. "A lot of people make that choice."

"I don't suppose Jean-Michel thought he had a choice. I *know* him. He wouldn't have cared to hide out in the underground for the next four or five hundred years."

Blake smiled at her. "You know I keep forgetting that part. I can't quite believe it, I guess. I mean, I feel okay. But maybe . . . well, maybe I thought I'd feel like a superman or something."

The building was empty and almost dark. They grew quiet and made no sound as they crept along inside.

Blake was suddenly aware of a glow to his left. He pulled Rio down and they watched as light grew upon a mountainside.

They were high up, along a cliff path. Far below lay fertile valleys, and sheep grazed. An ordinary bush now burst into flames and a tall, impressive figure strode out from a crevice. The bearded, robed humanoid began a conversation with the bush as Blake and Rio relaxed and started moving on, bent over and alert. At the exit, they turned a last time to see bolts of holographic fire leap from the bush to carve out symbols in rock.

In the next chamber they stood on a rock and watched Moses part the Red Sea far below, as the chariots of the pharaoh raced after the Jews.

"Are you after Jean-Michel just to avenge Doreen, or to punish him, or . . ." Rio hesitated. "Or to kill him so that . . . so that—"

"So that you will be free?" Blake shrugged. "I don't know. First things first. He killed Doreen for no good reason. He chose sides and he didn't switch back when he had the chance. He gave us no help in the Arena."

Blake started to leave the chamber, which now echoed with the thunder of falling water and the recorded screams of the Egyptian charioteers.

"Don't kill him," Rio said. "He can't help it . . ."

Blake laughed as they left the building and looked up and down the empty street. "You mean, he's the poor product of his environment? Poor little rich boy? You're confusing—"

Part of the doorway arch spattered behind them, and a long groove appeared in the wall. Blake lunged across the street, pulling Rio with him. They threw themselves beneath a patroncounter and rolled into the darkness within.

"Where did that come from?" he asked, his laser ready.

"It must have been from this side, further along," Rio whispered. "Let's creep through here and circle around."

She started to move, then Blake took her arm.

He grinned at her and said, "Suddenly a hunter? Now are you convinced?"

Rio didn't answer, only crawled toward the building. "Let's go in and find the back door," she said.

Inside, Samson was in the process of demolishing the temple when the second laser shot cut away a strip of Blake's tunic and the third put a hole through Delilah.

Blake fired back blindly, sending a shot into several different dark spots. He flung himself behind some fallen stones. Then the lights went out, and he heard running feet, followed by a grinding noise, many scrapings, and the whir and hum of machinery. In a few moments the lights came on again, and Blake found that he and Rio were no longer hiding behind stones. The temple of Dagon had been reconstructed, ready for the next visitors. Delilah stood serene and imperious, except that her right arm did not work. Samson in chains again stood over the motionless feasters.

"He went out that way!" Blake said, and started running.

Rio raced after him. They crossed through a backstage area—a workshop where a robed Philistine reveler lay gutted on a workbench—and wound up on a battle-field.

To the right were the Philistines, row upon row of animatronic warriors graduated in scale to give great depth. In front of these stood the giant Goliath, bearded and armored, a massive robot a meter higher than Blake. In the center was the watercourse known as the Terebinth, and on the left were the few Israelites. Before them, standing amid the corpses of the slain, was the young David, whirling his sling.

Blake caught a glimpse of movement in the ranks of the fear-frozen Israelites and cried out to Rio, "Down!"

Two long grooves cut into the fake rock near their prone figures, then Blake fired back. David hurled his stone, an Israelite warrior tilted oddly to one side, and Goliath uttered a great roar and crashed down. Blake jumped up and bounded across the ravine as David sawed at the monster's head and then raised it high.

Crouching behind the Israelite army, Blake saw nothing. He called out to Rio, then she joined him and they waited while the darkness reknit Goliath's head and David returned to the Israelite ranks.

Quickly, Blake and Rio passed by another David peering at a bathing Bathsheba, then skirted a scene of David's son Solomon in a luxurious setting with the dusky Queen of Sheba.

"He may have circled back," Rio said, and Blake agreed.

They moved to the right, passing out through a shuttered and deserted food-dispensing area that featured "Manna," "Fishburgers," "Goat's Milk Malts," and the "Original Menu from the Last Supper." Blake shook his head but remained alert.

They next looked in on a Noah's Ark that bobbed beneath threatening skies. Long lines of animatronic animals waited patiently to board.

"Let's go the other way," Blake said. He looked up, seeing some high-flying aircars. "I hope those aren't Army reinforcements," he said.

They entered a new area, this one done more in pastels than in the bold, almost gaudy colors of the previous part of Bibleland. They passed a stable filled with animals and a glowing child, then several crowds watching a silent mature Christ. Blake searched for Voss as an uninvited guest at the Last Supper. His eyes stopped on Peter, and in his mind he said, *You never thought it would come to this, did you? A pope with a laser, a lecher wearing the triple crown, robot Christs and electronic miracles.*

Blake saluted his predecessor with his laser, and he and Rio headed toward the scene of the Crucifixion with all their senses on alert. They were nearing the end of the big Biblical park and Voss had to be someplace

. . .

The Earth trembled and lightning slashed across a sky boiling with black clouds. Wind whipped at the robes of the centurion and his soldiers as they gazed upward at the three figures on the crosses. People were standing around the base of the hill, singing; but their number was too few for the great heavenly chorus Blake and Rio heard.

Blake tore his gaze away from the tortured figures and sought Voss in the crowd. One figure was not singing, and Blake caught the flash of a glittering eye as a robe fluttered open and a fistful of laser was aimed at him.

Blake fired. A praying figure at Voss's side lurched and fell.

Voss's millisecond pulse missed, slicing into the floor. He fired again, but Blake and Rio had already dodged behind a group of onlookers.

The room darkened until now only lightning flashes illuminated the diorama. Voss's laser bolts were more easily seen in the darkness. Blake fired between the legs of the Christians.

The thunder and the chorus made verbal communication impossible, so Blake finally poked at Rio and pointed toward the exit. They emerged into the dying daylight gratefully and sagged against the wall. Blake searched the doors and corners nearby as he spoke to Rio.

"Now what do you think? Is he on our side or not?"

"All right, Blake."

"Do you want me to spare him now?"

Rio did not answer. She swallowed hard, then asked, "Where can he be?"

"Only two places we haven't looked. The offices, which are down there, and over here . . . the hill . . ."

"There's something on the hill," Rio said as they neared it. Then she read the sign. " 'The Last Judgment.' Oh, Blake!"

"Stay here," he said. "There's no reason for you to go in."

"I've come this far."

"And you shouldn't have. I'm the one with the training, what there was of it. I'm the pope, too."

Rio smiled wanly. "Pulling rank?"

Blake nodded his head. He leaned over and kissed her, then went toward the door to 'The Last Judgment.'

The chamber was dark and quiet. Blake had no idea of its size, except that the building on the hill was fairly large. He glanced back at the light of the entrance and saw Rio's head. He waved her back and melted into the darkness to the left.

It's blackshirts and rip-offs, he mused. *Kid stuff, playing in the long halls and labyrinthine service corridors, Jerry and me against Bud Silva and Karen Blanchard, the Tigers versus the Werewolves, Deck 980 against those scrubs from Level Ten.*

Blake had learned stealth then, many years before. *Watch your shadows and watch for theirs. Don't rub against anything, it makes noise. Don't surprise a serviceman. He just might curse you and give you away.* If you were a blackshirt, you had to make the attack; if you were playing a rip-off, you'd had to hole up and let them find you. *Wear dark clothes, blend in. Use the slidewalks, skipping from lane to faster lane deftly. Learn to breathe without sound—through your mouth, not your nose.*

Use your senses. Listen for the scrape, the breath, the tinkle. Smell the sweat, the steam, the oil. Separate the clunk and throb of the machinery from the slither and scratch of the enemy. Feel for the vibes, out-doublethink the slobs, doublethink your moves, do the unexpected, react swiftly.

The music began softly, but it was startling to Blake. He instantly rolled, heard a "Hah!" and saw the faint ruby beam cut into the floor next to him.

He was in too awkward a position to fire, and by the time he had twisted around it was too late and he thought better of giving away his new position. He quietly edged away, taking his time getting to his feet, then found a wall.

The music grew into a symphony unknown to Blake, but a powerful theme, which gave him shivers of foreboding.

He *felt* the red light almost before he saw it, and threw himself back onto the floor into the darkness, rolled, hit a row of seats painfully in the hip, then crept between them.

The whole hemisphere over him now became churning clouds flicked with distant fires. Demons gobbled the perimeter, leering down at the empty seats trapped in a pit edged with flame. Blake risked one quick look over a seat but did not see Voss.

The music crescendoed, then paused dramatically for a shrill trumpet call. From all around the edge of the seats rose the dead, climbing into the light, toward the parting clouds. The light from the rift was blinding, illuminating the amphitheater brightly. The demons howled, the dead moaned, the celestial chorus sang, the music thundered, and something ripped off the tops of two seats just over Blake.

He reversed his motion and started to crawl backward; then something told him to move ahead. Quickly he reached the aisle, and looked around carefully. One of the demons in the shadow of a rising stream of dead moved curiously and Blake shot, but missed because of his position. The figure ducked, and Blake threw himself across the aisle and between the rows of seats on the other side.

He waited, all senses keen, trying to filter out the sounds of the climactic spiritual event going on overhead. It was no use. He had to rely on sight.

He gathered himself, then sprang up quickly in the middle of the row, moving his laser as he moved his eyes, sweeping the room in a swift search for Voss. A dark figure at the back of the amphitheater moved, and they both fired almost at the same time. But Blake's laser exploded a second after he fired, burning his hand and cauterizing a groove along the top side of his forearm.

He dropped the ruined remains of the weapon as he ducked again to the floor. Frantically, he replayed the last few seconds in his head. Everything had happened so fast he had not grasped it all. Again he saw the figure, felt his hand tighten on the firing stud, saw the faint red beam, saw the figure fire as it started to topple backward, felt the stinging explosion of his ruptured laser.

Blake waited a moment, using the light from the domed ceiling's projections to examine his hand. Then he crept out a side aisle and along the wall. He looked around beyond the last row and saw a motionless figure lying on the floor, illuminated·by the flickering light from the 'Judgment.' He watched it for several moments, but the body did not move. Cautiously, he got to his feet and stepped closer. The face was turned away, partially in shadow, but Blake saw who it was.

Vogel.

"Don't move," Voss said from the shadows beyond.

Blake did not move. Only his eyes did, and he saw the lean figure of the financier rising from the darkness. Overhead the dead were being separated. Some were rising, some were falling, and the demons danced in glee.

"You have been rather devastating to my subordinates," Voss said, moving into the light, a laser steady in his hand. "To say nothing of my plans."

"Why did you switch sides?" Blake asked.

Voss looked surprised. "Switch sides? I never changed allegiance. I've always been on the same side: *this* side, the side of power. I still am. Your revolution will fail. I will show them all their hero. You will be on every screen in the world, my pushy friend. You will tell them you were mistaken, you will tell them to stop, you will tell them it is hopeless."

"With a little help from drugs, I suppose."

Voss smiled. "Of course. They have made some excellent advances since my ti—since our time. Subtle changes can be made at the very core of your thinking, and from then on you will react normally, with your usual vigor and blind faith."

"Mind control."

"Just another way, another technique . . ." Voss waved to the scene above them,· to the celestial choir and the light in the clouds. "Just like that one. Fear. That's all it is: fear. Obey the rules, or suffer for all of eternity. Obey the rules, or I will kill you. Obey the rules, even when the rules are insane, because the alternative is more horrible. Drugs and hypnotraining are much easier on one than the truncheon. You might even enjoy it." He smiled wickedly.

"You think those dedicated fighters will stop just because I am captured?"

"Oh, no. But you will be a factor, just as you were a factor in the rebellion."

Blake looked up toward the scene of religious hysteria being enacted. "The Last Judgment is really about to commence, Voss."

The lean man laughed sardonically. "For you, yes."

Blake looked at him. "Why did you kill Doreen? She did you no harm. She was one of us."

"She was only a diversion, like all the others, just in case the future turned out not to have the kind of woman I was used to. I used her—successfully, I think—to keep you at bay when you were stomping around in that ridiculous Kong. But it doesn't matter about her, or Rio, or any of them. It *certainly* doesn't matter about *you*, except for your slight value as a tool."

"You never cared for Rio?"

"Rio is beautiful, charming, and was quite useful to me. But I find this world has many beautiful, charming women—who will be much more loyal and will have no taint of the Arena. Rio made her choice, so let her suffer for it."

"She didn't *choose* to be arrested!" Blake snapped angrily. "And you made no attempt to get her out."

"I couldn't afford to be associated with you anymore. It cost me almost everything I had to bribe my way to acceptance, then all of my wit and energy to get into a position of power. Your temporary success here will not stop destiny. The Army will come in. We will crush you here, then in all the rebellious parishes."

"And rule the world?" Blake asked bitterly.

"Why not? We have the perfect tool for it! Other conquerors have used steel, some have used the cross or the crescent. We have *both!* We can control their minds with the cross and control their bodies with the whip!"

"Why did you do it?" Blake asked. "You had everything back in our time. You didn't need all this."

Voss's mouth drew into a grim, harsh expression before he spoke. "I didn't want to die. I didn't want to grow old and feeble, ending up in some nursing home plugged into a wall of sensors and with most of me parts of other people stitched on. I didn't want to end up too feeble in body to wipe my ass, too senile to even know I had fouled myself. I took the chance, and I won! I always win!"

"Not this time," Rio said.

Voss was fast. He was firing as he turned, scarring a semicircle of wasted energy into the walls. Blake jumped at him, striking down the flaming laser, making it slice into the seats. He hit Voss hard, driving his fists into his face and stomach, striking with a rage he had never felt before.

The laser fell to the floor and broke as Blake's foot smashed down on it. He slipped, recovered by holding on to Voss's tunic, then struck at him again and again.

"Blake!"

He hit the saturnine face, feeling the teeth against his knuckles, ignoring the stabbing pain, driving his other fist into Voss's stomach.

"Blake!"

The bloody mess that had been Voss's face dropped back as the body fell from Blake's grasp. Voss's head hit the concrete with a sickening thump and he did not move. Blake swayed, staring down at the dead man with bulging eyes.

"Blake." Rio was at his side, holding him, looking up at him anxiously.

"Are you all right?" Blake gasped.

Rio nodded, and hugged him close. "I'm all right," she said. "Now I'm all right."

□

Blake and Rio sat on a bench in the deserted square. They were silent, and Blake felt nauseated from the aftermath of the adrenaline surge. The aircar slowly, cautiously drifted down, peeking over the treetops of 'Eden.' It settled down on the imitation cobblestones, and Blake took Rio's hand and they walked over to it and got in.

The area before City Hall was still filled with people, only now most of them were drunk. A guarded group of prisoners huddled within a circle of jeering revolutionaries.

As Blake and Rio descended from the aircar, they heard the loudspeakers announce that the Council of the United Churches had given its unanimous blessing to the new governments of North America, New America, the nations of Islandia, Allegheny, Nuevo Mexico, and Yukon.

They went upstairs and found Granville.

"They just went on leave," he exulted, "the entire armed forces of the Council of the United Churches. We told them their franchises were null and void and that new contracts would have to be negotiated. They didn't want to antagonize their potential employers, so they gave everyone leave!"

"We've won?" asked Rio.

Granville smiled, and hugged her tightly. " 'Winner and still champion,' the free spirit of mankind!"

"Not without casualties," Blake said.

Rio turned, following his gaze to see someone pull a blanket over Gali Bennett's face.

Kapuki came in just then and they told her about Bennett. She took the news impassively. "You never get used to it . . ." she said, "but you must go on."

322

"Well, what do we do now?" Marta asked, coming up behind them.

"They made me give up my toy," Kapuki sulked. "I think I'll open a gladiator school, or maybe sell my life story to the newstapes."

"Constantine says he is going to run for the new congress on the Satanist ticket," Marta said. "I'm thinking of going to Mars again." She looked at their expressions. "Well, I *thought* about going once before."

"I think we are going to some funerals first," Blake said. " 'Living happily ever after' has some dark days, too," he added.

□

They held services for Doreen, Neva, Rob, Bennett, and Narmada. The bodies were then sent down the chutes to the fusion torches, to be recycled through the mass accelerators. They never found Sergeant White's body, and presumed it had been recycled during the cleanup.

"Atomic dust unto atomic dust," Marta philosophized.

The remaining friends lingered, reluctant to part. Kapuki asked if they had heard that Lieutenant Cady had been found hiding in one of the lower cells of the Arena, dressed in a bloody retiarius costume. "They executed him along with the rest of the cadre," she added.

"A change of power can be so bloody," Rio shivered.

"I made my speech," Blake said, "but it didn't stop much bloodshed, I'm afraid. There were just too many years of oppression to get out of their system. I didn't want them to reject religion, I just wanted them to remember never to let it control everything, ever again."

"The old ways die hard, darling. New ways are not easily assimilated," Rio consoled him.

"Granville," Marta asked, "are you going to like being a Professor of Modern History?"

"As long as they let me soak up information outside my field," the older man said. "They are talking about building some starships again and reviving the colonies out on Mars and Callisto. If they really get a starship going someplace, I think I'd like to be on board."

Kapuki said, "Do you know what Linda Muirwood is selling in her shop now? Little animatronic robots of Christ and Satan. Fighting."

"Ah, commercialism combined with patriotism." Rio laughed.

324

"Maybe the outcome of the battle is optional," Blake commented.

"It always is," Rio said.

The friends parted, with promises of future meetings, but each was off to pursue his or her life. Marta was shipping out to the colony at Bradbury, on Mars, and no one expected her to return.

As they left the chapel, Granville cautioned Blake about those who might be thinking of either capturing his favor or of removing him from their path.

Blake shook his head as he and Rio took a slidewalk toward the helipad on the Bay side of *Fremont*. "I'm so tired of all the plots and counterplots," he said moodily. "All those pockets of resistance that are still being talked out of it . . . or subdued. Everyone wants his say in the new Constitution. And things are bogging down, nothing seems to be getting done."

Rio patted his arm. "Thank God for the Total Information Service. At least we can educate people better and quicker, and their choices and desires can be made known swiftly."

Blake blew out his cheeks in an explosive release of air. "Nitpickers, that's what Granville calls them—all those politicians. How few of them fought for the liberation. The ones that believed in it hard enough to lay their lives on the line soon got disgusted with all the talk-talk, and pulled out. Leaving the politicians."

Blake shook his head sadly. The reformation of most of the world's religious, political, and power structures was under way, but he knew it was far from finished.

"Now what?" Rio asked.

"To Rome. They've unsealed the Vatican, and pilgrims are pouring in from all over. The clergy are coming out of hiding."

"The Catholic Church—like the Jews—has had a lot of experience in survival," Rio said. "And has the philosophy for it. But those very facts made them dangerous to most of the new churches: the old ones had to go before the new ones could really take hold."

They switched slidewalks and crossed an area of carnage that was slowly being cleaned up. Rudely printed signs taped to walls pointed in the direction of Catholic churches, Hebrew temples, and Moslem mosques.

"The Catholics and Jews know how to lean with the blows," Rio said. "It sounds odd, the old religions going against total church control, but they were one of the biggest and strongest of the rebelling factors."

They came out on the helipad, and Blake showed his credentials as a member of the Western Revolutionary Council and commandeered an aircar to the airport.

"You're going to resign, aren't you?" Rio asked.

"I'm going to try. Cardinal Crowe seems to think 'Once a pope, always a pope.' They've never had anyone want to resign before." He patted Rio's hand. "But don't worry, you aren't going to end up a nun."

"Oh, I *know* I'm not. Nor the pope's mistress, either."

Cardinal Barbella was a large, florid man who had spent his years as an outlawed cardinal working as a butcher. He was uncomfortable and hot in his new robes, which smelled of mothballs and moist catacombs. He looked at Blake mournfully for a long time, then his eyes quickly scanned Rio, who stood in the background.

The red-clad fat man sighed mountainously. Then he looked briefly at the semicircle of monsignori, bishops, and other cardinals. His glum expression matched theirs.

"You are determined to do this?" he questioned in heavily accented English.

"Yes," Blake said. He looked back at Rio. "I'm not really the pope and you know it. I was never really elected by the College of Cardinals, and I'm tired of people asking me, 'Is the pope Catholic?' and having to say no."

"You could convert. From whatever you are—or were." The cardinal seemed frustrated and faintly angry.

"From what? Hedonism? Once I've licked them, join them?" Blake was beginning to become angry. "Look, I was handed a holy mission. I did it. Now I want out. Why the hell do you want to keep me, anyway? Surely I can't be someone you *want?*"

Cardinal Barbella looked both annoyed and embarrassed. "You are known as the pope. You are a figure of international acclaim. You are someone the various disunited factions could unite behind."

"A figurehead." Blake snorted. Cardinal Barbella spread his hands in an expressive gesture. "No, thanks."

One of the female clergy spoke up. "If His Eminence will permit . . . ?"

The cardinal made a gesture.

327

"*Señor* Mason . . ."

"See, *she* doesn't think I'm the pope," Blake said quickly.

"*Señor* Mason, please, may I speak?" The woman gestured toward Rio. "Is it because of the woman, Rio Volas? Perhaps—"

"Monsignora Graef!" Cardinal Barbella exploded. "Are you suggesting—"

"Never mind what she was suggesting," Blake interrupted. "Jesus H. Christ, this job is harder to quit than to get!" He leaned across Cardinal Barbella's ornate carved desk and pounded it. "Look, I'm quitting. I'm going. Now. Good-bye. Understand? Tell the press what you will. Excommunicate me. Tell them I'm retiring. Whatever you want. But I'm leaving!"

"And how will you make a living?" Monsignora Graef asked silkily.

Blake stopped his angry thumping and looked at the slim churchwoman. "I'll go back to what I did before. I was pretty good at it."

"Ah, but your reputation was based on your sensual designs, was it not? 'Devout hedonism' I believe the media of your time called your style."

Blake looked with new respect at the woman who had obviously dug into his past. He said, "Yes . . . Go on."

"Do you truly expect the permissiveness of your period to return overnight? If you do, you do not know history, *Señor* Mason."

Rio stepped to Blake's side and said, "She's right."

"And I believe your trust fund and other monies were confiscated by an interchurch department more than fifty years ago?"

"Are you saying I should stay in this nice, comfortable job, draw my pay, keep my mouth shut, and never have Rio?" Blake laughed briefly. "You just don't understand me, do you? Your sort of life—not to even mention the celibacy—is just not for me. Nor could it ever be. I was your—what did Network B call it?— your 'warrior pope' because I *had* to be, just to get the job done. But I don't need to do that now."

Blake put an arm around Rio. "Don't worry about

me, monsignora. I won't disgrace you by dying in the gutter with a bottle of sacramental wine in my fist. I'll get a job."

"Cardinal Barbella," the monsignora said, turning to the man behind the desk. "May I suggest something? It would not be, um, suitable for one whom the world thinks of as Pope Urban X to engage in, um, unsuitable vocations." Cardinal Barbella nodded his agreement, as did several of the other clergymen and -women. "The Church will need restorations, new churches, hospitals, many buildings. Perhaps *Señor* Mason could—"

"Ah, yes! Perfect, perfect!" Cardinal Barbella's face creased in a bright smile. "Yes?" he asked Blake.

Blake was shaking his head. "The Church is too steeped in the old forms. They would never like the ideas I have. I don't want to do repeats of forms already explored."

The fat cardinal just smiled. "You have new ideas?"

Blake said, "Yes, I do. New materials, new techniques can dictate new forms. A church is a place to worship, to meditate, to think, to focus the mind. There are materials that can give us soaring spires of crystal, underwater chapels surrounded by the living sea, orbiting temples with real stars in the ceiling, transparent—"

"Hooked," Rio said, amazed. "They've really hooked you."

"There are even forms no one has touched," Blake said. "Three-dimensional super-ellipses, floating in . . . Huh?" Blake looked at the smiles around him. A smile tugged at one corner of his own mouth, then broke across it. "Suckered," he said with a snort. "All right, I'll design some things for you."

He started to turn away, his arm around Rio, but the cardinal stopped him. "When can we expect the ceremony to take place?"

"What ceremony?" Blake asked.

"The marriage ceremony between you and *Señorita* Volas?" the cardinal said suavely.

"Marriage?" Blake looked at Rio blankly. "Why?"

The cardinal spread his hands again.

"Respectability," Rio said. "They want their architect to be respectable."

Blake looked into Rio's eyes for a long moment, reading what was there. He looked at Cardinal Barbella and nodded.

They went out under Bramante's arches, away from everyone, and embraced and kissed.

" 'Living happily ever after' will take up a lot of time," Rio said.

"We have a few dozen decades, remember?"

"Yes, I remember. Just enough time for me to try a lot of the things *I've* been wanting to do."

"Ah, a happy beginning . . ." Blake said.

They walked out toward the fountain in the center of St. Peter's Square. The moon was full and bright. Behind them they heard a choir begin to sing.

Hand in hand, they began to run.